CIRCUS PHANTASM

Naomi P. Cohen

Cover Art by K. Ryan buboplague.tumblr.com

Cover Design by Savannah Jezowski dragonpenpress.com

This book is a work of fiction. Names, characters, places, and incidents either are products of the author's imagination or are used fictitiously. Any resemblance to actual persons, living or dead, events, or locales is entirely coincidental.

Naomi P. Cohen

Visit my website at www.naomipcohen.com

Printed in the United States of America

First Printing: May 2019

ISBN 978-1-7339684-0-9

To my mother, who has been endlessly supporting and read through this tale countless times and to my father who journeyed with me to my inspirations

THE CIRCUS

ACT ONE

Friday January 20th

E mma woke to the sounds of irate thoughts and merry birdsong outside her window. Her parents fumed in separate rooms downstairs. She squeezed her eyes closed tighter, groggily wishing she didn't have to hear such thoughts first thing. Her attention drifted to the neighbors' morning musings.

The two little girls next door were eating cereal and watching cartoons. Their mother slept soundly, dreaming of visiting family in South America. Everyone in the dream spoke Spanish and it didn't hold Emma's interest. She scanned the other neighborhood thoughts, but most were sleepy and disoriented, or utterly nonsensical. These sentiments made her yawn, and she quickly tuned them out before they sent her back to sleep.

The sun slanted in her window and shone on her face. This worked more effectively for her than any morning alarm.

A bird sang its sweet heart out on the branch just outside, as if to combat the dark brooding within the house. Emma listened, remembering the things she had learned from the mind of a birdwatcher who lived down the street.

An oriole. She rolled out of bed and went over to check, smiling

1

sleepily at being right. The bird's plumage gleamed as bright and yellow as the morning sunlight. It watched her with a shiny black eye, dipping its sunshine breast as it continued to warble. With a flick of its wings, the oriole flitted away into the foliage.

Her parents' angry thoughts again flared up, driving the bird's song and the brief peace it had provided out of Emma's head. She grimaced and turned away from the window to get ready for the day. As she dressed, she listened in on their thoughts, trying to discern the problem. Knowing what they were angry about made it easier to face them and ignore their thoughts.

When she went down the hall, the bathroom door stood open and water gurgled in the sink. She rapped on the door and peered in at Nemo, bent over the sink, his white hair shaggy and mussed from sleep. "Heads up. Dad is mad at you. You left the TV on last night."

When is he ever not mad at me? Nemo thought grimly and rinsed his mouth. "It's such crap. *He* left the TV on last night. I just didn't turn it off for him."

Emma knew that from their father's thoughts. "Yeah, well, he thinks you should've. Can't you try to—" He gave her a withering glare, and she bit back the words, hunching her shoulders. "Whatever. I'm going downstairs. Mom is making breakfast, and it's almost ready."

Nemo came to the door and watched her walk toward the stairs. "Family breakfast, huh? Maybe you should bring a book. I know it's hard for you, being able to hear their thoughts when they're like this." She shrugged in irritation and refused to look back at him. He knew that but did things like this anyway.

"Good mornings" were exchanged when Emma entered the dining room. She covered a yawn and squeezed behind her dad to get plates from the cabinet.

Her dad read the morning news on his laptop, as he did most mornings. He glanced down at his empty mug and frowned. *Don't want to go into the kitchen...*

Emma picked up the coffee pot from the top of the cupboard and silently refilled the mug. Her dad looked up at her, and his eyes narrowed for a moment before he smiled wearily. "Thank you." She smiled and nodded. His irritated thoughts mellowed, which she appreciated. Angry thoughts sounded like a swarm of bees buzzing around the house. It was never a pleasant way to start a day.

2

Feeling more positive now, Emma ducked into the kitchen to help her mom finish breakfast. Her mother was sipping tea as she cooked, her thoughts muzzy with weariness and irritation. She waved a lazy hand at Emma and stared down at the pan.

The food was almost ready when her dad's thoughts once more became an annoyed rumble.

Emma peeked back into the dining room. Nemo sat at the table, wearing a bright pink shirt over his black jeans. A pair of black headphones contrasted sharply with his hair, and even from the doorway, she could hear rock music blaring.

"You shouldn't wear headphones at the table." Their father's eyebrows drew down into a scowl, and he closed his laptop with a snap.

"You shouldn't talk," Nemo retorted with a sharp smirk, his eyes sparking with anger, and Emma sensed the power in his voice.

Their father's eyes widened, and his face reddened, but his mouth stayed firmly closed. His face grew more flushed and finally his mouth popped open with a gasp. He fixed his eyes on his laptop, his thoughts tinged with fear. *I can't do anything with either of these kids. What even was that?*

Emma ducked back into the kitchen and clutched the counter, wrestling with anger at her brother for doing this. She wouldn't yell at him in front of their parents. When she could swallow back the feeling, she carried the food into the dining room. She kicked Nemo's chair as she passed. Guilt flashed over his face but settled into self-righteousness. *I did suggest you bring a book.*

She only gave him a steely look, facing away from her father so that he wouldn't see. Years ago, she had learned not to reply out loud to thoughts. She took particular care around their parents and wished Nemo would do the same.

Her mother came in a moment later, more awake and in a better mood now. She saw her husband's glower, heard the music and deflated noticeably, her thoughts growing unhappy and resigned as she sat down. Emma kicked Nemo's shin under the table and then pointedly ignored him. Her brother hunched over his food and kept his eyes on his plate while he ate.

Breakfast remained silent but for Nemo's music. When Emma couldn't stand the hush anymore, she checked the time on her phone. "Oh. Hey, Nemo." She nudged him to get his attention. He slipped the headphones down around his neck. "We have to leave in five minutes to get you to rehearsal on time."

"Okay." Nemo hurried out, keeping his eyes down still. Emma didn't feel sorry for him. He chose to make breakfast tense.

"Rehearsal?" her father asked. He closed his laptop and put it away in his bag.

"Yeah. He's in the school play. He auditioned for it while you were on your business trip," Emma said. "It's a musical so he's getting credits for drama and music class both."

"He has a lead role," her mother added, glowing with pride. "The Phantom. He sang one of the songs for me the other day. He's doing very well."

Her father's thoughts were conflicted. Emma stared at him, daring him to say the less pleasant aspects of his thoughts. She could feel an explosion simmering.

"At least he's dedicated," he finally said, and Emma let out a long breath. Her mother's thoughts softened toward him, and they exchanged smiles. Emma got up and put the dishes in the dishwasher as Nemo thundered down the stairs.

"We're going now! Have a good day!" She grabbed her car keys and backpack from the hooks by the door.

"You too!" Her mother called back and came to the kitchen doorway to see them out. "Oh! Don't forget. We're working late again tonight. I'll leave some money on the table if you want to order delivery." *Hopefully something healthier than pizza...*

Emma snorted as she went out the door. She would cook something instead, but her mother was dreaming if she really thought they might order something healthy. She wondered how her mom would react if she knew for certain Emma heard her thoughts. Emma winced. The few hints she had from her childhood, when she had slipped up and commented on something that hadn't been said aloud, didn't suggest it would be a pleasant reaction. Emma's mother usually kept her thoughts distant, and Emma suspected in a way she did know. After all, when Emma was younger she had occasionally responded to thoughts, or mentioned what Nemo was thinking. Her mother had drawn back as if stung each time, her face twisting. Those memories still caused an ache. Then there was her father...

She stopped on the bottom stair of the porch. Once more the wind shook the oak and made the tire swing sway like a pendulum. Memories assailed her, and she blinked against the burning in her eyes.

Flashes of her father's face came to mind: mouth hanging open and staring at her with wide eyes as the blood drained out of his face after she asked him about something he had been thinking about, and then he had reached for her. Unexplainable fear had struck her, and she had fallen off the swing and fled. From then on had held her tongue about what she heard that wasn't said out loud. She never wanted to see her parents look at her like that again.

Nemo staggered down the steps in his rush and bumped into her, sending them both stumbling forward. "Jeez, Em," he grumbled and looked at the tire swing. "Why do you always stare at that old thing?"

"I'm remembering when we started having secrets." She tore her gaze away and advanced toward the car.

Once on the road, she glanced at Nemo and frowned. He wore a gray shirt under his black sweatshirt now. "You wore the pink shirt just to annoy Dad?"

He shrugged and glared out the car window. "I'm allowed to wear pink if I want. I just don't want to wear it to school. You know better than I do that Dad thinks I'm gay."

"But you're not," Emma retorted. After hearing many of Nemo's recent thoughts, she knew that for sure. That alone often drove Emma out of the house, but there had been no escaping it at times. Nemo had hastened to figure out how to block his mind so she couldn't hear him anymore. "So why rub things like that in his face?"

"Because he's a jerk!"

Emma's explosion came with the screeching of brakes, and he thrust his hand out to brace himself against the dashboard.

"What the hell, Em?" he growled and whipped his head around, his mouth open to say more. Her furious expression silenced him.

"*You're* being a jerk. Maybe I shouldn't drive you to school and pick you up. You can take the bus like everyone else. Dad being a jerk does not give you an excuse to be one, too. Dad's trying, in his own way, despite you provoking him. I love you, Nemo, but the way you're behaving is awful. I can't believe you used your power on him like that."

Nemo's expression closed off, and he refused to meet her gaze. Emma sighed and pulled back on the road. The school was in sight before he spoke. "I appreciate your help. You know the bus would get me to rehearsal late. I wore the pink shirt because I thought it would be funny." Emma snorted, and Nemo's mouth twitched but she didn't call him on that bluff. "I'm sorry it made your morning bad, Em."

She pulled up to the school curb and drummed her fingers on the steering wheel. "It's not just my morning you made worse than it needed to be. Apologize to Ma, too." She hesitated and then added, "I won't ask you to apologize to Dad..." He stiffened, letting her know it would've been pointless to ask. "But you really should talk things out with him."

"Maybe," Nemo said, his expression and voice neutral. "I'll apologize to Ma. You're right. It was a dick—" Emma shot him a look and his mouth snapped closed. "Jerk move."

"Thank you. I hear too much of that crap in people's thoughts. I don't want to hear it out of your mouth."

Nemo chuckled and swung out of the car. "Have a good day, little brother!" she called right before he closed the door. He waved and took off across the school's lawn. Emma watched him until he disappeared into the building, her thoughts turning to her own day.

She wasn't looking forward to her last class of the week. *At least it's Friday.*

The drama teacher collared Nemo as soon as he walked into the auditorium. "How can you be late? Today of all days?" she nattered as she pushed him backstage. She snatched an armful of clothing off the costume rack, shoved it at him, and then hurried away to supervise the other students putting the costumes on over their clothes.

"No, no, no!" she shrieked at them. "You must go into the changing rooms and wear them properly!" Most of them looked as rattled as Nemo felt and shuffled away under her stern stare.

"Oh right. The full rehearsal." With all the family drama that morning, it had slipped Nemo's mind entirely. He looked down at the clothing. A white shirt with ruffles on the front almost glowed on top of a pile of thin black fabric: vest, tailcoat, cloak, and pants.

As Nemo changed into it, he wondered how much all this would weigh if made from proper fabric and meant to keep someone warm. "Heavy wool would really weigh a person down," he mused while he struggled with the clasp on the cloak. He felt a tingle, and the cloak immediately felt heavier on his shoulders. Nemo frowned and ran a hand over the fabric. It was still thin material, but every piece of it felt heavier. His power had never affected inanimate objects before. Fingering the fabric, he didn't know what to feel but then he shook off the uncertainty. *Oh well. It will help me get into character better.*

He fanned the cloak to the side dramatically, turned on his heel, and went out to watch the rehearsal begin. From his position backstage, he could make out a few people sitting in the front row beside the teacher. "Let the show begin," he whispered and smirked, feeling the Phantom muse he'd been developing settle onto him.

Emma's only Friday class didn't start until midmorning. Having arrived early, she took the chance to explore campus and get her bearings better, so she would get to her classes on time the next week.

With far fewer people on campus than the rest of the week, the noise level was more tolerable. She found an empty table in the student center and decided to do some homework.

As the morning slipped by, the room grew more crowded. Emma's shoulders itched with the sudden sense of being watched. She frowned and scanned the thoughts around her but didn't hear anything strange. Still, the feeling didn't go away.

Unable to focus on her homework, she doodled some flowers in her notebook, but the noise continued to intensify as the room filled up. Frustrated, Emma snapped it closed and left the student center. Her class didn't start for another half an hour, but she couldn't spend another minute hearing all that noise.

The feeling continued to plague her. Perplexed, Emma glanced over her shoulder at the people coming out of the student center. She still couldn't hear any thoughts out of the ordinary. She meandered over to the building her class would meet in and sat down on a bench.

A boy with mousy brown hair wearing a loose black shirt and baggy jeans sat down on a bench across the path. A moment later, a girl plopped down beside him and pulled her long, straight brown hair back with a knit green headband, a blue flower clip wobbling on it. The bright yellow blouse she wore over a pair of skinny jeans drew and held Emma's gaze. She nodded to them and turned her attention to her backpack. They looked a little young to be here, but it wasn't uncommon for high schoolers to take college classes.

The boy got out a handheld game and devoted all his attention to that. The girl watched some sparrows chase each other around the bushes on the side of the path. Their thoughts were uninteresting and easy to tune out. Emma's unease wouldn't go away, though. She got up and tested the classroom door. The handle didn't budge.

Emma turned to sit back down and saw the girl grinning at her. A wave of calmness washed over her with the same tingling sense she got when Nemo used his ability on her. Her eyes widened. "What are you doing?" *Does she have a power too?*

The girl laughed merrily and elbowed the boy. "See, Seth? I told you." He grunted and inched away from her. Undeterred, the girl swung to her feet and, in a few swift steps, stood next to Emma.

Emma took a step back, uncomfortable with the girl's proximity.

"I'm Adah," the girl chirped. Her bright clothing had already put Emma in mind of the oriole from earlier, and her energy only reinforced the image.

"Emma," she mumbled, increasingly unnerved. *What's with this girl?* "Do you...I mean...what did you just do?" She couldn't bring herself to put the question about powers into words. "That was really weird."

Adah bobbed her head. "Yes. You can do something too, right? Wonderful!"

The boy put away his game and came over. "Enough, Adah. We've confirmed it. We can move on now." His bloodshot eyes raked over Emma, and then he looked away.

Adah huffed and crossed her arms. "No. I want to get to know her." She turned back to Emma. "So what Blessing do you have?" she asked, bouncing on her toes.

"Blessing?" Emma's head whirled, making her feel faint. "Is that what you call it? Why?" Her interest was piqued, despite her discomfort, and she suspected the other girl was using her ability to keep Emma from panicking.

"Because that's what it is! You see, the elves once—" A woman walked up. Adah fell silent, a guilty expression crossing her face before her grin returned.

The woman glanced at them, unlocked the door to the classroom and went in. Emma fought down the urge to follow her and get away

8

from this strange girl.

Adah beamed once more at her. "I'm getting ahead of myself. Would you like to come have coffee with us? My treat. I'll tell you all you want to know."

"I have class," Emma said, glad for the out. She needed a chance to think. "But later. I need to know more about what it is that I can do. If you give me your phone number, I'll message you after my class."

"Great!" Adah whipped her cell phone out and rattled off a list of numbers. Emma fumbled with her own phone, hastening to get to her contacts. "See you later, then. Come on, Seth! Let's see who else we can find!" She turned and jogged off.

Seth and Emma exchanged cool, calculating looks. "We're in town for a few days," he finally said, his voice hoarse. "Get in touch if you want. No big deal if you don't. We'll see you again soon enough, either way." He smiled thinly and followed Adah around a corner.

Emma stared after them, disoriented. She gathered her wits and forced herself to go into the classroom. What did the girl mean about elves? It sounded completely insane, but so did what she and Nemo could do. The boy's words echoed in her head, sounding more sinister each time. Worry blossomed in Emma's chest and refused to be displaced. Should she call them, after all?

She needed to know more, but there was no way to get information other than calling them… She grimaced at that circular reasoning.

Either way, she needed to talk to Nemo.

Nemo always performed better with an audience, even if it was only a couple teachers. He channeled the morning's pent-up emotions into his singing, and his energy elicited an even better performance from the others. His voice rang through the auditorium as he sang his solo.

The bright lights made it hard to see anything beyond the stage, but he could dimly see the drama teacher sitting in the front row, entranced. In this theater, Nemo's abilities were truly appreciated. His grin widened at the teacher's amazed look. Then he spotted a group of shadowed newcomers proceeding along the side of the room, and he faltered in surprise. They took seats a few rows back, too far for him to see their faces.

"Nemo?" the teacher called when he missed his cue. The music flowed far past the lines he should've been singing.

Instead of starting over, he caught up the lyrics from where the music was, the words from the *Phantom of the Opera* coming easily to his lips. The teacher nodded in approval.

Nemo angled so he could see Ann, the girl playing Christine, and keep an eye toward the strangers. He felt a twinge as he sang his last line and resisted the urge to grimace. His power was becoming harder to control, particularly when he sang. Being around Ann distracted him enough, and the newcomers had diverted a lot of his attention.

He peeked at the girl, worried about what he would see. Sure enough, a flush crept up her neck and face as she took a half step back. Her eyebrows furrowed as she tried to remember her lines.

Relief washed over Nemo when she took a breath and launched into her part. He needed to be more careful. His gaze wandered once more to the group while Ann sang her lines.

He jumped right in when he heard her last line and smiled lazily in her direction. She didn't catch the grin, too focused on listening for her next part.

The drama teacher led the visitors, a man and a woman, closer to the stage while they continued to sing. Despite being accustomed to people watching him on stage, something about their attention made his skin crawl, and he nearly faltered again. *Concentrate!*

Pushing his misgivings aside, Nemo allowed the music to take all of his attention as the end of the song came. "Sing for me!" he commanded as the music swelled around them. Another surge of power escaped him, and this time he couldn't keep his frustration from showing in his expression. He twisted and covered his face dramatically to make up for it.

Ann sang a pure note far louder and clearer than she had managed in any of the earlier rehearsals. As it rang through the room, she broke down coughing. Nemo patted her on the back and berated himself for the slip-up. "Are you alright?" he asked, still rubbing her back. She shot him a venomous look that made his stomach flip, knocked his hand away, and crossed to the opposite side of the stage. Nemo jammed his fists into his pockets and looked away from her. He really needed to figure out how to control this.

The teacher gestured for them to come closer. "Sorry to interrupt the rehearsal. We have some unexpected guests. They're…" she trailed off and frowned. "Where did you say you're from again?"

"The Ark Light Company," the woman said smoothly. She looked extremely professional, standing ramrod straight and wearing a sky-blue business suit with a knee-length pencil skirt, the color complimenting her fair complexion. Nemo's gaze swept from her bright red hair, confined in a tight bun, to the dark red lipstick on her upturned lips, the color contrasting with her pale skin, and down to her curves. He struggled to look away.

"Such an amazing performance," the woman said and grinned. "Your voice is truly spectacular. It's really...something else." Her eyes glittered as she said this, as if excited by a discovery.

Shaken by the intensity of her look, Nemo only smiled and nodded. The woman turned her attention to the other performers, so he sat down on the edge of the stage and surveyed the dark-complexioned young man. Straight black hair framed a sharp boned face with a bored expression.

Nemo glanced around the theater and noticed a third stranger: a girl standing several feet behind the couple, half hidden in the shadows of the auditorium. She looked younger than him, wearing an overlarge purple sweatshirt. Long lavender hued braids framed her round, dark face.

The girl shifted uncomfortably, gripping one arm with her opposite hand. Her head jerked up suddenly and their gazes locked. Her eyes widened in surprise. She took a step forwards and raised her hand as if to tap the woman on the shoulder. She teetered in this pose for a split second, and then dropped her hand before stepping back further into the shadows, casting her eyes down.

The drama teacher handed him a water bottle, pulling his attention away from the girl. "Well done," the teacher said, turning her gaze toward the other students. "This is great exposure for you. You are definitely going places."

"Thanks," Nemo croaked and cleared his throat. His voice was a little sore from singing so passionately. His eyes were drawn back to the red-haired woman. Why did he find her attention so alarming? Ark Light Company. He'd have to look that up online. Still filled with the performance's energy, he got to his feet, unable to stay still.

The movement caught the dark-haired man's attention, and their eyes locked. The stage seemed to fall out from beneath Nemo. His breath froze in his lungs and iciness spread through his chest, and from there to his extremities, up his neck and to his head. He couldn't draw air in. He went rigid, and the teacher glanced at him in concern. "Nemo? Are you okay?"

He couldn't reply; he couldn't move at all. His lungs screeched for oxygen, and the room spun around him. The man smirked and took a step toward him. The cold increased and crept into Nemo's arms and legs. He swallowed and struggled to do anything at all.

The woman grabbed the man's shoulder, her manicured nails digging into his shirt. Breaking gazes with Nemo, the man turned to look at her.

Nemo slumped forward and sucked in a ragged breath. Eyes brimming with concern, the teacher reached out to steady him.

"Fine," he gasped and coughed. "I'm fine." He shook his head and retreated toward the back of the stage. He rubbed his face and then jerked his hand away, staring incredulously at the frost that rimed his fingertips.

Looking toward the group again, he saw the girl with the purple braids standing only a few feet away from the stage. Her dark eyes were wide and her round face alight with worry. Their gazes met, and he quickly looked away. Would something happen again? She retreated into the darkness that surrounded her and vanished.

Nemo rushed backstage to get away from them. This group must be like him and Emma. That explained why he sensed something odd about them from the start.

Still shivering from the cold, Nemo rubbed his arm, and someone jostled him as they passed, snapping him back into reality. Mechanically, he went through the motions of changing back into his clothing and listening as the teacher reviewed the rehearsal. A sick pit formed in his stomach, and he got his phone out to message Emma. *What do they want?*

N emo stood on the curb outside the high school and watched the students file into the parking lot or gather by the bus stop. A few smiled and waved to him as they passed, but nobody stopped to speak to him. Nemo stuck his hands in his pockets. Normally, he would stay a bit longer and chat with some friends. He didn't feel like it today, still shaken by the encounter with the strangers at the morning's rehearsal.

When Emma pulled up, he got in and they drove most of the way home in silence. She looked tired. He almost asked how her day at the college went but thought better of it. Judging by her expression, it didn't go well. He lapsed into thoughtful silence instead, playing his lines over in his head.

As Emma turned onto their street, she glanced at him. "Are you okay? Are you having a problem with something?"

Nemo frowned and quickly strengthened the barriers he kept around his thoughts. He knew Emma couldn't hear anything specific, but if he got distracted, she sometimes could catch the drift of his thoughts.

"Is it a girl?" she asked.

"No! It's not a girl." She raised an eyebrow, and he flushed. "I mean…it's not a romantic problem. Jeez, Em. What's with the questioning?"

"Just wondering, little brother. Seriously, though. Are you doing alright?"

Nemo leaned his head against the window, staring out at the passing buildings. "Something weird happened today," he said and then told her about the strange group at the rehearsal.

Out of the corner of his eye, Nemo saw her hand twitch off the wheel. "What is it?"

"I also met some odd people earlier." She recounted the details of her own encounter. Nemo stared, wide-eyed.

"Don't call them," he said as soon as she finished. "There's no way it's a coincidence that we met them on the same day."

"But we need to learn how to control our powers," Emma fretted. "We can't go on this way, we have to get more information."

"That's true, but I still feel cold from what the guy did." Nemo rubbed his arms. Emma reached over and clasped his shoulder. He smiled at her. "Let's think about it and decide tomorrow morning."

Emma stared straight ahead at the road, frowning. "Okay."

The car stopped, and he jumped out, eager to be alone for a bit. The two neighbor girls thundered down the porch stairs and knocked into him on their way to hug Emma. Nemo stumbled and caught himself against the railing. Emma crouched down and hugged them both.

"Mama said we could watch cartoons today if you said yes!" the younger of the two gushed, her tan face creasing into a grin. "We did our homework last night!"

"Okay, okay," Emma said, laughing and patting the girls' heads. "But apologize to Nemo first. He almost fell down."

"Sorry, Nemo," the girls chimed in unison as they tugged Emma up on the porch.

Emma shot him a rueful look and unlocked the door for them. "Do you girls want some hot chocolate? And I made cookies last night that you can have."

Glad I don't have to babysit them. Nemo slouched in after them with the girls' cheering echoing in his ears.

He leaned against the doorway into the living room and looked on as Emma set them up with paper and crayons and turned on some cartoons. "Mom and Dad said they're working late tonight," she told him as she plopped down beside the girls with a textbook. "I'll make dinner after I do some homework."

Okay. I'll be upstairs. Let me know when it's done. Or if you need any help with dinner. I'd rather the house didn't burn down.

"Shut up!" Emma shouted after him. The girls looked up in alarm, exchanged looks, and returned to their coloring, chattering in Spanish.

After Nemo disappeared upstairs, Emma stretched out on the couch and enjoyed the quiet of the neighborhood after the mental tumult at the college. Most of the nearby neighbors were still away from home, and the few minds she heard rolled along slow and weary from their long days.

The closest thoughts were the Spanish musings of the two little girls. Both familiar and indistinguishable and so easy enough to tune out. She focused on her textbook, optimistic about her chances to get some reading done.

The dry wording and large blocks of text quickly dispelled optimism, and she looked up eagerly when Gracia, the older girl, brought over a drawing and proudly showed it to her.

Emma studied it and hesitated, scanning the girl's thoughts for clues. She didn't want to guess wrong and hurt Gracia's feelings.

"It's a faun," the little girl said, her expression solemn. "Like Mr. Tumnus from Narnia. I saw him when we went for a walk in the woods on Saturday. He gave me a flower and then ran away before Irene and Mama saw him." She pointed to a second drawing of a flower and three smiling stick figures.

"I see." Emma studied the drawing. "You did a great job on this. You should take it and show it to the faun the next time you see him." Gracia nodded and went back to coloring on the floor.

Emma watched her, still amused. *Such an imagination!* She set aside the textbook and rolled onto the floor. "Want me to braid your hair?" That sounded like much more fun than homework.

Both girls scooted closer eagerly. "Your hair is getting long," Emma observed as she separated Irene's dark-brown hair.

"Yeah. But it's still not as long as Gracia's." Irene looked jealously at her sister.

Emma only smiled. The girls almost looked like twins. Gracia was just slightly taller, her black hair only slightly longer.

Their mother struggled to make ends meet, and Emma worried about them sometimes, but they were always happy when she saw them.

"I have to go start dinner," Emma said as she finished Gracia's braid. "I'll refill your hot chocolates," she added and took the mugs with her into the kitchen, wondering if the girls would eat with her and Nemo.

No sooner did the thought cross her mind than a knock sounded on the front door. The girls rushed down the hall and yanked it open before Emma could pull off her apron. She hurried after them. "Good afternoon," she greeted their mother.

"Hello." The woman smiled slightly, but her face remained reserved. She tucked her hair behind an ear. "Thank you so much for watching them. I hope they behaved."

"They were great! Oh! Here, you can take some cookies with you." She darted back in and grabbed a Tupperware container off the counter. "My mom and I made them yesterday for a potluck at her work, but there were leftovers. We try not to keep too many sweets around."

"Thank you." The woman accepted the container, and her grateful thoughts warmed Emma. "Say gracias, mis rosas." The girls echoed her, beaming.

"You're very welcome. Have a good evening, you three. I'll see you tomorrow."

Wanting some fresh air, Emma went out onto the porch and watched as they crossed the lawn over to their house, the girls chattering at their mother in Spanish and tugging on her hands to move faster. They waved at her from their porch and then disappeared inside. Emma wandered back into the kitchen to finish dinner, feeling better than she had all day. Children's energy always brightened her mood.

Researching the Ark Light Company turned up unexpected results. Nemo stared incredulously at the business website, scanning the plain text filled with technical descriptions of lamps and lighting. The company sold lighting appliances to ships in San Francisco.

This couldn't be more corporate bland. So why did that woman say she's a talent agent working for them? He tapped the edge of the keyboard, thinking hard, and then ran the CEO's name through a search engine. He scrolled down through a list of articles and more information, clicked through a few pages, mostly bored now, and then caught his breath. A grin spread over his face as he read through the website, not much different than when he had read it a few months before. A tentative knock came at the door.

"Come in!" Nemo called and spun his chair to face the entrance, still smiling.

Emma hovered in the doorway. Nemo raised his eyebrows, and she stepped inside. He hadn't let her in his room in a long time. "I'm missing some ingredients for the recipe I wanted to try, so I'm going to order take out, after all. What are you so happy about?" she asked, picking her way over the scattered clothing spread over the floor to sit down on his bed. She glanced around at the messy room, then stared at the immaculate fish tank with a single gold fish swimming around in it. Nemo could almost see the waves of disapproval rolling off her.

"Do you want to go to a show tonight?" he asked to curtail her saying anything about the state of his room.

"What?" Emma gave him a mystified look. "Where did that come from?"

"Internet. I read about an awesome show that's in town this week. It makes some very wild claims on the website, and I want to see if it's telling the truth. This is the last night they're performing here. We should go!"

Emma raised an eyebrow, and Nemo grinned coaxingly, some energy coming into his expression. "Come on, Em! I think you'll really like it." He paused and picked at the blanket. "And we might be able to find some of the answers we need there."

"I don't know." Emma rubbed her neck, weariness pulling at her. "I don't think I can take much more time in public. I've been looking forward to a quiet evening and going to sleep early." Sleeping provided the only way to get away from hearing the neighbors' thoughts, so Emma often went to bed early when they didn't have any family time planned.

He looked down. "Please, Emma? I think it will be good for you to get out for once. And if we stay here, we'll just keep worrying about those people. I think we need to get out and think about it with clearer

17

heads later."

Emma stared down at her hands, frowning. "What's it called?" She glanced at his laptop, but the black screen yielded no clues.

Maybe Nemo is right. Emma didn't have much of a social life. She had tried to be social during high school but retreated from all that in the semester she took off from school. People's minds were just too noisy.

"Circus Phantasm. They sound fantastic. If even half of their claims about their performers are true, they're better than Barnum and Bailey's! I really want to go!"

She crossed her arms and tilted her head. "What did you mean, we might find answers? Do you think they have powers? Didn't you just say we shouldn't call that weird girl who apparently has information? If I talked to her, at least I wouldn't have to stay out late. Besides, we don't know that this group is any more trustworthy."

He grimaced, but he couldn't keep a smile from plucking at his mouth. "Are you really a teenager, Em?" he teased. "Where's your sense of adventure? Please? We both need something to cheer us up. Especially after what that girl's friend did to me."

She couldn't argue with that. Despite his pleading tone, Nemo's brown eyes danced with humor. He knew she was curious. She sighed. "Okay. I'll be your ride to the show." Nemo whooped and jumped up to hug her. Emma held a hand up, and he stopped with his arms held wide. "Only if you ask Ma's permission to go."

The joy drained from Nemo's face. "You really aren't a teenager," he muttered and huffed. "Fine!"

"Just be glad Ma is getting home before Dad today," Emma pointed out. Nemo winced. "Also, that means I'm ordering something healthy for dinner. It'll put Ma in a better mood and improve your chances of getting a yes if we eat something healthier than pizza," she said over her shoulder as she left the room.

"But pizza is life!" Nemo shouted in protest. "And healthy take-out is a myth!" Emma only laughed.

Adah lay on the immaculate hotel blanket, her head at the foot of the bed and her long hair cascading over the edge. Seth sat at her feet by the pillows, hunched over his game. His eyes were even more bloodshot than that morning. "I don't think that girl is going to call," he commented.

"I know," Adah said, her voice dreamy and peaceful. "It was worth a try. She seemed really nice."

"She seemed flustered and confused. You should just take note of a Blessed and let the Collectors do their job. Explanations can come afterward."

Adah huffed and prodded him with her toes in reply.

The door clicked and opened. "It was unnecessary and unhelpful for you to scare the boy like that!" Rebecca yelled as the couple came in.

"Uh oh." Seth tucked his face down closer to his game. Caleb stomped across the room and pulled his coat off. "What happened?" Seth asked Rebecca. She dropped down next to Adah and pulled out the pins that held her braid up.

"Caleb scared the crap out of the Blessed boy we found. That was completely uncalled for." She glared at Caleb.

"The kid is fine," Caleb grumbled. "He'll be interested now. He knows we have Blessings like he does."

"That is not our job," Rebecca reminded him coldly. "We just find them and report it. The Collectors deal with the rest."

"Oh, will you just—" Caleb growled.

"We found a girl at a local college," Adah interrupted without opening her eyes. Serenity flowed from her and spread through the room. Seth chuckled quietly, and Adah smiled.

"Oh good. The Collectors love when there's more than one person to get in a town. Makes their job easier." Rebecca fingered her braid apart and shook her hair out.

Seth looked up from his game and frowned. "Hey, where's Gail?" He leapt to his feet, his game left forgotten on the bed.

"Huh?" Caleb looked around. "Oh, blast the girl. She must've slipped away again."

"She still doesn't have a key. She'll get bored and come knocking soon enough. Make her sing a song to come in when she does, Caleb," Rebecca said before disappearing into the bathroom. Caleb chuckled.

Seth glared at Caleb. "You're both awful," he grumbled before walking straight through the door to go find Gail. Adah knew he preferred Gail's company over theirs', but the room felt tenser without him. She sighed and pulled a pillow over her head.

19

Gail had practice in tuning out Caleb and Rebecca's arguments, and today was no different. Their bickering had filled the car, and then the elevator. When they had reached their floor in the hotel, instead of following them, Gail trailed absently over to a large window and sat down on the floor. She leaned her head against the glass to watch the raindrops rolling down just a few inches from her eyes. The glass cooled her skin and she felt the tension drain out of her. She wished she could just sit like this and go to sleep.

The carpet rustled with soft footsteps and the floor creaked. Seth plopped down on the floor next to her, got a Nintendo out of his pocket, and became part of the quiet.

Dark fell outside the window before he spoke. "It must've been tiring going around with them today. I haven't seen you this pensive in a long time. Not since—" he stopped and glanced warily at her.

Gail still did not look away from the thinning clouds. "Is it weird I'm always hoping we don't find anyone, Seth?" She rubbed her face. "Not so lucky this time. There was a boy with a Blessing at a school we went to today."

"Are you sure?" Seth slipped his game into his pocket and regarded her seriously. "You've been wrong before. Your sense of these things isn't as strong as Adah's."

"He saw me through my shadow, but I didn't tell Rebecca or Caleb. Please don't mention it to them."

Seth sighed and twisted around to peer out the window at the dark rain-washed twilight. "We're just Scouts. We'll report and...you never know. Maybe nothing will happen. There's too many Blessed around for the Collectors to come for everyone the Scouts find."

They both knew that to be unlikely. The Collectors would jump at a job in the same state as Company Headquarters. That sat unspoken and uneasy in the silence between them.

After a minute, Seth smiled tentatively. "Hey. Come on now, Gail. Cheer up. Adah is worried about you. She doesn't want to make you feel happier, but it's like an itch she can't scratch. I think she might give in sooner or later." His smile widened, and he raised an eyebrow, willing her to join in the joke.

Gail looked away. Seth bit his lip and reached through the wall until he felt icy rain on his palm. He cupped his hand to gather a small amount and then brought his hand back through and inched closer to her. "Look. Diamonds." The water droplets sparkled against his palm, but Gail's expression did not change.

Frustration flashed across Seth's face and he sank one shoulder into the wall so that he could face her straight. He put his arms around her and drew her close. "Please cheer up. I promised your brother I'd take care of you."

Gail snorted and put her head against his chest. "As if he cares about me anymore."

Seth didn't argue with her but stroked a hand over her braided hair.

"Your Blessing is so weird." Gail traced his shoulder where it fused with the wall. "I'm ready to go back," she said with a slowly widening smile. "If you take us straight through the door so that we can scare Rebecca and Caleb."

"Deal." Seth drew himself out of the wall and clasped her hand in his. The rain began pounding even harder against the glass. He glanced out the window at the rain drops for a moment, a pensive look coming into his eyes; then he shook it off and led the way down the hallway.

Gail reflected on the day's events as they walked. They needed to report anyone with a Blessing they found. That was their job. Still, she wondered about this boy. Very few people could see through her shadow. She frowned, remembering his uncertainty, and then his fear when he met Caleb's icy gaze. Seth's fingers tightened around her hand, bringing her back to the present.

When she glanced at him, he smiled brightly for her, even though she could see her own misgivings mirrored in his eyes, along with something else. She reached up and smoothed a finger over the slight crease between his eyes. "Don't be jealous. I don't know the boy."

Not yet, anyway. The Collectors will change that. She didn't say the thought aloud. They both knew it to be true.

The directions that came up on Emma's phone took them a strange route. They came to the edge of town and Emma let up on the gas pedal. The car slowed to a crawl as she peered out at the highway winding up the mountain.

"Keep going!" Nemo urged. "We can't get there late."

"I don't like this." But she sped up again, alert for nocturnal creatures that might emerge from the trees. The twists of the road quickly made her stomach feel queasy from the Greek chicken, the healthiest option she could find that delivered. Nemo's claim proved to be right. Healthy take-out was a myth.

"Turn right," her phone intoned.

Emma came to a stop, aware there were no cars behind her, and looked at the dark road her phone would have her turn onto. It curved away out of sight into the dark forest. "Go!" Nemo insisted.

She turned onto the road. "What kind of circus performs in the middle of nowhere? This seems really shady, Nemo. People die this way. Or worse."

"I won't let anything happen to you," he promised. The hint of power in his voice sent a shiver down Emma's spine.

She gave him a flat look over that use of his power, and he smiled sheepishly, but it had served its purpose. They both remembered the night he had protected her with his power. Memories of frigid water and pale faces chilled her.

Emma shuddered and turned her attention to the thoughts ahead and listened to them while they got closer. The minds bubbled with excitement. Further away, she could sense quiet, whispering thoughts that sounded like flowing water and eluded her attempts to make out anything specific. She turned into the dirt parking lot. *Time to see what Nemo's gotten us into.*

A s soon as the car stopped, Nemo leapt out and set off toward the trees. Emma ran to catch up with him, her purse swinging wildly at her side. Her brother came to a stop in front of a trail. The gray gloom of twilight made the trees to either side a black mass.

People flowed onto the trail, chattering and laughing, but Emma grabbed Nemo's arm to keep him from continuing. "What are those?" she asked.

Small, bright lights floated beneath the trees. They looked almost like fireflies but bigger and in a variety of colors. A swarm of red ones hovered the closest, but Emma could see gold, green, and blue lights flickering further away.

She took them to be some sort of automatic lights at first, but then she realized she could hear thoughts from them, high-pitched like a hummingbird's peeping. Entranced, she moved closer to the red lights and tried to make out what they were thinking. A flutter of indignation hummed off them and the lights scattered. But not before Emma glimpsed the tiny human-like figures amid the glow.

Nemo grinned at Emma's awestruck expression. "The website

called them Guardians of the Path. Fey lights guide the mundane visitors safely along the path to the Circus Phantasm," he recited.

Emma continued to stare. Nemo's smile faded, and he impatiently tugged her on. "Come on! We don't have much time before the show starts!"

They kept pace with many others going down the trail to the show. Emma recognized several people from the high school and college. Their familiar thoughts put her more at ease.

Wonder what special effects they're using to make those fairies?
Can't wait to see the show!
Wow! That animatronic is so lifelike!

Curious about that last thought, Emma walked faster. The path led to a clearing where people milled around an ornate wrought-iron fire pit. Flames licked up around the black metal, and smoke clogged the air. After the dark forest and the mild light of the Guardians, Emma's eyes fixated on the fire. The blaze left her blinded to her surroundings, so she didn't notice the change until a surge of excitement from the throng's thoughts caused her to glance around. People filed into a cave that hadn't been there a moment before.

Pulling her eyes from the flames, she noticed a great creature lying beside the cave, nearly indiscernible from the darkness. She watched in stunned disbelief as people filed past it with barely a second glance. "How are people just walking by that?" she whispered.

A pair of Asian girls leaned right up against the black dragon to take a selfie. They had to stand on tiptoe to grasp the horns on top of the dragon's wedge-shaped head. Emma's gaze roved from them, to the dragon's sinuous neck, and then to its wide shoulders. Its body seemed to be coiled among the trees at the edge of the clearing, but Emma couldn't quite tell. Perhaps it was a trick of the firelight playing on the dragon's dark scales, but its edges blurred out into a heat shimmer. The dragon was surely as big as a truck, but between one blink and another, it seemed to be different sizes, the blurry haze making it impossible to determine. Emma shuddered, and fear clenched in her chest, freezing her in place.

"It's just a statue, Emma." Nemo continued toward it. They had to walk by it to go into the cave. Emma followed him, her dread making her steps slow.

The dragon's eye, a glowing, molten bronze disk, moved to watch them. It lifted its nose just a few inches off the ground and curled a lip up to expose spikes of ivory teeth, the movement stiff and mechanically slow. Even so, those closest to the dragon leapt back, crying out in alarm, bumping into others and stepping on feet. The dragon returned to its former position and became completely still again.

The people laughed nervously, but their thoughts buzzed with uncertainty. The air of magic to their surroundings made it difficult to be certain what was real and what wasn't.

Smiling at their reactions, she kept shuffling along with the crowd. "The Gate Keeper," Nemo whispered as they drew level with the dragon. Its eye moved again, focusing on them. Emma stared into that great eye and came to a stop. Unlike the fey lights, she could clearly hear the dragon's mind. Her heart raced. This was no statue or machine. Curiosity mixed with her breathless anxiety, and she closed her eyes to listen.

The dragon was amused, but its mind was so deep she could only hear the barest whispering echoes of its thoughts. She listened harder, wanting to discern specific thoughts. The dragon's gaze sharpened and glared at her. Nemo tugged on her arm again. "Emma, you're blocking the entrance."

She shrugged him off and concentrated harder. She could almost hear. The dragon jerked its head to the side, lifted its upper lip, and gave a throbbing snarl.

Emma fell back onto her butt and scrambled away, scraping her palms against the pine needles and stones on the ground. A hush descended. Fear rippled among the throng. There had been nothing mechanical in that sound. The dragon coiled itself sinuously closer to the fire.

The crowd remained silent for a heartbeat and then took up their interrupted conversations and kept moving, skepticism keeping them from seeing what was before them. Emma climbed shakily to her feet and looked at the shallow cuts on her hands, picked at some sap at the base of her thumb.

"Are you alright?" Nemo asked as they hurried into the cave. A strange excitement leaked past the barriers on his mind. Emma only nodded, and he stepped closer. "Could you hear it?" So, he knew, or suspected these creatures were real.

"You should've warned me," she hissed, quivering with adrenaline.

The tunnel widened, and she stepped out of the flow of spectators into a rough corner. Her hands still stung, and she needed a moment to still the trembling.

Nemo stepped close to her, gripped her shoulder, and held it firmly until her trembling stopped.

"Thanks." She took a shuddering breath. "Yes, I heard it. I couldn't make out anything specific, though. Nemo, this place...is it..." she shook her head, unsure of what to ask. The reality of their powers and creatures like that dragon tumbled around in her head confusingly.

He held a hand up and smiled mysteriously. "Let's just wait and see. You can make your own judgement. Based on the website, there's still much to see."

I'm not sure I can handle much more, Emma thought, but she took another deep, steadying breath and they rejoined the stream of people.

The air felt different than she'd expected. She had been in a cave once before, during a family vacation; it had been a cool, moist place.

This cave felt warm and dry. A breeze of fresh air that smelled of pine trees blew from, curiously, further in. The light from the fire pit faded within just a few feet, when the tunnel twisted in a sharp turn. After that, pure darkness descended, and the slow shuffling of feet marked their passage. The gloom pressed in on them, stifling and thick. People bumped into the walls and each other. Whispered apologies and hissed expletives sounded all around them. Emma's heart began to pound, and her breath sped up. "Nemo?"

He opened his mind to her. *I'm here.* Emma reached for where the thought came from. He gripped her hand and squeezed her fingers. **We're almost through.**

Emma squeezed his fingers back in wordless relief. They shuffled onward a few more breathless moments, and then the tunnel opened onto a large cavern, dimly lit by flickering light from a fire pit identical to the one in the clearing. Stone stands lined the walls like a Roman amphitheater. Above that, the cave walls glittered with crystal. People crossed a hard-packed dirt floor to the stands and selected seats. A single Corinthian column towered on either side of the cavern, their tops lost in the thick darkness above them.

"Okay," Emma said in stunned disbelief. "What the heck? There's a coliseum in a cave in a small California forest, and nobody has heard about it?"

Nemo chuckled. "Amazing, isn't it? The circus brings the architecture with them."

"Brings it with them?" She stared at him, eyebrows raised.

He only shrugged. "That's what the website said."

They skirted the fire pit on their way to the stands, and Emma realized no smoke rose from the fire. The breeze of fresh air seemed to be coming off the flames, smelling of the pines outside and so chill that Emma glanced up, wondering if the cave opened to the sky. There was only darkness above, with no stars visible. "I'm definitely dreaming," she muttered. They tromped up the stone stairs and found an empty section of the bench to sit on.

A troupe stood around the firepit when Emma glanced over again. They stood with their backs to the flames to form a circle of oddly shaped silhouettes. More than that, Emma noticed their silence. She couldn't hear thoughts from any of them. "Are those the performers?" she asked.

Nemo nodded. "They call themselves Phantasms. Hence the name of the circus."

Emma studied them more intently. It was odd to not be able to hear anything at all from them, considering she had been able to hear the fey lights and the dragon. *What if they really are ghosts?* She couldn't just laugh off the notion after what she had seen already that evening. "Nemo, do you have any theories from what you read on the website?"

"I'm not sure. I was thinking maybe they're—" The fire went out and the whispers that filled the cave were extinguished with it.

"Ladies and gentlemen," a voice called. "Please find your seats. The show is about to begin." A low glow emanated from beneath the stands, just enough light for the stragglers to find seats. Emma glanced toward the tunnel. The entrance disappeared while she watched, fading away into solid stone.

The glow slowly brightened to illuminate a young man standing by the fire pit. He was younger than Emma expected, appearing to be in his mid-twenties. Despite that, he truly looked the part of a ringmaster. A coat with interchanging bright blue and gold diamonds contrasted sharply with his dark complexion and long dark curls. He held a blue silk top hat upside down by the rim, pressed against his chest. A long, golden brown feather pinned to the hat gleamed dully.

"Ladies and gentlemen," he repeated, with a wide, toothy grin.

"Welcome. Welcome. Welcome to a show that will delight and amaze you." His voice echoed, rich and hypnotic. Puffs of smoke rose from the fire behind him, twining and twisting into peculiar shapes. "It may also, perhaps, frighten you but, I assure you, you will depart enlightened to a world beyond your wildest dreams. Welcome to the Circus Phantasm!"

He tossed his hat up, flicking his wrist so it spun in the air. The fire flared up behind him in a great pillar, and the two oddly shaped figures leapt up into the air. They unfurled great wings, one tawny brown, the other pure black. Their feathers gleamed in the flickering light and Emma couldn't look away, dazzled by their plumage. One caught the hat as they ascended. They flew up, keeping out of the spotlight so they remained shadowed. Separating, they glided to the columns and disappeared into the darkness.

Emma craned her neck to try to see the one on the column closest to them, but the darkness didn't allow her to discern anything more than a few feet up.

When she returned her attention to the ringmaster, his hat sat atop his head once more and he stood next to a single dark figure. The firelight gleamed strangely off this person's arms and chest, and Emma realized he wore black plate armor.

"We begin our show in a forest," the ringmaster whispered as he took several twisting steps away from the armored man. A greenish glow reflected off the crystalline walls and bird whistles rang out somewhere above them. "Forests are filled with many wonders, but this brave knight sought a very special one."

The knight whistled. A black horse appeared at the far end of the arena and trotted into the firelight. It stood still for the knight to pull himself into the saddle, his armor clanking as he did. He took up the reins in his gloved hands and pulled them to the side to direct the horse to trot along the wall of the stands. "The knight's quest was certainly unusual," the ringmaster continued, "as well as perilous. The creature the knight sought was known to be fierce and dangerous when looked upon by men."

The horse started its second circuit of the arena and a gold glow replaced the green light. A white horse cantered into view on the other side of the arena. No, not a horse. When Emma looked closer, she saw that the creature was more slender than a horse, with thin legs like a deer, and a whippy tail with a tuft on the end. Most prominently of all, a curved gold and silver horn protruded from its head above intelligent dewy gold eyes. It turned its head as it surveyed the audience, so that everyone could get a good look at it. Emma realized she was holding her breath in awe and let it out in a rush.

Advancing gracefully into the center of the cavern, the unicorn turned, as if inviting everyone to admire it. On the far side of the stands, the horse wheeled around to face the unicorn. The horse snorted in alarm and tossed its head, sidling as it tried to turn away. The knight yanked the reins and forced his steed to stand its ground.

"While beloved of maidens the world over, the unicorn detests the armed man." Despite the ringmaster's breathy tone, his voice carried across the cavern and could be heard clearly. The unicorn pawed the ground once, then lowered its head and charged at the knight.

The horse leapt to the side, sending the knight clattering noisily to the ground while it turned and galloped away. It vanished before it went more than a few feet. Everyone's attention, to judge by their thoughts, was riveted on the knight, and nobody noticed the horse's disappearance.

The knight rolled hurriedly out of the unicorn's path, dust forming brown smudges on his dark armor. The unicorn turned aside before it ran into the stands. That gave the knight the chance to scramble ungracefully to his feet and draw a long, thin sword.

"The knight had taken a solemn oath to capture the marvelous creature and bring it back to his lady love," said the ringmaster, still standing impassively by the fire pit. "The fair maiden who held his heart had fallen victim to a terrible illness only the unicorn could cure."

The unicorn raised its head high and regarded the man. Then it stuck a leg out straight and bowed its head over its leg. The man bowed at the waist in return, and then they saluted one another: the knight with his sword, the unicorn with its horn.

Emma had seen plenty of swordfights in movies, but the display that followed was unlike any of those. The man dodged and wove around to avoid the deadly horn. He moved desperately, giving the illusion that his life was truly at stake.

More than once, he clumsily stumbled back when the unicorn lunged at him, its movements graceful and assured.

More than once, it caught the knight's blade with its horn and sent it swinging wide. Its opponent always hastily recovered, and the unicorn did not press the split-second advantage the maneuver gained it.

"Alas, the knight proved to be no match for the unicorn's skill," the ringmaster intoned. "He had diligently trained for many years with the great sword masters of the king's court, but the unicorn possessed centuries of experience. It bested him with ease." The unicorn once more caught the knight's sword and sent it swinging. The knight lost his balance and couldn't recover as quickly as before.

The unicorn lunged forward and held the tip of its horn right above his heart, forcing the knight to go still, his arm held at an odd angle. He dropped the sword and sank to his knees. The unicorn tilted its head and paced forward to keep its horn pressed against his armor.

"The knight realized he was surely about to die." The armored man raised his hands in supplication. "He implored the unicorn to grant his final wish: that it should hasten to his beloved and cure her of her ailment." The creature blinked slowly and tilted its head. "The unicorn agreed and told the knight his life would be spared. However, he must swear never to venture near his beloved again. For he, who had shed so much blood in his lifetime and would even have shed the unicorn's blood, was unworthy of one purified by the unicorn's magic."

The knight slowly inclined his helmeted head, his shoulders slumped in defeat. "He agreed and so swore. The unicorn left him there. He succeeded in his quest but would be lost in spirit forever more." The unicorn turned, bounded into the darkness, and vanished. The knight remained on his knees, staring after it, and the soft golden glow slowly faded into darkness.

No applause sounded. Nobody seemed quite sure how to react. Emma could hear the amazement and shock the narrative inspired echoed in many thoughts.

The bird calls petered out, replaced by the soft strains of a harp. One by one, small lights blinked on high above. A few people glanced up, and their thoughts prompted Emma to look up as well. Her eyes widened in wonder. She poked Nemo and pointed. The darkness above them was strewn with star-like lights.

Most of the audience weren't aware of the change. A few took note and their wonder grew. Titters of laughter from above echoed around the cavern. Everyone looked quickly up.

Three girls, clad in dark garments lined with glittering crystals that winked and sparkled in the renewed golden light, flipped and swung around.

Their faces stood out like pale moons under their black hair. The trapezes they used were painted black as well, so they truly seemed to be gamboling weightlessly among the stars. Their melodious laughter continued to fill the room and brought smiles to the faces of the spectators.

Emma became so fixated on the acrobats' tricks that she didn't notice the increasing heat until sweat beaded up on her face. It swiftly became uncomfortably hot. Emma yanked her sweatshirt off, trying to keep her head clear as alarm filled the spectators' thoughts.

A thunderous boom shook the stands and yanked her attention back up to the ceiling. An image formed out of the darkness. A volcano on a planet, or perhaps a moon, erupted out into space. Large chunks of blue-gray ash fell, and the acrobats made a game of dodging them. Emma snatched a piece out of the air. It disintegrated into fine silver dust in her hand. She let it run through her fingers, dispersing lightly into the air.

The heat faded along with the image. The temperature plummeted. Emma bit back a curse and pulled her sweatshirt back on. Nemo chuckled beside her, and she elbowed him.

New celestial bodies shone above them: great, icy spheres lit up with blue and green light as the acrobats continued to frolic laughingly about. One of the stars grew bigger, and the others faded out of view. The acrobats kept to the edges and avoided this star, no longer laughing. Emma realized they were looking at the Sun, when it once more got warm. She refused to take her sweatshirt off a second time though, so she fidgeted and continued to watch. With a blinding flash, the Sun disappeared, leaving the room in pitch black once more.

Flames licked up from the fire pit as applause thundered around the cave. The ringmaster leaned against the twisted metal, his arms crossed, and his head tilted a little to look up at the ceiling. He didn't move until the audience began to wonder what came next. "Oh," he said in patent surprise. He uncrossed his ankles, pushed himself off the metal, and stepped lithely away from the fire pit. "Welcome back. Did everyone enjoy the celestial journey? I'm afraid you caught me with my head still up in the clouds." He doffed his hat and fanned himself with it while he walked over to one of the columns. He leaned against it and twirled his hat. "Let's see. What's next?" He peered up, as if expecting an answer. When no reply was forthcoming, he put his hat back on and resumed his stroll.

A large tank of water appeared in the center of the room and the man almost walked into it. "Oh, that's right!" he exclaimed. Emma blinked several times and looked at the dirt floor. The tank hadn't been there a moment before, and then it simply was.

You're such a ham during shows, Gabriel. The thought sounded loud and clear from within the tank. A smile twitched at the ringmaster's mouth, and his expression twisted slightly as he tried to remain solemn.

Did he just hear that? Emma stared at him wildly while her mind whirled with the possibility.

"As with forests," he said after he regained his composure, "the ocean has hidden many wonders over the centuries. And as with the unicorn, many tales have been told of these wonders. Some delightful. Many dark." He paused for dramatic effect, his eyes scanning the audience. Emma felt something brush against her thoughts and shivered.

A pale face peered through the glass over Gabriel's shoulder and then flashed away. *Oh, do hurry it up. I just want to get back to my room and have a smoke. We've been working this town too long.*

Mermaids can smoke? The ludicrous idea made Emma chuckle. Nemo gave her a questioning look. She shook her head, and he quickly refocused on the show. Emma stared at the tank, sensing the cross mood of whoever was in there. It puzzled her. The mermaids she and Nemo saw that horrible night hadn't projected thoughts the way humans did.

The magic of this place evaporated and left her feeling disillusioned. Nemo leaned forward, his face alight with eagerness to see the mermaid. She envied him not being able to hear the performer's thoughts, but looked back to the tank, determined to enjoy the show anyway.

The ringmaster stared directly at her, his expression curious. *They are people too. Some smoke, just like humans.*

Emma blanched. He looked away and continued his narrative, but she didn't hear it, too astonished. *Did he just speak into my mind?*

The mermaid leapt suddenly out of the water, twisting in midair, and dove back in. Her damp skin gleamed a pale silvery-blue, and long dark hair streamed around her head. Strings of sparkling pearls, emeralds, and sapphires looped around her tail. The glitter of the gems was the last thing visible as the mermaid splashed back into the water. Emma started and tried to concentrate on the show. Her attention kept wavering and returning to the ringmaster, and she couldn't follow his narrative or the mermaid's theatrical antics.

Emma remained in this daze the rest of the show, only partly aware of the performances, of the music and sounds that echoed around the cavern. Later, she wouldn't be able to describe any of the middle acts. She fidgeted, impatient now for the show to finish. Nemo gave her a few odd looks but otherwise ignored her.

The music cut off abruptly, and the dragon appeared on the floor. It filled up the amphitheater floor and brushed up against the stands. Its bulk shouldn't have fit, but again its edges blurred out into heat haze. Emma frowned, sure this time that not all the dragon was visible.

The ringmaster sat at the base of the dragon's neck, his coat bright against the creature's black scales. He beamed around at the spectators. "Well, ladies and gents," he said in a relaxed tone before yawning hugely. "I am weary, as I am sure many of you are. I release you now." He gestured grandly to the cave wall. The dragon breathed out an inferno of blue-green flames that licked against the stone. When the blaze died, the tunnel entrance had reappeared in the wall. "Go back out into the world but speak not of what you have seen. I bind you to silence."

Emma felt something brush her mind again. She pushed back against it, and the ringmaster's gaze flicked in her direction a moment before he and the dragon disappeared.

The spectators sat in awe and utter silence. Their thoughts of the show were hushed and vague, reminding Emma of how dreams sounded. She suspected these people wouldn't remember much of what they saw here when they woke up the next morning. The show would simply fade from their minds as if they truly had dreamed it.

She remained in her seat, mulling these things over, as the people vanished into the tunnel in twos or threes. Nemo made no move to get up either.

"I want to talk to the ringmaster," Emma said.

"Why?" he asked, his voice overly casual.

Emma shot him a suspicious look. "What are you planning?" She probed his mental defenses and tried to hear his thoughts.

He recoiled from her, both physically and mentally. "Don't do that," he muttered and scooted away from her.

"They're still there."

Gabriel Hightower, ringmaster of the Circus Phantasm, glared at the speaker.

"I know that, Donovan. I can still hear the girl's thoughts." He leaned back against the rough stone wall and rubbed his temples. "I need some pain meds and a drink. Why aren't they leaving?"

"They are Blessed," a deep voice growled. The darkness of the tunnel behind the two men shifted around until a copper eye glared at Gabriel. "The girl is a telepath. Deal with it."

Straightening, he inclined his head. "Yes, sir." He smoothed a hand over his hair and twitched his coat to hang properly. "Are the brothers still in there?" he asked the other man.

"One of them is," Donovan said, his voice fading out as Gabriel stepped forward and teleported, one moment in the tunnel, the next appearing back in the amphitheater, right at the bottom of the steps.

The girl's thoughts skipped with excitement at his sudden appearance. Gabriel inhaled deeply, wishing he could escape to the quiet of the caves. Donovan would just teleport him back if he tried. "Well?" he called up to them. They leapt up and hurried down the stairs to stand before him.

You can read minds, the girl thought eagerly, peering up into his face. He sensed a small bit of apprehension behind this admission, but her excitement overpowered it. *I can too! Can you tell me more about our powers?*

Gabriel only smiled and crossed his arms, dropping back into the mysterious ringmaster he portrayed in performances.

"Are you going to make me say it out loud?" the girl asked, her eager expression fading into irritation. Despite the bravado, he sensed her anxiety spike in her thoughts at revealing herself this way. She knew she had thrown caution to the wind.

He chuckled and shrugged. "I don't know what you're talking about. You children really should be getting home. I'm sure you have a curfew."

"We want to join your circus," the boy blurted.

Caught off guard, Gabriel could only stare at the white-haired boy, unable to hear thoughts from him.

The boy flushed. "We're like you," he added. Gabriel's eyes narrowed in irritation at the implication he was anything like this teenager, and the boy hastened to explain better. "I mean…not normal. I can—"

"Nemo!" The telepathic girl cut him off and grabbed his arm. "What are you doing?"

The conversation was not going the way Gabriel thought it would. He glanced at the telepath and recovered his balance.

"How old are you, Nemo?" he asked dispassionately. "Fifteen? Sixteen? Certainly not old enough to be making such decisions."

"I'm seventeen," Nemo snapped, the flush spreading down his neck. "I know you're interested. Your talent scouts noticed my ability. You're Gabriel Hightower, right? A group came by from Ark Light Company, run by a Mr. Hightower."

Gabriel took an involuntary step back and clasped his hands. He sensed the avian's attention sharpen from the top of the column high above. *Darn it all. Didn't I take my name down from the circus website?*

I must have missed it on one of the side pages.

"Is that so?" He kept his face pleasant and voice pitched to hide the slight tremble. His mind raced. "What about you, girl? Have you had any encounters with this group?"

She stared at him, her thoughts scattered and confused. "I did meet a couple people this morning. They knew that I had an ability," she said. "A girl named Adah. She called it a Blessing. But this is all beside the point! We can't run away and join a circus, Nemo! That's insane!"

"I'll let you join," Gabriel interrupted. His certainty that he needed to keep the younger telepath out of the Company's hands if possible outstripped his burgeoning apprehension.

Nemo's face lit up, but the girl fixed Gabriel with an incredulous stare. He kept his eyes on Nemo. "We're leaving tonight," he lied, quickly analyzing the logistics. Donovan would have to close off the caverns completely, to be safe. "You have three hours. Get your things and be back here, or we leave you behind."

"Deal." Nemo swung around toward the tunnel. His excitement seeped through his mental barriers that prevented Gabriel from hearing his thoughts.

"Wait a minute!" The girl grabbed her brother's arm to stop him. "We can't just..." she shot a desperate look at Gabriel, but he kept his face impassive. *This isn't the conversation I wanted to have with you!*

"We can't just run off! What about Mom and Dad? What about your show, Nemo? And I have..." she trailed off again. *The semester just started. How will I focus on lectures and homework with all that noise?*

Gabriel blinked, aware that the girl hadn't aimed that thought specifically at him. He had to admire her resolve to keep dealing with people with the constant mental overtones. It made no difference, though. He couldn't allow these two to stay behind knowing about the Circus, waiting for the Collectors to find them.

"What is there for you in this town?" Nemo asked, guessing the train of thoughts Gabriel could hear. "Think about it, Emma. Is there really anything you want to do here? I've seen how exhausted and unhappy you are. This is your chance to do something better. To find out about your ability and how to use it."

Emma looked between Gabriel and Nemo, a confused mix of anxiety and anger roiling through her mind and showing on her face.

36

"If I may," Gabriel said smoothly and took a step forward. "I see now that I was wrong to deny the fact that I can, as you said, read minds. As you can, Miss. That is a unique skill, and I would be delighted to teach you how to perfect it. Allow me to properly introduce myself. I am Gabriel Hightower." He bowed to Emma and then looked at Nemo. "I believe you said you have an unusual talent as well?"

Nemo shifted his weight. "Yeah. I can...well, I'm not sure how to explain it. I have some sort of power with my voice. I can influence people with it. Sometimes, I can make them do what I want." An excited idea flashed past his barriers.

"Don't even try it," Gabriel said, his facade slipping enough that his lips dropped into a frown. "I've been trained to defend myself against most Blessings."

"Why are they called Blessings?" Emma's interest renewed itself in her thoughts. Gabriel repressed the urge to chuckle at her wavering indecisiveness. "That girl, Adah, said something about elves."

"I would love to teach you about the history of our abilities," Gabriel replied, his showman's façade returning with a smile and a dip of the head. "But not right now. I'm tired. Come with us, and I will happily answer your questions later."

Emma hesitated and glanced at Nemo. He smiled smugly back at her. "I'm not saying yes yet." She glared defiantly at her brother. "We'll discuss this on the way home. Come on, Nemo."

Gabriel watched them walk into the tunnel, tension snapping between them even though they didn't look at each other. The girl's thoughts drifted back until she exited the cave and the sound cut off suddenly.

A rustle of wings and a heavy thump sounded behind him. He turned to face the avian. Firelight burnished the man's wings to a reddish-gold. "Follow them, Avery. You heard there's Scouts in town. They've already noticed these two. It's not unusual for Scouts to keep watch over their finds to discover their Blessing. If those two are being watched, the Scouts might find us. We'll need to move quickly if they're onto us."

Gabriel's head spun with the possibility. His shoulders slumped. Dropping heavily into a chair that appeared behind him, he clasped his hands, and stared at his fingers, dusty from the performance. He couldn't still the trembling in his fingers now that he had stopped putting on an act.

"I won't be seen," Avery promised. "And I'll make sure those two get back safely. It's important the Company doesn't get another telepath." His features darkened with a worried scowl.

Gabriel continued to stare at his hands, silently cursing his fear. "I share your concern, but if they know the girl's a telepath, Virgil might be in town. If there's any danger, you get back here first. I can't risk them getting wind of the Circus. Understand?"

The winged man didn't reply, and when Gabriel looked up, the flickering illumination showed something close to anger in Avery's face and eyes.

Gabriel forced himself to stand and look at his friend squarely. "I know it's hard, but we really can't take the risk. Please."

Avery took a deep breath and fluffed up the feathers on his head. "I understand," he muttered and took wing, disappearing into the darkness.

No lights shone in the windows of the house when Emma pulled into the driveway. Nemo went in immediately, but she sat in the car and stared at the house before trailing up the porch. The tire swing struck the trunk of the oak tree with a dull thud, and she felt her eyes sting as she closed the front door behind her.

When she passed Nemo's bedroom, she peeked in and saw her brother stuffing rolled up shirts into a half-packed suitcase.

She could only stare in breathless anger for several moments, and Nemo's shoulders hunched under her gaze. "You planned this!" she hissed, pushing the door open a little wider and stepping into the bedroom.

Nemo looked up guiltily and shoved the shirt he held down on top of the forming pile. "I wasn't sure," he muttered. "But with the performing feats the website described, I suspected the show was run by people like us after I found out Gabriel was connected to the Ark Light Company, and I wanted to be prepared. If they were anything like the guy I met earlier, I wouldn't have said anything, and we could have slipped away with the crowd."

Emma bit her lip. The ringmaster's tantalizing promises still rang in her ears. More than that, she knew she couldn't talk her brother out of this, and that frightened her. Would he leave her here alone if she refused to go? Ever since Nemo went into theater, Emma had feared he would leave town one day, relegating her to the past and occasional visits. "I can wake Mom and Dad up right now."

Nemo stiffened. "Don't you dare." Power rang through the words, and she pushed against the compulsion squeezing like iron bands on her mind to keep her from acting on the threat. "I'm serious, Emma. If you do that, I will never forgive you. You might be happy to stay in this town, take care of kids, and deny your Blessing for the rest of your life, but I won't be trapped here."

The words stung, and she drew back, staring at Nemo as he reddened and looked away.

"We're not kids anymore. I'm just months away from graduating high school. I've already done the work I need for that. I'm only taking electives this semester. My role in the play..." he ran a hand over his white hair. "I won't let this chance pass by for their sake. If I allow things like that to stop me, this town will never let me go. That's how it works."

A few tears slipped down Emma's face before she could stop them. She wiped her sleeve over her cheek and sniffed. Nemo's arms closed around her, and he hugged her briefly before stepping away.

"I want you to come, Em. You deserve better than what this town can offer. But I won't let you stop me from going." He turned his back to her and continued packing.

Indecision kept Emma frozen for a minute. What did she want? She considered the silence from the performers. Could she feel normal, living with them?

"I'll go with you. We've always been there for each other, Nemo. All these years, when Mom and Dad had to work late, and we were sick or..." she shook her head and rubbed her arm, trying to dispel the goosebumps rising from the chill in the air and her apprehension. "If this is what you really want, I'll go with you. There's no way I'm letting you go alone." *No way I'm letting you leave me behind.*

Nemo looked at her over his shoulder. "Don't go just for me or to keep being a protective sister. Think about what you want."

Emma stood up straighter and smiled. "I want to learn about my Blessing. I want to know where these powers came from and how I can use them to be more than a nuisance. This sounds like a great adventure for us both!"

39

An excited lightness filled her chest, contrasting sharply with uncertainty and sadness for their parents. The emotions slowed her down as she packed. She lingered over many things, debating what to take and what to leave.

Even so, it took surprisingly little time to pack what she considered essential. When the suitcase was full, she considered the many mementos of her childhood she had to leave behind. Her eyes alighted an ornate music box with a carousel dragon. She wrapped it in a faded shirt and placed it carefully into her backpack. Memories of dancing to the tinkling music from it with her mother plagued her as she went down the hall, and she ran her hand over her parents' door as she passed.

She returned to her room and wrote out two notes. She left one on the desk and went down the stairs. The other note, enclosed in an envelope fat with her savings, she tucked behind a flower pot on the next-door neighbors' porch. *That should be enough to help her find a babysitter for Gracia and Irene.*

Within an hour, she and Nemo climbed once more into her car. The backseat and trunk were stuffed full, but it still seemed like very little to take with them after living in the same house their whole lives.

She gripped the steering wheel and looked at the house for several moments. Then she tore her gaze away and saw Nemo balancing a fish bowl on his lap. "You're bringing your goldfish?"

Nemo's shoulders hunched defensively. "Of course! I can't leave my undead fish. It's resilient and gives me courage."

Emma roared with laughter. More laughter than was warranted, but she couldn't help it after the stress of the week, coming to such a peak that evening.

Nemo had won the fish at a fair in junior high. About a year after he got it, one day he had gone into his room and found his pet on the floor. It had jumped out of the bowl when he was downstairs. It had been late at night, and he hadn't wanted to deal with a dead fish right then, so he'd dropped it back into the bowl and gone to bed. It must've been not quite dead because when he woke up in the morning, he had seen the fish swimming around, alive and happy. It never leapt out of the bowl again.

The laughter eased the tension in Emma's chest, and her heart beat sped with excitement for their adventure. Neither of them noticed the shadowy figure on the house roof that took wing and followed them.

Saturday January 21st

Emma woke up and stared blearily at the golden light streaming in through the window. The slant of the light was different than usual, not reaching her face and giving her no clue of the time the way it did in her bedroom. She studied the unfamiliar room with a groggy detachment.

It looked like a cabin. The walls were all wood paneling, with whorls and grains that drew her eye. She rolled onto her back and looked up at the canopy of the four-poster bed. Vague images of unicorns, dragons, and mermaids flashed through her mind. They had been greeted by a knight and a unicorn after they drove along a dark, mountain road. Nemo had brought his crazy fish with him, and the water sloshed at each bend in the road. The knight greeted them as "newbs" and showed them into a cave with several other cars.

Emma's eyes drifted closed. "What an odd dream," she mumbled and rubbed her face. "Why am I in a cabin?" She must still be dreaming, because she couldn't hear a single thought. Maybe she should get up and explore. She considered that for a moment but curled up instead. The thick blanket on the bed felt so soft and warm she couldn't bring herself to pull herself out from under it.

Someone cleared their throat. Emma's eyes flew open and she scrambled up against the headboard. The room had been empty, and no approaching thoughts warned her of anyone's presence. Now, a man stood by the window, tawny wings folded against his shoulders, the tips brushing his hands. The sunshine gave the crest of feathers on his head and his tan skin a golden glow.

Emma gaped at him. The smile on his open, freckled face wilted under her stare. He shifted, tugging on the tip of his wing while his crest pressed down flat against his head.

"Good morning. Sorry about this. Donovan asked me to show you around. I thought you were already awake, so I said yes, and he shifted me into your room."

"I...what? What?" Her face reddened over how stupid she sounded, but that explanation hadn't made any sense. "Okay." She took a deep breath. "Okay. Last night actually happened. That show...and..." her mouth went dry. "We ran away with a circus." A slightly hysterical chuckle escaped her as a confusing tangle of excitement, sadness, and anxiety struck her.

A smile twitched at the man's lips. "Yes, I suppose that's one way to look at it." He glanced around. The room was bare except for a wooden chest of drawers with an attached mirror against the far side. "How about a chair, Donovan?"

Emma stared at him and wondered if he was mad. Her confusion quickly turned to shock when a chair appeared behind him. He sat down, carefully positioning his wings over the back so they wouldn't be crushed or caught on anything. Emma swallowed and pulled the blanket closer around her. She still wore her jeans and shirt from the day before, but the blanket provided a surprising amount of security.

"I would say you found a good place to learn about your Blessing. The only safe place I know of," he added.

"People keep saying that word without telling me what it's about," Emma grumbled and then took a deep breath, shoving away her sadness over having left her parents and the two girls. She couldn't think about that right then. "Okay," she said once more. "You're here to show me around?" The man nodded, and Emma noticed her suitcase standing by the dresser. Had that been there when she looked before? "I need to change clothes first."

"Of course." The man swung to his feet. "I'll wait in the hallway for you." He took a few steps toward the door but glanced back as Emma pushed the blanket to the side. "I'm Avery, by the way. Welcome to the Circus Phantasm, Miss Emma."

He went out and closed the door before it occurred to Emma that she hadn't told him, or anyone in the circus, her name yet.

Gabriel stared up at the ceiling, his eyes gritty and aching from a lack of sleep. When gray light crept in through his window, one of the few on the edges of the caverns, he swung up, splashed cold water on his face to clear his head, and dressed quickly. He knew what he needed to do.

Years of practice had taught him how to move through the cavern system quickly, and soon he came to a stop at a fork in the tunnel. He glanced once into the amphitheater, just visible at the end of one path, but then turned aside into a smaller cave where the performers waited for their cues. "Tristan."

Tristan jumped and dropped the thick brush he held. The horse turned its head and peered at him. "It's okay," he crooned and stroked the creature's mane reassuringly. Small bits of hay stuck to his gray tunic and in his frizzy cloud of brown hair, giving Tristan a slightly crazed appearance. "Was it necessary to sneak up on me?" he muttered, leading the horse through a wooden gate set into the cave wall. He latched the gate and dusted his hands off. "Well?"

Gabriel tossed and caught his hat, a nervous habit. "Those two kids told me about a group of Scouts in town. I gleaned what I could from their thoughts. I think Caleb is on this team."

Tristan stiffened. "That doesn't make any sense. Caleb is a Ranger." He paced to the end of the room and back. "Is Balthasar on the team too? After what…what I did to him, he might not have been any good as a Ranger anymore."

"I don't know," Gabriel replied. He put his hat on his head and straightened his coat.

"We need to leave town now! Scout teams have people with them that can sense Blessings. If they find us—"

"We will leave this morning," Gabriel said. "But there's something I need to do first." He took a deep breath and explained his plan to his friend.

"Are you crazy?" Tristan demanded. "You're going to get us captured."

"Very possibly," Gabriel said with a thin smile. "But you've known my mental state for years now. If you don't want to go, I'll find someone else. Or go alone."

Tristan sighed and stared into space, his eyes unfocused. "Okay. I told Lady Celeste that I'm going out. Let's get this over with."

"You and that unicorn," Gabriel muttered under his breath as they came to a large cavern where the circus kept their cars. He swiped a hand over the roof of his car, leaving a trail in the dust. It had been a while since he had left his sanctuary. *It will be a while before I do again*, he reassured himself.

Tristan drove, his hands clenching the steering wheel so hard his knuckles stood out stark white against the black leather. As they entered town, he glanced at every passerby.

Gabriel kept his eyes closed and scanned the thoughts around them. "Will you relax?" he muttered. "I'll know if I sense any of the Scouts' minds. I haven't forgotten what their mental voices sound like. Especially not Caleb's or Balthasar's."

"I don't like this," Tristan replied and continued to mutter under his breath as they proceeded. The underlying layer of sound made it that much harder for Gabriel to concentrate as the town's thoughts came at him from every direction. He rubbed his temples as his head began to pound. He always got a headache when subjected to this level of mental noise.

When Tristan came to a stop, Gabriel opened his eyes and surveyed the neighborhood. "This is the address Avery gave you, right?" Tristan asked.

"Yeah." Gabriel eyed the tire swing moving like a pendulum just a few feet away. "Stay here. I don't sense the Scouts' minds anywhere nearby, but that could change. We might need to leave quickly."

"What?" Tristan stared at him, his brow furrowed. "I thought you wanted me to come for my strength! You could've had anyone drive you!"

"I do want your strength. But only as a backup to just driving away if things go south." He listened to the thoughts inside the house. "She hasn't noticed the kids are gone yet. She's going to be freaked out enough without facing both of us."

Tristan muttered under his breath and reached to undo his seatbelt. Gabriel glared at him. "Fine!" he snapped. "Fine! I'll stay here like an obedient dog!"

Gabriel stiffened and stared at him in shock. After a moment, Tristan looked away. "I'm sorry. It's just hard when you get all authoritative and give orders. It reminds me of how things were before. It makes you look like—"

"Don't you dare compare me to him," Gabriel snarled. He grimaced and took a deep breath. "Just wait here. I'll be back soon."

Gabriel caught the tire swing to still its movement. Advancing up the porch, he snapped a charming smile onto his face, knocked on the door, and slipped fully into his showman façade yet again.

Nemo walked through a roughly hewn tunnel, following the strong scent of food, his feet falling quietly on the hard-packed dirt floor. Strings of lights lined the crease between the ceiling and wall on both sides, casting a yellowish glow on the stone walls. It felt like a mine and that made him worry about Emma. She disliked enclosed spaces. His stomach growled loudly. He would go find her…after he ate. Food came first.

The aroma led him to a pair of heavy wooden double doors. They looked wildly out of place set into the stone of the tunnel. Nemo could only stare for a moment, and then he shrugged, too hungry to wonder about it anymore.

The smooth metal handle chilled his hand as he pushed one door open and stepped from the dirt floor onto slick black tiles. The moment he released the door, it swung decidedly shut once more. Nemo barely registered that, too intent on the room before him.

The walls were the same roughhewn stone as in the tunnel, but lamps hanging from the ceiling cast the room in dim light.

It looked like a dining room in a fancy restaurant. Rows of round booths lined the walls on either side. Round tables with red table cloths were spaced evenly in the middle of the room. At the far side, he saw a solid wooden door next to a stereotypical pass-through window. Clanks, thumps, and snarls came from the kitchen.

Nemo could hear several people speaking, but they were ensconced in the booths, so he couldn't see them. He stood by the door for a few moments, uncertain where to go, before walking over to the corner booth where a man with long, straight black hair sat by himself. "Excuse me."

The man looked up from the book in his hands. His eyes glinted, proud and unreadable. He looked Nemo over coolly before he tucked his hair behind a pointed ear and raised an eyebrow.

"Do I order food or what?" Nemo asked, struggling not to stare.

The elf tilted his head. "Just go up to the pass-through and ask for a plate," he said quietly and returned his attention to his book with an air of dismissal.

Nonplussed, Nemo wove through the tables up to the window. "Hello?" he called.

The snarling and thumping cut off. A wild-looking man stepped up to the window and peered out at Nemo. His ears came to points like the elf's, but his short black hair stood nearly on end in messy spikes. His yellow eyes were most prominent of all, with slit pupils like a cat's. "What?" the man rasped in a hoarse voice.

"Are you serving breakfast?" Nemo asked, growing more and more disoriented. Had he fallen down a rabbit hole?

The cook withdrew from sight, and the clanking resumed. Nemo fidgeted. *What now?* The smell coming from the kitchen made his mouth water. His stomach growled again. He debated going through the door into the kitchen and turned in that direction, when the door creaked open. The wild-looking cook and a man with pasty white skin walked out, both carrying plates.

The wild-looking man placed the plates he carried on the nearest table and gestured. "Sit," he ordered and took a seat himself. Nemo's appetite evaporated as he sat down across from the man.

The cook leaned forward and regarded him intensely. "You are the new Blessed," he commented as the elf from the corner also sat down at their table. The pale man had taken the other two plates to the next table.

"Yeah," Nemo said uncertainly. The elf and the cook continued to stare piercingly at Nemo as he began to sweat. "Please leave me alone so that I can eat." His voice rang with power, but by this time he was so irritated he hardly cared.

The room fell silent. "You will pay for that impudence!" The elf half stood, reaching toward his hip.

The cook held a hand up. "Peace, Lucien," he rumbled, his eyes not leaving Nemo. "The boy is quite impudent, but I will not have violence here."

Nemo glanced around, hearing people taking up their conversations again. His attention arrowed back to the cook when the man leaned forward and tapped the table. "I like your fire, but you will not use your Blessing on me again, boy, or I will roast you."

The elf studied Nemo as he slowly sat back down. His scowl gradually lightened. "I don't think he can control it."

The cook glanced at the elf. "You believe so?" he asked in surprise. The elf nodded, his gaze still lingering on Nemo. The cook huffed. "I see. Then he'll need a teacher." He scratched his chin and looked at the pale man. "Donovan, are any of Gabriel's people qualified to teach someone with a vocal Blessing?"

"Not that I know of," the man replied, examining his bitten off fingernails. The two plates of food he had brought out still sat untouched on the other side of his table.

The cook huffed again and swung to his feet. "Alright then. I will teach you," he growled and jabbed a finger at Nemo. "Eat up, boy. You will need all of your strength." He turned on his heel and stomped back into the kitchen. The elf rose lithely and returned to his corner booth.

The pale man watched Nemo with a faintly curious expression. Nemo turned his back to the man and took a tentative bite. The food tasted amazing and successfully diverted all his attention into shoveling it into his mouth.

When he looked over a few minutes later, the pale man frowned down at an open notebook that had not been at the table before. "You have a lot of courage," the man remarked.

"Why is that?" Nemo asked. His mood was much improved now that he was full.

"Not even Gabriel would speak that way to the Gate Keeper," Donovan said glibly and got up. He circled the table and pulled the other two chairs out.

Nemo blanched, and the blood drained from his face. "The Gate Keeper. You mean…that man…the cook is…

"A dragon, yes." Donovan smirked. "He meant it quite literally when he threatened to roast you. You'll have your work cut out for you as his student."

Nemo's stomach turned over, and he breathed in slowly to keep his breakfast down. He replayed the conversation, picturing having it with the great black dragon from the night before.

The peculiarity of his situation struck him all at once, and for just a few moments he wished he could retreat into his messy bedroom. His head thumped down on the table, and he didn't look up when the door opened a few seconds later.

"Welcome," Donovan called. Nemo turned his head to the side and glanced around. Emma and a winged man walked up to Donovan's table.

Being unable to hear the winged man's thoughts perplexed Emma. They walked in silence for a few minutes while she probed his mental defenses, trying to discover why she couldn't hear him. His mental defenses were much stronger than Nemo's. She couldn't even sense a hint of his emotions.

They came to a fork in the path, and Emma noticed their surroundings for the first time. The wonder from the night before returned. "The Circus lives in these caves?" she asked, giving up on hearing his thoughts. "How does that work with travelling around?"

Avery hesitated. "I'm not sure how to explain that," he said and shifted his wings. "It's magic. Donovan is Keeper here, and he teleports the caves from one place to another."

"Okay," Emma said and nodded her acceptance of all this. Avery gave her a strange look and she smiled. "I'm a mind reader, standing next to a...um..."

"Avian," Avery supplied.

"Right. Standing next to an avian. To say nothing of the other creatures I saw last night. Why shouldn't some wizard and teleporting caves be thrown into this crazy mix?"

"Mage," a nasal voice said right behind them. Emma jumped and whirled around. She found herself face to face with a man with an extremely pale complexion, unkempt black hair, and dark rings under his eyes. He hadn't been there a moment before. Emma took several steps back, closer to Avery. "I am a mage, not a wizard."

"Morning, Donovan," Avery said cheerfully. "You look well. Did you actually get some sleep last night?"

Donovan's flat gray eyes focused on the avian. "A few hours, yes.

Thank you for the concern. After you show Miss Emma around some, will you please bring her to the dining room? Nemo is headed there now. Gabriel went out early, but he'll be back soon. He'll probably want to speak with Miss Emma some over coffee in a short while."

"Will do," Avery said. Donovan disappeared as abruptly as he appeared. "The teleportation thing is one of his abilities as a Keeper," Avery explained. "You'll get used to it. He can also pop us around. It's quite useful. Newcomers always get lost a lot at first. And I think he just likes to mess with us, popping us around the caves at random. But you didn't hear it from me."

Emma chuckled and replayed the man's words in her head. "Does he know everything that happens in the caves then?"

"I believe so, yes. I think that's the main thing of being a Keeper." They came up to an archway leading into another cave. "Ah, here are the baths," he said and bowed. "My lady," he added with a grin.

Emma snorted. "Clown," she said as she passed him. The echoing of water dripping into a pool masked the gasp that escaped her when she saw past the archway. Steam gently rose from the pool, covered with ancient mosaic tiles, many of them cracked or chipped. She went up to the edge of the water and dipped a hand in. It was pleasantly hot, just on the edge of comfort, like a jacuzzi. Her fingers stung ever so slightly as she pulled them back out. She cast her eyes around the cavern once more. Short marble columns lined one side. "What is this place?" she wondered out loud. "It's so beautiful. It looks Roman, like the amphitheater."

"Darned if I know," Avery said in a bright tone. "I just live here." Emma gave him an incredulous look that he smiled at. "Now that you know where the bathroom is, want to go get breakfast? We shouldn't keep Donovan waiting."

"Okay." She looked around one more time before reluctantly following the avian out. She would have to come back here later.

Avery led her through a series of tunnels and caverns that twisted and turned until she knew she would never find her way back to the bathroom or her own room. Finally, they came to a set of carved wooden doors. Avery opened one door and again bowed her through, winking as she stepped past him.

Emma didn't believe anything could surprise her after what she had already seen, but the room she entered made her pause. It was even

49

more incongruous than the bathroom. Like her cabin bedroom, the dining room simply did not fit with the caverns that surrounded it. She stared, dazed for a moment, before she spotted Nemo and flew towards him. His presence provided the grounding factor she needed.

Nemo had his head down on the table, and he looked sick. Donovan sat at another table with two plates of food. He beckoned them over. "Timaeus, the cook, has already closed the kitchen for the morning," he said. "I got you some food before he did." He nodded to them as they sat and then disappeared.

"Good morning," Emma called to her brother. "How are you doing so far? Adjusting?"

"Yeah. I just got...apprenticed...or something...to the dragon. I don't think that I can..." Avery gestured urgently at Nemo. "What?" Nemo snapped.

"Don't speak about Timaeus in the dining room," Avery whispered. "He has very good hearing, and his temper—"

"What are you saying, bird-man?" a voice boomed. A crazed looking man walked out of the kitchen and leaned on the door post with his arms crossed. He scowled at them.

Avery grinned sunnily in reply. "Good morning, Timaeus. How are you doing, sir? Your cooking is wonderful, as always.

Timaeus snorted. "Suck up," he grumbled. "If you enjoyed the food so much, you can wash the dishes."

Avery flinched, and Timaeus smiled maliciously, beckoning. The charming avian sighed and looked at Emma. "I will sacrifice my time so that you all may eat. I hope you appreciate it." He bowed his head and disappeared into the kitchen. Timaeus followed, and the kitchen door fell closed with a heavy boom as Nemo dragged himself over to Emma's table.

They stared at each other. "Timaeus," Emma said, and her lips twitched with the urge to smile. "There are some who call me...Tim." Nemo snorted, and they both burst out laughing. The others in the room glanced at them curiously, but nobody questioned them.

"I see your morning's been interesting too," Nemo said when he regained his composure.

"It's been unique, to say the least." She glanced at the kitchen door. "Tim is the dragon?"

"Apparently," Nemo muttered, his mirth evaporating entirely.

50

"That bad?" Emma asked. Nemo groaned, put his head on the table again, and covered his face with his arms. Emma chuckled and patted him on the back.

The entrance door creaked open to admit Gabriel and another young man. Their faces were slightly flushed, and their hair ruffled as if they had just come in from outside. The man stood a head shorter than Gabriel and looked to be about Emma's age. He wore a blue tunic over loose pants and kept his long, straight brown hair tied back at the nape of his neck. They walked over to the table where Emma and Nemo sat.

"Emma, this is Tristan," Gabriel said and gestured at the man. "He led you in last night."

"I'm the knight," Tristan said. "Have you settled in? You seemed disoriented when I greeted you last night. I think you were starting to feel the effects of the mind trick Gabriel does to make everyone forget."

Emma smiled uncertainly at him. "Did I? I'll admit I don't remember last night very well. Whatever Gabriel did to make everyone forget is very effective."

Tristan nodded, and Gabriel beckoned to them. "Come with us. Donovan is going to be shifting the caves, and he wants us all together in the arena. We can talk more there."

Avery watched them go out, elbow deep in soapy water.

Timaeus looked up from the meat he was carving, seeing that Avery had stopped washing. "You seem troubled, little bird."

The avian set aside the clean plate, wiped his hands dry on his pants, and scratched his shoulder. His feathers made his skin itch sometimes. "Just wondering how Gabriel will do as Emma's teacher," he remarked. "She'll be his first student. And well...he doesn't talk about his teacher very often. That didn't end well." Avery tilted his head, remembering Gabriel telling him the details of that through the bars of a cage. His feathers itched even worse at the memory, and he resisted the impulse to pluck one out.

Timaeus grunted. "Such is life. If you have finished with those dishes, help me with this. I am going to cook a proper feast to welcome those two new humans."

Avery chuckled and approached the dragon-man. "Any excuse will do?" he teased, ignoring the burning look Timaeus gave him.

"I am going to teach that scrawny boy to control his voice. He will need to build up his strength. He needs more meat."

"God help him," Avery said and then leaned back to see out the door. "Oy! Lucien! Come be useful! If I must help, then you have to, also!"

Entering the arena made the reality of Emma's situation come crashing down. Leaving home. Abandoning those two little girls. Sadness made her eyes prick, and she glanced around for a distraction. Nearly a dozen people sat in the stands, partaking in various activities. Two dark-haired girls leapt and swung from the trapezes high above. They caught sight of Emma and waved. The elder of the two let go of the trapeze and straightened out, floating weightlessly. "Welcome to the circus!" she called down. The other girl flashed in and out of view as she continued to move.

Emma smiled and wiped her sleeve over her eyes. "Thank you!" she called, grateful to the girl for the words.

"Our acrobats," Gabriel said proudly. "Arielle has a levitation Blessing, and Adelle invisibility." As he spoke, fragmented memories of last night's show flashed through Emma's mind.

Then something else brushed her thoughts. She blinked, and the memories slowly grew clearer, as if a light were coming on in her head. She glanced over at Gabriel. Curiosity pricked her, and she thought her question.

"Sorry," he said. "I cast that on the whole audience, so they wouldn't remember us. I would prefer your memories were whole, though."

"Cast?" she repeated. "It's a spell?"

"No. Memory manipulation is an ability of my Blessing. I'll teach that to you sometime. First, I'm going to teach you how to close your mind off. I prefer not being able to hear anyone's thoughts here. It makes me feel normal." He walked over to a pair of stools and sat down.

Emma sat across from him. Eagerness to learn about her ability and make new friends chased thoughts of home away.

"Close your eyes and picture a wall," Gabriel instructed. "Good. I can see it clearly in your thoughts." His voice sounded pleased. Emma smiled and opened her eyes. "No, you let it go. You need to focus. Keep it ever present, with the rest of your thoughts behind it. Once you get used to it, you don't have to do it consciously anymore. Your mind will keep the wall up subconsciously. It takes practice, though. Keep at it."

Nemo watched them, feeling out of place; a common enough feeling. He'd always felt a step removed from the other teenagers at his high school, even those he told himself were his friends.

Tristan sat cross legged on the side of the arena floor, speaking quietly with the unicorn lying beside him. He glanced up at Nemo and said something to the magnificent creature. She nodded and surged to her feet, pacing away. Tristan got up as well and came over. "Do you want me to teach you some sword fighting basics?" he asked with a shy smile. "That's a skill any dragon's pupil should have." His mouth twitched as he spoke, and his eyes crinkled with repressed laughter.

"Yeah!" Nemo followed the older teen to the center of the room. A short while later, he lunged one foot forward in a dueling move, and the dirt floor jerked unexpectedly under his feet. He lost his balance and tumbled down, raising a cloud of dust. The ground shook ever so slightly under his palms.

Tristan approached and offered a hand. "Are you okay? Sometimes transitions are a little bumpy, especially ones as big as that one. Gabriel wanted to take us far from that town."

"Why?" Nemo asked. The way Tristan said it made Nemo think there was a distinct reason for it. An uncomfortable lump formed in his throat as it sank in that there really wouldn't be any going back now. He coughed to clear it and blinked several times to keep his eyes from watering.

Tristan's expression went blank, and he cleared his throat. "Well, that's because..."

"I don't like performing in the same state very long," Gabriel interrupted, coming up behind Nemo and startling him. Nemo whipped around. Gabriel smiled thinly. "We're a circus. We move around a lot. Usually just where the whim strikes me or Donovan to go. Please don't ask too many questions about that."

"Okay then," Nemo muttered. *That's not suspicious at all.* Emma watched them from the other side of the room, her face unreadable. Their eyes met briefly before she looked away.

Doubts assailed Nemo, but he stood up straighter and resumed practicing with the wooden sword. He had gotten them into this, and he wouldn't make them regret it.

Adah leaned back against the park bench. Letting her long hair dangle over the back, she closed her eyes and sighed in contentment. "I love the way parks feel. People tend to be happy here."

"Uh-huh," Rebecca said absently. Adah opened one eye and saw the young woman sitting with her legs crossed and her foot jiggling impatiently. "Do you sense anything other than how happy everyone is?"

Adah sighed again. "Why do we have to rush?" she grumbled. "We have all day." Still, she closed her eyes again and tried to sense anything more.

A pair of joggers passed them, their emotions drawing Adah's attention. She opened her eyes to peer after them, and Rebecca exhaled loudly.

"Calm down." Adah regulated Rebecca's mood, mentally picturing turning down a volume knob, and tried again to sense any Blessings. "I don't think there is...Oh. Those two." She nodded to two children chasing each other around the playground, giggling. "They're both Blessed."

Rebecca studied them, a thoughtful look on her face. "It's interesting how often it runs in families," she said. "And how often it doesn't. The boss told me once that he was the first Blessed born in his family for several generations. And now there's Michael and—"

"I'd rather not talk about that," Adah interrupted.

"Right." Rebecca got to her feet. "Come on, then. Let's see if we can find anyone else."

"Let's go on the slide, Gracia!" one of the girls yelled. The other girl called back in Spanish.

Adah looked back towards the girls and smiled. "See you soon."

The intoxicating smell of roasting meat filled the caverns and tunnels for two whole days, making it hard to focus on the rehearsals and day-to-day tasks.

Food proved scarce, even at mealtimes, since the cook remained preoccupied with the feast preparation. Hunger made concentration even more difficult.

"Is this normal?" Emma asked Avery on the second afternoon, after a long day practicing how to guard her mind. Avery had once again showed her the way to the baths, where they now sat with their feet in the water. Emma found the steady plinking of moisture off the stalactites and into the pool quite relaxing after the day's mental strain.

Avery shrugged, his wings rising and falling with the motion. "It's not particularly odd. Timaeus takes any excuse to go into a cooking frenzy. It usually doesn't last more than a day, but once or twice he went this long. One time, he took five days. We were about ready to storm the kitchen and risk his wrath by the time he finished preparations."

Emma chuckled at the image.

"How are you settling in?" he asked. "There will be a show tonight.

It won't be any different than the one you saw, but I've heard newcomers say the first show they see as a member of the circus is quite special."

Emma smiled and drew her knees up to her chest. "I am excited for tonight's show but I'm still feeling a little lost," she admitted. "It's all still so…" she trailed off as a golden glow emanated from the tunnel. The unicorn entered, accompanied by the acrobats: Arielle, Adelle, and a third girl who also had dark hair but stood slightly apart from the other girls, her expression aloof. Arielle and Adelle cast knowing smiles at Avery and Emma.

The avian pulled his feet out of the water and stood up. "Did you want some girl time? I'll be on my way."

Emma got up hastily and followed. Light-hearted laughter floated out after her. She flushed a little in embarrassment that she'd run from interacting with them and rubbed her face. "Will you show me back to my room? I need some time alone before the show and…storming the kitchen for dinner."

"Sure thing," Avery said, an understanding smile making his freckled cheeks scrunch up.

Emma smiled tentatively at him. "Thanks. Your help with finding my way around here means a lot. I'll learn my way soon, hopefully."

"There's no hurry," Avery said. "I enjoy meeting interesting people, and it's been a while since we had any newcomers."

"The feast is ready!" The roar echoed through the tunnels as Emma and Nemo walked towards the dining room, starving and hoping to scrounge anything at all. They looked at each other in surprise, and then they suddenly stood in the dining room.

Emma bit back a curse as dizziness hit her from the sudden transition. Nemo bumped into her, knocking her onto one knee. "Darn it, Nemo!" she hissed and shoved him away.

"Sorry," he said in a dazed tone. When she staggered to her feet, she saw the buffet table set with a grand amount of fare, lit with flickering colored lights from the pixies fluttering over it.

"Oh," she whispered and took several steps forward as more people appeared around them.

A beef roast crowned the middle of the table, between a golden-brown turkey and a baked ham. Fresh bread, tureens of mashed potatoes, roasted ears of corn, platters of cheese and berries…and more besides filled in the gaps between the platters of carved meat. A bowl of salad sat on one corner, looking like an afterthought, although when Emma examined it, she founds bits of turkey mixed in.

The black dragon stood on the other side of the table, his head raised proudly and the tip of his tail twitching like a cat's. The rest of him faded into the darkness behind him. "Welcome, Emma and Nemo Reeve," he rumbled, grinning in a way that showed his teeth. "Step forth."

Emma's stomach growled loudly, but she walked around the table and up to the dragon. Nemo followed just a step behind her. "Kneel," the dragon ordered. Swallowing back a sudden burst of fear, Emma obeyed without question.

Gabriel stood in front of her suddenly and put a hand on her shoulder. "You may rise, Emma. You've already blocked your thoughts. You're more than welcome in my sanctuary. I look forward to teaching you more about your Blessing." Emma got to her feet and followed Gabriel around the table, leaving Nemo kneeling before the dragon.

He regarded Nemo with his burning copper eyes. "Nemo Reeve. Your Blessing is special and unique. An ability that can be great when refined and controlled. It will be my joy to teach you. Rise, and let us feast together."

Nemo got to his feet as the dragon arched and twisted around, his body shrinking with a rustle of scales and a few unusual pops until he stood in his human form. He clapped the teen on the shoulder. "Sit at my left hand, my student." Nemo nodded, his eyes bright with joy.

Timaeus sat down at the head of the table. The elf sat at his right, Nemo at his left, and Donovan on Nemo's other side. Emma sat between Gabriel and Avery at the other end of the table. Everyone else sat along the single long table. Pixies hovered over and around them, occasionally stealing bits of fruit. Happy chatter and laughter filled the room as the troupe relished the wondrous feast.

"So how does the shifting thing work?" Nemo asked Donovan. Avery's head jerked up, and he waved frantically at Nemo. Nemo raised an eyebrow but remained focused on Donovan. "With moving the whole cave system, I mean."

Donovan's eyes lit up behind his glasses. Avery clapped a hand to his face and groaned. The sound ran like a soft current up and down the table.

Emma looked at the avian in confusion then glanced at Gabriel. The ringmaster stared fixedly at his plate, his eyes glassy. A hush fell over the table in the wake of the groan, so Emma could clearly hear Donovan when he spoke.

"It is a complicated process, and one of the main reasons so few mages train to be Keepers. It takes an exceeding amount of mental strength to fulfill the requirements," Donovan said in a monotone, staring straight at Nemo. Despite the gleam Nemo's question had elicited, his eyes were still weary and a little bloodshot.

Nemo stared back in growing befuddlement. "First, I need to find a place in the area I desire to relocate to. It must have a convergence of the lines of natural energy. It also must be in a gap with minimal spiritual warfare occurring. Fortunately, these two requirements usually coincide as the spread of humanity weakens natural energy and increases spiritual conflict."

Donovan paused for breath and took a drink from his goblet. "Next, I must loosen the physical fusions I have made with the current location. This is tedious. If I sever them entirely, we would be cast adrift and be unable to return to the physical plane. Then I must begin creating bonds with the new location. The farther away it is from the current location, the more difficult this step is, and things are very precarious at this point. I must both strengthen the bonds in the new location and slowly dissolve the remaining fusion to the previous one."

He took yet another deep breath and fingered his goblet. "If I fail, the cave would suddenly be in two places at once. As this is a physical impossibility, it would be destroyed along with everyone and everything within."

The respectful silence held while Donovan spoke, but by the time he concluded his monologue, everyone stared glassy-eyed into space. Timaeus still ate, chewing slower than before, and looking grouchier than ever. "Is that simple enough?" Donovan asked with a slight smirk.

Nemo swallowed. "Well..." he said and grimaced. "It was very informative," he said politely. "Thank you for explaining, sir."

Emma snorted and covered a smile. She reached for her own goblet of apple cider and brought it her lips, only to feel something quite solid brush her lips. A yelp escaped her, and the goblet fell to the floor. A pixie crawled out of it, a wide grin splitting its round face and its scrap of a tunic soaked with juice. Avery and several other performers laughed, breaking the silence. Conversations resumed around the table.

Nemo moved down the table to sit by her and glanced uncertainly at Gabriel. "So, what now? Can I perform with the circus?" Hope touched his voice.

Gabriel took a drink from his goblet and regarded them. "We can incorporate you," he said slowly. "You need to learn to use your voice. You can do a lot with that. In the meantime, perhaps you can get a singing skit in one of the performances. Or help me narrate." His eyes lit up. "Your voice would be perfect for the knight and unicorn story."

"Gabriel," Tristan interrupted. "Lady Celeste wanted me to tell you that she's going to sit out from the shows for a while."

They stared at each other, and Emma heard an indistinct mental communication pass between them, like listening to someone speak far off. Gabriel's mouth twisted into a frown. "I see. I won't ask her to perform in that delicate state. I suppose I should've seen it coming. She's been acting oddly ever since she visited that unicorn herd last year. Will you still be performing?"

"I will until Lady Celeste needs me to stay close to her," he promised. "I have that vow to protect her to consider, you know."

"Yes, I know." Gabriel rolled his eyes and looked once more at Nemo. "There are other parts you can narrate. We'll work on that. What about you, Emma? Any dreams of being in the show?"

Emma shook her head vehemently. "I just want to learn about my Blessing and anything else I can here. I'm sure there's plenty."

"Very much so," Gabriel replied, amusement lighting his face. "Go ahead and explore to your heart's content. Get yourself situated. You'll have duties with the circus soon."

"Dessert!" the dragon bellowed. Donovan waved his hands and the plates from the buffet disappeared to be replaced by platters of cherries jubilee and tureens of ice cream.

Tristan got up and patted Nemo on the back. "Don't let that big lecture get to you," he whispered. "Donovan catches someone being curious every now and again, usually when the person is new. He loves the chance to haze them like that. Good luck settling in." The teen straightened and bowed to Timaeus. "May I be excused, lord dragon? I would like to take some ice cream to Lady Celeste."

"Go," Timaeus grunted. Tristan grabbed two bowls of ice cream but paused. He looked uncertainly from Gabriel to her and Nemo, as if he knew something they didn't. When he saw Emma had noticed, he grimaced and fled.

What's that about? She glanced at Gabriel, but he was looking pointedly away now.

She put it from her mind so that she could enjoy the dessert. "Why cherries jubilee?" she asked Avery. "Seems like an odd choice. Did he make everything? What about the ice cream?"

Avery chuckled. "He didn't make the ice cream. Timaeus doesn't mess around with cold stuff. Meat is his specialty, but he enjoys branching out. Cherries jubilee was favored by some dragon king in medieval times. Timaeus honors that bit of culture whenever he gets around to making dessert."

Emma laughed but Avery's face remained composed. "Wait, are you *serious*?"

"Perfectly," Avery said as solemnly as he could. He failed, and his lips twitched into a smile. He never seemed to be without one for long. "Ask him sometime. Cherries jubilee is part of dragon culture."

Emma gave him a suspicious look that he returned with a bland smile. She huffed and looked away, sure that he was pulling her leg.

The performers dispersed as they finished eating. Each one asked Timaeus to be excused before they left. Emma had swallowed her last bite and couldn't possibly eat any more, when Gabriel got to his feet and regarded them sternly.

"Tristan and I went out to speak to your mother this morning," the ringmaster announced.

Emma choked on the water from her goblet.

"She wants you to call her." He frowned at their horrified expressions. "What? Did you think this was like a movie, where your parents simply stop existing because you ran away? As your new official guardian, I had an obligation to speak to them." He bowed to Timaeus. "If I may be excused, lord dragon?"

Timaeus nodded, and Gabriel left the room at a speedy clip. Emma and Nemo stared after him, wide-eyed.

"Well," Avery murmured into the silence. "I don't envy you two." Emma turned her shocked eyes to him. He grinned and patted her on the back. "Best not to put it off. See you in the morning." He rose lithely, bowed at the dragon-man, and went out.

Emma took a deep, shuddering breath. "Let's get it over with." "Come back to my room with me. I need to charge my phone, but that won't take too long. I think I saw an outlet in the wood paneling earlier. Powered by magic, I guess."

Unnecessary drama, Nemo thought for her to hear, refusing to be distracted by the evidence of magic in their new home. He got up and slouched after her.

At the door, Emma glanced back, wondering if they'd be committing a faux pas in not asking the dragon to be excused. "Go," Timaeus rumbled, smiling grimly. "Have fun with that. I expect you to be in the kitchen early tomorrow, Nemo."

Emma bit back a groan at the thought of the coming conversation and walked out, her feet dragging heavily. The door fell closed behind them with a jarring, disheartening boom.

Gabriel collapsed onto a couch pushed up against the stone wall of a cave lit only by a dim blue shine.

"What a delightful banquet," a dark-haired woman murmured, settling next to him and stretching her pale legs along the couch.

Gabriel smiled at her, reveling in her low, quiet voice, and stroked her knee absently. "Timaeus does love the occasional formal ceremony."

The woman chuckled and ran a hand over Gabriel's forehead and hair, her fingers cool and light on his skin. He leaned into the touch, his eyes drifting half-closed.

Her smile widened to show gleaming white teeth, and she tugged on his hair with just enough force to cause him a twinge of discomfort.

"I take it you've decided to keep the issue with the Company a secret?" she asked. "I heard you prevent Tristan from telling the boy the truth about why we moved so quickly. Why?"

Gabriel rubbed a hand over the spot she had tugged on. "It's okay now that we're away from that town. I was just worried that Virgil might've gotten word that the Scouts had found another telepath." A tremor ran through him.

The woman sat up, put her arms around his shoulders, and lowered her chin onto his shoulder, rubbing his back.

"I can't trust these two until I get to know them. They seem impulsive, agreeing to come with us the way they did. I saw nothing wrong with the family life they had." He squeezed his hands together. "It's important we keep the girl here so that the Company doesn't get her abilities. More than that..." His gaze went distant. "Virgil would break her so that he could control her easier." His hands shook, and he squeezed them tighter. "He would find out about us."

He put a hand over his eyes. "I can't go back there. I won't let Virgil ever get into my head again, and I won't let him get her. I *won't* let him do that to someone else."

The woman hugged him tighter. "You don't have to explain yourself to me. I'm here for you, whatever you choose, my angel."

"Thank you." A slight smile touched Gabriel's mouth, and he turned to kiss her. "That's all I need."

Silence reigned in Emma's cabin room after the phone clicked off. Their mother's emotional voice still rang in her ears, making the silence even heavier. One glance at her brother put all that from her mind. His lips were pressed tightly together. He stared hard at the wall, his eyes flashing with fury and repressed tears.

"Nemo..." She stood up from the bed and went over to him. A hug wouldn't do much to ease his pain, but at the very least she could remind him she was here for him. She would always be here for him.

He lurched to his feet and moved out of her reach. "Don't try to defend him. He wasn't even there. He didn't even know!"

"He went on his fishing trip." The words sounded pathetic to Emma even as she spoke them. "He left in the early morning, before mom found my note or Gabriel came to talk to her. We knew about his plans before all of this happened."

Nemo's face reddened as his rage burned hotter. "You're really protecting him. I can't believe he still went on that stupid trip. Nothing will ever prevent him from going out fishing!"

Emma could only fumble for any words that might soothe Nemo's pain. She needed to say something. Anything that would calm him.

Nothing came to mind, and Nemo stomped out. Emma flinched as the door slammed. Silence descended like a shroud again.

Caleb watched in bemusement as Seth and Gail walked through the closed door into the hotel room with their hands full of plastic grocery bags. Seth promptly tripped over a pile of suitcases and fell full length on the floor.

Adah burst out laughing from the bed.

"I see we're leaving today, after all," Seth commented from the floor. Gail stepped over him and gathered up the sandwiches he'd dropped.

Their morning flight had been cancelled. After receiving a text message saying as much, Rebecca stormed out to deal with making new flight arrangements. In the meantime, Seth and Gail had gone out for food.

"In the morning," Caleb said from the other bed, lying back and putting a hand over his eyes. Frost blossomed along his fingers.

"Headache?" Gail asked sympathetically. She dropped onto the bed next to Adah and watched Seth scoot along the carpet on his belly toward his backpack. "Maybe you should take some medicine."

"It'll pass," Caleb grunted and pressed his ice tipped fingers to his temples. "Rebecca is in a mood. Ever notice her voice gets really strident when she's ticked off?"

Adah giggled. "Better not let her hear you say that, or it'll be the floor for you when we get back home."

Caleb lowered his hand to glare at Adah. "It'll probably be the floor anyway. Think I'll crash in Tsar's room for a few days. He's probably still out on a Collecting job right now anyway."

Adah's smile faded, and she glanced uneasily at Gail. The other girl was leaning over the edge of the bed and watching the handheld game Seth played. If she heard, she didn't show it.

A heavy metal song screeched from the heater at the far end of the room. Caleb made a face and sat up to grab his phone. "Hello?"

"Hello, my name is Mr. Reeve, and I am contacting you about a business card you left for my son at his school."

"Oh." Caleb blinked and tried to clear his head. "R-right. I am a representative of the Ark Light Company. We left a business card at your son's high school due to the talent he displayed. Did you or your son have any questions?"

"Damn right I have questions," the man snarled, and Caleb winced as his headache spiked. "My son ran away with some pretentious circus led by a Mr. Gabriel Hightower. Care to explain what you're doing getting kids to pull stunts like that? I want to speak to your boss." Caleb went very still, and ice spread over the phone. "Hello?"

He heard a rustle behind him as Seth got to his feet. Adah and Gail also slipped off the bed. All three of them retreated toward the door. Seth kept himself between the girls and Caleb, his wary gaze fixed on the man. "Adah?" he breathed.

"Trying," she muttered. "You know his temper is usually too much for my regulation."

The door swung open to admit Rebecca. She looked at their expressions and then rushed over to grab the phone from Caleb's icy fingers. "I'm sorry, sir. A technical issue occurred. Will you repeat your inquiry?"

"What the hell?" the man on the other end yelled. "What kind of business are you people running! I want to speak to your boss, *now!*"

She glanced at Caleb's darkening expression. "I'm sorry, sir. We are a field group and cannot transfer you to a manager. We will return your call to address your complaint within twenty-four hours," she said and hung up before the man could respond. "Caleb, what's wrong? Are you okay?" She reached toward him, but he whirled around and stormed out of the room. The three teens skittered out of his way, their eyes wide and frightened. "Stay here, Seth. I'll bring him back when he's calmed down."

Caleb barely heard her words. He stomped silently down the carpeted hallway, his rage building until he couldn't contain it anymore. He grabbed the small table by the window and upended it. The vase on it shattered loudly between the carpeting and the table. A dark spot seeped out from under the wood and porcelain shards as water soaked into the carpet.

He turned and watched Rebecca approach him cautiously. "Caleb?" she breathed. "Calm down, now. Tell me what happened." She put a hand on his shoulder, and ice blossomed on her skin, making her yank it back. She frowned and sent a burst of heat into her fingers to hold off frostbite.

Caleb's face contorted into a mask of fury. Ice spread along his neck, down under his shirt, and up to his chin. Rebecca put her hand against that ice, her fingers growing hotter. The ice melted and dripped like tears onto the carpet. "Tell me what's wrong."

"The boy. From the high school," Caleb ground out. "With the vocal Blessing. He signed on with Gabriel."

Rebecca sucked in a sharp breath but kept her voice calm. "That sucks. It's not such a big deal though. We'll cross him off the list. We found plenty of others to report to the Collectors and—"

"Gabriel was in this town! He's taking more people away from us!" The ice bit into Rebecca's hand, and she gritted her teeth against the pain. Caleb stared into the air between them, ignoring her struggle to melt the ice on his skin. "How did we miss that! We should've sensed him!"

"You might be right," Rebecca soothed. "But we didn't. It's not the end of the world. The boy isn't a terrible loss. We have bigger fish to fry." She stroked her hand down his neck and pressed her warmth over his heart. "Calm down, honey."

Caleb heaved a heavy sigh, and his shoulders hunched as he deflated. He closed his eyes and drew in deep breaths as the thin layer of ice on his skin slowly disappeared. "Alright. I think I've gotten it under control." He opened his eyes and met Rebecca's concerned blue eyes. "I scared the others, didn't I?" His mouth twisted wryly.

"They're used to it," she said with a dismissive wave. "Just buy them some ice cream." She took his hand to lead him back to their door. "Seth," she called through the thick wood. "Everything's okay. You can let us in."

The door opened just a crack and Seth peered out, eyeing them for several moments before opening the door wider and stepping aside to let them in.

Gail and Adah sat propped against the headboard of one bed and watched. "Is everything alright?" Adah asked, one arm around Gail, who leaned against her and watched them with worried eyes.

"Yes." Rebecca picked up her phone. "We just received some unexpected news, that's all. We need to call Michael. Tonight. We need to report to the boss that we've found out what his son is up to."

Nemo crept into the dining room, holding his breath and listening. Without any windows, he couldn't get a sense of the time. The brisk air wafting through the tunnel suggested it was early morning, but nobody was up and about yet. He made his way through the small tables, which had been replaced just as they had been before, leaving no trace of the great feast.

The kitchen was locked. Nemo muttered under his breath and tugged on the metal sheeting that covered the pass-through.

"What are you doing?" The nasally voice made him jump, and he slammed his hand against the metal.

He glared at Donovan, shaking his stinging hand. "Did you have to startle me?"

Donovan tilted his head and crossed his arms. Nemo huffed and unzipped his sweatshirt to reveal a tiny animal's pointed face. It looked around, its ridged ears swinging wildly. "I found this fruit bat in my room. It's not native to this area, so I'm not sure where it came from. I wanted to get it some food."

"You couldn't wait until breakfast?" Donovan asked. He looked at the bat curiously, and his mouth twitched. He refrained from smiling though. "What do you think, Lucien?" He turned as the elf appeared in the room, mid-stride. "Should we get the bat some fruit?"

Lucien's eyebrows shot up, the only sign of surprise the elf's face showed. "Is that..." he tilted his head and chuckled quietly. "Have a seat, boy. Timaeus will be here shortly and will be pleased to see your eagerness to start your education. I will retrieve some fruit for the creature."

The elf unlocked the kitchen door and went through. Nemo looked suspiciously at Donovan. "What aren't you telling me?"

Donovan reached over and stroked a single finger over the bat's head. "That's for her to tell you. When she chooses to," the Keeper said before disappearing.

Nemo frowned darkly and took a seat, carefully cradling the bat against his chest. He lifted it close to his face and peered into its brown eyes. "There's nothing mysterious about you, right, sky puppy?" The bat yawned, closed its eyes, and folded its wings up around itself.

A few minutes later, the dragon appeared with a crack. His black bulk filled the room, even magically distorted as it was in the usual heat shimmer, and he impatiently batted aside several tables to make room for himself. His eyes fixed on Nemo, and he advanced, shifting his leathery wings against his back. The bat nibbled daintily on a peach, its pointed tongue flashing in and out of its mouth around the fruit. When it caught sight of Timaeus, it squeaked in alarm and flew away into the darkness of the ceiling, dodging Nemo's attempts to grab it.

"You bully! There was no call for that!" He sensed he was using his power again, but irritated grogginess made it hard to care.

The dragon's copper eyes narrowed dangerously. His jaws parted, revealing his great fangs...and then he burst out laughing and shifted into his human form to stretch and yawn. "I like this kid," he said to the elf before regarding Nemo sternly. "We're going to work on that voice of yours first thing. You need to learn when not to use it or you're going to get yourself into a lot of trouble. Most creatures are not as forgiving as I am."

Nemo glanced at the marked-up peach and wondered if he dared speak. "I would like some breakfast first." The elf gave him a withering look that he met calmly. "I won't be able to concentrate on an empty stomach."

"That's reasonable. Donovan, bring the girl here," Timaeus ordered.

Nemo glanced around but didn't see Donovan. "Lucien will give you two a little history lesson while I fry up some breakfast for us."

Emma appeared, still in pajamas and distinctly ruffled, and stumbled, bumping into a table. She blinked owlishly at Nemo. "What's up?" she asked, her voice thick with sleepiness. Lucien took one look at her and strolled away into the kitchen after Timaeus.

Nemo chuckled. "Pulling a girl out of bed. Have you no shame, Donovan?" he said to the air, much as the dragon had.

Emma gave him a venomous look, not understanding the joke and in no mood to think about it.

"We're going to get a lesson," he said and plopped down. Emma half fell into a chair beside him, rubbed her eyes, and yawned.

The elf returned, carrying a silver tray. On it were several ceramic cups, a small sugar bowl, a silver pitcher, and a few cups of milk. "Do either of you like tea or do you want coffee?"

Emma covered another yawn. "Normally, I'd take the tea, but if you want me to be awake for your lesson, coffee will be faster."

"I will not be repeating this," the elf said in a clipped tone and watched while Nemo and Emma prepared the drinks to their liking.

Emma took a sip and closed her eyes while the sweetened liquid warmed her. "Okay," she sighed after a few moments. "I think I'm awake enough to at least listen. No promises how much I'll remember later." Lucien's eyebrows drew down into a scowl.

"I'll fill in the gaps for you," Nemo promised quickly, to stave off an angry tirade from the elf.

Lucien regarded them coldly. He took a deep breath and steepled his fingers. "Let us begin then. The history of elves and humans is long and complicated." He paused and eyed their groggy expressions. "I will do my best to simplify it to focus on the topic of the Blessing."

He stirred his tea with a small spoon, his face thoughtful. "Elves originated in Europe. We lived in the deep forests and rarely associated with humans. There have always been mages among humans, and they initiated some limited contact with elves. Through them, the elves knew the state of the human clans."

His eyes grew distant, and his voice fell into a sing-song tone. "My people looked on as invading forces from first one land and then another came, fought, and fell. We decided humans were a violent, tumultuous race." A smile touched his face, and he laughed quietly, a bell-like peal.

"We vowed to not take sides in their bloody conflicts. Then the humans began to perish from other causes. Diseases my people possessed the ability to cure with simple spells ravaged the human populations. Many elves felt sympathy toward the humans and chafed at the vows to not interfere."

The elf stared down at the table, tapping a staccato rhythm. "I will not go into elven politics. It took many years for a consensus to be reached, and by that time, that particular bout of disease had ceased. That made no difference. My people abide by our decisions."

A loud thump from the kitchen interrupted him. He frowned, rose to his feet, and went to peer through the open door. He returned a moment later, shaking his head.

"The spell the elves cast was a great undertaking," he said as he sat back down, "and required all my race's most powerful spellcasters. The spell encompassed all of humanity, not just the immediate clans we knew. It gave humans unique abilities that would aid them so that they could stand on equal footing with the more powerful races and the human mages. We layered the spell so that it wouldn't become genetic or otherwise run too strongly in any one family. The elves Blessed humanity."

"So that's why our abilities are called Blessings," Emma murmured. She still looked rumpled, but her eyes were bright and excited. "That's awesome!"

The elf smiled thinly. "Yes. Awesome is a fitting description. The elves never had attempted a spell of that magnitude and have not done so again. The Blessing of humanity is a point of pride for my race. Despite the fact humans no longer need it."

"Why do you think that?" Nemo asked. Before the elf could reply, plates of bacon and eggs were plopped unceremoniously in front of them.

"Breakfast," Timaeus grunted and sat down next to Lucien. "Eat. After you're done, you may go, girl." So saying, he began shoveling food into his mouth greedily.

Emma blinked a few times, shrugged, and ate. Nemo sighed, sensing the history lesson was over. He would've liked to learn more.

No sooner did Emma take her last bite than she abruptly disappeared. Her fork clattered loudly onto her plate. "Donovan doesn't mess around," Nemo commented.

"Not when it's an order from me." Timaeus grinned savagely. "Let's begin with your proper lesson, boy. It's past time you learned how to use your voice."

When Emma woke up again the breakfast seemed like a dream. She got dressed, mentally repeating the elf's lecture so she would hopefully retain it. It had been a lot to learn that early in the morning. She would speak with Nemo later to make sure she remembered everything properly. She wondered what to do now and had walked halfway to the door when there was a soft knock.

She cracked it open to see Avery and his brother Martin waiting outside her room. She regarded them warily. She already trusted Avery. His open, freckled face beamed at her when she came into view. Martin was another matter. He was as dark as Avery was fair, and his expression under his crest of black feathers was closed off. "Good morning," she said.

"You're with us today," Martin said brusquely. "Gabriel wants us to spend the day teaching you how to find your way around the tunnels. Avery has shown you some basics, although he told me that you could barely remember that." He bit out the words as if he begrudged every syllable.

"I've only been here a few days," Emma muttered, not looking at Avery. The idea of him talking to Martin about her like that irked her. But they were obviously close siblings, and she couldn't fault Avery. She would just have to be more careful and remember that not everyone here would be friendly.

"Be that as it may," Martin said roughly, "we're going to fix that today. This is your home now, and you should know your way around. Donovan isn't a babysitter." He turned and started down the dimly lit tunnel.

Avery gave Emma a reassuring smile before following his brother.

"Home," Emma murmured. She swallowed back a surge of emotions, good and bad, and looked around at the rough stone walls. "Yes, this is home. Remember that," she told herself sternly and trotted to catch up with the winged brothers. Exploring her new home would be its own adventure.

Tuesday January 24th

Michael Hightower brought the mug to his lips and nearly spat out the stale coffee that chilled his tongue. The surprise snapped him out of the stupor he'd fallen into, and he realized he hadn't taken in a word of the memo he'd been staring at. He sighed, rubbing his eyes before glancing at the digital clock perched on the corner of his desk. 8:13 PM. That gave the young man another jolt. He'd been expecting a phone call at 8:00 and lost track of the time, a habit he'd been trying to break himself of for years. Having no appointments that day had caused a relapse.

A yawn bit at him as if in response to knowing the time. He got to his feet and took a turn about the office to wake himself up.

A headache prickled behind his multicolored eyes. He frowned irritably and rubbed at them again. The visions came no matter what he did to prevent them and never showed him what he most dearly hoped to see.

Michael returned to his desk, picked up his coffee mug, and went over to the window. Only dregs remained, but habit prompted him to hold it while he looked out over the city. The lights of San Francisco glittered like so many fairies, as if trying to hide the hideousness that dwelled within the darkness below. The barest whispers of those thoughts reached Michael, and he turned away.

It had taken him a long time to recover from the shock of his brother fleeing San Francisco four years before. His visions had given him no hint of Gabriel's intentions. Deep down, he had suspected. His brother had never been happy here. Steel and heights hadn't offered Gabriel any protection against the city's thoughts.

Without thinking about it, he raised the mug to his mouth and choked as the cold, bitter liquid filled his mouth once more. He forced himself to swallow it and set the mug down, irritated he was giving in to so many habits.

The phone blared, shattering his reverie. He picked it up instinctively. "Michael Hightower speaking."

"Sorry to call you so late, Michael," his secretary said. "I just received a call from Adah Roth's Scouting team. They're back in town and wanted to schedule an appointment. Adah said it is urgent."

Urgent? Michael frowned. "Tell them I'll see them at..." he glanced again at the clock. Were they still at the airport? Even if they weren't, it would take them a while to get through the city traffic. "Nine. Send them in right away when they get here. Oh, and will you brew me some fresh coffee?"

"Decaf, right? I'll brew enough for the Scouts, too," the secretary said and got off the phone. Michael sighed. He would've liked actual coffee. His secretary needed a reminder that she was his employee, not his mother, despite their ages.

He glanced into his cup. The glint of the desk lamp off the black liquid caught his eye and expanded into the vision his headache had heralded. Not of the future, but of the past, as often happened with his Blessing in the last few years. Ever since he stopped looking toward the future and craved only for the past. A memory from years before played out like a movie.

Gabriel, as Michael had last seen him all those years before, stood on the pier, staring out at the ocean, his face pensive. He glanced up when Michael approached, and his face twisted. "Why are you keeping me out of your mind? You don't want to talk that way anymore?"

"It's just a precaution," Michael said. "I don't want Virgil hearing my thoughts."

"Virgil left town on a Collecting job yesterday," Gabriel snapped. Michael had no answer to that, and Gabriel's eyes narrowed. "Since when did you wear a suit?" he snapped. "You trying to become Father's twin instead of mine?"

"You're being childish. You can speak aloud if you want to say something to me," Michael retorted. "I'm allowed to have my own thoughts. You've been so weird ever since you came back from that fishing trip, Gabriel."

"Whatever." Gabriel looked over Michael's shoulder as Caleb, Tristan, and a tall dark-skinned man approached.

Caleb's face lacked the angry lines that would form in the coming months. He laughed loudly and jostled the dark-skinned man. "Hey Michael, did you hear? We get to go to Europe!"

"Father put me on a Ranger team," Gabriel added. "Guess he wants me gone for a while. You should be happy. With both Virgil and

me out of town, you can have your mind all to yourself. Maybe I'll just stay away all the time and neither of us will have to worry about my Blessing as much."

Gabriel turned and stomped away, Tristan following in his wake. Michael looked up at the dark-skinned man. "Take care of him, please, Tsar. I'll make sure Gail gets by okay while you're gone."

Balthasar smiled, the expression reaching past where scars would soon mar his face. "I will," he promised.

Michael pulled his gaze away from the coffee and set the mug down so hard that the cold coffee slopped over the edge.

Rebecca, Caleb, and Adah walked in to Michael's office at 8:55, surprising Michael as he stared dismally at his mug of decaf. "Light traffic?" he asked, snapping his business smile onto his face. "Welcome back to San Francisco."

Rebecca smiled wearily. Caleb's face was closed off and thunderous. "We sent the others to the House," Rebecca said. "We have some news and…well, I thought it would be best we didn't get Gail anymore mixed up in this than she already is. Tsar…Balthasar would be angry at us if we did."

Michael tensed, and his smile faded. "That bad?" He glanced around at the walls. "Virgil is out on a Collecting job. You don't have to guard your thoughts."

Rebecca relaxed visibly. She took a deep breath and looked at Caleb. His expression didn't lighten in the slightest. He met her gaze, and she nodded. He took a deep breath and told Michael about the morning's phone conversation. Michael went very still.

"I see." His mouth twitched. "A circus. I didn't see that one coming." Caleb's expression grew even darker. "This isn't going to leave this room, Caleb," Michael said sharply.

Caleb took a step forward. Rebecca's hand shot out to press against his chest. "Adah, I'd appreciate your help here."

"I'm regulating him as much as I can," Adah retorted. "He's never been easy to get a handle on. That's why they put you on the team, too."

"You aren't going to do anything?" Caleb ignored the women and glared holes in Michael.

Michael looked at him wearily. "What should I do? Gabriel will

73

have moved on. We don't know where he is. I won't send Scouts on a wild goose chase." He took a deep breath and clasped his hands on his desk. "If my father hears about this, that's what will happen. He might even send your team. Can you imagine Balthasar's reaction if he comes back to find out that you took Gail along on that job?"

Rebecca flinched. "Good point," she whispered. "Balthasar would never forgive us."

Michael stared down at his hands, frowning in thought. "I'm going to keep your team here until Balthasar comes back, Go to the House and tell the rest of your team that they're not to tell anyone about this. I'll find you assignments in the city in the morning."

Rebecca nodded and went to the door. Her hand closed around the door knob before she noticed Caleb was still staring at Michael. "What happens when your father does find out?" he asked. "He will, eventually. You won't be able to protect everyone."

Michael's eyebrows shot up. "I don't see why not. Gabriel isn't in the picture anymore. All I want is for it to stay that way. He didn't take a powerful Blessed. Let him have his circus and recruit whom he may."

"I'd choose to face Balthasar's anger over the boss's. If I feel the boss's Blessing again because of the crap Gabriel is pulling..." Caleb trailed off bleakly, fear overcoming his usual anger.

Michael looked away. "You won't be facing either." He got up and clapped Caleb on the shoulder. "Calm down. I won't let that happen again."

Caleb studied Michael's face and, seeming satisfied, he nodded and went out, followed closely by Rebecca.

Adah rocked on her toes, hovering by the desk. "Are you going to be okay, Michael? Sorry I couldn't do more to curb Caleb's temper. I know that's why you made me leader of the team, and I do keep trying."

Michael went over to her, kissed the top of her head, and for a moment, just enjoyed being near her. "Don't worry about it. Caleb's temper is something else." He smiled. "Go on. We'll have plenty of time to figure things out."

After the door closed behind her, Michael picked up his mug of decaf coffee and went back over to the window. "What are you doing, Gabriel?" he whispered and leaned his forehead against the cold glass. It rained softly outside, water streaming down the glass like tears. "Keep your head low, or I won't be able to keep protecting you from father."

THE PHANTASMS
ACT TWO

April 1st, Toronto, Canada

Julia Mercer had never been much of a runner, despite her strength. Now, she regretted never improving her legs. She sucked in frigid air that made her lungs ache fiercely and then fogged around her face when she forced it back out. Lake Ontario came into view, bright with reflected moonlight. Footsteps pounded behind her, and she sped up as much as she could, driven by terror. Her legs already trembled with the exertion, and the effort felt in vain.

Where did that feeling go? She tried to bring it back. That unexplainable, compelling urge to escape, to find Lucien. It swelled within her and gave her the burst of speed she needed. Her pursuers fell back once more. She wouldn't be able to keep this up for long though. She needed to get out of the city. Swallowing back her fear, she dashed across a street and continued along the deserted sidewalks of Toronto. How did it come to this so suddenly? The evening had started so normally…

Julia leaned against the railing and raised her phone to take a picture of the moon rising over Lake Ontario. The sound of water lapping against the stones below always calmed her, and she needed that peace before starting her shift. After listening to it for a few more stolen moments, she turned away and walked to the door of the Cove Night Club.

The night was young, but there were several people already in line at the entrance. "Hey, Julia," Sam said as she walked by. He was checking the IDs of a trio of young women and didn't look up as she pushed the door open. The women glared at her, obviously thinking she was underage. "I'll be inside later," he said over his shoulder. "Don't get into any fights."

"No promises," Julia said and gave the women a wide grin. They pulled back and hesitated to follow her in. Julia put them from her mind and looked around the club while she crossed the empty dance floor. Fake stone walls glistened with round fish tanks and patches of mosaics, barely visible in the shifting blue light that the Cove was known for. Pillar glass tanks of jellyfish lined one side of the dance floor, with colored lights shining through them. Julia paused next to them and straightened her loose black shirt. A few of the regulars nodded to her as they crossed the room to the bar or were escorted by the host into the small restaurant in the next room. Judging by the noise coming from the restaurant, the club would be much busier later.

Her scan of the room complete, she continued to the bar and plopped down on a stool at the far side. A mermaid swam back and forth in a large tank over the bar. Mirrors on the far side reflected the tank. Idly, she watched the mermaid in the mirrors until the bartender walked over.

"Hey, Jul," he greeted her with a grin.

"Hey." Julia gave him a quick nod before turning her gaze onto the dance floor. The light played over his gold-blonde hair and bright blue eyes. Julia often saw women sit at the bar, drink way too much, and almost drool while they stared at the bartender.

She refused to be like that.

Two women crossed the dance floor and came up to the bar to order drinks. They were tall, wearing form-fitting dresses that hugged their curves, and high heels to accentuate their long, slender legs. Dyed blonde hair tumbled around their shoulders in huge curls, drawing attention to the plunging necklines on their dresses.

"Hello, ladies," The barkeeper said suavely and gave them a grin that displayed his even, white teeth. "I am Tip Moore, and I will be serving your drinks tonight. What may I get for you?"

The women tittered, gave their orders, and then batted fake eyelashes at Tip while he made their drinks. He slid the glasses over to them, and they waved to him as they went back across the dance floor. Tip waved back, still grinning.

When he turned back to Julia, his grin was gone, replaced by a neutral expression. Julia sighed and kicked her legs against the stool. Being just over five feet tall, with no curves to speak of, seeing women like that made her feel like a child.

"You just love using your name like that, don't you? Tiberius," she said with mischievous glee to hide her disappointment. He never smiled at her that way.

Tip pulled a face. "Don't go there, please." He perched on a stool on the other side of the bar and rested his chin on his palm. "What's up? You seem on edge."

"Nothing," she muttered, looking away from him and ignoring how her pulse sped up when his gaze focused on her. "It's just odd, seeing you like this. I still remember the awkward, nerdy boy you were when we were kids."

Tip's eyes narrowed. He looked away and turned a bottle on the wood of the bar. "Was I dorky? I don't remember that. I was just interested in different things." A smile touched his lips. "And you were there to punch anyone who teased me for it."

Julia's tension eased, and she chuckled. "Yeah, that's true. I guess I was always destined to work as a bouncer. My small size aside." Tip leaned back and crossed his arms. Julia glanced at him questioningly, but he wouldn't meet her eyes.

The dance floor was beginning to pick up some. Julia turned so that she could watch it. "What does the crowd look like so far tonight?" she asked.

"Normal, I think," Tip said. There was an odd note in his voice. Julia followed his gaze to a man sitting at a table in the corner. That spot had one of the best views of the lake, but the man sat with his back to the window and watched the dance floor. "He's been there all evening. Only ordered one drink," Tip said. He hesitated and then added, "I think you should switch with Sam and work the door tonight."

Julia's eyebrows flew up. "What are you on about? You know I hate door duty."

Tip looked away but not before Julia saw the concern in his eyes.

She scowled. "I can handle any trouble that guy causes. Don't treat me like I'm weak. I got this job long before you started working here. I've always done just fine."

A waiter came out from the restaurant and handed Tip a list of drink orders. He busied himself preparing them.

Still annoyed, Julia went over to her stool against the wall where she could see the whole room. She perched on it, arms crossed, and glared around, daring anyone to come near her.

Tip kept casting anxious looks in her direction when he wasn't preparing drinks. That did nothing for her mood. After months of working together, there was no reason for him to be this jumpy because of one man. He well knew how strong she was. Soon, the bar got too busy for him to pay attention to her, and she calmed down.

Around midnight, halfway through Julia's shift, the man made his move. She was circling the room and noticed him getting up from his table. He wove through the dancing crowd toward the three young women who had come in to the bar when Julia first came into work.

The trio, clearly inebriated, stumbled around on one corner of the dance floor. The two blondes had found dance partners but the third, who was dressed more comfortably, seemed content to bounce along on her own. Julia slid around the edge of the crowd to a spot where she could watch the scene playing out.

The man started dancing with the third woman. At first, she laughed and accepted his advances. He began inching her subtly away from the other two women. Julia watched, keeping an eye on the rest of the crowd as well. Soon, the man managed to position the woman in the corner, caught between a jellyfish tank and the wall. His hand slid up her arm, gripping her tightly so that when she tried to dash around him, she couldn't pull free.

Rage coursed through Julia at the panicked look on the woman's face. Still, she kept her face calm when she approached the man and tapped him on the shoulder. "Excuse me, sir. I'm going to cut in. The lady isn't interested."

"Get lost," the man barked without looking around. "It's none of your business."

"Is that so?" Julia said pleasantly. She grabbed the man's arm and twisted it behind his back. The man struggled and yelled curses at her. "You see?" Julia leaned close to say it in his ear. "It's unpleasant to have someone grab you and not let go." She jerked him out of the corner and looked around for the manager. He was standing by the bar. He caught her eye and nodded to her. Julia angled the man toward the door and shoved him forward.

She was almost to the door when a drunk staggered off the dance floor and bumped into her, knocking her off balance. The man saw his chance and stomped on Julia's foot. A yelp escaped her, and she stumbled back. The man yanked free, twisted around, and punched her in the gut.

Julia's vision blanked.

She blinked, surprised to find herself on her back on the floor. The man darted back toward the dance floor. She could hear Sam and Tip shouting as if from underwater.

Rage ripped through her once more, and this time she didn't hold it back. She flipped to her feet, took several long strides forward, and grabbed the back of the man's shirt. Displaying more of her unnatural strength than was wise, given the number of people watching, she lifted him clean off his feet. "You do not treat people this way, asshole!" she screamed. She stomped to the door and threw him bodily out of the club.

People stared at her. Julia looked wildly around. The patrons averted their gazes. Even the young woman she'd saved.

"Are...are you okay?" Sam asked, his face pale and stunned.

The manager and Tip pushed through the crowd to her. "Hold down the fort for a few minutes, Sam," the manager ordered and then cautiously put an arm around Julia and propelled her into the kitchen. "Are you alright?" he asked urgently.

Julia sat down and rubbed her hands together, trying to still their trembling from the adrenaline. "I...don't know." Her stomach roiled, and her eyes prickled. She took a deep breath. She wouldn't cry or be sick. She was not weak.

Taking another deep breath, she tried to smile up at them. Their concerned expressions only deepened.

"Stay here with her," the manager told Tip. "I don't want to leave Sam out there alone for too long. I'll take the bar for a little while."

The manager ducked out, and Julia gave up on her forced smile. "I hate men," she muttered and wiped her eyes. With just Tip in the room, she didn't need to hold it together quite as much.

"I know," Tip said softly. Julia's head jerked up, and she caught just a hint of his sad expression before he looked away.

Julia grimaced, repressing the urge to apologize. She got to her feet instead. "I should go back out. We need someone to do door duty if Sam is going to take over the floor."

Tip gave her an incredulous look and blocked her way. "You can't be serious. Tell the manager you want to take the rest of the night off. I'm sure he'll let you."

"What's with you? Would Sam ask to take the night off because of a tap like that? It's part of being a bouncer. Sam knows that, and so do I. Don't hold me to different standards, Tip."

A hurt look flashed across Tip's face. "I didn't mean you were weak. I would've given Sam the same advice." He reached out toward Julia. She flinched back, and he dropped his hand. "I'm sorry."

Julia looked away. He had just been going to pat her shoulder. Why did she still shrink back from men touching her? Berating herself and still feeling sick, she shook her head and pushed past Tip. "Forget it. I'm fine, Tip. That's all that matters." She hesitated and then patted him on the shoulder, grinning impishly.

Tip managed a smile and a quiet chuckle, but his eyes were still distant. "That's all that matters," he echoed. "Let me know if…well…you don't feel okay. You can trust me, Julia."

"I do trust you," Julia told him, surprised by his words. She gave him an uncertain look but then shook off her confusion and walked across the club. She ignored the gazes she sensed following her.

The line outside had grown long during the incident. "I got door duty, Sam," she told the other bouncer. Relief lit up Sam's face, but he took one look at Julia's grim expression and ducked inside without a word, wise enough to not say anything. Julia began checking IDs. That occupied her for a large part of the second half of her shift.

By two A.M., she had her coat pulled tight against the icy air, with the hood up and heavy gloves on her hands. They closed the door half an hour before the bar closed, and she spent a few minutes by a heater vent before going to help Tip clean the bar. There was still a tenseness to his shoulders, and he didn't meet her eyes as they worked.

Sam and the manager called taxis for the last few patrons, giving Julia the chance to corner Tip when he went to the end of the bar to grab a couple of glasses. "Are we cool?" she asked.

Tip hunched his shoulders and shrugged. "I suppose. I'm not mad at you or anything. It's just..." he stared at the glass he was holding. "I'm not sure how to say it."

"Take your time. Don't strain anything," she teased, hoping to lighten the mood and avoid the serious conversation she sensed brewing. Tip gave her a scathing look and she grinned back.

A movement in the mirrors on the far wall drew her attention. The mermaid in the tank above them was still swimming back and forth. Julia's smile faded. *When does that swimmer get off her shift?* It seemed odd that she'd never wondered that before.

"I need a ride tonight," Julia said, tearing her gaze from the mirrors. As soon as she looked away, she forgot about the mermaid. "My car broke down while I was out doing errands earlier. I'd rather not take a taxi home."

"Of course," Tip said automatically. "Let me just change out of this uniform. I got more than one type of drink splattered on it tonight. I don't want to get the alcohol smell in my car." He wiped down one more bottle and then walked out from behind the bar and into the kitchen.

Julia leaned against the bar and looked around. This room felt so familiar, but she hated it. She chose the job because she thought she could do a good thing for women by working here.

And yet... She sighed. Nothing had changed. She still flinched back when men she trusted reached toward her. Fury still coursed through her at what she saw here most nights. Maybe she needed a change of setting. To get away from those thoughts and let her anger cool so that she could live life without it. So that... Tip's smile filled her mind, and she grimaced. *Oh, come on,* she scolded herself. *I'm just his awkward childhood friend. I don't stand a chance.*

A flash of movement drew her attention to the other side of the room. The mermaid was gesturing urgently at the mirrors. Her tail flipped in agitation. When she saw Julia looking, she pointed frantically. Julia's head whipped around. She could just make out half a dozen shadowy figures crossing the dance floor in the dim blue light.

"Hey!" she called. "We're closed!" She walked toward the end of the bar. The manager stood at the board that divided the bar from the club, blocking her way. Julia frowned and stopped. His expression was oddly blank, his eyes dull and staring. "Sir?"

The manager lunged forward and grabbed her wrist. A fearful chill cut through her, and she jerked away so swiftly he stumbled. While he was off balance, Julia pushed past him and darted out from behind the bar.

The six figures were now just a few feet away. Julia could make out two of them: an older man with a scruffy salt and pepper beard and a tall man whose dark skin made his features impossible to discern. They all watched her. Julia's mind was growing muddled for some reason. She ran onto the dance floor.

"Not that way!" Tip shouted, plunging in from the kitchen. He looked at the men, and his expression went blank. The bearded man snatched at Julia, catching hold of her purse strap. When she pulled back, the strap snapped, and the bag fell to the hard floor. Her cell phone clattered out and slid several feet. The black man stepped forward and snatched it up.

Tip's fingers closed around Julia's hand, and he pulled her to the back of the club where there was an emergency exit. The manager charged at them. Tip released Julia's hand to swing at the manager, catching him squarely on the cheek just below the eye. The man dropped.

"Since when did you know how to punch like that?" Julia asked, her voice slurred. Tip shot her a concerned look before towing her through the exit.

The frigid air outside cleared her mind a little but not enough. "Snap out of it, Julia," Tip said. He came to a sudden stop. Julia ran into him and stood blinking up at him. He cursed and looked around. The alleyway the exit led onto was a dead-end, and she could see people blocking the other way. As she watched, the two men from the bar came into view. Tip cursed again.

"What's going on?" Julia asked and shook her head, trying to clear it.

Tip bit his lip and ran a hand through his hair in agitation while he turned slowly to fully survey the narrow alleyway. "Very well," he said, apparently having come to a decision. "Listen to me." He put his hands on the sides of her face.

That alarmed Julia, and she tried to pull away. He tightened his fingers so that she couldn't. "Tip, let me go!" she said and tensed up. Suddenly she couldn't move.

"Calm down and listen," Tip said forcefully, and his voice cut through the fog in her mind. His following words rang with a strange power. For a moment, Julia had a flash of memory: a group of men standing around her, using a similar power. Something much different than her own peculiar ability.

"I need you to go find Lucien. Tell him what's happened. You'll be safe there, and he'll carry word to people who need to know."

"Lucien," she whispered. Tip's magic carved the name into her mind, clearing it even more. "I can't leave you, Tip!"

"You can, and you will." He kissed her gently. Warmth flooded through Julia, her unacknowledged feelings rising to shove aside her anxieties, and her resistance to the unusual compulsion crumbled. He released her and kicked aside a crate to reveal a jagged hole in the wooden fence. "Go," he said and walked toward the group at the entrance of the alleyway. A man came out of the club door and grabbed Tip from behind. That was the last thing Julia saw before she crouched down and crawled through the hole.

Footsteps pounded the pavement as soon as she straightened up on the other side. They were coming for her. Julia sobbed and ran, unsure where she was going or why.

She just knew she needed to find Lucien.

May 1st, Calgary, Canada

Nemo stood in the dining room, facing Lucien. Tension loomed between them. The elf scowled and crossed his arms. "Well, human? Have you given up on this foolish scheme? I have much better things to do with my time."

Nemo seethed at the elf's arrogant tone. "You jerk," he said hoarsely under his breath. "I'm not even close to giving up." He straightened and squared his shoulders. "You will obey me, elf," he ordered, filling his voice with as much power as he could muster with his sore throat. He pointed to the line of round tables. The elf had shifted them to the edge of the room earlier so the dragon could move comfortably. "Put that table back where it goes."

Lucien didn't display the barest hint of strain. He shook his head. "Not even close," he said smugly.

Nemo sagged. They had been working on this for hours.

Timaeus snorted out a puff of smoke. "Give the boy some credit. That was a reasonable attempt." Lucien's composed expression pinkened ever so slowly, and the dragon chortled. "You came close to breaking down Lucien's resistance. He would've still been able to fight your command, but you are certainly making progress." He shifted back into his human form and stretched. "Get going, boy. I'm going to start on dinner, and I know you're needed at rehearsal."

"Right, rehearsal," Nemo muttered as he went out. His eyes felt dry from the early hour he'd woken up, and with his scratchy throat he wouldn't sing well, but he couldn't skip rehearsal. He'd only walked a little way down the tunnel when Lucien caught up with him.

"Drink this." The elf handed him a paper coffee cup. It warmed Nemo's hand, and he wrapped his fingers around it. "It's tea that should help your throat." The elf smiled a bit. "Good work today. You're going to be a force to be reckoned with by the time Timaeus is done with you."

"Thanks," Nemo said in surprise. The elf nodded and returned to the dining room. Nemo walked to the amphitheater cavern in a much better mood.

Several months had slipped by since he and Emma had joined the Circus. In that time, Nemo had learned how to avoid using his Blessing unintentionally. Wielding it as a tool was a much greater challenge. He had managed to use it once on Tristan but couldn't repeat the achievement. Most of the time, everyone was too busy with rehearsals to work with Nemo, so he practiced on the elf, with dismal results. Timaeus did not allow him to give up, though.

Arriving in the brightly lit cavern drove all of that from his mind. He advanced into the tumultuous activity and forgot the struggles of his lessons.

Emma closed her eyes and listened. She could sense the minds of everyone in the caves. She brushed briefly against Timaeus's mind in the dining room, then Celeste's, in her own room with Tristan. For just a moment, she could hear him thinking about practicing his sword work, and then he silenced his mind. Emma grinned. Even after several months here, the silence of the caves still made her giddy after so many years of hearing the minds of everyone around her.

"Focus, Emma." Gabriel's voice pulled her back to the task at hand: learning how to break through mental defenses. "Don't let your own mental protection slip during this. If your target has any sort of telepathic ability, they can get into your head while you're distracted."

Emma nodded and found Avery's mind on the far side of the cavern. He often volunteered to be the subject of her search. The feeling of his mind was quite familiar now but getting into it was another matter.

Her shoulders slumped, and she opened her eyes. "No good."

Gabriel crossed his arms, his frustration obvious in his frown.

"You're not trying hard enough. You really need to..." he realized Emma wasn't listening and trailed off. Her head was turned away from him, and she was gazing at Avery.

The avian lifted his wings and flew over to them. "No luck?"

Emma made a face and shook her head. Despite the expression, a smile hovered at the corner of her mouth. Smiles came easily when Avery was near.

"Don't worry about it," Avery said. "You'll get it soon enough. Maybe we should go—"

"Avery," Gabriel interrupted. The avian turned to him questioningly. "Go away. I need Emma to hear what I'm saying right now. This is hard enough without you distracting her."

"Oh." Avery deflated. "I got you." He ruffled his feathers up. "See you later then, Emma." He cast her a smile and then flew over to where his brother sat playing guitar.

Gabriel shook his head and sighed when Emma gave him a withering look. "Do you want to be able to do this or not?" he asked dryly.

"I do! We've been working on this one thing for days!" When Gabriel didn't answer, she scowled at him. "Can you do this? It seems weird to say you don't like hearing people's thoughts and then try to teach me how to break through their mental barriers." Gabriel went very still, and Emma's mouth snapped closed. "I'm sorry," she said, though she wasn't entirely sure what she was apologizing for.

"No," he said slowly. "It's a reasonable concern. I haven't taught anyone before, and it's showing." He ran a hand over his hair, his gaze unfocused. "I have an idea that we can try tomorrow. For now, I should go supervise the rehearsal. You can go do whatever it was Avery was going to suggest. Have fun."

Gabriel headed over to where the performers were gathered in the middle of the floor. Emma watched him go, feeling guilt over her words and foreboding over his. She reached for Avery's mind and pushed ineffectively at his barriers. A frustrated huff escaped her.

"I take it your lesson didn't go well today?" Nemo asked from behind her.

"Gabriel thinks I'm not taking it seriously because of Avery," she explained indignantly. A knowing smile spread over Nemo's mouth. Emma glared at him. "Don't look at me like that! I am being serious with this!" She knew it wasn't quite true, though. She found it hard to keep her mind on her lessons when Avery started joking with her.

"Let's trade lesson partners. I'll try to boss Avery around, and you can scrape away at Lucien's mind." Emma swatted him, and he chuckled. "It's not your fault. Avery is just way too easy-going. He makes it hard to take anything seriously."

Emma couldn't argue with that. "Are you going to be singing with Martin and Avery then?" she asked, glancing over to where the two avians sat together.

"Yeah." Nemo shrugged. "It's not a long song, just an introduction piece that Gabriel helped me write to open the performance tonight."

Emma's gaze caught and held on Gabriel and Tristan arguing. Tristan stood with his feet apart and arms crossed, his expression dark. Gabriel jabbed a finger at him demandingly, and he shook his head.

"Wonder what Tristan's deal is?" she mused out loud.

Nemo glanced over. "Don't know. Tristan's been really distant and distracted whenever I've seen him the last few days."

Tristan disappeared, spirited off somewhere by Donovan. Gabriel whirled around and tersely issued orders to the performers. Nemo nodded to Emma and trotted over to Avery and Martin.

Nobody looked up when Emma left the cavern. Ever since Martin had shown her around, Emma had made a game of exploring, enjoying the blissful silence of the caves. She loved simply walking through the tunnels and hearing only the slight sounds from her immediate surroundings: the drip of water from the roof, or the scratching of some small creature.

She usually got lost while exploring. This time was no exception. Her feet were beginning to ache when she came to a dead end some hours later. She turned around to see Donovan standing in the middle of the tunnel, his arms crossed and a resigned expression on his pale face. "Must you always lose yourself? Couldn't you use a trail of breadcrumbs or some string?"

"It's not my fault this place is as bad as Daedalus's labyrinth," Emma retorted cheerfully and walked over to him. Her jacket pocket clattered against her leg with every step she took, full of interesting crystals and rocks, and she was in a much better mood after the time alone.

Donovan raised a single eyebrow. "I've seen Daedalus's labyrinth. The caves aren't nearly as bad as that. But I will let it slide. I have to help Gabriel with letting the audience in soon, so if you'll come with me…"

"Hang on." Emma went over to the dead end and put a hand to the wall. She could hear a thought, whisper soft, from somewhere nearby. Frowning, she turned around and walked past Donovan. Where was it coming from?

Donovan heaved a long-suffering sigh and followed.

She came to the fork in the tunnel she had passed a little earlier and went into the other passage. The whispering thought wasn't growing any louder, but she knew it was nearer. This far out from the main caverns many bulbs were burned out, making the tunnel dim. A brighter light that must have been recently installed shone a little way off. Emma hurried toward it.

Tristan sat under the light at the mouth of a cave, leaning back against the wall and holding the sword he used in the shows. He looked up when Emma approached, and his face darkened. "Did Gabriel send you? I'm not going to perform tonight."

Emma looked at him blankly. "Nobody sent me. I heard some thoughts from here," she said, perplexed by his attitude. She started to pass into the cave, but he jerked the sword up to block her way. Emma took a hasty step back to avoid cutting herself on the sharp blade.

"Tristan!" Donovan hissed and came behind her. "This is getting out of hand. I won't have you threatening people."

"It's okay," a voice trilled from within the cave. "Let her in, Tristan." Emma recognized the unicorn's voice. Tristan reluctantly lowered his sword.

Emma looked between him and Donovan and remembered Gabriel's earlier anger. She didn't know what was going on, but nobody seemed to be happy with Tristan about it. Curiosity got the better of her, and she stepped into the cave.

The room she entered was dimly lit and half open to the outside. Snow, piled high on one side of the cave, gleamed bright and crystalline in the moonlight. Emma's gaze caught on that first, and she crossed half the cave before she spotted the unicorn lying against the wall. In the silvery light, her fur shone as purely white as the snow.

"Beautiful, isn't it?" the unicorn remarked. She made her voice audible to Emma physically, instead of using her telepathy. "I have always loved snow," she added and then rested her muzzle on her shoulder. "Wake up, little one. We have a visitor."

These words drew Emma's attention to the black creature nestled against the unicorn's side. She gasped in wonder and knelt in front of the unicorn before her brain caught up with her movements.

The tiny black unicorn blinked large dark blue eyes at Emma, and the whispering thoughts took on a warmer tone. "He's beautiful," she breathed and scooted even closer. Her fingers twitched with an urge to reach out and scratch the baby's head around his short gold horn. She only just managed to stop herself and looked sideways at Celeste. "May I?" she asked, hoping it wouldn't offend the unicorn.

"Of course," the unicorn replied, sounding amused. "Unicorn foals are not fragile like newborn humans. He has been asking you to pet him ever since he saw you."

"Is that what I was hearing?" Emma tilted her head, trying to make out the whispering while she scratched the baby unicorn's forehead.

"He isn't able to think in words yet. He's trying different things out." Celeste nuzzled the baby. "I have named him Davet."

"Hello, Davet," Emma said. "I can see the stars in your eyes." The black unicorn sneezed and radiated bashfulness. Emma chuckled and moved her hand to stroke his short mane.

"He likes you," Celeste said. She lifted her head as raised voices echoed in from the tunnel. A tremor ran from her neck down to her flank, and Emma sensed her sudden worry.

"I'll see what's going on." Emma smiled reassuringly at Celeste before going back out to the tunnel.

Donovan stood by the opposite wall, his arms crossed and his face stern. Gabriel and Tristan were a few feet off from the entrance of the cave. They seemed to have resumed their earlier conversation.

"What are they arguing about?" she asked Donovan. Tristan and Gabriel were good friends, and she didn't know what to make of this.

"Ask them," Donovan grunted back. His expression was closed off, displeasure in the set of his shoulders.

"I need you to perform, Tristan!" Gabriel shouted, his face

reddening with anger. Then he straightened, took a deep breath, and composed himself. "Please don't make me change the line-up last minute. I need you to do this." He noticed Emma watching. His eyebrows shot up. "Emma will stay with Celeste. She can communicate with Celeste telepathically, so she will do an excellent job watching over them. I just need you for a little while, and then you can come back."

Tristan hesitated, glancing at Emma. "Maybe." He picked up his sword and strolled into the cave. Emma leaned over to peer in. Tristan advanced across the cave and knelt in front of the unicorn, holding his sword tip down at his side. "Lady Celeste, may I be excused from your service for an hour's time?"

The unicorn regarded Tristan with a stern, golden eye, before lowering her head to tap him on the shoulder with her horn. "You may," she said and turned her head away to dismiss him from her presence.

Tristan bowed his head once more before getting to his feet and coming back out. "Alright," he said to Gabriel before looking sternly at Emma. "You keep close watch over them."

"Stop with the drama," Donovan said derisively. "I am more than enough protection for the unicorns, and Celeste knows it."

Tristan didn't seem to hear Donovan. He fixed Emma with a serious look until she nodded. "I'll stay with them," she muttered. His intensity was making her uncomfortable. Donovan disappeared, taking Gabriel and Tristan with him.

Feeling even more uncomfortable now that everything was silent, Emma crept into the cave and crouched down by Celeste. Icy wind blew more snow in, making the cave exceedingly cold. "Is this alright for him?" Emma asked to fill the silence.

The unicorn nudged Davet with her nose while he struggled to get his spindly legs under himself. The gesture knocked him flat. Frustration emanated from him, but he tried again. "He is fine," Celeste said. "It is true we are creatures of spring, but it is not unheard of for foals to be born in the winter. They grow to be fierce warriors."

"Interesting." Emma tried to picture a fierce warrior unicorn. She wasn't quite able to. "Do you have many warriors?"

Celeste fixed her with a disapproving stare. "You ask too many questions," she said haughtily and shifted to get more comfortable. "Humanity has forgotten the awesome ferocity of the unicorn," she muttered, disgust leaking out from behind her mental barrier. She turned her gaze onto the foal, and then she opened her mind to Emma. Centuries-old memories of European forests and villages filled Emma's head. She shot a hand out to steady herself against the wall, the barrage making her dizzy. The rough stone under her hand helped ground her with her surroundings.

Foremost in the memories was a great black unicorn, much larger than Celeste. An image presented itself of the great creature driving a handful of hunters from a thick forest.

Celeste pulled her memories back behind her mental barrier, radiating smugness. "You see?"

"Yes. That unicorn is Davet's father?" she asked and sat up straighter. Davet had gotten to his feet and wobbled slowly to the center of the cave.

"He is," Celeste said, arching her neck and raising her head proudly.

They lapsed into silence after that, watching Davet make his slow, clumsy way around the cave. He came over to Emma and butted his head against her knee. Emma smiled and stroked along his muzzle.

His dark eyes shone with happiness, and Emma stared, hearing his powerful mind churning with indistinct thoughts. Something caught and held her. She grew rigid and gasped as a jolt went through her. Suddenly she saw herself through Davet's eyes. She watched with detached interest as her hand fell limply onto the stone floor. Her eyes were vacant and staring.

A clatter of hooves reached Davet's ears, and he turned his head to watch his mother scramble up. *Davet, no!* The reproving thought from his mother was for his mind alone, but Emma heard it clearly.

His head whipped around again to see the human girl fall over. Other humans appeared around her. His mother spoke frantically to them, displeasure and worry colliding in her thoughts. Emma identified them to Davet as Gabriel, Donovan, and Tristan.

I've seen Tristan before. He's so very serious, Davet told her mentally. Davet's thought caught Gabriel's attention. The man's hands shot out and grabbed Davet's head, startling the baby unicorn.

Stop it! Emma protested mentally. Then she felt another jolt, and a rushing sound filled her ears. Davet objected silently as she fell into darkness.

headache pounded behind Emma's eyes when she drifted back into consciousness. "Emma?" Gabriel's voiçe said somewhere above her. She opened her eyes slowly to allow them to adjust to the light and looked around Gabriel's office. She had only been in this room once before, but she recognized the piles of books and heaps of papers that surrounded the cot on all sides. Far-off thoughts reached her. The show must still be going on.

The headache reasserted itself. A groan escaped her, and she put her hands over her eyes.

Cool fingers brushed her temple. "I have some pain medication," Gabriel told her. "But you should eat something with it. Are you able to sit up?"

"Yeah," Emma croaked and pushed herself up on her elbows. Gabriel solemnly handed her a piece of bread. She nibbled it, testing how her stomach would react. It roiled uncomfortably, but she didn't think she was going to be sick. "What happened?" she asked as he handed her a glass of water and some pills. "What about the show?" she added in concern. She scanned the distant thoughts. They were as amazed as the thoughts she'd heard at every show since they came. Nothing amiss there.

"Nemo is finishing it. I announced there had been an emergency, and I had to go make sure my student was alive," he said and shifted his weight. "I'm telling Nemo the words as he goes," he added. A smile touched his lips. "Putting words directly into someone's head. That's another thing I'll have to teach you."

Emma nodded absently but then realized he hadn't answered her question. "What happened? What was it that Davet did?"

Gabriel shifted again, staring fixedly at the floor. The movement disturbed a stack of books. They went tumbling down, knocked into some papers, and both the books and papers fell to the stone floor. Gabriel looked at the mess dispassionately. "Unicorns and...other creatures, have the ability to draw people into their minds. It allows the person to hear the creature's thoughts and see through their eyes. It's...well, quite intimate. It shows an extreme amount of trust and respect. I don't think Davet meant to do it, and he certainly didn't understand what he was doing. Celeste was very upset with him."

A shiver went down Emma's spine as she remembered watching herself collapse. "I don't think I'd like to ever do that again. It was creepy."

Gabriel chuckled and got carefully to his feet to avoid knocking anything else over. "There's little chance you ever will. But when it's done properly, it's not that bad. Normally, you'd be aware it was going to happen and position your body accordingly."

"That still sounds unpleasant. Has it ever happened to you?" Emma asked and swung her feet over the side of the cot. She didn't want to step on papers, so she brushed them aside with the flat of her foot before standing.

Gabriel reddened very slightly. "Once or twice," he said with feigned casualness. Emma gave him a questioning look, and he shook his head. "We're not going into that. Donovan will take you back to your room to rest. I need to get back to the show."

"I'll take her." They both looked to the entrance of the cave and saw Avery's winged silhouette. Emma's heart skipped a beat. She smoothed a hand over her hair. "I finished my act, and Nemo wanted me to check up on Emma," the avian said as he entered.

Gabriel shrugged and stepped over a pile of books. "Alright. Don't keep her up, Avery. She really does need to rest."

Avery chuckled, and Emma blushed as she realized the implied meaning. "You should get a desk and organize this room," she muttered. It was a weak retort, but it was the only thing that came to mind with her headache. The room really was very messy.

Gabriel laughed. "Desks are like suits. Way too confining and—" His words cut off abruptly as Donovan teleported him away.

Emma shook her head. "Gabriel's so strange." She made her way carefully though the office, raising her feet high to avoid the heaps. She nearly made it out of the messy radius without anything falling, but then she tripped over an encyclopedia and stumbled. Avery shot an arm out and stepped forward quickly to catch her.

"Are you okay?" he asked in concern.

"Fine," she gasped and hurried out of the cave before he could see her flush. He dropped his hand slowly and turned to follow her out into the tunnel.

"You gave us a scare. Donovan interrupted the show and whisked Gabriel and Tristan away. Martin had to cover for me, I was messing up my music so badly." He rubbed the back of his neck, glancing away. A smile tugged on Emma's face, but Avery hurried on before she could say anything. "Nemo was really freaked out, but he agreed to take over since Gabriel knows how to help mental ailments."

"Does he?" Emma asked curiously. "Gabriel sure knows a lot about his Blessing. I wonder if someone taught him all this stuff."

Avery's face went blank. Emma glanced at him pointedly, but he remained silent. She didn't press him. "Thanks for checking in on me."

"Of course." They had reached her room. Avery opened the door with a low bow. Emma huffed at his dramatics.

"Oh. I have something for you." She turned in the doorway and raised an eyebrow. He pulled a handful of round stones from his pocket. "I noticed the quartz you put in your window. These would look nice there. I found them in a stream, so they've been smoothed. They sparkle in the sunlight." He shifted and looked away when Emma didn't say anything right away. "It's fine if you don't want them."

"No, I would love them," Emma said, a little stunned he had noticed that. She reached out, and he dropped them into her palm. Emma hesitated and then hugged him quickly. "Thank you." She released him and stepped back with a rising panic. "Good night!" She rushed into her room and closed the door before he could reply and then winced. She should've given him a chance to say something. It'd be even more awkward to open the door again, though.

Several moments passed before she heard the slow tread of his feet move away up the tunnel.

Weariness washed over her. She placed the stones in the windowsill and fell into bed. She could hear the quiet whisper of Davet's thoughts still, amused and content. It seemed he'd made some sort of connection between them. Was it intentional?

As her eyes fluttered closed, her musings strayed once more to wonder about the reason for Avery's gift. She fell asleep with a smile on her lips.

Persistent squeaking reverberated through the cave and pierced Nemo's dream. His eyes flew open, and he stared into the large eyes of the fruit bat, gleaming in the dim light. It hung from the headboard to peer into his face.

"Good morning to you, too," Nemo mumbled, wondering what time it was. "I left you some fruit over there." He gestured vaguely at the darkness around him. The bat squeaked again, its ridged ears swinging madly.

Nemo groaned and covered his eyes. "Going back to sleep. You can find it." The bat squeaked again and buffeted his face with its leathery wings. He cursed and sat up, knocking the bat onto the blanket. It clung to the fabric and squeaked indignantly. "Sorry," he said thickly, rubbing his eyes. "I really need to sleep, little one." His voice was hoarse from narrating the show, and he grimaced at how scratchy his throat felt.

Hopefully, he wasn't getting sick.

The bat climbed up to Nemo's chest on the blanket and regarded him reproachfully before launching into a flurry of high-pitched squeaks that hurt his ears. "I'm awake," he muttered, but his voice was still slurred. He held his hand out and the bat climbed onto his palm.

His toes protested the cold floor, and he sucked in a sharp breath as he hurried across the room. "Why can't Donovan let you out of my room, huh? He's constantly shuffling us around."

When he opened the door, Lucien was standing in the tunnel, his hand raised to knock. "Oh good, you're awake. Timaeus wants you." He turned on his heel and strode away down the dark tunnel. The bat took wing and flew away out of sight in the other direction.

Nemo watched them both go, cursed again, and rushed to get dressed. Timaeus's name served to chase away the bleariness. It was only a few minutes before he burst into the dining room. "You asked for me, sir?"

Timaeus raised his head off his talons and eyed Nemo's disheveled appearance. "Knowing your habits, I wasn't expecting you for at least an hour. Perhaps two," he growled. "I do appreciate your punctuality." He heaved his bulk up, scraping past several chairs and a table.

"A bat woke me up." Nemo couldn't keep his remaining irritation from his voice.

The dragon snorted. "Wise creature, that one. She must have heard Lucien coming." He changed into his human form and stretched his arms over his head. "I went hunting last night. I need your help cleaning the kills, and then you'll deliver the furs to Aoife."

"The mermaid?" Nemo's brain was short circuiting without caffeine. He wasn't sure he had heard correctly.

"Yes, the mermaid," Timaeus grunted irritably, setting up a bulky wooden frame.

"Why does the mermaid need them?"

"Don't ask questions right now." He took a few steps toward the kitchen and then glanced back at Nemo. "Judging by the timbre of your voice, I do not think you are up for a lesson. After you finish aiding me, you may have the day off. You should go outside and get some fresh air.

Take your sister. She could use it after last night."

"What happened last night?" Nemo asked, concern for his sister overpowering Timaeus's command. Nobody had told him exactly what happened to Emma, only that she was okay and asleep, so he should get some rest as well to be prepared for the next show. A tight knot of worry still clenched in his chest.

"Ask her yourself later," the dragon replied. He looked up and nodded to Lucien as the elf came in. "Leave a note on the girl's door that Nemo wishes to spend time with her later, and then come back and help us clean the kills." Lucien turned on his heel and went right back out without a word to either of them.

Nemo sighed and set his mind to the unpleasant task ahead. At least he would have the day off after this was done.

Timaeus showed Nemo what to do and then wandered off. The work quickly became the most disgusting thing Nemo could remember doing.

Blood coated his hands and crusted under his fingernails. He peeled the animal's skin down and sliced through the membrane between it and the meat the best he could, but clumps of coarse fur still came off on his hands and clung to the raw meat underneath. The metallic tang of the fresh blood made him gag. He quickly turned away and brought a hand to his mouth. His fingers stuck to his face and left a scarlet handprint.

Bile rose in Nemo's throat. He sat down hard on the nearest chair and took deep breaths, glad he hadn't eaten anything before starting this. His stomach roiled, and he doubted he would have any appetite for breakfast. He hadn't done anything remotely like this since the only fishing trip he had accompanied his father on. Memory of his father's disappointment when Nemo failed to learn these skills stilled Nemo's hand. He stared blankly at the knife for several moments.

Lucien entered, took one look at Nemo, and took the knife from him. "It does take getting used to," he said, his voice kind. "Human society has become very far removed from death."

"I've just never seen meat like this," Nemo muttered self-consciously. "The stuff you can buy at a store doesn't look anything like animals anymore."

"I wouldn't know," Lucien said. He somehow managed to keep his hands relatively clean as he worked.

Nemo watched, trying to figure out how while his stomach settled. When he didn't feel he was going to throw up, he took a final deep breath and went over to help. "It's not a big deal," he said as casually as he could. "I'm not going to be a vegetarian or anything over this."

Lucien nodded, and they worked in companionable silence for a few minutes. Nemo retreated once, heaving, but Lucien did not comment. His silence made Nemo feel better. There was no condemnation here.

A question formed in Nemo's mind as he swallowed back his disgust enough to resume working again, and he glanced at the elf, turning it over in his head. "Lucien, may I ask you a question?" he said, remembering the dragon's rebuke to not ask anything.

"You just did," Lucien retorted. "You do not need to ask permission. Timaeus may not be in the mood for them sometimes, but he will not forbid questions permanently. I will always answer your questions."

That simple statement struck Nemo, and he swiped his sleeve over his eyes. "Why does everyone bow to Timaeus? Like, asking him to be excused from meals and calling him lord."

Lucien took the hide he cut free and put it in the corner where the pelts were stacked, his expression thoughtful. "It never ceases to surprise me how little history humans remember," he said. "And what little knowledge remains, they call myths and legends."

He rubbed his hands together and his gaze grew distant. "We revere Timaeus for he is one of the few dragons that remain, and of those, one of the oldest. I believe there are only two dragons older than him. Lord Timaeus was young during the zenith of the Roman empire."

"He's that ancient?" Nemo dropped his knife, just barely managing to not cut his foot. He snatched it up again, aware that Lucien watched him, and went over to the sink to wash it off.

"Indeed," Lucien said. "The elves revere the dragons for their power and their wisdom. For that alone, they are considered as royalty among the elven courts. Their prestige is only enhanced by their scant number. I believe there are only a few dozen left the world over. Of those, less than six remain of the ancient dragons that held sway throughout Europe during the Middle Ages. King Arthur and his Blessed knights used their abilities to kill several in the name of making the land safer for humans. The dragons withdrew to wilder haunts long before the elves felt obliged to. Most of the dragons that remain are only a few hundred years old and dwell with the elves for safety. Timaeus does not care for the elven courts, though, so he has remained tucked into these caves. This is his domain, and we are all his guests. That is why we show him deference."

"I see," Nemo said. He looked down at the beast he was skinning. "But he hunts and cooks for us," he said slowly. "He's a good host." He frowned and set to work with more vigor. His stomach was still uncomfortable, but he shoved away any urge to stop. He would prove his worth to Timaeus and to Lucien both.

The darkness in the cave was absolute and heavy. Emma sucked in a deep breath, and the sharp scent of mint made her sneeze. Her fear rose up, almost choking her. The silken blackness pressed in around her, and her breathing sped up. Emma stumbled forward blindly, and her foot splashed down into icy water. She hissed and took several steps back, the darkness and the swish of water reminding her terribly of the night all those years ago.

Donovan had told her he was taking her to where Gabriel would teach her this morning and then teleported her here. Wherever here was.

She wrapped her arms around herself and slowed her breathing. Her eyes were still adjusting to the dim, blue-tinged light when she heard a quiet splash and a low chuckle of laughter. Realization chillier than the water hit her along with renewed fear. "Hello?" she called tentatively, hoping to be wrong. She moved back further, feeling behind her for the wall or anything that might set some parameters to ground her.

"Gabriel stepped out to fetch something," a raspy voice replied. "Come closer. Let me look at you."

"No, thank you," Emma said and winced at how squeaky her voice sounded. Cold memories of pale faces floating above her in the dark water almost paralyzed her.

She heard the laughter again. The blue light reflected like moonlight on the water, showing the ripples as the mermaid swam closer.

The mermaid's pale skin shone silver, and her dark hair flowed like ink around her. She grinned up at Emma as she reached the edge of the pool. Emma took another step back. "Jumpy, aren't you?" the mermaid breathed. "Don't worry. Gabriel has some fun planned for us."

Emma did not like the sound of that. She swallowed, trying to dispel her fear. "I've been wanting to talk to you," she said, her mouth dry. "Avery's mentioned you a few times. Your name is Aoife, right?"

"That's right," the mermaid purred. "And you're Emma Reeve. I hoped you would come and visit. I'm a little sad you're only here because Donovan brought you." She sighed morosely but then brightened. "I suppose it's just as well you didn't come before. This will be a wonderful way for us to get to know each other." While she spoke, the mermaid swam over to the other side of the pool and pulled herself up on some stairs.

Even more confused and alarmed, Emma laughed, a forced sound. "I'd like to get to know you too," she said softly. "As long as you're not trying to drown me."

Emma meant it as a joke, but the mermaid placed her chin in her webbed hand and regarded her unblinkingly. "We'll see.".

Gabriel strolled in carrying a backpack. "Let's get this over with," he said, ignoring Emma's tense posture. "Tristan is sitting out of the show, so I need to reorder the lineup before the performance tonight." He met Emma's eyes and looked away. "You've been having trouble breaking through mental barriers. Once you have the feel of it, it's not as hard, depending on the strength of the person's will. For example, nobody could ever get past Timaeus's barrier."

"Okay." Emma raised an eyebrow when he didn't continue. "So, how do I get the feel for it?"

"That's the catch," Gabriel said. "If you can't do it after all our practice, we have to force it." His eyebrows drew down into a troubled expression, and he moved closer to her. "Do you trust me?"

"No," Emma said without giving it any thought. Gabriel and Aoife laughed, and she turned red. "I mean...I don't distrust you. You've been a good teacher these last few months, and I feel more at home with the circus than I ever did in my hometown. I know you're a good person."

Gabriel smiled thinly. "You don't need to explain your reasoning." He shifted and took a deep breath. "Let's get this over with," he repeated.

Before Emma could react, Gabriel lunged forward and pushed her into the water. The shock drove the air from her lungs, but it wasn't as cold as the river in her memory. She quickly swam to the surface and paddled for the edge. A splash to her right gave her just a few seconds warning before a hand closed around her ankle and yanked her back under the water.

Hampered by her clothing, she struggled to twist around to see the surface. Instead, she came face to face with the grinning mermaid. Aoife gripped Emma's wrist and ran a hand through Emma's billowing hair. Emma stared at the mermaid's faintly glowing skin as the fear she had been suppressing came rushing in, choking her nearly as much as her burning lungs. For a moment, she was eight years old again, trapped in a submerged car with a grinning, pale face between her and her parents in the front seat.

Nemo's Blessing had saved them that night: commanding the mermaids to rescue them. This time, she was alone in the water.

The mermaid's hand was still closed like a vice on Emma's wrist, and her lungs ached horribly. She struggled frantically against Aoife. The mermaid allowed Emma to bob to the surface.

She gasped in two breaths and saw Gabriel leaning low over the water before Aoife dragged her down again.

This time, Emma was ready. Determination to save herself with her own Blessing drove out her fear. She closed her eyes to concentrate and hammered at the mermaid's mental barriers. Her lungs cried out for air, and her vision blurred around the edges. She pushed harder, scrabbling desperately with her ability.

Merfolk follow an old faith that humans have begun to abandon. We have ancient texts of this belief, lost at sea throughout the

103

centuries. We believe it all. The good and the bad. The fierceness of God, and the wonderful love. We do not cringe away from the judgements. Perhaps because we have remained so much fiercer than humans through the centuries.

Emma couldn't hear it clearly, but she barely considered that. She needed air. She ineffectively kicked at the mermaid. *Let me go!* She screamed mentally.

Aoife instantly swam Emma up to the surface. Gabriel was kneeling at the edge of the water. He slumped in relief when he saw them. "Thank you for keeping your promise, Aoife," he said and helped Emma out of the water.

"Did you really think I would've drowned her?" Aoife said, crossing her arms and glaring.

Gabriel shook his head, but his expression said otherwise. "Sorry. Old stories and all. You know I still struggle not to believe them sometimes." He busied himself putting a blanket around Emma's shoulders and didn't look at Aoife.

Aoife huffed and turned her attention to Emma. "What did you hear?" she asked.

Emma was still panting. Shivers continued to wrack her while she stuttered out the thoughts she had heard in the water.

"Good," Aoife said before turning to Gabriel. "She didn't hear everything, but that was a good amount of it."

Gabriel smiled and rubbed Emma's back. "Are you okay?" he asked in concern.

Emma's gaze sharpened as her mind caught up. "Oh, don't even start," she growled and jerked away from his touch. "I can't believe you just did that!"

Gabriel's face blanked but hurt flickered in his eyes before he blinked it away. "I didn't know how else to teach you this," he said stiffly.

"How did you learn?" Emma snapped, struggling to get up. Before she rose more than a few inches, her foot slipped on the damp stone, and she crashed back down, adding a painful bruise to the indignities of this lesson.

Gabriel drew back to the edge of the cave. "My teacher threw me off a ship into a maelstrom of merfolk," he said and rubbed his face, suddenly looking exhausted. "Very angry merfolk."

The sorrow and weariness on Gabriel's face caused Emma's anger to deflate. "I just wish he would've warned me," she muttered, pulling the blankets tighter around herself.

"The lesson wouldn't have worked if you were expecting it and knew you were safe. Sorry." Gabriel leaned against the wall and crossed his arms.

"Well." Emma wiped her drenched sleeve over her nose and shook her head. "Let's agree to discuss it next time."

Gabriel nodded, his features lightening a little. "Agreed. I swear we'll find a better way next time. Sorry again." He came over and patted her shoulder. "I need to get to the rehearsal. Aoife will take care of getting you dried off."

Aoife reached up and stroked Emma's ankle when the door closed. "He really did feel bad about trying this. He just didn't know what else to do."

Emma nodded as another shiver rocked her, as much from the mermaid's clammy touch as from her sopping clothing.

Aoife frowned. "Let's get you out of those wet clothes. Donovan, will you please take her to the other side of the room?"

The shift occurred seamlessly. Emma didn't even feel anything, but she was suddenly sitting on the floor on the other side of the cave. Aoife swam across the pool and heaved herself out of the water. Her dark hair curled against her shoulders like inky tentacles. The image made another shudder rip through Emma.

As Aoife's tail came up onto the stone, it split and transformed into slender legs. She got to her newly formed feet and slipped a black robe over her shoulders.

"I didn't know you could do that," Emma said through chattering teeth. She stood up to get away from the cold stone. "How come I never see you around, if you can leave your pool?"

"I like to keep my secrets," Aoife said with a mischievous smile. "I come around sometimes. I was at the welcome feast for you. I just keep to the background and observe when I go out. Humans are fascinating to watch." She touched a lamp. Golden light brightened the room, illuminating furniture: a four-poster bed like Emma's, racks of clothing, three wooden wardrobes, and a table with an old-fashioned Singer sewing machine. Piles of fabric cluttered the table and half of the bed. Wooden frames with deer hides stretched over them leaned against the far wall. "Let's see," the woman mused and began looking through the racks of clothing.

"I could just go back to my room," Emma muttered. She went over and sat on the stool next to the table, shivering miserably. "Is Gabriel going to be okay? He seemed quite upset."

Aoife went still, considering the clothing. "He doesn't talk about his past very often, so you certainly touched a nerve, but that's not necessarily a bad thing. I'd guess he's feeling more guilty than angry. It wasn't a good thing that was done to him, and he knew it wasn't a good thing to do to you. He just didn't know how else to teach you."

"I see." Emma could understand that, but she would reinforce discussing lesson plans beforehand with him later. She lurched to her feet. "I really should go back to my room. There's no reason for you to find me new clothing."

"No!" Aoife darted over, crouched down next to the stool, and clutched Emma's hand. "Please let me dress you up! I never get to dress anyone up! Celeste is a unicorn, and the girls don't come to me for clothing nearly enough!" She looked down. "Besides, it's the least I can do to make it up to you for that scare."

Emma stared into Aoife's puppy eyes and felt a bubble of hilarity rise in her chest. It burst, and a laugh escaped her. A smile touched Aoife's lips, belying her guilty expression.

"Okay, okay," Emma relented. Aoife let out a whoop and darted back over the clothing rack. "Why do you have all this clothing anyway? There's no way you wear it."

"I wear some of it," Aoife retorted lightly. She pulled a dark blue blouse off a hanger. "Not nearly enough for how beautiful these things are. I'll have to help you fill that closet you have." Emma chuckled. "I make the costumes for the show," Aoife added. "Sometimes, when my room gets too full, Gabriel talks me into leaving some things at thrift stores. He hasn't succeeded with that in a while, though." She tossed her head, sending water from her wet hair striping the cave floor. "Take those wet things off," she said and gestured toward a screen on the far side of the bed.

Emma made a face and went behind the screen to obey. As cold as she was in wet clothing, she was even colder without it. Her clothing disappeared before it hit the floor, caught by one of Donovan's spells to keep belongings in their owner's room. Emma frowned. Magic still disconcerted her at times, despite how long she'd been with the Circus now.

She put on the dark-blue blouse and a flowing ankle length black skirt before coming out from behind the screen.

"Sit," Aoife ordered and pointed to the stool in front of a large mirror mounted to the cave wall.

"How do things even work here?" Emma muttered and peered at the edge of the mirror, trying to figure out how it was attached to the stone.

"Donovan is a world-class mage who had the nerve to seek out a dragon and ask to serve him," Aoife pointed out as she walked over with a brown plastic bottle and a hairbrush. "Don't try to apply normal logic to magic, especially Keeper magic. You'll just give yourself a migraine. Now sit!"

Emma sat, and Aoife attacked her wavy gold-brown hair with the hairbrush and conditioner. Once it was untangled, she began braiding it. "Tell me what happened with Davet last night. Celeste is close mouthed about it."

Emma hesitated. She didn't know if she should tell the mermaid if Celeste didn't want her to know. Her lips twitched. "I'm not sure how I feel about gossiping about the unicorns with the mermaid doing my hair."

"Oh hush. It's not gossip. I can tell you more about whatever it is. Gabriel only hinted at it. I think he would be happy if I explained it to you."

"He explained it last night," Emma said, but she smoothed a hand over the skirt and told Aoife anyway. She didn't see the harm in the mermaid knowing, and she might get more insights into it than Gabriel could tell her.

"I see," Aoife said, drawing the words out. "Do you still feel like you have a connection with Davet?" she asked, her hands moving deftly over Emma's hair.

Emma blinked. "Yeah. I don't know if it will last, but I've been able to sense him all morning." She closed her eyes. "He's not really directing any thoughts at me, but I feel like he could. Even if he keeps a barrier around his mind from others."

Aoife burst out laughing. "Oh, that is *rich*! No wonder Celeste is so miffed! Her newborn son went and formed a compact with a lowly human!"

Emma stared at Aoife as the mermaid continued to laugh. "I don't understand. A compact?"

Aoife regained her composure with deep breaths. "That wasn't an accident. Some creatures just know when they encounter someone they want to connect to mentally, no matter how young they are. Celeste is a proud creature and doesn't like to think about connecting with humans, although she practically has one with Tristan. She puts that off by calling him her knight." Aoife resumed brushing Emma's hair. "Timaeus and Lucien also share a telepathic bond of that nature. It's possible Timaeus is considering Nemo for it as well."

"Nemo might end up as a dragon rider?" Emma asked, unable to quite wrap her head around the idea. "A lot of stories have dragons having bonds with their riders like that."

Aoife smiled. "It's not that simple in modern times. But yes, that is what it amounts to. Young dragons will usually only accept one companion, but as they get older sometimes they will have several. Especially since human companions come and go with time." She finished the braid. "Beautiful."

Emma looked in the mirror and grinned. Aoife had managed to tame her wavy hair and no hairs escaped from the tight braid. "It is! Thank you. I feel a lot better." She got to her feet. "I should go find Nemo. He wanted to spend some time together this afternoon before the show."

Aoife nodded and hugged Emma. Emma stiffened for a moment before returning the embrace. "I hope there really are no hard feelings for the lesson Gabriel wanted to teach you. He was really conflicted about doing that to you." She stepped back with her hands gripping Emma's shoulders and peered into her face. Emma shook her head, still smiling. "Good. He's trying his best to teach you things, but I'm glad he agreed to do better in the future." She patted Emma's shoulder. "You come back so we can play dress-up again. I hope we can be good friends now that that rough introduction is past."

She walked Emma to the door, not even blinking when they shifted in-between steps so that they didn't walk into the pool. "You're going to be just fine," she added. "I could tell how worried Gabriel was after last night, but now I know it was unfounded. You're doing well. See you later." She waved to Emma and closed the door. Before Emma was more than a couple steps away, Aoife jerked it open again and poked her head out.

"What size shoes do you wear?"

Music thrummed through the stone slab that served as a door to Nemo's cave. Emma knocked, wondering if he would be able to hear. The music faltered and then continued. The slab crunched as it was pushed open. Avery's freckled face peered out at her, his surprise plain. "Emma! Your hair! And..." his eyes drifted to her skirt. "You're not wearing jeans. You look very nice!"

Emma grimaced as she walked in past him. His reaction had made her self-conscious. "I spent the morning with Aoife," she said dryly.

"Ah. That makes sense," Avery said. He cleared his throat and his feathers fluffed up a little bit.

Nemo sat on his bed with a guitar on his lap. Martin sat next to him, a shadow nearly invisible against the dark wall behind him. Nemo raised an eyebrow at Emma and snickered. "I don't think I've seen you in a skirt since we were kids," he said hoarsely. "My voice is shot, so Martin is teaching me how to play guitar," he added. He stood up and handed the instrument to Martin. "Are we going to go exploring?"

"Are we?" Emma asked. This was the first she had heard of it.

"Timaeus thinks we could use the fresh air," Nemo said. "We're starting to look like ghosts, haunting these caves the way we've been. Not even Gabriel is as pale as we are."

"True," Emma conceded. "It's snowy outside, though. I'd have to change." She shifted, all too aware of her bare legs. "And it seems a shame to waste Aoife's effort on my hair."

"The wind is very calm today," Avery put in. "Martin and I went flying earlier. It's cold outside, but it's sunny."

"Okay, okay." Emma laughed. "I give. I'll go out with you." Avery beamed at her. Martin's face remained as inscrutable as it had been the handful of times Emma had encountered him since moving into the caves. He kept to himself a lot of the time. "How about you, Martin?"

Martin looked at Avery and then back to Emma. "I'll pass. Avery might be willing to catch a chill for you, but I'm not." He shouldered the guitar and left the room.

Nemo looked between Emma and Avery, much as Martin had, frowning in thought. "We'll meet by the exit then," he said as he got to his feet. "I need to change too. These clothes aren't nearly warm enough."

Avery nodded and bowed before disappearing.

"What do you think about Avery?" Nemo asked. Emma gave him a surprised look, and he raised an eyebrow. "I've noticed you two spend a lot of time together. I'm curious."

Emma turned pink. "I'm not sure. He's just cheesy. I doubt he means a lot of the absurd gestures he makes. The bowing and all that."

Nemo turned appraising eyes on her. She suspected he didn't believe her. "See you later then."

Donovan teleported Emma to her room while she considered what Nemo and Martin were implying with their hints and thoughtful looks.

A windy snowstorm the night before had left the air crystal clear, and the beauty of the landscape left Emma speechless. The brisk temperature and slight breeze made Emma pull gloves out of her coat pockets. She slipped them on as they crunched over the fresh snow and looked around.

"Tell me what happened last night!" Nemo said, poking Emma in the side when the silence stretched past a few minutes.

Her breath clouded in front of her face while she told Nemo about finding Celeste and her baby, and the following events. Avery listened without comment, his eyes troubled.

"Wow," Nemo said and grinned. "I guess this means you found a new friend."

"It's not that simple. Especially considering Davet's age," Avery snapped, his tone startling Emma.

Nemo looked equally stunned and hurt by the unexpected outburst. He shrugged and forged ahead, stamping the snow down to make a path for the others to follow.

Avery glanced at Emma, his expression growing more troubled. "I'm sorry, but—"

"Don't worry," she hastened to say. "Aoife told me about it. I know it's serious."

Avery's shoulders sagged in relief and he smiled. "Good. I got worried. With modern human society the way it is, there's too much room for misunderstandings to leave both humans and magic creatures hurt."

Avery wore a leather coat with button closed flaps in the back to allow for his wings. He fluffed his trembling feathers up slightly and tightened his scarf around the bottom of his face.

"Not used to the cold?" Emma asked. Avery rarely talked about himself. Excitement sparked at the chance to learn more about him.

Avery shook his head. "Martin and I are from Great Britain. It's plenty cold there. I've just never liked being out in it much. I'll take sitting by a fire with some apple cider any day."

"That sounds nice right now," Emma said. The air brought color to her face, and Avery's eyes lingered. "What?" she demanded. Nemo's question still nagged at her.

"Nothing." Avery hopped forward, using his wings to leap up several feet. Nemo was quite far ahead by now. Emma shook her head

111

and smiled at Avery's antics. She still wasn't sure how she felt about him, but he could always make her laugh.

"Look!" Avery said a few minutes later and stopped dead. Emma bumped into his wings. He stepped off the beaten path so that she could come up beside him and peer at the clump of trees he pointed at.

"What am I looking for?" Emma breathed, catching on to his excitement.

He leaned closer and pointed again. "Look for the white feathers. Their heads stand out against the dark trees," he whispered. His breath tickling her ear.

The sensation almost distracted Emma, and then she saw what he was pointing at and caught her breath. Three bald eagles perched in the dark branches, glaring regally down at them. "Amazing," she said and grinned. "How funny to see bald eagles for the first time when I'm in Canada."

"Borders mean nothing from the sky," Avery said. He took a step back and straightened while Emma turned to face him. His face broke into his habitual grin. "Would you like a closer look?"

"Yeah!" Emma's eyes lit up and she lifted a foot to hurry forward. His arms closed around her and the ground fell out from beneath her feet before she could take a step. The wind stole Emma's breath, and she could only gasp as they ascended.

Avery angled his wings and flew them over to the trees, the noise of his wings filling her ears. The eagles shifted when Avery and Emma landed on a thick branch midway up in a tree. They were only a dozen feet away, but the birds didn't move. She gulped and clung to Avery as the branch swayed beneath them. She wished she was as fearless as the eagles. "You're okay," Avery said, rubbing her back. "I won't let you fall."

Emma couldn't answer. The breeze, so gentle on the ground, rattled the branch they stood on and shook the tree under them. She stared at the ground. Nemo stood nearby and waved up at them. The tree swayed again, and Emma clenched her teeth.

"Look up," Avery suggested. "Looking down makes it worse." Emma took a deep breath and pulled her eyes up to the eagles, focusing on them to calm herself.

The insanity of the situation made a hiccup of laughter bubble up in her for the second time that day. It emerged as a grin, and Avery beamed in return.

Eventually, she looked away from the birds and took in the view. Snow covered mountains rose on the other side of the forest, crowned with the tattered remains of the night's storm.

"Beautiful, isn't it?" Avery asked in the moment that another gust of wind shook the tree. Her hold on his arm tightened, and he winced.

"I'd rather enjoy the view from the ground," Emma said, staring down again. It would be an awfully long fall.

"Deal. I'd rather keep circulation in my arm." He gripped her tightly around the waist and stepped off the branch. They plummeted. Emma shrieked and squeezed his arm in a vice-like grip while he whooped and laughed. He snapped his wings open just a few feet from the ground, lifted Emma up a foot, and landed hard. His legs folded, and he fell to his knees, but he set Emma lightly on her feet. "Not a feather out of place," he said and smirked at her.

"Yeah," Emma gasped and forced herself to release her frozen grip on him. He rubbed his arm and grimaced.

"You have quite a firm grip."

"Sorry about that," she muttered and took a deep breath.

"It's fine," Avery said. "My fault. I didn't know you had an issue with heights."

"I don't mind them. I just prefer having a solid surface under my feet when I'm dealing with them. As for flying…" she frowned. "It was like a rollercoaster." She managed a slight smile. "It was exhilarating. I'd do it again."

Avery's grin lit up his freckled face, and he pointed toward the mountains. "Maybe we could—"

"No more flights today," Emma said quickly. Avery's face fell. "It's too cold, and I don't want to mess up my hair before the show tonight. It took Aoife a while to do this braid."

Avery cast his eyes over her hair and nodded. "That makes sense." He looked away, stuck his hands in his coat pockets, and started stomping down a path for them. "It looks really good. Your hair."

"Thanks," Emma mumbled, looking away and rubbing her neck. A snowball whizzed suddenly from between the trees and struck her shoulder. She whirled around and spotted Nemo dashing away.

"Take cover!" Avery bellowed and pursued Nemo, slipping around on the snow. "I'll take down your assailant, my lady!"

Emma laughed and followed Avery's path in the snow, stepping in the indentions he made for her.

Lucien.

Emma stopped dead and looked around. "Hello?" she called, trying to locate the person's mind. It sounded close. Nemo and Avery were shouting at each other on the other side of the trees and didn't hear her.

Lucien. The thought, terribly soft, came from deeper in the copse of trees. She glanced back once and then set off through the trees. She heard the thought several more times and peered around. The sun was setting, and the pine trees cast deep shadows under their boughs.

"Hello?" she called again, louder. She could barely hear Nemo and Avery now, but she couldn't wait for them and risk losing the thread of thought.

A twig snapped a few feet away, and Emma's head whipped around. The deer froze, its body twisted around to look at her. Emma took several deep breaths. She was being too jumpy. She took a slow step backward, not wanting to frighten the motionless deer.

The thought sounded again, right behind her. She turned to look, and the ground gave way beneath her, sending her tumbling down the embankment. The deer darted away, its hooves barely leaving indentations in the snow.

Emma sat up and rubbed her head. "Ow…" She was in a gully, the embankment rising steeply above her. Lines of pain along her arms and side marked scratches from the fall, but she patted herself and didn't feel anything worse. It wouldn't be too difficult to climb back out.

Lucien. Emma jolted and peered around again, trying to see through the gloom. She could barely make out the hunched figure on one side of the gulley. Leaves and pine needles crunched under her boots while she walked, but the figure didn't look up. She knelt beside

114

the figure. The woman's pale face stared through her without seeing her.

A chill went through Emma as she took in the woman's dull gaze and blue-tinged lips. "Miss?" She put a hand on the woman's shoulder. The woman jerked away and toppled over.

Emma bit her lip and looked up at the slope again. She could climb up, but it wasn't likely she would be able to do it supporting this woman. Even less if the woman wouldn't cooperate. "Miss, let me help you," she whispered and moved closer. The woman stood up. Her eyes now stared sightlessly up at the sky. There was something unnatural in her gaze, more than just succumbing to the cold.

"What do I do?" Emma muttered. Only the whisper of distant thoughts reached her. Would anyone hear her if she shouted? Maybe. But she didn't like the idea. What if something else came? Did grizzly bears live in this wilderness?

Emma didn't want to find out.

"I'm here to help you," she told the woman and listened for her mind. All she could hear was the woman chanting Lucien's name. When she tried to push past that, she ran into a barrier.

"Okay. I can do this when I'm threatened with drowning. Well, if I stay here I'll freeze." She gathered her mental strength and hammered against the barrier.

It broke with surprising ease, and Emma fell into the woman's mind. The unnatural feeling was amplified here. Emma recognized magic a moment too late. Her thoughts became sluggish and she went stiff, staring straight at the woman and unable to move as the deep sorcerous cold spread from the woman into her.

A shadow loomed at the top of the slope. A puff of steam rose around a large muzzle as the creature looked at the two prone figures.

Lucien.

11

A very and Nemo panted, their breath streaming into the air around their faces, while they watched the elf lope across the snowy field towards them. "Hey, Lucien," Avery called and waved.

"The sun has set," the elf called back. "Donovan wants everyone back inside so that he may begin preparations for our next transition after tonight's show." His eyes skimmed over them and then over to the copse of trees a little distance away. "Where is Emma?" he asked.

"She's—" Avery looked around and frowned. "Huh. I thought she was staying clear of our snow war and watching."

"Emma?" Nemo called, projecting his voice so that it carried. There was no reply. "Weird. She must've wandered into the trees."

Lucien's expressionless eyes swept over the trees again and then widened. His normally detached expression cracked with apprehension. "A spell just spiked over there," he said in a rush and sprinted toward the trees.

"A what?" Nemo asked blankly.

Avery's face paled. He cursed and took wing after Lucien, leaving Nemo to bring up the rear, much slower than either of them.

A dark beast turned its head and watched their approach, snorting in alarm. It lowered its head so that its great antlers threatened the approaching figures. The elf skidded to a stop and stooped low, gripping the hilt of a dagger in his boot. "We mean you no harm, great one. We are here for the girl."

The moose pawed the ground, its deep brown eyes glaring at them. Avery muttered restlessly and leapt over the large animal, pushing his wings down so that he cleared the creature's back by several feet.

"Avery, wait!" Lucien protested. The moose swung its head around, but the avian was already descending into the ravine.

He landed heavily and knelt. Emma was slumped over on the gully floor, staring blankly at the ground. "Emma!" He shook her gently, but it elicited no response. "Come on, Emma," he whispered, stroking a hand down her face, her skin cold to his touch. His hands trembled with his growing fear. He scooped her up and extended his wings to take off, before catching sight of another woman sprawled out in the snow a few feet away. A curse escaped him. "Lucien!" he shouted, his arms tightening around Emma. "There's another woman down here! I need your help!"

Lucien's face peered over the edge of the precipice. "I will be down momentarily. I'm convincing the moose to leave us be." Nemo jogged up to the elf and bent over, breathing heavily.

Avery stooped down, still holding Emma close, and waved a hand in front of the woman's face. "Stay up there! I'll bring Emma up and then fly back down for the other woman!" He flapped his wings and landed next to them a moment later. He carefully laid Emma down on the ground, stroking her face again. "Her skin is cold. Both her and the stranger are unresponsive."

Nemo crouched down and reached for Emma's hand, but Lucien shoved him back. "Don't touch her," he ordered.

"What the heck?" Nemo growled and pulled away from Lucien's hold. "What's your problem?"

"She's fallen under an enchantment," the elf said stiffly. "It's possible it might be spread by physical contact. I would've stopped Avery from touching her if he hadn't flown off on his own." His gaze went distant and unfocused. "I have contacted Timaeus. He will be out shortly. He can bring her inside where we can examine her."

Avery landed beside them, carrying the stranger. Lucien bent and studied the woman's face.

"Anyone you know?" Avery asked. "You're from this area, aren't you?"

"This general area, yes. I did not have much experience with the mage community, however." He tilted his head, took the woman's hand, and traced the blue veins visible in her pale skin. "I do not think this woman is a magic user. I sense no magic in her other than the spell."

They were thrown into darkness for several moments as a shadow passed overhead. A heavy thud shook the ground, and the sharp cracking of trees approached. Lucien grimaced. "Timaeus will tear the copse apart. Please take the woman out to him, Avery. I will bring Emma." Nemo shot him a furious look, and he sighed. "I can contain the effect of the contact."

Avery gave Lucien an annoyed look. "You're getting awfully bossy."

"Do it!" Lucien barked. "We need to deal with this swiftly, or the spell will damage both women more than it already has!"

Avery took off immediately.

Timaeus withdrew his serpentine head from among the trees and breathed in deeply over the two young women laid before him. "This is an elven spell," he murmured. Lucien stiffened. "I will need more time to study it." The dragon reared back onto his hind legs and picked the women up in his claws.

"Hey!" Nemo shouted. "Aren't you going to break the spell? Lucien said it will hurt Emma more the longer it's on her!"

"Hasty action would cause more harm than the spell can in a brief time," Timaeus rumbled. "Particularly if it's an elven spell. Put your mind at rest, Nemo. I will do all that is in my power to heal your sister from this ailment."

Nemo ducked his head and ran his fingers through his bleached hair until it stood on end.

Avery clapped him on the back. "I know how you feel, but trust Timaeus. He'll keep his word."

"Right." Nemo looked up and saw a flash of white against the pine trees. Celeste stood at the edge of the forest, Tristan on one side of her and a tiny black unicorn on her other side. They watched as Timaeus took off toward the caves and then followed silently. "She better be alright," Nemo muttered.

"She will be." Avery sounded as if he was reassuring himself as well. Nemo gave him a considering look, and they walked back to the cave side by side.

Emma's thoughts wandered. She was aware of voices, but they were garbled and echoed. Gentle hands touched her, and she knew that she was being moved, but she couldn't bring herself to care. She could also hear the woman nearby, still chanting Lucien's name. *Who are you? Why are you looking for Lucien?* she asked silently.

The chanting did not falter. Emma stopped listening.

The voices moved away for a time and then came back. She was warmer now, and that was a relief. Davet's thoughts flitted through her mind, and she sensed his concern. She tried to reassure him. It must've worked because he withdrew from her mind, radiating his relief.

Then a very different presence mentally brushed her mind. *Sorry about this.* His voice was familiar but different than she knew it. He sounded infinitely weary. She was arduously piecing together a response when a cacophony of thoughts swamped her.

It solidified into a multitude of visions, complete with sound. The splash and quiet laughter of the mermaid in her pool. The dragon raised his great black head and snorted in front of a cave entrance. Celeste nuzzled her baby while Tristan looked on, still holding his sword. Farther away, a mouse scuffled through a hole. A cricket chirped forlornly by the cooling fire pit. On and on it went, every detail from every inch of the caves, continuously.

Emma's back arched, and she scrabbled at the fabric her hands fell on. A new vision barraged her senses. She saw herself thrashing about on a bed, mouth wide in a scream she heard through both her ears and the unusual vision.

It cut off as abruptly as it had begun, and Emma collapsed back, panting and staring up at the stone ceiling with her own eyes, blurry with tears. She turned her head to see a handful of faces staring at her, gape-mouthed and pasty white.

Her face burned, and she knew she must be bright red. Her head began to pound from the horrific barrage. "What—" her voice cracked, and she coughed. Nemo silently offered her some water. She struggled to sit up, and Avery helped her get propped up against the bedframe. She accepted the water and drank it all. "What was that?" she croaked, when the glass was empty.

Donovan cleared his throat softly. He stood a few feet off, looking mortified. "We weren't sure how to rouse you," he said. "We decided one of us should try to reach you mentally. Timaeus and Lucien are with the woman still, so I opened my mind to you."

Emma stared at him, expecting him to continue. "That's it?" she said when he remained silent. "You just let me hear your thoughts? That's what's going through your mind all the time? How do you function?" Her voice rose a bit. She knew Donovan was aware of the entirety of the caves. It never occurred to her what that might be like. Horror gripped her, and she stared at him, appalled.

Donovan smiled faintly. "I was trained as a Keeper," he said in his monotone. "It's the magical field I specialize in, and I knew what it would be like before Timaeus employed me. There are plenty of benefits to being a Keeper that make up for the mental strain. Especially in being a dragon's Keeper." Avery shifted, and Donovan nodded to him. "At any rate, that's not the issue right now."

"Oh yeah!" Emma exclaimed, the events from the forest coming back to her. "What happened? Is that woman okay? How did I get in here, anyway?"

The door banged open before anyone could answer. Gabriel stomped in, glaring furiously at Donovan. The mage's smile faded, and he looked expressionlessly back at Gabriel.

"Timaeus brought you in," Avery said, looking between the two men. "Whatever spell the woman was under spread to you. Timaeus and Lucien took the spell off both of you, but you didn't wake up, so Donovan did...whatever that was that he did." He sounded concerned and swallowed. "Lucien and Timaeus are with the woman now."

"Ah, that's right," Donovan said. "I need to go attend them and do what I can to help." He hunched his shoulders. "Stop glaring holes in my back, Gabriel. It was not my intention for you to hear my thoughts too. It was a desperate measure to wake Emma."

Donovan disappeared, and Gabriel sighed. "Sorry, Donovan. It just gave me a headache," he said and rubbed his eyes. "You need to stop having accidents, Emma," he said wryly. "I ended the show a little early since so many of my key performers were dashing around dealing with this."

"Sorry to inconvenience you," Emma grumbled and then realized what he had said. "Wait. The show is over? How long have I been out?"

"Four hours," Nemo put in, checking the time on his phone.

Emma leapt up. "I need to go see what I can do for the woman," she said. Avery blocked her way, frowning. "What?" she asked and frowned right back. "Let me by."

"You should rest, Emma," he said. "You got really chilled while you were under the spell. I would be surprised if you didn't catch a cold."

"I feel fine," Emma retorted, appreciating his concern but unwilling to be diverted. She ducked under his outstretched arm and darted away before he could grab her shirt. "That woman is looking for Lucien."

"What?" Gabriel said over Avery's protest. He stumbled and cursed when they were suddenly both shifted into another room. A single oil lamp illuminated the cave, and the shadows flickered wildly around them while Gabriel clapped a hand over his mouth. The sudden transition had left Emma feeling a little ill as well.

"The woman is awake," Timaeus growled. His bulk filled fully half of the room. The flame of the oil lamp glimmered off his black scales and gleamed in his copper eyes. "She won't speak to us, however. She withdrew into her mind and closed us out. We need Emma to

121

communicate with her. Judging by her reaction to us, it would be too invasive for Gabriel to do it." His eye moved and bored into Emma. "You say she is looking for Lucien?"

"Yeah." Emma averted her eyes away from the dragon's burning gaze. He still made her nervous. She was all too aware of his ivory fangs and foot-long talons.

The woman sat on a cot pushed against the wall, leaning against the rough stone with her knees drawn up to her chest and curled into a ball. Her eyes were squeezed shut, her mind closed off.

Emma crouched down beside the cot. "Miss? Will you speak with me, please? We need to know who you are and what's going on."

The woman stirred slightly but otherwise didn't respond. Emma hesitated and glanced back at Gabriel. "Go ahead," he told her.

Despite his reassurance, Emma swallowed back guilt as she listened for the woman's mind. In the forest when they were both freezing. Now, it felt like an invasion of privacy. The barriers she encountered in the forest were back up, heightening Emma's feel of wrongness, but they weren't as strong. The unnatural sensation was gone. Emma pushed past them with ease. "Julia," she whispered a moment later.

The woman's eyes flew open. She looked at Emma incredulously before her gaze fixed on the men. Her eyes narrowed, and she squeezed them closed again. Emma sighed. "Julia, that man is Lucien."

Julia gasped and leapt off the cot, knocking Emma aside as she rushed forward. "You are Lucien?" she demanded, grabbing a fistful of the elf's shirt. A soft snarl emanated from the dragon, but the woman took no notice. "You need to help Tip!"

"Tiberius Moore," Emma added, having caught the man's full name in Julia's unguarded thoughts.

Lucien's head whipped around, and he stared at Emma. "Oh. I see." He put a gentle hand over Julia's fingers and pried them open.

"You know him?" Gabriel looked between Timaeus and Lucien.

Lucien shook his head. "I know of him. If he's involved, then it's likely this involves the Company."

122

Gabriel stiffened and couldn't repress the flash of fear that crossed his face. He shook his head at Lucien, shifting his gaze pointedly sidewise at Emma.

She looked between them, frowning. "What Company?"

Silence reigned. Lucien put an arm around Julia and guided her back to the cot. "Lie down and get some rest, Miss," he whispered. "I will do what I can to get help for Tiberius."

The woman shook her head frantically. "You must help him now!" she insisted. Lucien looked across at Timaeus. The dragon breathed out an unusual word. Julia's eyelids drooped, and she collapsed onto the cot. She was asleep in moments.

"The enchantment was a tracking spell," Timaeus commented. "Elven magic. Placed on the woman to guide her to you."

Lucien nodded. "That makes sense. It must have happened when we were by Toronto. I would've been the closest elf, so Tip sent her to me. Then we shifted before she reached us, so the spell warped trying to readjust to our new location." He sighed and rubbed his eyes. "What a mess."

"What Company?" Emma repeated and stared at Lucien. "What's going on?"

Lucien frowned at her. Gabriel stepped between them, desperate to avoid this conversation. "Nothing. Forget about it," he ordered. "You don't need to worry about this anymore, Emma."

"Don't give me that," Emma snapped. "I want to know what happened to Julia and Tip. Who are the people that took Tip?"

"Take her out of here, Donovan," he said. "We're not having this conversation, Emma. Forget about all of this. It's not your concern."

Emma scowled, opened her mouth...and vanished as Donovan shifted her away.

"I have locked her door," the Keeper said. "She needs some rest after all this."

"Thank you," Gabriel said and breathed a heavy sigh of relief before turning to Lucien. "What are you planning?"

The elf now stood by Timaeus, speaking quietly and rapidly to the dragon. He looked up, his long hair obscuring part of his face and unease in his eyes. "I will do what I must. A half-elf has been abducted by humans. I must go to the nearest outpost and report it."

Smoke curled up from Timaeus's nostrils, his eyes narrowing. "I don't like it," he growled and twisted away from the elf.

Lucien's frown deepened, carving lines into his ageless face. "It is my duty," he said simply. "I cannot let this go. There's too much chance of a spell message being misunderstood."

"And what will the elves do when they get word of this?" Gabriel interrupted. Lucien blinked as if surprised to see Gabriel still in the room.

"I don't know. But something needs to be done. Do you not agree?"

Gabriel rubbed his face and hunched his shoulders. "I agree," he said roughly. "Just..." he cleared his throat. "Come back quickly and tell me what the elves plan."

Lucien nodded and strolled from the room, leaving Gabriel alone with the sleeping stranger and Timaeus.

"You need to decide where you stand on this matter," the dragon growled.

"I know," Gabriel replied wearily.

The fog cleared from Tiberius's mind to reveal a room that appeared to be straight out of an old movie. A plush red armchair sat on either side of a matching couch, facing a stone hearth. Tip was standing in a knot of about a dozen people in the middle of the room. There were a few girls, but they were mostly boys. None looked older than their early twenties.

A second group stood by the hearth. A young man in a suit watched everyone. On one side of him, there was a red-haired woman and a dark-complexioned man. A tall African-American man stood on his other side.

Tip's eyes went to that man. He seemed familiar, but Tip couldn't place him. For that matter, he couldn't remember how he got here either. He frowned, probing for memories as disconcerted and alarmed murmurs rose around him. He cast his eyes up to the crystal chandelier, trying to block the voices.

Someone had placed the obscuring fog in his mind; Tip had been waiting for it, and he had prevented it from happening to someone else.

His memories fizzled out at that point. The person he had protected was important to him, but he could not bring a face to mind. It left an empty feeling in him.

He looked over at the group of observers. His gaze locked with the suit's multicolored eyes, one blue, one green. A jolt shook through him. He could sense that everyone in the room was Blessed, but this man was on a different level. His Blessing was rare and unlike anything Tip had encountered.

The youngest in the room, a girl that looked to be around seven or eight, began to cry. "Where are we?" A slightly older girl who resembled her hugged her.

The terror in her voice caused fury to ignite deep inside Tip. He took a deep breath and forced it back. His old memories were resurfacing and, with them, the knowledge of why he was here. He couldn't allow his personal feelings to control him. That wouldn't help anyone.

The red-haired woman advanced into their group and drew both girls close in a warm embrace. The man in the suit followed just a step behind and smiled kindly down at the girls.

"You are in San Francisco, dear," he said soothingly. He looked around at all the confused youths. "I am Michael Hightower," he announced. "You've all been brought here for your own sakes. You are Blessed, with abilities bestowed on you that other humans do not have. I am Blessed as well, so I know the difficulties we face among the world."

For a moment, Michael's face fell as a shadow crossed it, but then he took a deep breath and brightened with obvious effort. "We have brought you here to be among others like yourselves." He scanned their expressions, his gaze skipping from one face to another.

Tip's face was thoughtful, but many of the others were making no effort to hide their anger and fear.

"I know you're all confused and disoriented right now, but please, don't be afraid. My colleague..." Michael nodded to an elderly man with thin salt and pepper hair and a scraggly beard. "Has blocked your unpleasant memories so that they won't haunt you and make it harder to

126

settle in. This is your home now, and we will do all that we can to make you feel welcome."

Confused and uncertain murmurings followed Michael as he walked back to the elderly man. The man spoke softly to Michael, who nodded. Tip sensed the elderly man scanning their minds and hastily buried his memories and thoughts about his assignment. The man's eyes lingered on Tip for a moment. Tip tensed, holding his breath, but then he looked away, and Tip exhaled heavily.

"Rebecca, show the girls to the rooms," Michael said while he walked to the door. "Balthasar, take care of the boys," he added to the tall man. "I have business to attend to." He looked over his shoulder and smiled brightly. "Again, welcome to the House. I will see you at dinner tonight."

"Come on, girls," Rebecca said as calmly as if this was the most natural thing in the world. She kept her arms around the two little girls and led the others out just behind Michael.

Tip moved closer to the two men by the hearth. "You are Balthasar?" he asked. He recognized the man from the bar, but he kept his face neutral and kind while he offered a hand. "I am Tiberius Moore."

"I know," Balthasar said, his voice a low, gravelly rumble. He didn't look directly at Tip, and moved his hand up slowly, as if searching, to grasp Tip's hand and shake it firmly. "It is a pleasure to meet you. Welcome to the family."

Blind, Tip realized. Now that he was closer, he could see a faint white line across Balthasar's eyes. *Blinded. By an accident?*

"Thank you," Tip said and forced his gaze away. The other man was looking at him coldly, and he didn't want to stare.

"All right. I'm Caleb, and that's all the introduction you'll get from me," the man said briskly, and the boys' muttering stopped. "Don't worry. I won't leave you in Tsar's less than tender care." He elbowed the tall man and snickered. Balthasar cracked a smile. "Come on."

Caleb led them out into a hallway. The moment they stepped out of the room, Tip began to construct a floor plan in his head. If he kept track of the house, he would be able to navigate it quickly later. They went up a staircase and into a spacious but plain hallway. The walls were painted white with no decoration at all. Windows shuttered from the outside marked one wall every few feet. Finding his way around would be a challenge.

Giving up on searching for distinguishing features, Tip looked around at the others. Their increasingly open and curious expressions didn't give him much hope of finding allies.

Then he saw the young man who was walking directly behind Caleb. His dark-brown hair curled thickly down his neck and along his forehead. The man's expression was pleasantly curious, and he wore a smile, but his eyes flicked around warily, also taking note of the hallway.

Their eyes met briefly and then the man looked away. This man would take some watching. Tip needed to move carefully, though, so he wouldn't be observed himself.

They turned a corner, and Caleb opened a door that led into a narrower hallway. The wooden floor creaked under their feet, and Tip took note of exactly where, so he could pass undetected later.

"These are the bedrooms." Caleb indicated a series of white doors. "The white ones are occupied. The blue ones are free," he added and opened the first blue door they came to. "All of the rooms are identical," he said and stepped back so that they could peer in. "Two to a room. You don't have to pick a roommate until tonight but go ahead and mark the door of the room you want now." He handed out chalk to each of them.

The group sized each other up. Two boys with curly red hair immediately dashed off to a door on the far side of the hallway with their chalk. "Nothing crude," Balthasar barked, making them jump.

Tip moved closer to the man who had been looking around in the hallway. "We may as well pick now," he was saying to the others. "We're all strangers, anyway." He turned his kind smile onto Tip. "How about you? Roomies?"

"Sure," Tip said with an answering smile. This was the best option, given his feeling that he needed to keep an eye on the man.

"Name's Neilan," the man said in a distracted tone and then made a face. "Just Neil, please."

Tip grinned. "Tiberius. Just Tip, please." Neil chuckled, and a sincerer smile flashed across his face as swift as lightning before he began drawing a detailed dolphin onto the nearest blue door.

"Don't mind at all," he said as he drew. "Guess we both had parents that liked big, old-fashioned names. My parents were born in the last century or something, I swear." Confusion flitted over his face before he hid it behind his pleasant mask. "Not that I remember them now," he added with the slightest bitterness to his tone. "But I've always thought that. Guess they didn't take that from me."

Interesting. "Yeah," Tip said. The words about the last century made him uneasy. *Is he like me?* He couldn't be sure. If he was, he was a very good actor. Tip would have to move carefully indeed.

"Remember when we got a room together when we were boys?" Caleb was asking Balthasar with a grin.

Balthasar chuckled. "Yes. We tried to kill each other that first night. I got frostbite from the fight. Gail was so upset..." He trailed off, a pained look on his scarred face.

"Just talk to her already," Caleb said. "I'm tired of you two missing each other and acting like we don't all live in the same house."

Balthasar only turned away.

Caleb bit back a curse and shook his head. "Be that way then." He turned his attention to the milling boys and Tip quickly turned away, so he wouldn't be caught eavesdropping. "C'mon guys. You can glare at each other in the living room."

Tip glanced around and saw that most of the group was still sizing each other up over the roommate situation.

He continued constructing his floor plan while Caleb led them through the House to a large living room. It was brightly lit from the broad, round skylight overhead. Couches and armchairs formed a semicircle around a central fire pit with an overhanging chimney. A large-screen TV, flashing with a sci-fi space battle, was on the far wall with another line of chairs facing it. A few people lounged around the fireplace, working on various projects. They looked up when the group entered. "Newcomers," Caleb said, and their attention returned to their tasks.

One young woman was crafting a dagger out of a silvery substance floating over her lap. Neil went over to watch, and most of the others followed.

Tip shuffled around the fireplace and saw a teenage boy lying with his feet over one arm of the chair, his head resting on the other, and a handheld game in front of his face. A dark-skinned girl sat on the chair next to him, leaning over to watch the game. "What are you playing?" Tip asked.

The boy squinted up at him through shaggy bangs. "Flame Insignia." He looked back at the game and mashed several buttons in quick succession, frowning intently. "Do you play?" he asked without looking up again.

"I did. I didn't exactly get to bring my games with me here."

The boy looked up again and really saw him this time. "Oh. Right," he said and grimaced in sympathy. "Well, it happened to all of us at one time or another. Once you start working, you'll get some spending money and can buy new consoles. You don't have to pay for food or a bed, so any money you earn is yours. It's a sweet deal once you get used to it."

"Get used to not being able to leave?" Tip said and dropped into a chair. He was more tired than he expected. He must've been quite active before they released him from the mind control. The boy shrugged. "When did it happen to you?" Tip asked to keep the conversation going. Maybe he could learn something useful.

"All the core members of the House were brought in as children," Balthasar rumbled, cutting off Tip's probing. The man loomed over them. Tip was not short, but Balthasar stood head and shoulders over him.

The girl tensed and looked down fixedly. The boy slid down a little and raised the game to cover his eyes. "Gail?" Balthasar said, his deep voice very soft. "I want to talk to you. It's been a long time since we were at the House at the same time."

Gail stiffened at the sound of Balthasar's voice and slid down in the chair. She flinched when he directed his words at her and shot him a venomous look that was lost on him. Then she sighed and got up. "Okay, let's talk," she said and strolled out of the room.

Balthasar followed.

"Well, brother?" she said when they were in the hallway. She turned to face him and crossed her arms.

"I know you're still angry with me," Balthasar commented. She snorted, and his frown deepened. "It was for the best, Gail. The Boss wanted me to stay on a Collecting team, despite my impairment. But I don't want you anywhere near Collecting." His head dropped a little. "It's dangerous. One accident was enough. I don't want something like that happening to you. Besides, your ability is more suited to Scouting."

Gail's shoulders hunched. "I don't care. I didn't want to be put on separate teams. I knew we'd never see each other if that happened. But you don't care about that." She reached up and stroked her fingers along the scars over his eyes. "If I'd been with you, the accident might've been avoided."

"Or you might've been hurt as well," Balthasar retorted. He grabbed Gail and drew her into a hug. "You're with good people on the Scouting team. It's a better job for you, little one." He stroked her purple hair and smiled. "Some of my early memories have leaked past Virgil's barrier. Just random ones, here and there. I can remember holding you when you were a baby, and how I felt in that moment. How I wanted to always protect you."

Gail relaxed into Balthasar's hold. "I'd still rather we got to be together more. It's hard, dealing with things without you. At least Seth has helped. He stands up for me against Rebecca and Caleb. But it's not the same without you around." She pressed her face against his shirt. "I've missed you, Tsar," she said, her voice muffled by the fabric.

"I've missed you, too," Balthasar said and squeezed her. "I think Michael wants me to stay in town for a while. Let's not waste the time we have together avoiding each other." A smile touched his lips. "The others will be happy. They've been on eggshells around us both." Gail chuckled and returned his hug.

"Why are you keeping Gail in the city?" The words lashed out, harsh and angry. Balthasar sat in Michael's office and glowered sightlessly at the other young man. "Caleb told me last night you had reassigned their Scouting team to positions here. What are you planning?"

Michael grimaced. He had been hoping to put off this discussion. "My father is busy with other matters," he said, stressing the statement. "I wanted some of my friends around me for a while. My twenty-sixth birthday is coming in just a few months. The party will be fun."

Balthasar tilted his head. "So that's it. If there's going to be trouble with your father, I want Gail well clear of it."

Michael steepled his fingers. "Your Collecting team may still be in the city as well. You're the one I want here most, and I'm sure you want to stay close to Gail."

"Very much," Balthasar said. "That means Virgil will be around, though. Will that be okay?"

"It's not ideal," Michael said, rubbing his eyes and thinking about the long week ahead. "But we've learned how to guard our minds from him. Nobody will give us away. They've been warned."

Balthasar mulled this over. "You're keeping something from me. But that's nothing new. You are the next boss. I don't expect you to tell us everything." He clenched a fist. "Just remember, if you put Gail in danger, I will make you regret it."

"I'm sure you will," Michael said. "That's not my intention. I just want to protect everyone."

Balthasar stared sightlessly at Michael. The young businessman looked back sadly, remembering his friend's formerly quick smile and bright eyes.

"Everyone?" Balthasar said, drawing Michael back to the moment. "Even the members of the Company that deserted?"

"We're not an army," Michael said wearily. "As much as my father might like to think otherwise. I will protect *everyone*."

The door of the cabin room scraped open. Emma sneezed and clutched her music box close. Eyes watering, she watched as Nemo shuffled in, balancing a tray of food and tea. The door swung shut behind him without being touched. He glanced back in surprise, and Emma huffed in frustration. "Donovan's been keeping me in here. I think he enchanted the door."

"Well, you're sick," Nemo pointed out, as if she needed reminding. "It's better for you to stay in bed and rest. Avery is also under enforced bedrest right now. Timaeus told me it's standard practice to keep the illness from spreading." He glanced at the music box. "At least you have your good luck charm from home. You're fine. I'm sure he'll unground you soon." A small table and two chairs appeared, and he set the tray down.

Emma blew her nose and climbed out of bed. "It's not a good-luck charm. The music is relaxing," she said, her voice hoarse. "But it's making me feel homesick on top of the cold."

"Lucien took off, so you'll have to settle for the crappy tea I made,"

Nemo said.

Emma joined him at the table. "Lucien left?" she asked. "Donovan's been spiriting me food, but I'm going crazy in here. What's going on out there?"

"He went to report the abductions to an elven outpost. Timaeus is distraught over Lucien being gone, so the food has been awful." Emma glanced at the burnt eggs, and her appetite dropped despite her hunger.

"I did notice the quality of the food going down. I thought it was just Donovan being weird." She took a deep breath through her mouth and blew her nose with a trumpeting sound that caused Nemo to make a face. "I don't think Donovan is keeping me in here just because I'm sick."

Nemo raised an eyebrow, so Emma told him about what she saw in Julia's mind and how everyone got weird after a company was mentioned.

Nemo whistled. "They really could use a lesson or two in discretion. They practically screamed at you that there's a secret here."

"I've been thinking while I lay around in here. Didn't you say something about a company the night we joined the Circus?"

"Yeah, I vaguely remember that." Nemo frowned. "Some talent scouts came to the school. I thought they were from the Circus, but I haven't seen any of them around. I completely forgot about that." He scratched his head. "I can't remember what they said the name was. I know there was a reason I assumed they were with the Circus, but now I couldn't say why I did."

Emma studied his troubled expression with a growing unease. "I could try to see the memories in your head," she said. "I started to do that with the woman the other day."

"I'm not letting you in my head," Nemo said quickly. Emma glared at him, and he scowled right back. "Glare holes in me. I don't care. I don't want you poking around in my head."

"Oh, come on! I won't see anything that didn't happen months ago!"

"I don't know that," Nemo retorted. "Gabriel's been teaching you all sorts of mind tricks. I have no clue what you can and can't do anymore." He crossed his arms and shook his head. "No." His voice reverberated with power.

Emma flinched. "Don't use your Blessing like that on me. I know you have better control over it now. That was uncalled for." She looked down, a hurt expression on her face. "Why are you reacting this way? Don't you trust me?"

"Don't give me that," Nemo snapped. "You know it's not about trust. I need my mind to myself. And don't tell me not to use my Blessing while you're asking to use yours on me." He leaned back and glowered at the table. "I thought you always appreciated not being able to hear my thoughts. After all, before we joined the Circus, you could hear everyone else's. I learned how to block my thoughts for your sake as much as mine."

Emma traced a fingernail along the wood grain on the table. "I appreciated it a lot. But this is important, Nemo. Tip was kidnapped. Julia only just got away. It has something to do with their Blessings and this Company, and I don't like that Gabriel is hiding things from us."

"Are you sure you're not just being nosy? Gabriel has the right to his secrets just like anyone else."

"It involves people being kidnapped, Nemo! This isn't something Gabriel gets to be secretive about!"

Nemo rubbed his eyes. "You don't trust Gabriel?"

Emma caught her breath but forced herself to consider the question. "I'm not sure. I don't think he's involved or anything like that. But it is weird he's being secretive."

Nemo sighed. "Fine. I'll let you look at my memories. But I think we should leave it alone. Lucien went to report to elves. Even if we had all the information, I don't see how we could be helpful."

Emma had no answer to that. She closed her eyes and listened while Nemo hesitantly lowered his mental barriers. Nemo's thoughts grumbled at her. "Relax," she breathed. She chose a memory at random and worked her way back from there, skipping over long stretches of irrelevant information. It took her a few minutes to get back to when they joined the Circus. She was aware of Nemo fidgeting, but she kept her eyes tightly shut and blocked it out.

She was almost to the memories she needed when she ran into a wall. The sensation nearly shattered her concentration. She pushed against it, and it dissolved into something that felt like a fog bank. It was opaque, and she could sense none of the memories inside it. "What the?" she muttered and heard Nemo's questioning thought. She opened her eyes and stared down at her empty plate.

"What is it?" Nemo asked. His barriers were already back up, making the room silent physically and mentally.

"I'm not sure," Emma said, baffled. "Your memories are…foggy. No wonder you can't remember."

"Foggy?" Nemo said, raising an eyebrow.

Emma reddened slightly. "I don't know how else to explain it. That's just how it felt. I can't see those memories."

"Ah." Nemo got to his feet and looked around the room. "Donovan, do you have a sleeping bag?" He asked the air. "Or a pile of blankets?"

The air shimmered next to Emma's bed, and a futon stacked with blankets and pillows flumped down onto the wooden floor.

"Why do I need that?" Emma asked, struggling to pull her thoughts away from what she had felt in Nemo's mind.

"You don't. I do," Nemo replied and flopped down onto the blankets. "I'm going to sleep in here tonight since you're sick."

Emma chuckled and poked Nemo with her foot. "Like when we were kids? Mom got so exasperated that we both always caught every cold because we snuck into each other's beds whenever one of us got sick."

"Just so." Nemo fell back, spread-eagle on the futon. His smile faded. "I always appreciated it, though. Especially that time when Dad didn't take me on that fishing trip because I got sick." His mouth twisted. "He never would cancel fishing trips to stay with me."

Emma opened her mouth to say their dad did cancel a fishing trip once, to see Nemo's play in elementary school, but then she remembered their dad's attitude the whole weekend and closed her mouth again.

"Let's not think about that. We're here now." The words felt weak even as she said them. She grimaced. "I mean…well…"

"I know what you mean." Nemo took a deep breath. "It's not your fault. You've always been there for me, and I appreciate it." He covered a wide yawn. "Sorry. Got up early to help Tim in the kitchen."

Emma stepped over him and half fell onto her bed. "It's okay. I'm wiped out too."

Her eyes drifted closed, and she began to doze almost instantly, the cold medicine she had taken with the meal making her sleepy. Even so, she felt it when Nemo reached up and grasped her hand. She smiled and squeezed his fingers.

"I'll make sure we're okay, even if we can't trust Gabriel," Nemo whispered. Emma heard him, and her eyes eyes flickered behind her eyelids, but she drifted off before she could form a response.

A fever had plagued Julia for an indeterminate amount of time. She thought she was in a cave, but when she became lucid enough to examine her surroundings, she saw a comfortable bedroom with pale cream-colored walls and soft, moss-green carpet. It gave her the sense, oddly, of being in a forest. Serenity stole over her, and she dozed off again.

Recollection struck her the moment she woke up. "Tip!" she gasped and leapt up. Her feet sank into the carpet, and she looked wildly around, the serenity shattered.

"Easy there," a voice said from the corner. Julia tensed and clenched her fists, ready for a fight. A chuckle sounded in response. A woman with long dark hair and wearing a flowing sapphire-blue dress rose from the stool she perched on. "Emma was right. You *are* scrappy."

Julia scowled. "Who are you? Where am I? Is…Lucien here? He needs to go help Tip!"

The woman tilted her head and surveyed Julia. "You delivered your message. Lucien has gone to see what he can do. You are safe here. That was, I believe, the main reason this man of yours sent you here."

"He's not mine," Julia mumbled, but even as she spoke she remembered Tip kissing her. Her face grew hot. The woman raised her perfectly arched eyebrows, and Julia looked away. "You still haven't told me where I am," she growled to move the conversation along.

The woman gripped the edge of her dress and curtsied elegantly. "I am Aoife," she said. "You are with the Circus Phantasm, and through the ability of our mind readers, we have aided you even though you came to us addled with fever. You are welcome here, Miss Julia Mercer. Your Blessing of strength will be a welcome addition to the show, or simply to our troupe in general."

Julia's eyebrows furrowed. *Mind readers?* she thought skeptically. Then her brain caught up with the rest of the woman's statement. They knew her name and about her strength. "Alright." She drew the word out. "Thank you, I guess. I don't know about joining a show, but I'd like to look around and...meet the others. These mind readers sound interesting."

Did these people really have such abilities? She wanted to reject the idea, but then she remembered the mermaid and the compulsion Tip had placed on her, so different than anything she had encountered before. Not to mention her own unusual strength. Curiosity and restlessness nipped at Julia. She needed to get out of this room, stretch, and think through all this.

"It will be my pleasure to show you around," Aoife said, and her eyes travelled down to the loose shirt and jeans Julia wore. "I will have to get you some clothes that fit you better. Emma's clothing is a little too big for you."

Julia shrugged as she followed Aoife out. "I don't care about clothing."

Aoife scoffed. "Well, I do. Nobody dresses badly here. It is not permitted."

Julia bit back a retort and looked around at the cave walls just outside her room. She really was in a cave. *Curiouser and curiouser.*

Nemo closed his eyes and let the music flow from his fingers. It echoed through his cave and returned to harmonize with the new strains of the guitar. The resulting sound sent a shiver through him. He opened his mouth and sang without words. He didn't need words to form a melody. After so long working with his voice, it was a relief to sing without any thought.

A squeak jarred its way through the musical reverberations. Nemo kept his eyes closed, pretending he didn't hear it. The door was closed, and he had looked around his room just moments before. There were no bats in the room.

Another squeak sounded, closer this time. Nemo's fingers faltered. A moment later, leathery wings buffeted his head, almost causing him to drop his instrument. He cursed, fumbled to keep a hold on it, and swatted at the bat with his other hand. The small creature dodged out of his reach and landed on the table, looking up at him with its large, puppy-like eyes. "What even are you?" he growled. "How the heck did you get in here?"

He set the guitar on its stand and rubbed his temples. So much for a little while to relax by himself. "I brought fruit in for you," he grumbled and pointed at a peach on the table behind the bat. "It's better than what the rest of us are eating right now."

The bat blinked slowly and squeaked again. It leapt up, flew at the door, and then circled and landed on his knee, looking back and forth between him and the door.

"What are you?" Nemo asked again, thoroughly confused.

The bat flitted forward, nipped his earlobe, and tugged.

Nemo cursed again and swung at it. "You're pushing your luck little guy! You're cute, but if you give me rabies or something, I swear I'll—"

"You need to go to Timaeus." The voice, whisper soft but distinctly female, came from the bat's tiny gaping mouth as it bobbed in front of him. Nemo's mouth dropped open. The bat squeaked impatiently and dove at his hair.

Nemo jerked back and grabbed the bat. It squeaked in alarm and went limp, staring at him. "What are you?" he shouted at it. It blinked and yawned. "Whatever." He released the bat, stood up, and stretched. "I'll go see Timaeus then. Happy?"

The bat squeaked, flew in an arc, and then careened into the peach so hard the fruit toppled and rolled off the table, the bat clinging to it resolutely all the way to the floor. Nemo snorted a laugh and left the room. If the bat was still there when he came back, he would squeeze some answers from it. He suspected it would somehow manage to get back through his closed door again and be gone by then, though.

The bat faded from his mind as he hurried to the dining room. The door seemed heavier than usual, and he put his weight against the wood to shove it open. The barrier swung quickly when it finally gave in, and he stumbled into a pitch-black room. The dining room had never been dark in the time Nemo had been with the circus. The performers kept odd hours, sometimes stopping in for a snack after a show or coming for breakfast in the afternoon. Timaeus kept it lit and ready as a recreation room.

Now Nemo couldn't see an inch in front of his nose. "My lord?" he called. Timaeus didn't hold with formality, but this situation made Nemo uneasy, and he had learned to respect the dragon in the last few months.

He shuffled forward, his hands held out in front of him. He expected to bump into a table or trip over a chair at any moment, but he kept going forward without encountering anything. "I must find Timaeus," Nemo muttered, his voice ringing with power. He wasn't sure why he said it out loud or why he allowed his Blessing to creep into the statement. Both things simply felt right to do.

A flickering light appeared in the darkness. Nemo was sure he'd walked at least halfway across the room, but the light looked far away, further than the room was long. The sense of magic caused an icy trickle down Nemo's spine. He swallowed nervously and continued forward, his arms still out in front of him even though he no longer expected to encounter anything.

The darkness pressed in on him. It felt close, and soon he found it hard to breathe, as if the blackness were squeezing the air out of him. He wasn't claustrophobic like Emma, but this was something else. He sucked in a deep breath, and his steps quickened. He pushed forward until he came to the light. It proved to be an opening into another cave. Golden light spilled out from the crevice, and his fingers brushed stone. He leaned against the cave wall and peered in.

140

A vast library spread before him like something out of a fairytale. Books and scrolls, many of them brown with age, were piled on the stone shelves that stretched along the wall further than Nemo could see. The smell of the room attested to their age: the scents of aged paper and leather mingled with smoke and a musty smell he couldn't place.

A plethora of small drawers and cupboards along the bottom of the shelves had been ripped open and emptied of their contents.

Nemo's eyes went from the damaged wood to the dragon, who lay on a heap of gold and jewels from those drawers. With one more deep breath, he crept through the opening into the room.

Timaeus stirred restlessly, the coins and jewelry clinking under him. He stiffened and bent around to scratch at his tail. Coins scattered several feet through the room. His eye fell on Nemo, and they stared at each other. Nemo didn't know what to say, and the dragon seemed shocked by his presence.

"Interesting use of your voice," he rumbled, and sparks flickered along his roiling jaw. Nemo took a step back. Timaeus turned his head aside and sneezed. "Don't worry. I won't roast you. Did Donovan show you how to come here?"

Nemo shook his head. "That bat again."

Timaeus snorted. "Interfering little wretch. I should've kicked her out of the caves years ago. Serves me right for letting her stay underfoot."

"Unless you're going to tell me what 'she' is, let's talk about something else," Nemo said irritably. He hated how every time he brought the bat up, Timaeus dropped hints about it being more than it seemed but refused to elaborate.

"Don't be impudent. I am not in the mood. Though I suppose that is why she sent you." He twisted around and bared his fangs as some of the jewels dug into him between his scales. He sighed and closed his great eyes. "I was not expecting Lucien to be gone this long."

"Is that bad?" Nemo asked and moved closer, stepping lightly. Coins clattered with each step he took, so he knew Timaeus was aware of the movement. Receiving no rebuke, he climbed up on the pile and sat down, leaned just a little of his weight against the dragon's side,

141

ready to move away in an instant. Timaeus's scales were hot from his inner fire but not enough to burn Nemo.

"Oh, not in the way you might think." He sighed once more, his side moving like a bellows and sending a jet of hot air and smoke into the room, raising the temperature. "The elven courts are, by nature, beguiling and tediously slow in their machinations. I have never cared for them. Lucien did not either. It has been over a century since I visited the court where he resided and took him as a companion. I fear that he might have gotten caught in some scheme or other to draw him back into a court."

"Wouldn't they respect his decision to not be in one?" Nemo asked. His brow furrowed as he tried to follow what Timaeus was saying.

The dragon opened one eye and stared at the floor. Then he touched Nemo's mind. Images of a great white stone palace flashed in front of his dazzled eyes. Graceful elves moved regally through a great hall. Timaeus took up one whole corner. Lucien sat leaning against him, reading aloud. An elf woman with a dazzling smile twirled over, took Lucien's hand, and drew him away to dance. Lucien whispered something to the woman. She laughed, and Lucien's face lit up with a slight smile.

The vision ended, and Nemo slumped, smelling smoke as Timaeus brooded once more. "We left the court because we could not find the solitude and quiet we desired. I detest the idea of returning to the court to find Lucien. Or even worse, perhaps he has decided he wishes to end our contract, and I must once more endure the social niceties required to find a new companion."

"I don't think that would happen. He seemed happy here. A century…I can tell you two are very good friends."

Timaeus chuckled. "Humans simplify things so wonderfully." His gaze turned onto Nemo, and again his thoughts brushed Nemo's mind, though not providing any distinct images this time. "Perhaps this is why she sent you. I am in no humor to cook, but I am sure Donovan and Gabriel will see to the humans' needs. In the meantime, perhaps you might entertain me while we await Lucien's return."

Nemo snorted. "I'm not a clown. But I don't mind performing for you some."

"Not even anything as much as that. Simply pick out a book and read to me. Use your Blessing. I will contribute some magic. Let us see what wonders we can create."

Nemo got up and skidded down the pile of gold over to the nearest bookshelf. He picked up a book at random and was surprised to find it was one of Grimm's fairy tales. He let it fall open and read about a bird. The dragon focused on him, and a fiery blue bird circled the room overhead as he read. Nemo's voice faltered. The bird flickered and almost vanished. Nemo resumed reading, watching it out of the corner of his eye. He moved on to another story and then another before picking up a different book. The illusions grew bigger and more elaborate until he and Timaeus were no longer in the cave but looked around at the sitting room of Bilbo Baggins' hobbit hole. Dwarves rushed around them with plates of food, laughing and singing.

Nemo's voice cracked, and he stopped. He had been reading for hours with no water or break. Timaeus yawned and scratched his chin with a talon. "That is enough. You look weary, and I am too. I feel better than I did though. She is right. I shouldn't lie here and brood. I have more than one companion, after all."

Nemo sat down carefully, frowning down at the gems and gold coins under him. Sitting on such treasures was unnerving.

An idea flitted at the edge of his mind. He struggled to catch it and grinned as it took shape.

"Hey, Tim," he called, tapping Timaeus's scales.

The dragon's head jerked around. "What did you just call me?" he asked in a mystified tone.

"Never mind that. I have an idea that you might like."

14

The first few days at the House fully tested Tip's patience. The newcomers' measurements were taken, and they were each allowed to order a week's worth of clothing, which arrived the same day. A doctor and dentist came to check their basic health. That took all of one day. The next day, a tutor spoke privately with each newcomer. That took even longer. Tip, being the oldest, was last. He played games with Seth while he waited.

When the tutor called him in, Tip learned they assumed the Blessed captives might not have received a full education. The tutor questioned Tip at length to check his knowledge of all the basic subjects, much to Tip's irritation. After he was dismissed, he retreated to the room he shared with Neil to think. All of this showed an amount of organization and wealth that Tip couldn't help but marvel at. This system didn't develop overnight. But how to get word out? There had been no chance.

On the third day, they got around to the examination Tip had suspected was coming and dreaded the most. They were tested to find out what Blessings they possessed so they could be placed with appropriate teachers. That was the first time all the House residents were gathered together.

The red-haired woman, Rebecca, sat next to Caleb on a loveseat. Balthasar was on a couch next to Gail and Seth, who were leaning their heads together playing handheld video games. A teenage girl was on a chair talking to Balthasar. When she saw Tip watching, she looked up with a kind smile. "Hey. You're Tip, right? I'm Adah."

"Nice to meet you," Tip said warily and felt a wave of good feeling push at him. He moved away from Adah. The last thing he needed was for someone with a mood-stabilizing ability to relax him into letting something slip.

Like the other days, they were examined from the youngest to the oldest. The two little girls, Irene and Gracia, went in first, holding onto Rebecca's hands, and when they came out they were both assigned to Adah as students. "Irene has a vocal Blessing but she's a bit young to do more than just learn how to sing," Rebecca told Adah. "Gracia can create illusions. Michael thinks you might be able to help her learn to project that better."

Tip watched with interest as the others went in and came back out to receive instructions. More than half were assigned to people who weren't present. Tip gathered that meant they wouldn't be staying at the House. He frowned. *How big is this?* He would have to figure out a way to report in soon. He wasn't sure yet how he would get a message past the House Keeper and the defensive spells. He would watch and wait for his chance.

A few boys were assigned to Caleb. The red-haired brothers were assigned to Rebecca. She showed them a flame over her palm, and they grinned, sparks playing over their own hands.

When Neil came out, he was given Seth as a teacher. "Almost the same Blessing," Rebecca said. Seth didn't even look up from his game when this was announced, and Tip chuckled. Neil gave him an exasperated look and then sat beside Seth and Gail to watch them play their games.

Then Tip was called into the examination room. Adah got up and followed him in. He gave her a puzzled look and then examined the room to hide his alarm. She hadn't been in the room for any of the others. It worried him they'd change the set-up for him.

Michael Hightower and Virgil, the grizzled man from before, were seated at a table. Adah slid into a chair next to Michael.

The young man stood up and offered Tip his hand, flashing a winning smile. "Tiberius Moore, right?"

"Tip, please," Tip said and shook Michael's hand. *I should put that on a shirt so I can stop saying it.*

Michael nodded, and Adah made a note on the paper sitting on the table in front of them. "Very good. Please have a seat. I've already introduced myself, and I believe you met my assistant, Adah, out front." He glanced at the other man. "This is Virgil. One of my father's associates."

Tip sat down across from them and glanced warily at the older man. *He's the telepath.*

When he looked back, Adah was watching him intently, and again, he felt her using her ability to calm him. He forced a more comfortable, relaxed look onto his face so that she let up. He couldn't lose his concentration.

"Balthasar reported you're quite strong," Michael mused, flipping through the papers in front of him. "Is that your Blessing? That's the ability Balthasar has. It's relatively common as Blessings go."

"I suppose it is," Tip said and glanced again at the telepath. How should he play this? He might be able to find out their methods, but it would be a risk. His thoughts were carefully blocked except for some nervous dithering about the interview. Then he glanced at Adah and saw her face was scrunched up in confusion. Could she sense Blessings? That would complicate things. "I've never noticed anything unusual about my strength. But maybe most people can't lift things I can? I don't know." He shrugged.

Michael turned to Adah. He said nothing, but they were clearly adept at communicating without words, no magic or Blessing required. "I don't know," she echoed, sounding troubled. "I don't sense any particular abilities from him. If I hadn't heard Tsar's report, I'd say he was a normal person."

146

Michael pulled his chair closer to the table. "Okay. Virgil?" Tip tensed and quickly activated a spell, ignoring the look Adah gave him as she sensed his sudden spike of tension. It was none too soon. He felt Virgil lift the fog in his mind and the fake memories flooded his mind, of a childhood and adolescence spent in a suburb of Toronto.

The man scanned over Tip's false identity with a practiced efficiency. He paused and pulled a particular memory to the front of Tip's mind. Tip flinched when he saw it, shuddering even though it wasn't a real memory. A calm feeling struck him as Adah acted against the stress the memory caused. Then it skittered back to the past as Virgil lowered the fog again. "His family got into a boating accident when he was a child," Virgil growled. "The accident triggered strength Blessings in both him and the woman that Balthasar met in Toronto."

Tip clenched a fist under the table but didn't let these words affect his mood. *That's right. Julia was included in those fake memories. Are they still after her?*

Virgil glanced at him. "I would strongly suggest sending a team back to Toronto. He is very good at blocking his thoughts. People don't usually develop that skill unless they know someone who can read minds. You might find a new telepath for me to teach."

Michael nodded, his eyes raking over Tip. "Tell me, Tip, have you ever heard of the Circus Phantasm?" Adah gave Michael a sharp, alarmed look.

Tip's pulse quickened. That was the group Lucien and Lord Timaeus traveled with. He took a deep breath. He couldn't give Julia and the Circus away. He forced his expression to show confusion so that Adah would notice. She might not consciously be aware of it, but if he didn't, she might remember that later. "Circus?" he asked. "No, can't say I have. Why?"

"Forget it," Michael said. "Balthasar will be your teacher. You may go." Tip pushed back his chair and got up, moving slowly. "Adah, compile the list and get it emailed to my father by this evening. He'll want to know what assets our new workers have. Virgil, please don't bring up your telepath theory in the meeting tomorrow. We will send a team back to Toronto, but this isn't an appropriate time. I'll make note

147

of the potential, and it will be on top of the location list for later."

The door swung closed behind Tip, and he breathed a sigh of relief. They didn't suspect him, and Julia was safe. That was all that he could've hoped for at the end of a meeting like that. Adah was one challenge, but Virgil was another matter entirely. The only thing that reassured him was Virgil was apparently the only telepath the Company employed. Holding onto his fake human identity was hard enough without his mind and emotions being monitored.

Gabriel knew when Emma entered the dimly lit amphitheater. He kept his eyes on his book and turned a page, but the words became confusing black marks and swam before his eyes. He struggled to regain the peace of this stolen moment of solitude before the day started.

"Good morning, Gabriel," she greeted, climbing the stairs toward him. He didn't look up from his book, hoping against hope she might be in the room for another reason and would leave him alone to read.

No such luck. She sat beside him. "I've always wondered about this cave," she commented. "It's so peculiar."

"You'd have to ask Donovan or Timaeus," he said, glancing up. Her shoulders were tense, and the look in her eyes suggested something was bothering her. "The cave is theirs. Well, it's Timaeus's, but Donovan has been here for a long time, too. I've—the Circus has only been here for five years. Well, almost five." He refocused pointedly on his book.

Emma scuffed her boot against the bench in front of them, and the silence held for nearly a full minute. "What are you reading?"

Gabriel sighed and snapped the book closed, resigned to giving up his time alone. Emma clearly needed to get something off her chest, and that worried him. Perhaps he could satisfy her with a chat. *I'll have to take a little break in my room tonight before the show. Seems that's the only way to get some quiet.*

"Jack London," he said aloud. "I love reading about what San Francisco and other cities used to be like."

"San Francisco in particular? Jack London lived there, right? I did a book report on him a few years ago."

"He did," Gabriel said with a widening grin. "He was an oyster pirate as a teenager."

"Wait, really?" Emma laughed. "Not sure what that is, but it sounds amazing. He was quite an adventurer."

"The oyster pirates of San Francisco Bay are an interesting little bit of history. You see, in the late 1800s there was a monopoly on oysters, keeping the prices high. Oyster pirates would go diving and steal from the oyster beds. There was actually some violence over it in other areas. Look up the Chesapeake Bay Oyster Wars sometime."

"That's really cool. I'll have to do that. Jack London was quite the rogue." She looked down at the arena and seemed to be considering her next words. Gabriel braced himself. "You know a lot about San Francisco, huh?"

Gabriel shrugged, ignoring the twinge in his chest at the thought of that disgusting city as he knew it. "You pick up a lot when you grow up hearing everyone's thoughts. My—" He cut himself off and stared into the darkness for a moment. "I knew another Blessed boy, who had visions. He saw a lot of past events and shared them with me." He looked down at his hands for a moment, sadness gnawing at him. *How is Michael doing now?*

"I'm sure you have your share of stories about your hometown?" Gabriel continued. His tone made it into a question, and he hoped he could divert her into talking about her home before he dwelled anymore on his own.

"Not quite." She leaned back and looked at the darkness above them. "But I learned all sorts of things from the college students that lived next door. I was getting a beginning knowledge of German from them when you came to town."

Gabriel laughed at this, loud and warm. It felt good to laugh like that occasionally. "You're just a sponge for knowledge, aren't you? It's refreshing to hear your take on this Blessing of ours."

"What about San Francisco?" she asked. "You must've learned all sorts of cool things there."

"No." Gabriel's good humor vanished as quickly as it had appeared,

149

leaving him feeling even more sour than before. He took a deep breath and forced the words to come. "San Francisco isn't like a small town. It's..." his gaze went distant, looking into the past despite his resolution to not talk about this. He found he wanted to, after all. He wanted to speak to someone who would understand what it was like to hear all those thoughts.

He took a shaky breath and smiled crookedly. "Well, obviously it's a big city. But it's more than that. In my travels, I've realized San Francisco is especially terrible. All cities are cesspits. The thoughts show every depravation of humanity, but I despise San Francisco especially. It's there that I realized how terrible humans truly are and that not even family or teachers can be relied on."

His words sped up as he spoke, and his mouth stung after he fell silent. Emma stared at him in shock, and he looked away. The sympathy he saw in her eyes only irritated him.

"Gabriel—"

"I don't want your pity." He stood up. "Forget it. I can see you don't understand. I guess I shouldn't have expected you to, seeing as you grew up in a small town and you and Nemo have stayed so close as you grew up." *Why did I think she would understand?*

Emma twisted the hem of her shirt in her hands. "I have been to cities," she said, not meeting his eyes. "I do know what it's like, hearing all those thoughts. But I...well, I decided I shouldn't judge people by that. I try my best to judge people at face value; what they actually do and say, not what they think. They deserve the privacy of their own minds to think things that would never come out of their mouths."

Gabriel snorted, his irritation growing. "What idealistic nonsense. I knew better than that when I was just a kid," he muttered and walked down a few steps.

Emma ducked her head. "I might think differently if I grew up hearing a city's thoughts like you did, but I stand by what I believe about people." She took a deep breath. "And is it idealistic nonsense that what you did to Nemo is wrong?"

Gabriel's heart sank. He turned slowly and gave her a cool look that didn't match the tempo of his pulse. "What are you talking about?"

"You blocked some of Nemo's memories, didn't you?" Emma got to her feet to face him, and Gabriel regretted going down the stairs and giving her a height advantage. "I tried to find the memories he had of those talent scouts that he met right before we joined. He can't remember them."

Gabriel forced his expression to remain neutral and swept his gaze over the empty amphitheater while he collected his thoughts. *I should've known this would happen sooner or later. That's a cursed way to use this Blessing.*

"Emma, I'm going to be honest with you." He kept his eyes focused on the theater below them. "I want to keep teaching you so that your Blessing can flourish. That said, to lie here would not serve me in the future." He jerked his head up and met her furious eyes. It seemed unlikely he could convey further sincerity with this alone, but he needed to try. "Yes, I blocked Nemo's memories. He encountered Company agents, and I didn't want him to wonder about them. You need to understand. You don't want to get mixed up in things where the Company is involved. I know you're curious, but please forget about it."

Her gaze hardened, and he clasped his hands behind his back. "I'm just trying to protect you. Don't trouble yourself about this anymore. I don't want anything to happen to you."

Emma's face twisted with frustration. "Protect me by keeping me in the dark? And doing that to Nemo—" she broke off, color flooding into her face. "Why is just knowing about this Company dangerous?"

"Knowledge precedes action. If the woman hadn't been so adamant against letting me into her mind, I would've kept you far away from all of this. You need to forget what you saw."

Emma clenched her hands into fists around the hem of her shirt. "Are you saying we aren't going to help Julia? You're just going to leave Tip to his fate with this...Company?" She opened her mind just enough to throw Julia's memories of Tip at him. They were clear and sharp as daggers, even though Emma had never met the man.

Gabriel struggled to keep his resolve. "I won't risk my friends. They're Blessed, Emma. I'll tell you that much. They have very powerful Blessings and have trained extensively on how to use them.

Rescue attempts would just end with more people being taken." He shook his head vehemently. "No."

Emma stared at him and her anger retreated behind an implacable mask. "Okay."

Gabriel studied her expression, but she kept her face as blank as his had been before. "You worry me, Emma. Just stay out of it. There's a high chance the matter will be settled without any of us getting involved."

"Right." Emma glanced again at the book in Gabriel's hand. He could sense the tone of her thoughts changing, cooling into something harder. It worried him. "So how is that story? I haven't read that one."

Despite his anxiety, Gabriel accepted the change of topic with relief, and they discussed books for a little while.

Emma checked the time on her phone. "I have to go," she said. "Aoife asked me to spend some time with Julia now that I'm better."

"I really do just want to protect you, Emma," Gabriel insisted. Emma only nodded, not looking at him, and Gabriel's heart sank. "Oh, and you should go see Avery. He's still sick."

Emma watched as Gabriel hurried down the stairs to direct those who came in to begin rehearsal. Nemo stood by Timaeus, speaking animatedly to Gabriel, but Emma couldn't hear what he said. Gabriel listened, nodded, and hurried on to the next group. Emma considered going over to Nemo, but he and Timaeus shifted out of the cavern as she got to her feet.

She sighed and rubbed her face. Her guilt over not having not asked about Avery mixed with her anger over the revelations of the morning. When she came to speak to him, she hadn't wanted to believe Gabriel had blocked Nemo's memories, but he hadn't even tried to deny it.

What sort of life has he lived? She tried to remember what she knew about San Francisco while she descended the steps and wandered out of the amphitheater.

Her feet meandered for a while. She didn't want to keep fuming though and forced her mind onto other things. Perhaps she should go scrounge for whatever food Donovan had found and take some to Avery. She turned in that direction, but then she became aware of Davet's presence swiftly approaching. She had been trying to shield her mind from his, without much success. He zeroed in on her presence and moved faster.

A moment later, the little unicorn came skidding around a corner, clumsy on his long spindly legs. He spotted Emma and let out a joyful trumpeting sound before barreling into her. She tumbled to the cave floor with the baby unicorn on her chest. A dozen pixies clung to his dark mane. Their high-pitched laughter and thoughts buzzed above Davet's excited mental babbling about the new things he had seen while he explored the caves. "I'm happy to see you too, Davet," Emma gasped and stroked his soft face.

He pushed closer, peering into her face. *Why haven't you visited?*

His clear blue eyes made Emma's chest feel tight. She grinned and pulled herself to her feet. *Sorry. I've been sick.*

Davet sighed heavily and hung his head. *Mama has been preparing for a show, and she won't let me watch the rehearsals. She wants it to be a surprise.* He was so morose that several of the pixies flew around to his face and poked at him. Their antics successfully distracted him, and he pranced about the tunnel pursuing them.

Are these your babysitters? Emma asked. The pixies' tinkling high-pitched laughter made her chuckle quietly.

Babysitters? Davet stared at her. *Well...they are sitting on me.* He shook his head and dislodged a few. *So, yes?*

Tristan sped into view, out of breath and red in the face. He spotted the small unicorn, and relief crossed his face before he set his features sternly. "Davet! How many times do I have to tell you not to run off like that?"

The black foal snorted and stomped a hoof. *Tristan is watching me while Mama is at practice,* he told Emma. *I don't like that. He doesn't let me run, and he can't hear me like you can. I wish Mama would ask you to watch me instead.*

Emma patted Davet's head and gave Tristan a sympathetic look. "I can watch Davet. You should be at the rehearsal."

Tristan drew himself up and puffed out his chest just a bit. "Lady Celeste asked me to watch Davet for her. It's *my* task."

Emma's eyebrows shot up. She couldn't understand the weird dynamic between Celeste and Tristan. "With Donovan watching over the caves, is it really necessary for anyone to chase after Davet?" It seemed like a reasonable question, but Tristan reddened even more. "You really should be at the rehearsal. Aren't you working on a new act?"

The teenager looked away with a conflicted expression. "Lady Celeste trusted me to keep an eye on Davet."

"Oh, stop being an ass," Donovan's voice said from the air over their heads. "I won't let anything happen to the little one. Celeste knows that full well. It encourages her to be even more mischievous when you act this clueless. Stop enabling her."

A look of outrage crossed Tristan's face. "How dare you talk that way about Lady Celeste! I'll have you know that she—" his words cut off when Donovan shifted Tristan away, probably to the show cavern. Emma snorted. *What a silly boy.*

Davet frisked around the tunnel with a crown of pixies flitting around his head as bright as rubies and sapphires against his black fur. *Now that Tristan is gone,* he thought slyly, *may we go out and see the snow?*

Emma chuckled, glad Donovan couldn't hear that. He would have a fit. *No, we may not,* she thought back as sternly as she could be with the unicorn.

Davet whined and head-butted her hip in protest, angling his head so his horn wouldn't hurt her. *Nobody's any fun.* He sulked, with his head still pressed against her. *Everyone's been so serious ever since that elf visited Mama before he left.*

Emma caught her breath. Here was a chance to have a conversation Gabriel and Donovan couldn't monitor. She crouched down and rubbed Davet's neck while she opened her mind to him alone, so he would be able to sense her deep curiosity and interest. *What did your Mama and the elf talk about?*

He raised his head and blinked at her. His eyes went distant as he tried to remember that far back. His memories were shallow, mostly impressions and sensations. He hadn't yet developed the attention span to focus on conversations that didn't interest him, and he only vaguely recalled this at all. *Serious stuff,* he thought, focusing hard. *About a report, and a company, and a half-elf.*

Half-elf? That surprised Emma, and she pictured the image of Tip from Julia's memories. Julia hadn't known that about him, and this shook Emma. It certainly added another layer to the mystery. In her lessons with Gabriel, she'd learned that most of the elves in North America had moved up into the untouched areas of Canada and Alaska and usually shunned human company. That there would be a half-elf in Canada wasn't all that surprising, but why would he be in a city working as a bartender?

Davet wandered off and licked an oddly colored stone a few feet away. Their minds were still open to each other, and Emma heard him marveling at the texture and taste against his tongue.

It's cool and gritty, he reported to Emma when he sensed her attention on him.

Emma got a cookie wrapped in a napkin out of her pocket. She broke half off and held her hand flat. *Try this.* He came closer, emanating curiosity. *Can you remember anything else?*

As he lipped up the cookie she monitored his thoughts for any other clues. The memory of the conversation had faded to the back of his mind though and was even more indistinct. As the taste of the cookie filled his mind, it faded away even more, and Emma couldn't study it at all.

This is wonderful! He sidled a few steps to the side and then back. *It's so sweet!* He gingerly took the other half from her palm and then whirled and ran to the corner, tossing his head and snorting. *Play with me!*

Emma's mind raced. *Okay. But only if you'll do something for me.*

He came to a stop in front of her, quivering in excitement.

*If the elf or Donovan or Gabriel or Timaeus...*she sensed the question in his mind and showed him their faces. *If they talk to your Mama, please pay attention to what they say. I'll give you more treats*

155

if you can remember their words for me.

Okay! Davet spun around so quickly he almost lost his balance. It took him some effort to straighten himself again, and she felt a pang of guilt over asking him to spy on his mother. *Let's run!*

He took off. Emma swung into motion after him. As she fought to keep up with the baby unicorn, she remembered Avery and even more guilt filled her. But Davet demanded her attention, so she shrugged away thoughts of the avian. She would see him later.

Tension blossomed when the three acrobats appeared in the cave Timaeus had chosen to rehearse in.

Nemo looked between the dragon-man and the three women. The women were all dressed in black with the pale moons of their faces blank. Their eyes flicked from Nemo to Timaeus and back.

"You wanted to perform with us?" the oldest of the three girls asked, her voice accented and soft. She stood straighter and pulled her long dark hair into a ponytail. The other two, Arielle and Adele, stayed by the wall. Nemo marveled at how similar they looked: nearly twins but for their age differences. He had spoken with them only briefly, and he wasn't quite sure which one was which; their names were so similar. He knew their Blessings were invisibility and levitation, and that was all.

Nemo glanced at Timaeus, but the dragon-man didn't reply. "Timaeus and I are going to choreograph a scene for all of us to do together. I thought you would suit it, with your Blessings and skills."

Smiles touched the girls' mouths. The youngest, no more than thirteen or fourteen, laughed lightly, ran over, and hugged Timaeus. "I have always wanted to perform with you, lord dragon!"

She bounced with excitement and the tension broke. Timaeus grinned, ruffling her short dark hair. "I am going to enjoy this as well, little one," he rumbled and shifted into his draconic form.

Nemo watched as the sisters floated upward holding hands. When he glanced down, he saw the oldest girl had come closer to him.

"It is good to finally speak with you, Nemo Reeve," she said, her eyes dancing in amusement as if at a joke. She held her hand out to him. "I am Lian."

Nemo shook her hand, trying to recall if he had done anything to warrant her amusement. "It's good to meet you, too, Lian."

Her lips twitched, and she laughed as merrily as the younger girl.

"What's so funny?" he asked, not appreciating being the butt of an apparent joke.

Lian took a step back from him as Arielle floated back down for her. "You will see one day. Maybe." She grasped the other acrobat's hand and floated up.

Nemo watched her go, puzzled, and then shrugged and climbed up onto Timaeus's back. "I don't understand women," he said to the dragon.

"I don't understand humans," the dragon retorted. "My advice is to not try too hard. Just accept them for what they are. You'll save yourself some headaches that way." He raised his eyes and took off, and the sensation of flying for the first time put any thought of Lian's laughter out of Nemo's head.

Julia half fell onto a boulder, thoroughly lost among the twists and turns of the tunnels. She hadn't seen anyone during the hour she had been wandering and didn't know which way to go to get back to her own room.

"Should've used a string or trail of bread crumbs," she muttered, and her shoulders slumped. *What now?*

At least the cavern was beautiful. She had stopped in one covered in crystals gleaming in the electronic lights. She reached out and touched one, the point almost sharp enough to cut her. "I suppose there are worse places to be lost in," she mused, and something tickled the edges of her memory. Of being lost in a forest, and a strange group chasing her, moving with unusual speed. One among them looked familiar. Julia frowned. When had this been? The memory was dim with age, but it couldn't have been that long ago. She tried to glean more information from it, but it faded away out of her reach.

Julia rubbed a hand over her hair and looked around, recalled to her current predicament. "Oh well. Not going to accomplish anything just sitting here."

She stood up, and a young woman appeared in front of her. One moment she was alone, the next the woman was there, seemingly having been in mid-step, for she stumbled and smashed her foot against the wall. Several strong words escaped the woman while she hopped on one foot to rub her toes.

Julia watched, bemused but smiling a little despite that. "Anything else you want to say?" she asked. The woman spun around and stared.

"Julia. I didn't know you were out here," she said, much to Julia's increasing confusion. "I was headed toward your room."

"And you are?" Julia asked. "Not to be rude. I had a fever the last few days, and I don't remember much..."

"Oh. No problem. I'm Emma. I'm the one who found you out in the snow." She beamed. "It's good to see you're doing okay. I got sick as well, or I would've come and checked on you before now."

Julia nodded and smiled back. "Well, thank you. Your timing works just fine again. I'm lost. Do you know the way?"

Emma looked around, her smile fading into an intent frown. "Not sure."

Julia's heart sank.

"Can you help us, Donovan?" Emma asked, and Julia raised an eyebrow. "Oh, wait. I hear running water. This way." Emma broke into a jog. Julia leapt up and followed.

The spring of water flowed briskly along the side of the tunnel until they came to a closed stone door that the stream disappeared under.

"Aoife?" Emma called. "Are you in?"

"Come in," Aoife's voice called back.

Emma pushed the stone, and it gave way with a grinding noise. She slipped in and held it open for Julia to follow. Inside, Aoife leaned over the pool of water, wringing her dark hair out. Her eyes lit up when she saw them.

"Hey, Aoife," Julia said. Her eyes went to the pool. "Is there any particular reason you have a moat?"

"I'm a mermaid," Aoife replied seriously. "Didn't I tell you that before? No matter. Since you're both here, I'll give you the clothes I've made for you. Donovan, if you will."

All three of them were shifted to the other side of the pool. Aoife flitted over to the nearest clothes rack and pawed through it.

Julia sat down hard on the floor. Emma stayed standing and looked thoughtfully at Julia.

"I take it you don't want skirts?" Aoife asked over her shoulder.

"No," Julia replied faintly. "They're too hard to move in. Pants or nothing." Aoife tittered and continued her search.

"You're taking this all very calmly." Emma studied Julia. She was surprised by the other woman's calmness "It's a lot to adjust to, but you seem to be taking it all in stride."

"You did, too, Emma," Aoife said. "It's not that uncommon for humans to respond this way. Your race is very good at adapting to unusual circumstances."

"I read minds," Emma retorted. "And I'd seen mermaids before. The Circus didn't require a huge leap of faith."

While they were speaking, Julia stood up and effortlessly lifted a boulder with one hand. Emma's jaw dropped, and Julia grinned. "It's not such a leap of faith for me either," she said and set the boulder down, making sure she didn't drop it on her foot. "Also, there was a mermaid at the bar I worked at," she added and frowned. "Wonder if that woman was an actual mermaid?"

Aoife tensed, her hands balling into fists around the clothing she rifled through. "Was there?" she asked, her tone cheerful. Emma glanced at her uncertainly. She'd never seen the mermaid react to anything this way. "Did you ever speak with her?" Aoife moved away from the rack and leaned against a wardrobe, facing them with a blank expression and crossed arms.

Perplexed, Emma listened. Aoife's mind was so firmly closed off that Emma couldn't even hear a whisper that might indicate the mermaid's emotions.

"No," Julia said. "I assumed she was a hired swimmer at first, but I started to wonder when I never saw her outside the tank..." Aoife turned and fixed Julia with a withering glare. "Are you suggesting she was a real mermaid?"

Aoife returned her attention to the clothing rack. "Try these pants on. I'll find you a matching top."

Julia got up and obeyed. "She warned me when those men came. I would probably have been captured without her. Why was she there? Was it a job like yours?"

"No," Aoife said stiffly, her shoulders hunched. "There's a trade in...magical creatures. A company in San Francisco handles it." Emma looked up sharply. "They sell whatever they can catch, but their biggest commodity is the merfolk they fish up from the sea." She took a deep breath and picked out a frilly blouse.

The pants fell from Julia's fingers, her mouth hanging open in shock. "Then we need to help her! We can't just leave her there!" Aoife held out the blouse. Julia shook her head and stepped back. "How can you still be thinking about clothes?"

A bark of laughter escaped Aoife. "Why? Because there's nothing I can do!" she buried her face in the fabric. Emma put a hand on her shoulder. "Gabriel promised we would stop the trade once. We rescued a few creatures and many Blessed, but now he's too scared of the Company taking notice to keep working on that."

"What is this Company called?" Emma asked, quiet fury building deep within her. Aoife sniffed and peered at Emma over the blouse, her eyes red-rimmed. She straightened and wiped her eyes.

"No. Gabriel would be furious with me." She looked down at the blouse, now damp with her tears. "This was too frilly anyway, huh?"

"Yeah," Julia said, her voice subdued. "Do you have anything plainer?" She studied them for a moment more and surveyed the pants in a mirror. "These are okay, but I don't want any fancy blouses to go with it."

"Very good." Aoife returned to a bubbly excitement as she flitted among her wardrobes, but Emma could hear her brooding just under the surface.

A little while later, Donovan shifted Julia back to her room with a pile of clothing. Determined to get some answers now, Emma advanced

161

on Aoife.

The mermaid waved her away with a pleading expression. "Oh, Donovan, please."

Emma opened her mouth to protest, but Donovan shifted her to her bedroom. She spun around and darted out the door. She wouldn't give Donovan the chance to lock her in again.

There was no reply when Emma pounded on Nemo's door. Incensed at being ignored, she pounded again; pain blossomed in her hand, but she didn't care. She could sense Nemo inside, and she wasn't going away. She focused and slipped easily past his mental defenses. After practicing with Aoife and Gabriel, his defenses were weak. *Nemo, let me in!*

A crash and a cut-off expletive answered her. Nemo's mind flinched away, but she could still hear his disgruntled thoughts. The door jerked open and he glared at her. "Don't do that!"

"Then don't ignore me," she growled and shoved past him. "Please close the door. I don't want anyone to overhear us. It's bad enough Donovan will." A squeak drew her attention to a bat clinging to the stone wall. She looked back at Nemo.

He frowned darkly at Emma and kicked the door closed. "What's wrong with you?"

Emma grimaced. She wished she could have this conversation silently but knew Nemo wouldn't go for that. Besides, Donovan was aware of all this anyway. She squared her shoulders and told Nemo everything: that Gabriel had blocked some of Nemo's memories and what Aoife had just told her.

Nemo sat heavily on his bed and listened with a solemn expression. "I see," he said when Emma finished. He lapsed into a long silence, tracing the pattern on his blanket.

Emma held her breath, waiting, and then stomped her foot. The lack of a reaction stoked her temper even hotter. "Well?"

Nemo looked away. "Hear me out, Em. After we talked before, I tried really hard to remember what happened at rehearsal that day. It bothered me that I couldn't remember." His finger paused at a crease, and he straightened the blanket out. "All I was able to bring to mind was

162

that those people scared me. And with what you just told me, it makes sense. A company of Blessed that kidnap other Blessed and trade in magical creatures? I think Gabriel is right. We should stay out of it. Let the elves handle it."

Emma glared at him. "We don't know that they're going to do anything at all! Lucien has been gone for a while now, and we haven't heard a peep."

Nemo shook his head. "If Gabriel is scared of these people, why do you think we could do anything? We'd just get ourselves in trouble."

His words tugged at her thoughts, turning them toward his logic. She smacked Nemo on the shoulder.

His head shot up, and he looked at her indignantly. "What was that for?"

"Don't use your Blessing on me like that! I won't have it!" She was aware of this discrepancy after she just used her Blessing on him, but her emotional turmoil swept it aside. "This is important, Nemo!" She whirled around and stared at the wall, trying to get hold of her temper.

"I know it is! I was only trying to get you to calm down and see sense! If you agree with me, that has nothing to do with my ability!"

"I'm not going to turn my back on Tip and Julia. Or…or the mermaids Aoife wants to help and…and pixies and who knows what else?" She was rambling. Breathing hard, she fixed an imploring gaze on her brother.

Nemo wouldn't meet her eyes. "I trust Gabriel."

Emma caught her breath. Seething, she turned on her heel and stomped out.

Avery leaned against the wall next to Emma's door and shifted his wings, turning a pinecone over and over in his hand. Aoife had found him a little while before and told him in a great rush about her conversation with Emma. She hadn't needed to ask him to do something. He'd rushed to Emma's room only to find her gone. He paced for a few minutes, debating whether to go look for or her not, and then settled down to wait, fidgeting anxiously.

This decision was rewarded sooner than he expected. Emma came around the bend. A relieved grin lit his face. Emma only glowered at him.

"Did Donovan tell you to come?" she said while she stalked past him and gripped the door handle.

His smile faded at her tone, and he took a step back, feeling like she'd slapped him. He'd never seen her in a true temper. "Aoife told me what happened. She's really worried about you."

Emma bit her lip to keep and tightened her fingers around the knob, but she didn't turn it. "You're going to tell me it's a bad idea to keep poking my nose in this?" she said instead.

Avery shrugged one shoulder and his grin returned. "I wouldn't dare." Emma gave him a wary look, and his smile widened. He shot an arm out and caught her around the waist.

Emma let him pull her away from the door. He presented her with the pine cone. "A sweet flower for a sweet lady."

Emma's eyebrows shot up. "You're so cheesy," she said, her voice calmer now. "And that's a pinecone, you dork."

"What are pinecones but wooden flowers?" Avery replied grandly. "Immortal wooden flowers that will never wilt but may grant you joy forever."

"Did you study Shakespeare or something?" Emma asked, giving him a reluctant smile.

Avery's theatrical expression faltered. "You think I'm that good?" he asked, his tone caught between amused and flattered.

Caught up in his playfulness, Emma grinned wickedly. "I do. You're very cute, Avery." She reached up to pat him on the head.

Avery caught Emma's hand. "Cute? Now you wound me." He pressed a hand to his chest and brought her fingers toward his lips. "Speak not such barbs, dear lady, but let sweet words ring out in thy soothing tones—"

Emma yanked her hand free and took a step back, staring at him. He straightened up and blinked at her, stung by her reaction. His face reddened, and he took a few steps away to face the cave wall.

"Sorry," Emma mumbled.

"Don't be." Avery cleared his throat but didn't look at her. His feathers ruffled as he resettled his wings.

Emma walked up to him to bump his shoulder with hers. "Aoife sure knows how to handle people."

That made him chuckle. "She certainly does. Gabriel's a changed man since he met her."

Emma stared at him. "Gabriel and Aoife? Seriously?"

"Yeah. You didn't know?" He hesitated and then reached out and gently took her hand. "Come with me." He turned and towed her through the tunnels, his eyes alight despite the darkness.

"Where are we going?" Emma whispered, as if they were sneaking somewhere.

Avery put a finger to his lips. "You'll see," he said and continued to guide her deeper and deeper into the warren of caves.

"I've never been this way," she said with a touch of wariness.

"This is where Martin and I live. He wanted rooms further from the main tunnels, and Donovan emptied out some lower caverns for us."

Bird song greeted them as they entered a cavern bright with moonlight. Emma blinked and looked around. "Some bird is very confused," she said and tried to imitate the bird call. Silence fell, and she chuckled. "Guess it didn't like that."

"It's a nightingale. It made its nest in here last year when we were in Europe and has traveled with us ever since. Sometimes, when I can't sleep, I come in here and listen to it singing." He sat down on a rock and settled his wings, bleached silver in the faint light.

Emma sat beside him and listened while the bird resumed its interrupted song. "It sounds lonely."

"Maybe. I wish I knew where we were when it came. I would ask Donovan to take us back there and release it. Though it can fly out whenever it wants. Even so, it keeps coming back."

Her eyes drifted to him, and she frowned before touching a spot on his wing. "Your feathers…what happened?" She moved closer to get a better look. "They're all bloody!"

"It's nothing." He looked away, self-conscious. "Sometimes I pluck some out. It's a nervous habit like chewing your fingernails."

"Chewing your fingernails doesn't hurt unless you chew them too short. It's not the same." She gently ran her fingers along the reddened plumage on his wings. Her eyes gleamed with gathering tears at the sight. Avery felt a pang over causing her pain. "There's a bald spot here. What made you so nervous?"

He shifted to a more comfortable position and considered his answer. "The idea of something happening to you, and then being confined while I was sick," he admitted. "But there's no reason to worry! The feathers are already starting to grow back!"

Avery brought his left wing around and pushed the feathers aside to show a bigger bald patch. "This is a spot where I kept plucking the feathers the moment I got pinions, so the feathers stopped growing. It won't be as bad as this."

"That doesn't make it better." Emma kept a hand on his wing and wiped her eyes with her sleeve. "What happened to cause that other spot?"

The avian stared into space for a long moment, possibilities for this conversation spinning through his head. He decided on the truth. Perhaps that was the best way to dissuade her from anything hasty.

"Gabriel caught me and Martin and transported us in cages toward the Company headquarters." Avery looked up, longing suddenly to see open sky or stars.

"Gabriel kidnapped you?" She stared at him, her eyes flashing with renewed anger. "To be sold?"

Avery's feathers fluffed up at the memory. "Gabriel is a much different person than he used to be, especially when I first met him. A Company executive broke his mind after he helped Aoife escape and then sent him out to Europe to do some hunting and recover his wits. Tristan and some other Company Rangers were with him."

He rubbed his face, and his gaze focused somewhere distant. "Martin and I were living on our own, out in the wilderness. It was a tough life without any modern amenities, but we were free. We had thought it was the best option until Gabriel's team of Rangers showed up, and there was no one there to help us." He swallowed. "After they caught us, they kept hunting and found Celeste. Or maybe Celeste found them. Aoife had been tracking Gabriel and went to Celeste for help."

"Tristan blinded one of the men to save Celeste, and then she undid the damage to Gabriel's mind. He set Martin and me free, and then Celeste brought us to Timaeus's caves to request sanctuary. Gabriel went back to San Francisco to get the Blessed who wanted out of the Company." A smile touched his lips. "Instead of selling us, he founded a circus with us. It worked out."

Emma shook her head, struggling to take all this in. One question plagued her, diverting her thoughts. "How can you ignore others, the ones it didn't work out for?"

"I can't take on the world," he said. "I help where I can, same as Gabriel. He accepted you and Nemo into the Circus to protect you from the Company. He knows the scope of the Company better than almost anyone. If he says it's too dangerous to act here or there, I believe him. I choose not to risk my own neck. If we're captured, we can't help anyone at all. Maybe that's just cowardice. I don't know."

"I don't know either. With all our Blessings and abilities, shouldn't we be able to do more? Couldn't we help free people, mermaids and such, and shift away before the Company got news of it?"

"We've done just that a lot. But they're difficult to find. We can't exactly go around asking about mermaids." He rubbed his neck. "It's hard to accept, but that's life."

Emma huffed, and Avery ruffled her hair fondly. "You've gotten so adept at your Blessing. Gabriel will probably let you help soon. The only reason he hasn't yet is because he wanted to protect you. Please don't run off in the meantime."

"Okay," Emma said reluctantly and leaned against him.

Avery allowed the quiet to hold and slowly wrapped an arm around Emma's shoulders, worried she would pull away again if he moved too quickly. They sat together in the serenity and listened to the bird until she dozed off against his shoulder.

He stroked a thumb over her cheek. "Good night, Emma," he whispered a moment before Donovan shifted her into her bed.

T ip spun away from Balthasar's kick and threw a punch toward the man's face. The blind man twisted to the side, fast as a snake, and then charged forward. Tip braced himself but then changed his mind and allowed Balthasar to tackle him. They fell onto the mat and wrestled for a few seconds before Balthasar pinned him down and touched his throat. "Dead."

"Three-zero," Caleb called from the opposite end of the gym where he and Rebecca ran on treadmills. Tip glanced over. They wore earbuds but had watched him lose repeatedly as if it were a show. When he and Balthasar went over to the water dispenser, they focused on the television in front of the machines.

"I'd hate to be in a serious fight with you," Tip panted and drained a cup of water. He got a second cup and sipped it.

Balthasar grabbed a towel from the table and wiped his neck. They'd been exercising since early that morning. It was a regular habit of the older members of the House, and Tip was becoming extremely familiar with the small but well-equipped gym.

"I never fight seriously," Balthasar said grimly. "It wouldn't be a fair fight against anyone but someone else Blessed with strength, and I don't want a serious fight with a Blessed." He rubbed his face. "Maybe an elf could match me, but there's no way to ever find that out."

"The tutor said there's still elven cities up north. They must be very well hidden," Tip said in a mildly interested tone. Balthasar had prevented him from questioning the younger House members. Perhaps if he could get the man to see him as harmlessly curious, that would let up.

"They're not my concern," Balthasar grunted before jerking his head toward the mat. They resumed their sparring. Balthasar instructed Tip after each loss, ignoring Caleb calling out the score. But Tip still couldn't hold his own for more than a minute.

Balthasar frowned darkly at him. "Stop holding back because I'm blind. I promise but you won't be able to hurt me."

Tip rubbed the back of his head. "Sorry. I'm not doing it because of your eyes. Holding back my strength is just ingrained in me." It was something Julia had said to him once when she came to the club as a patron and drank a little too much. It made sense that those with a strength Blessing would have to hold back.

Balthasar pinned him again. "Let's take another break." He got to his feet, offered Tip a hand, and pulled him up.

"Why do I need to learn how to fight, anyway?" Tip asked. "It seems like an unnecessary skill. I can understand getting stronger, but fighting is different."

"It's just an extension of strength. The Company likes for the Blessed to develop our talents. Martial skills are required for strength Blessed. Boxing and wrestling are always occupation options for people like us. You must learn how to hold back just enough. Or you could be a laborer. The ships are always looking for strong workers. Sailors recommended by the Ark Light Company don't have to hide their strength."

Tip wrinkled his nose. "I don't want to be a deck hand or a fisherman," he grumbled. "The idea of doing something where I don't have to hide my strength does sound nice, though."

"The elves didn't give us these powers so that we could live in

169

hiding. The Ark Light Company is trying to create a sanctuary for the Blessed." The conviction in his voice gave Tip pause.

"So I've been told repeatedly since I was brought here and my memories were erased." Tip kept his voice carefully neutral and drank more water.

Balthasar grimaced. "You sound skeptical." He sat down on the seat of an exercise bicycle, his face turned in Tip's general direction.

"Taking children from their homes is very rarely acceptable. It's a noble ideal, but the memory thing is a little weird, you have to admit." Tip glanced around, glad the couple had left. He wouldn't want to rouse Caleb's temper.

"It can't be helped. We're a family here, and memories of their old families would only cause them pain. It's for their own good. I was taken as a teenager, and my memories were erased just like you and the others. I'm happy to be here."

"Are you happy Gail is here?" Tip asked and didn't miss the brief twisting of the man's face. He'd seen the way Balthasar often put himself between Gail and most of the residents of the House.

"Observant, aren't you?" Balthasar tapped his cup. "Gail is happy here as well. That is enough for me to want her here. I'm just careful. A lot of Blessings can be dangerous. Accidents happen."

Was it an accident that made you lose your eyesight? The question burned on Tip's tongue, but he didn't ask it. He didn't want to push the conversation anymore.

"Enough rest," Balthasar declared. Tip groaned and heaved himself up.

Tip limped into the living room and collapsed onto the nearest couch. It wasn't even five P.M, but he wanted nothing more than to just go to bed. He needed dinner, though. If he didn't eat after a workout like that, hunger would wake him up in the middle of the night. He would arouse the Keeper's suspicion if he wandered around at night.

He surveyed the room, taking note of the residents who were there and those who weren't. Adah, Rebecca, and Neil knelt in the corner playing a board game with the two little girls. Neil had his elbow sunk into the floorboards and was moving the pieces around while the girls stared, openmouthed.

Seth was setting up a smaller TV in another corner. Gail lay on the floor, watching Seth. He plugged it in and then plopped down next to her and handed her a remote while the game started up.

Tip watched them play for a few minutes, and then his gaze drifted to the movie on the big TV. He was tired and neither screen could hold his interest. His eyes closed, and he slipped into a dream.

He was leaning against his mother's knees after a day of exhausting training and spellcasting with his father. She rubbed his back and shoulders, singing softly to him.

Several peaceful moments passed before Tip realized someone was actually touching him. He jolted out of his doze and twisted around to meet Adah's merry brown eyes.

"Do you mind?" she asked, still kneading his shoulders. "I just can't stand to sense so much discomfort."

"I don't mind. It feels very nice. Thank you." He let his eyes drift closed again but remained alert. "Michael didn't need you tonight? I thought you were his secretary."

"He took the evening off to have dinner with his father," Adah told him with a guarded tone that Tip was quite familiar with. The House residents used it often around the newcomers.

"The mysterious head of the Ark Light Company?" Tip asked.

Adah's hands stilled, and his eyes opened. "The very same," she said with forced lightness and resumed the massage with vigor.

Tip relaxed and enjoyed it, with plenty to think about now. She'd looked almost frightened when speaking about the head of the Company. Interesting.

Neil walked by the chair and caught Tip's eye as he passed. Tip ducked out from under Adah's hands. "Thank you for the massage. I feel a lot better, but my legs are stiff. I'm going to take a walk around the house."

"Okay," Adah's eyes flicked to the doorway, clearly having sensed Neil there. She didn't miss a trick. They needed to tread carefully.

In their dorm room, Neil sat at the desk, reading. "This book is really interesting. I found it in the library."

Tip crossed the room and read over Neil's shoulder.

"The field of Keeping is a very specialized field of magic and requires a strong personality. Keepers are magically bound to a physical location and possess awareness of all that happens within that location. They exercise control over all comings and goings. They are often employed in large homes, businesses, or schools. They are an excellent form of magical security."

"Interesting," Tip said casually and stretched his arms over his head. "Let's walk some. I really am stiff."

They wandered the halls, chatting with easy comradery about the day and their differing lessons from Seth and Balthasar. When Tip's legs felt a little better, they went into a sitting room. It was the room they'd been in when the mind control lifted.

They settled by the cold hearth. Neil pulled crumpled papers from his pockets and lit them with a lighter. His eyes flicked lazily around the dark room while the flames licked up the paper. His face was thoughtful, and Tip knew he was thinking about the Keeper knowing what they were doing.

"Why don't we play a word game?" Tip suggested and got a small notepad and a pencil out of his pocket. He explained the rules and they began passing the pad back and forth.

"Think the Keeper is paying attention to what we're writing?" Neil scribbled hastily down before passing it to Tip, angling it so it was half closed.

Tip shook his head and then grimaced and rubbed his neck. *"I can get us out of here,"* he wrote, his face creased with thought, as if he were considering a move. *"I need to get a message out. Ideas?"*

The pad made several rounds after that with quick, inconsequential words written. Then ideas flowed, and a plan began to form. Tip made a few tweaks to it, and when the pad was passed to him again, he grinned.

"I have an idea!" He quickly wrote out his plan, snapped the pad closed, and passed it back to Neil, who opened it very slightly.

"Risky move," Neil commented and tapped the pad against his chin thoughtfully. He thumbed through the pages and gripped the pencil tighter, but before he could write anything more, the door burst open.

The two young men spun around, fear and guilt flashing over their faces as they half rose to their feet. The two little girls rushed in and threw themselves against Neil. He gasped as he went down under their combined weight, holding the notepad high. Then he twitched and twisted around under their hands, stressed laughter escaping him.

Tip lunged forward, grabbed the notepad away from Neil, and looked up as Rebecca and Caleb came along the hallway, their faces grim. Neil rolled onto his side, trying to scoot away from the tickling.

"Stop, stop!" he demanded breathlessly.

A foot kicked the coffee table, and Tip grabbed a glass vase before it fell. "Oh, come on." He quickly ripped the last few pages out of the notebook and poked them into the fireplace just before Rebecca cleared the doorway. She hissed and gestured. The fire extinguished with a fizzle, but the papers crumbled away into ash.

"Care to tell me what was written on those?" Caleb demanded. "Why are you two sneaking off on your own?"

"Drawings," Neil gasped, shoving away from the girls. He looked meaningfully at them. "Adult stuff I didn't want them seeing. We were just messing around."

Rebecca's expression soured, and she crossed her arms in disgust. "Let's go," she muttered at Caleb, and they walked back out.

"Seth told us you would play a video game with us," the younger of the girls said. "You must come!"

"Okay!" Neil gasped, and they backed away, grinning. Neil grabbed a chair leg to heave himself up off the floor, his face red and blotchy. "I'll be out in a moment. Give me a moment, please."

The girls wandered out, casting reluctant looks back at Neil. He flopped down on a chair and groaned. "I did not see that coming."

"That's what you get for playing with kids," Tip retorted. "They never leave you alone once you do. Let's not do anymore drawings for a while." He slipped the notepad into his pocket and went out, leaving Neil to recover as well as he could.

Michael had hated the family meals in the opulent dining room ever since his mother left. The grand room with the absurdly long banquet table brought back too many memories of when they had eaten there as a complete family. They had often invited guests, but when they didn't, their mother had joked over the absurdity of the four of them eating at one end of the long table.

After she left, her empty chair made the table seem that much larger and terrible rather than comical. Dinners became silent, solemn affairs for the rest of his childhood.

Now it was just him and his father.

Michael arrived before Dante and stood at the window overlooking the large back garden. Memories of long hours playing with his brother among those trees and flowers assaulted him, their minds open to one another so they knew each other's thoughts instantly and didn't need to speak. Their silent communication had always frightened their mother a little.

Dante strode into the room, his polished black shoes tapping a quick rhythm against the hardwood floor. "Sit. I want no delays. I have a phone appointment in an hour."

As he sat down, it was all Michael could do to not glance at the chair Gabriel used to sit in. He could count on his fingers the number of times he and his father had eaten in here just the two of them. They didn't feel like family dinners anymore, and guests were never invited into this room.

Dante Hightower sat as rigidly as a statue at the head of the table. He still possessed a powerful bearing, but his face was grayer than when Michael had seen him a few weeks before. His father had been to his doctor for some tests but refused to tell Michael the results.

"Did you review the Collectors' report?" Dante asked over bowls of fish chowder. "The team that just came in."

"I did. There was nothing I felt necessary to send to your desk."

"Send it. You aren't the head of the Company yet. Virgil told me you've kept several reports from me while he was gone."

Michael kept his face and mind blank. How did Virgil know that? "It was nothing important. You've been so busy. I was just trying to alleviate some work for you. I thought you wanted me to handle the Collectors, since you manage the Rangers and Fishers." He tried not to think too much about his father's management of those. Protecting the Blessed was the most he could do right now.

Dante's face became, if possible, even graver. "Do not coddle me, boy. I do not need it. You do not make executive decisions of this type. You will keep me informed of what the Scouts and Collectors find." He dropped his spoon into his bowl and looked around for the servant, tapping his foot impatiently.

"Yes sir," Michael said and bowed his head. He had already destroyed the reports that mentioned the Circus Phantasm. That was all that mattered.

"I would also like to know why you reassigned the members of a Scouting team to your staff and took Balthasar from his Collecting team. I do not want Balthasar to remain in town. He might be blind, but his Blessing is suited to the duty of a Collector."

"I will place him back on the team in a few months," Michael said. "The ship captains have been reporting frightening occurrences when they net merfolk. I am considering sending Balthasar out with the Fishers to help with that."

Dante slapped his hand down on the table. "Where is the next course?" A young man hurried in from the kitchen. Dante glared at him. Sweat beading up on the server's forehead. "I finished my soup minutes ago. Are you trying to test my patience?"

"N-no, sir," the man stammered. His hand shook as he placed the plates on the table, and he looked ill.

Michael twisted his napkin between his hands. "Father, stop. Please. There's no reason to use your Blessing."

Dante turned his eyes away from the server and the man fled. Michael felt a painful twinge in his chest as his father looked balefully at him, but he kept his face calm.

"You are taking way too much on yourself, Michael. You do not have the proper authority to make these decisions without consulting me. I will let this one slide. I know the real reason you want Balthasar in town is for your birthday. Stop making excuses, boy." He glared down at the table and dropped his napkin on top of the food. "I have no appetite. I'm going to rest. You remember what I said, Michael. You will consult me on all decisions."

"Yes, sir." Michael watched silently as his father went out. "Not qualified?" he muttered and ran a hand through his hair. At the last family dinner, his father had told him to take on more responsibilities.

He got to his feet, glaring down at the food, and bunched up his napkin to throw it, when his vision became blurry. Pain lanced through his head. He gritted his teeth and kicked a chair aside, so he could fall into it as the vision took him.

Gabriel stared up at him, pale and terrified. Michael bit back the urge to say anything. This was Gabriel as Michael had last seen him, several years before.

He stared up at Michael, his mouth gaping as he gasped in ragged breaths. "Please," he whispered, and his voice cracked. He ducked his head, and a sob shook him.

"Where did the mermaid go?" Virgil's voice asked from somewhere behind Michael. He didn't bother turning around but stared down at his brother, his fingernails biting into his palms.

"I...I don't know," Gabriel sobbed. "She left. Please. No more." He stiffened and shook his head frantically. "Stop it! Get out!"

"Lower your guard," Virgil growled. "If you're telling the truth let me see your memories!"

"No!" Gabriel threw his head back and glared defiantly at Michael. "My mind is my own. I've made my memories, and I'm keeping them. I will not be just another grunt whose memories you erase and rewrite whenever you want!"

"Idiot boy."

The new voice made both twins blanch. Their father marched into the room, swinging a cane thoughtfully.

"Father," Gabriel whispered, his voice trembling with fear. "Father, please."

Dante glanced once at Gabriel and then away. "Go ahead, Virgil.

A good block should sort this out. We'll keep him away from the ships after this."

Gabriel screamed in wordless rage and lunged against the ropes binding him to the chair. The sound cut off abruptly. His face went smooth and blank.

Michael covered his eyes and forcibly ended the vision. The pain lessened, and when he lowered his hand, the dining room swam around him. He put a hand to his cheek and frowned down at the tears flowing freely down his face.

"Enough is enough, Father," Michael growled, his resolve hardening. He would continue to wait and watch for a chance to make his move. If his father's health was, in fact, declining, it might come sooner than he had thought.

If it doesn't, I will take the initiative.

Neil lay awake that night, staring into the darkness. "Not being able to remember my family has been really bothering me," he said softly. "Does it bother you, Tip?"

Tip lay facing the wall, his head pillowed on his arm. He couldn't tell Neil that he remembered his family perfectly. He vividly recalled the last time he saw his father. Tip hadn't wanted to be sent on this investigation, but as a half-elf he could pass more easily as a human. His father had ended the argument by casting a series of spells on him that decided the matter. Bitterness simmered in him at the memory, and he shoved both away. He would deal with that later.

"Tip?" He heard a rustle as Neil sat up. "Did you fall asleep?" Neil sighed and lay back down. His voice was so dejected that Tip couldn't ignore him.

"No, I'm still awake. I was just trying to remember. I don't miss my family, but there's someone else..." He couldn't remember Julia's face. All the memories of his time in Toronto were hazy. "All I can remember of her is that she is also Blessed. When they came, she ran. I can't even remember what she looks like or what exactly was between us. They took that from me." His voice shook with genuine anger, but he quickly detached himself from that emotion and examined it. Did he really care that much about the human? The idea disturbed him. He needed a distraction.

He sat up and felt around on the bedside table. "We both need pick-me-ups. I nabbed some chocolate from Seth earlier."

"Chocolate right before sleep?" Neil asked. "You might not have to worry about getting fat, but my lessons aren't nearly as intense as yours."

"Do you want some or not? Don't tell me you're on a diet or some crap like that."

"Of course not!" Neil stumbled in the darkness and cursed. Tip reached out to steady him and sent a memory spell to free Neil from the block through the contact. Neil caught his breath. "What did you just do?" His voice hitched in a quiet sob.

Tip turned on the lamp. "Are you okay? Are you hurt?" He widened his eyes meaningfully. *The Keeper is aware of this.*

Neil turned away from the light but not before Tip saw the tears rolling down his face. "I'm fine. Just hit my foot really hard against the bed."

Tip patted his shoulder and handed him a chocolate. "Guess my gift wasn't a good idea."

"No." Neil took a deep breath. "I appreciate it." He got back in his bed and set the chocolate down unopened. Tip turned the lamp off.

"I realized," Neil said a few minutes later. Tip was half-asleep by then, but he made a noise to show he was listening. "I'm not sure if it's worse to forget your family or to remember them and not be able to go back to them."

"Neither. The worst is to remember them and not want to go back," he whispered without thinking.

Neil didn't reply, and Tip slipped into slumber, blurry images of Julia flitting through his final dazed thoughts.

Crystals glittered all around Julia as she completed a set of stretches. The pull of muscle calmed her more than anything else and cleared her head.

Emma had invited her to spend the evening with everyone after dinner, but Julia had refused and found her way back to the crystal cavern. Events had unfolded so fast. She needed to be alone and think all of this through. Gabriel and Emma had shown her beyond any doubt that they could, in fact, read minds. She could accept that, but she still shied away from the idea of mermaids, unicorns, or dragons. The thought caused a cold pit that felt like fear to form in her chest.

She groaned and leaned back on her hands, rolling her head to stretch the muscles of her neck. "At least this place is pretty." She eyed the crystals on all the walls and jutting from the ceiling, feeling like she sat in the middle of a geode.

The beauty of the place did not damper her restlessness. She longed to tell Tip about her day, to exercise with him, and spend a quiet evening reading before their shift at the Cove.

I want my life back. Tears formed in her eyes and she dashed them away angrily. She would not give in to such self-pity. Leaping to her feet, she jogged laps around the room and then launched into a series of kicks and punches. Movement kept her from moping.

A rustle of feathers caught her attention as a creature advanced into the cave and shattered Julia's sense of normalcy.

Green feathers tipped with gold flowed into amber, black spotted fur. A beak dipped to pick a pebble out of a paw. It lifted its head again and then leapt at Julia with a screech.

Julia dropped to let the creature fly over her and regained her feet to face it as it scrabbled at the dirt to slow its momentum. The young woman charged the creature before it could recover its balance and grabbed two fistfuls of feathers. The creature screeched again and thrashed, but Julia exerted her strength to drive it to the ground. The feat took more of her Blessing than she had ever used. It thrashed against her, and Julia had to strain to keep it down.

After one long minute, the creature went still and regarded her with its stern, black eyes. "I concede," it announced, startling her again. Its voice was scratchy like a parrot's.

"Great." Julia released the creature and scooted away but kept a close eye on it. That beak and the claws flexing out of its spotted paws looked deadly.

The creature angled its head to preen its feathers, rumpled and bent from the struggle, before standing and bowing its beak to her. "You have earned my respect. I would like to form a compact with you."

"A what now?" Julia stared at it. Now that it wasn't trying to murder her, she could see there was a fierce beauty to the creature.

A hiss issued from it, and it reared its head back as if offended by the question.

"Sorry. I'm new here," Julia added but couldn't stop the smile plucking at her mouth. The pit of fear in her chest dissipated. She had faced one of these unusual creatures and it had not bested her.

"Very well. I will give you time to consider it. I would be honored to be your companion, though. You are the strongest human I have encountered in a long time. To show you my sincerity, I will free you of the spell you are under."

"The what?" Julia's relief disappeared with a pop. Fear flooded back in. Something shifted in her mind and her mouth dropped open, the fear turning to horror. "No."

Her childhood memories of Tip dissipated like smoke. In their place, she now recalled a group of elves chasing her through a forest until they caught her. She swallowed, tears flowing freely as Tip's face swam in her mind, watching grimly as the elves invaded her mind and enchanted her. He went home with her that day, acting as if they had been out hiking together. *And then he enchanted me himself, to make me come here.*

"I accept," Julia whispered. "Your…contract or whatever it is. Just give me some time alone, please." She wiped her eyes and struggled to reconcile Tip's kindness at the Cove with this revelation.

Candlelight flickered over the hand-painted playing cards, worn with age. Nemo carefully organized his hand of cards, not wanting to bend them at all.

Feathers rustled, and scales hissed as the other players fidgeted.

Nemo looked around at the avians, dragon, and ringmaster, with his bright coat still around his shoulders. The trio of acrobats and a few other Blessed performers sat beside Emma. Silence reigned as they considered their next moves by the light of the tall candelabra, the only illumination Timaeus kept in his library.

For a moment, Nemo could only reflect on how strange his life had become. And then Martin threw down his cards triumphantly. Timaeus reared his head back, flames flickering along his jaw and dripping down onto the stone floor where they sizzled out. "You cheated!"

Martin smirked and held his hands up without a trace of fear in his eyes. "I did not. Go ahead and search the deck if you don't believe me."

Timaeus's eyes went to the antique playing cards, and he settled back into a crouch, grumbling under his breath. "I'm not playing with you anymore. Get out."

"When a dragon tells you to get out, you get out," Donovan said dryly and waved his hand. Everyone vanished.

Nemo blinked and looked between the Keeper and the dragon. "I'm not banished?"

"I want you to read to me for a while." Timaeus heaved himself up and moved over to lie on his gold pile, shoved to one side of the cave for their game.

"Oh, okay." Nemo got to his feet and went to select a book. His voice was hoarse from their lessons earlier, but he could read for a short while. "Any requests?"

"Whatever you want to read is fine." Timaeus glared irritably down at the floor.

Nemo sat down right up against Timaeus's side and began reading. Magic flowed half-heartedly, fairies chasing each other around the room, fizzling out before they got more than a foot or so.

"Enough," Timaeus snapped. "I am in no mood for this. Begone."

"Sir, is there anything at all I could do to cheer you up?" he asked tentatively. "I know you miss Lucien, but maybe—"

"I said begone!" Flames spewed out of Timaeus's mouth, coming so close to Nemo the heat scorched his face.

He tossed the book aside and slipped on Martin's floored cards in

181

his haste to flee.

The dimmed lights made it difficult to know which way to go. Nemo was lost before he slowed enough to get his bearings. Donovan usually shifted him in and out of Timaeus's library, so he had only walked there and back a few times since using his Blessing to find it.

Nemo looked both ways, then sighed and trudged down the way he hoped was correct.

A frantic squeaking erupted from the darkness and reverberated off the stone walls, the only warning he got before the bat flew out of the darkness and straight into his face. He grunted and stumbled back a step, his hand shooting up and brushing against the bat's furry back.

The creature clambered up onto his head. It was trembling, and its toes were icy and damp against Nemo's skin. It dove into the back of his shirt, making him gasp and squirm. He looked over his shoulder, trying to figure out what was wrong with it, so he didn't see the thing that bowled him over a moment later.

Paws as big as his hand with lethal claws cut into his shoulders as the creature tore at the back of his shirt, ripping fabric and skin indiscriminately. The bat's frantic squeaking filled his ears.

"Stop!" he screeched, his voice pitched high with pain but filled with power. Silence descended like a curtain.

Nemo arched his back to get his hands onto the floor and shoved himself up, gritting his teeth. He clambered to his feet and felt at his torn shirt. Deep gashes underneath bled and made the fabric stick to his skin.

The bat clambered up the back of his neck and came to rest on his hair again. He pried it off his head and cradled it against his chest as he studied his assailant. The large creature gazed balefully at him a few feet off.

It was a cross between a leopard and an eagle with piercing yellow eyes. Even accustomed to Timaeus, the feral ferocity of this creature made him take a step back. His shoulders stung where they pressed against the wall. He ignored the pain and remained focused on the creature.

Griffin. The word came to Nemo, for what good knowing that might do. His eyes roved over its golden plumage.

It leaned its head forward and opened its beak a few inches. "Unhand the flying creature I was hunting," it commanded imperiously in a strident, piercing voice.

"Hunting?" Despite how scratchy his voice sounded, he forced his power to continue flowing through it. "This isn't your territory to hunt in."

The creature recoiled and hissed.

Nemo's stomach rolled, and he fought to keep from looking at the blood seeping down his shirt. "Timaeus permits this bat to live in his domain. You're overstepping yourself to hunt here at all." He didn't feel confident at all, but he kept his voice even and assumed a haughty expression to match that of the griffin.

The griffin drew itself up and looked ready to scold Nemo, but before it could speak, Donovan's nasally voice came out of the darkness.

"Lord Amadis," he called as he shuffled into view. "My lord is expecting you. I informed him of your arrival, and he will receive you now."

The griffin resettled his green-tipped wings and turned his disapproving gaze onto Donovan. "I was pursuing a snack. Are you aware your caves are infested with bats? I will change that if I'm to spend time here with my companion. Also, I expect the humans' manners to be remedied. This boy is unbelievably impertinent. He referred to Lord Timaeus with no title. Your master never used to allow such vermin. You are being negligent as a Keeper. I will be telling your master about this."

Donovan bowed his head. "The human is my lord's newest companion. He is quite displeased you have injured the boy. The bat is my student," he said, his eyes narrowing. "If you would please come with me, Lord Amadis, I will take you to my lord. Nemo, after Lord Timaeus excuses me I will find you and cast a healing spell."

The griffin dipped its beak in a nod and took a few steps closer to Donovan. They both disappeared. Nemo exhaled loudly as his tension eased all at once.

The bat squirmed against Nemo's hands. He let it go, and it perched against the opposite wall, regarding him upside down.

"Don't give me that look," Nemo muttered. "I just saved you from being eaten by Lord Ama-what's-it. And what does Donovan mean, you're his student?"

"Amadis," the bat said and shook its wings out. "One moment. I need to change out of this form before something else tries to eat me." It took a deep breath, making its body expand several inches, then took wing and flew into the darkness.

Nemo stared after it, frowning in pain and bewilderment. He was just considering heading to his room to wait for Donovan when the leader of the acrobat trio walked into view, the shadows clinging to her long dark hair and black clothing. A blue flower-shaped mask obscured the top half of her face, its leather petals rising a few inches above her forehead. Her deep brown eyes looked out of the round eye holes with concern.

"Lian?" His voice sounded distant and fading even to him. "You're the bat?"

"Are you alright?" she asked and stepped around him to examine his shoulders. A hiss escaped her over what she saw. Donovan appeared beside her. "Teacher, will you instruct me how to do some healing spells? I need to repay him."

Donovan nodded. He summoned a chair and pointed to it. "Sit down, Nemo."

Nemo gratefully sank into the chair and closed his eyes. His stomach roiled from the pain, and his head felt light. They talked in low voices behind him. Lian said something in a louder tone, and then his shoulder blades itched furiously. He hitched his shoulders up and gritted his teeth, but it was over as quickly as it began, and the steady throbbing stopped.

"Thanks." He turned to smile at them. Only Lian still stood behind him, Donovan having shifted away.

She nodded. "It was the least I could do. I still owe you for all that fruit you gave me." She traced a finger over the tunnel wall. "By the way, I don't see well when I'm a bat, so you don't have to worry about..." She shrugged and walked away.

The reminder made Nemo flush. He reviewed in his head all the times she had come into his room. He valued privacy, and the idea disturbed as the implications sank in. But she had done so much to help him get in Timaeus's good graces, and if she really couldn't see while she was a bat...

"L-Lian," he called after her. She turned and looked at him. He couldn't see her expression behind the mask, but her eyes were questioning.

"You're—" he swallowed. "You're still welcome to come in my room anytime you want," he said, his hoarse voice cracking. "I'll keep fruit for you, even though you're not really a fruit bat."

A smile dimpled Lian's face. "We'll see. It's not as fun once someone knows. But I might consider it. I love hearing you sing and speak." She flashed him a toothy grin. "Good night, Nemo."

Nemo stayed staring after her long after she was out of sight. Donovan returned a little while later and shook his head over Nemo's expression.

Nemo didn't notice. He barely even noticed when Donovan shifted him back into his room, but went about getting ready for bed with mechanical, jerky movements. His mind was whirling, and there was an odd feeling in his chest. He knew what it was.

He just didn't know what to do about it.

Nemo knocked on Gabriel's office door before strolling in. The ringmaster looked up from his papers. "Yes?" Gabriel asked, raising his eyebrows. He sat surrounded by precarious, haphazard stacks of papers and books.

Nemo cleared his throat and bounced forward on his toes nervously. "I wanted to ask about Lian."

"What about her?" Gabriel shoved aside a handful of papers and gave Nemo his full attention.

"Just...in general." Nemo shrugged. "You know about the performance I'm planning with the acrobats. Things have been a little weird between Timaeus and those girls, Lian especially. They're with the Circus, but Timaeus speaks about Lian as if she's not."

"Ah." Gabriel nodded. "The two younger acrobats are members of the Circus. Lian already lived here when I came to Timaeus and made the deal to let us live in his caves. She's Donovan's student: Blessed with shape shifting abilities, but also a mage, which is rare."

He paused, and his eyes went distant. "There aren't strong politics here, I'd say, but there are loyalties. Lian's loyalty belongs only to Donovan, and that doesn't give her a steady position. Timaeus employs Donovan as his Keeper, and I have something of a tenant renter deal with him for the Circus. Lian is just here. She wouldn't be if he really minded, but I don't think he particularly likes it."

"I see," Nemo said, rubbing his chin. He could see the truth of what Gabriel claimed about loyalty. There seemed to almost be factions, although they all submitted to Timaeus. Nemo chuckled. "The dragon rules all."

Gabriel smiled. "Indeed. The dragon rules all. It's hard to argue with an ancient, fire-breathing being when you're living in his lair."

"Thank you for answering my vague question." Nemo went out, feeling more at ease about doing a performance with the trio of acrobats.

Timaeus thought having company might draw him out of his melancholy. Lord Amadis proved a bad choice. The griffin's attack on Nemo caused the beginning of their visit to be spent in brooding anger, and things remained tense the entire time. By the time the griffin left in the early morning, Timaeus was in a far fouler mood than before the griffin showed up.

Nemo was at the rehearsal. Timaeus brushed the human's mind and felt a prick of jealousy that the Circus possessed as much of a hold on the boy as he did. He hadn't been so irritated by it when Lucien was present to keep him company when Nemo was busy. Now it irked him greatly.

He twisted around restlessly, making the gold coins dig between his scales. He usually kept his treasure meticulously organized but, in his boredom, he had pulled it all down to make this pile. After all that, lying on top of it just didn't give him the peace of mind it had when he was younger. He couldn't sleep any better for having made this mess. Trying to sleep in a human bed at Nemo's suggestion a few days before had resulted in the destruction of an ancient bedframe as soon as he fell asleep and returned to his natural form.

He closed his eyes and resolutely shoved away the nagging worries.

He would get some sleep, and then Nemo would come and read to him to keep the thoughts at bay the remainder of the day.

He was just on the edge of consciousness when there was a rap on the door. "Go away," he snarled. A presence appeared before him anyway. Furious, he jerked his head up and glared at Donovan. The Keeper knelt with his head bowed respectfully. "What do you want?"

Coins clinked and clattered while the dragon heaved his bulk around and his tail thrashed. "You are becoming awfully impertinent, Keeper. If you think having those humans here changes your position, you are mistaken. You are my subordinate, not Gabriel's."

"I have not forgotten, my lord," Donovan said softly. "Gabriel has had a vision, and I thought it important enough to disturb you. Forgive me."

Timaeus's interest stirred. Even so, he scowled and blew some smoke into Donovan's face for good measure. "You may speak. What has Gabriel seen?"

"Lucien is on his way back." Timaeus twitched, and Donovan fell silent for a heartbeat. "Gabriel wasn't sure of the timing, but after scrutinizing his vision, Aoife assured me it would be soon." Timaeus gathered his bulk to get to his feet, but Donovan abruptly held up a hand, and the dragon froze. "Lucien just entered the caves."

Timaeus's mood elevated instantly. It seemed he wouldn't have to leave his caves to find a new companion from the elven courts after all. "Bring him here now," he ordered Donovan. "Bring Gabriel and Celeste as well. Let's get Lucien's report over with so I may have some peace and quiet."

"Yes, my lord," Donovan said. The formality, which had served to appease Timaeus before, now grated on the dragon's nerves for the delay it caused.

Gabriel, Celeste, Davet, and Lucien appeared before the dragon. Lucien wore garb in the manner of the elves: a dark-green tunic and leggings under a thick black wool cloak. His hair was secured back by the silver circlet on his brow. The elf immediately went down on one knee. "Forgive my absence, my lord," he said. "I arrived at the outpost to discover my brother was in residence. He called on my honor to demand I pay a visit to my family, which has both lost and gained members since the time I went into your service. I was obliged to go with him and linger for a time to become reacquainted with my family."

"They had no right to make such demands of your time," Timaeus growled. "You belong to me. Perhaps I should remind that court the required etiquette for approaching a dragon's servant."

"Unfortunately, families don't tend to work that way, sir," Lucien said, a touch of amusement in his voice though he wore a blank expression. He bowed over his knee. "I am at your service once more, my lord."

"Dispense with formality then. You know I never cared for it." As Lucien rose, Timaeus bumped him with his snout. "Welcome back, my friend."

"It is good to be home," Lucien said with a smile. He stepped carefully onto the coins to get to Timaeus's side. Gripping one of the dragon's horns for balance, he faced the group that had waited patiently during this exchange.

Emma!

Emma was curled up on her bed reading, and the call made her jump up. The book tumbled to the floor. She rushed to the door and peered out. There was nobody in view. She put a hand to her temple and closed her eyes, listening hard both physically and mentally.

Emma! Davet's voice rang out in Emma's head. *Listen!* His thoughts were excited and frantic.

I can hear you. What is it? she thought back, alarmed by his intensity. *Is something wrong?*

Instead of a reply, she felt a sensation like a small child pulling at her hand, like when Irene or Gracia had wanted to show her something. She sat down on her bed and allowed Davet to tug her along into his mind.

She was suddenly looking up at Celeste and Gabriel from a low angle. Donovan was visible in the corner of her eye. Her vision shifted, and she looked up at Timaeus and Lucien. *Listen and watch,* Davet thought faintly. *The elf is back.*

Gabriel glanced sharply at them, but then she worked out how to listen through Davet's ears and focused on what he was hearing.

"Tiberius was dispatched to investigate what is happening to the Blessed," Lucien was saying. "They have been disappearing from Canada and the Northern U.S. cities, and the elves have taken notice."

"So, the elves are finally making their move," Timaeus commented. "When Gabriel came here and told us about the Company, I wondered if they would get involved."

"They are still divided on what to do about the Blessed, considering modern human society. Blessings aren't very beneficial for humans anymore. However, in the matter of the disappearances, they have agreed to take a hand. They are simply waiting for word from Tiberius."

"Good," Gabriel said over Davet's head. "Then we don't have to do anything." He looked down straight into Davet's eyes as he said this. "We'll simply keep watch and reunite Julia and this Tiberius later."

"Are you really okay with doing nothing?" Lucien asked. The elf observed Gabriel thoughtfully. "The Company won't go down quietly. There could—"

Gabriel jostled Davet's mind, and Emma lost the connection the unicorn had provided. She frantically tried to reach him and heard his confused thoughts, but she didn't know how to tap into his senses without his help.

She paced her room a few times, twisting a shirt in her hands and replaying the little bit she had heard. What had Lucien been about to say? She took a deep breath and sat down at the small, round table. As she expected, she didn't have to wait long before a knock sounded at the door. "Come in."

Gabriel strolled in and sat down in the chair across from her. He crossed his arms and stared at her. "Did you or Davet initiate that?"

"Davet," Emma said. "I don't know how to. Is that something I could do?" She could tell Gabriel was annoyed, but he was also still her teacher about these things. She hadn't exactly done anything wrong, and she refused to feel guilty.

"It depends." Gabriel gave her a dark look. "It's not something I ever learned formally. I was discouraged from sharing thoughts with non-humans." He grimaced. "From what I've gathered while experimenting, both individuals need to have telepathic abilities and be willing participants. I've only ever been able to do it successfully with Aoife. Celeste would be angry if she knew Davet had let you that far into his mind. She's never approved the connection you have with him."

"I'm sorry," Emma muttered. "I didn't mean it to happen like that, and I'm sure he doesn't understand it very well. He's just a baby."

Gabriel leaned his head back. "I take it you did mean for Davet to spy on us, just not in the manner that he chose to do it? It's likely he chose that method exactly because he's 'just a baby.'" Emma winced, and Gabriel smiled faintly. "Well, now you know. We don't need to do anything. Tip is going to be just fine."

"Lucien thought you would be worried about the Company," Emma said tentatively. She wasn't sure if that was what Lucien had been inferring.

Gabriel's face went blank. "That's none of your concern," he said, his voice brittle. "We aren't getting involved."

"You *are* worried," Emma said, unable to hide her surprise. Why would Gabriel care about such people? More than ever, she felt he wasn't telling her everything.

Gabriel got to his feet and turned away from her, clasping his hands behind his back. "It doesn't matter. I won't risk my friends and my new home to protect a home I chose to leave. The Company workers..." Emma couldn't see his face, but she could sense his conflicted thoughts. "They might not be there by choice but, for the most part, they could leave if they really wanted. I did; and those who wanted to followed me out." He was silent a moment, his shoulders hunched. "Enough of this. I just came to make sure you'd given up pursuing this."

"I have," Emma said softly. She got up as well and walked around the table. "Are you going to be okay, Gabriel? Are you sure?"

"Drop it," Gabriel snapped. "And make sure Julia understands our position. She can just wait."

Emma watched him go out, feeling more helpless than ever.

The dripping of water from the stalactites into the pool of hot water was one of the most soothing natural sounds Nemo had ever found. It was a truly pleasant sound in the early morning. After bathing, he put on some pants and sat with his feet in the hot water. He was groggy, and he just wanted to relax for a few minutes. To keep himself from falling asleep, he grabbed a washcloth and rubbed it over his damp hair. His chestnut-brown roots were beginning to show. He would have to dye his hair again soon.

There was a rustle behind him, and then a thump. Nemo looked around and saw Lian straightening up and dusting herself off. "Good morning," he said. "Did you need something before the rehearsal?" She hadn't come into his room as a bat again after he had found out her secret. He wasn't sure how he felt about that. It was somewhat of a relief. She didn't squeak and wake him up at odd times anymore, and he did prefer his privacy.

A smirk crossed Lian's lips, and she eyed him shamelessly, making Nemo acutely aware of his bare chest. His hand shot out for his shirt. He pulled it towards himself but then stopped. He would not be bashful in front of her.

"Just enjoying the view while I have human eyes," she said in her lilting accent. Nemo's face settled into a scowl that hopefully hid his reddening features.

"I was just kidding," Lian rushed to say. She scuffed her foot against the floor. "I actually have very bad eyesight, even in this form. You're just a blur."

That helped mollify Nemo, but he was still irritated. "I have to go help Timaeus prepare breakfast." He climbed to his feet and walked toward the exit.

"I want you to sing for me," Lian said in a rush when he passed her. Nemo blinked and stared at her. She wouldn't meet his eyes. "I have trouble sleeping. Living in the caves and changing into a bat so often has messed up my..." she frowned. "I don't know the phrase you use in English. Something about a clock. Listening to you sing before you slept

192

each night was helping me. I swear I couldn't see much at all when I was in your room. And I am sorry if that upset you."

Looking closer, Nemo could see the dark smudges around her eyes that attested to her words. He remembered that most mornings when he woke up, she had been hanging above his bed as a bat, sound asleep.

"Okay," he agreed. "I can sing for you some before I go help Timaeus. Do you want to do it in your room?"

The girl shifted uncomfortably. "No," she muttered and looked down. "I don't let people in my room," she added quickly when he gave her a questioning look. He frowned and opened his mouth. "I just don't," she said, cutting off his question. She scuffed her black boot against the ground. "Would you care if I sleep in your room while you're not there?" she asked softly before she changed into a bat and landed on his shoulder. "Like this."

Nemo shrugged, jostling her and making her cling to the fabric of his shirt. "I guess not," he said. "You've already slept in my room while I wasn't there quite a bit," he said and snorted. "I can't count how many times you were in there sleeping when I left in the morning."

The bat squeaked and rubbed her velvety head against Nemo's neck. He felt the telltale warmth creeping into his face again, so he set off to distract himself.

By the time he got to his room, Lian had migrated to the top of his head. He muttered under his breath over having just washed his hair but didn't fight it. The moment he walked into his cave, she squeaked and fluttered up to her favored spot above his bed. Nemo sighed and rubbed the back of his neck. He couldn't bring himself to deny her.

His stomach growled, recalling him to the present. Timaeus would be annoyed if he didn't get to the kitchen to help soon. Lian looked at him expectantly, her wings wrapped tightly around herself and her claws clinging to the stalactite.

Nemo closed his eyes and sang the first thing that came to mind. It was the Phantom's love song to Christine that he had been rehearsing several months before. He vaguely remembered that the members of the Company had come around the last time he rehearsed this. He frowned and tried to recall their faces. He couldn't. From the Music of the Night, he transitioned into another song from that play, his thoughts beginning to wander.

The song ended, and Nemo's voice faltered. He opened his eyes. Lian's wings wrapped snugly around herself, her only movement caused by her breathing. He smiled to himself and left the room.

The crystal cavern had become Julia's sanctuary as time flowed slowly on. None of the others came there, not even Emma after finding Julia there once and hurrying away. The telepath had been avoiding her. That suited Julia just fine. She hated the idea of anyone messing with her mind again.

She worked through her normal set of exercises. That took all her morning and left her famished. She'd skipped breakfast, not wanting to go to the dining room. It always seemed like everyone watched her when she ate there. She still didn't want to go, so she sat down and schemed how to steal food from the kitchen.

The slightest rustle warned her a split second before something large bowled her over from behind.

That was all the time Julia needed to brace herself for the fall. The griffin pinned her shoulders with its heavy paws and snapped its beak just inches from her head. Julia arched her back and got one hand under herself to heave them both up. A squawk of surprise rewarded Julia's efforts. She gained her feet and threw herself at the griffin.

They tumbled down, the griffin batting at her, the edges of its retracted claws scraping her a little. She grabbed fistfuls of its feathers, and it gripped her shoulder with its lethal beak. They stayed locked that way for several breathless moments, and then Julia burst into out laughing.

Amadis licked her shirt, its pointed black tongue appearing for just a moment before it straightened up and closed its beak with a clack. She reached up and stroked the griffin's neck. "It's good to see you."

"Likewise." The griffin settled back on its haunches. "Something is troubling you? You didn't hear my approach."

Julia rolled over and leaned against the griffin, stroking its fur. A low rumble issued from its chest. "I'm just trying to understand what happened. Why would elves enchant me into thinking Tip was my childhood friend?"

Tip's smile and kindness haunted her thoughts like a ghost, tainted by the false identity the elves had placed in her memories. Thinking of him caused a deep ache in her.

Amadis tilted its head to look at her. "They have their own machinations."

Julia covered her eyes. "I miss Tip still. I don't want to. He's not the person I thought he was. All those false memories." Her breath hitched, and she clenched her fists. "But I don't believe our time together at the Cove was a lie."

"Elves cannot lie," Amadis told her. "Half-elves, like the boy in your memory, can bend that rule, but I've never met one that could successfully deceive me. His actions suggest a concern for your well-being."

She mused that over and sprang up to pace the cavern. "I want to see him," she decided. "To get his side of it. I'm so sick of cooling my heels here. Where is he?"

"Patience," Amadis advised, crossing his front legs and resting his beak on them. Julia threw up her hands and broke into a jog to run laps again. The griffin watched, amusement curling in the corner of its beak.

After yet another day of hard exercise, Tip collapsed onto a couch beside Gail and Seth. The others were still at lessons, so the two were playing their game on the main television. Neil was sitting in a chair with a book. "I see how hard your lessons are," Tip grumbled.

Neil grinned and waved to him before returning his attention to the pages. A phone beeped from Seth's pocket, and he promptly paused the game. Both he and Gail pulled out their phones. Tip peered over Seth's shoulder at the app game they were playing. "Is that a multiplayer game?"

"Yeah," Seth said absently. "The House members formed a group about a year ago. Most of them have lost interest, but Gail and I still play."

"Wish I could play." Tip kicked his foot back against the couch. "I'm so sore I can barely move. I'd give anything to be able to play a game for a few hours in the evenings."

Seth shot him a sympathetic look. "It's hard when you're first settling in. You'll get more freedom later. Until then you're welcome to play with us." He gestured vaguely at the paused game.

"Are you free to come and go?" Tip asked, his voice curious. He glanced at the television, and his hands twitched with the genuine urge to pick up a controller.

Watch it, Tip. He needed to remember what he was here for. It was not to befriend these people.

"Within some boundaries," Seth said. "Normal ones. I'm only sixteen after all. I have a curfew, and I have to tell someone where I'm going." He snickered. "Going out is overrated. When I'm not out on a job, I just stay home and play games." He dropped his phone on the couch cushion and picked up a controller. "Want to play now?"

Tip considered his blistered hands. "Maybe not tonight."

Seth followed his gaze and grimaced. "I'll tell Michael we need a Healer to hang around for a while."

"Balthasar won't approve," Gail said quietly, staring at the floor.

Seth snorted. "Not everyone has Tsar's pain tolerance. I'll tell Michael having Tip loll around in pain has been bugging Adah." He pressed play. Game music and sound effects filled the room. "Hey, doesn't Tsar still have that game on his phone? He doesn't play anymore, maybe he could let Tip borrow it."

Gail gave Tip a wary, sideways look. "I suppose I could ask," she said softly and went out of the room. Seth switched the game to single player and continued to play.

A few minutes later, she came back with a phone in her hand. "He said you can borrow it in the evenings. It's disabled for anything but games. No calls or texts."

"That's plenty. Thank you." He gave Gail a blinding smile. She smiled shyly back. Tip swallowed his guilt and started the game.

196

"Are you sure you're okay? If you screw your face up any tighter you might— Ow!" Avery winced and rubbed his arm where Emma had hit him. "What was that for?"

"You're not helping!" Emma covered her face and groaned. "I don't get it. I did it with Aoife, and then with Julia. Why can't I get past your barriers?"

"I don't think you really want to," Gabriel said. He sat a few feet off, reading a book.

Emma glared. He calmly turned a page without looking up. "You are a terrible teacher," she muttered and closed her eyes to try again. Avery's mental barriers weren't as strong and alien feeling as Aoife's defenses, but her life didn't depend on getting past them. She couldn't manage it. Shouting in annoyance, she threw up her hands. "I can't do it, Gabriel!"

Gabriel closed his book with a snap. "And you'll never be able to if you're holding yourself back out of fear of what you might find out in the person's mind."

"I'm not scared of that," Emma protested. *Am I?* She thought hard about the efforts she'd made for the last several mornings since they resumed lessons. She hadn't been holding back!

Gabriel gave her an exasperated look. "Your subconscious concerns have been leaking through your mental barrier since we started this. You're worried what you might see in Avery's mind."

Avery looked between them, his feathery eyebrows furrowed. "I don't get it. Why should she be worried about that?"

Emma turned lightly pink and looked away. Gabriel heaved a long-suffering sigh. "I'm not going to lay it out for you. Figure it out. In the meantime..." Gabriel leaned over and whispered in Emma's ear. "Once you get this, you can share almost anything mentally with a person. It doesn't even have to be words. Think about all that Davet has shared with you about his emotions."

A grin spread over her face. To be able to communicate that effectively without the struggle of finding the right words...Emma clapped her hands gleefully and bounced on the bench. "You've tested that?"

"A lot," Gabriel said gravely. "That should give you some incentive to get into his mind. Just imagine the possibilities." Emma's grin widened even more.

Avery scooted away. "I'm not sure I'm comfortable with this anymore. I'm going to take my leave now."

"Don't you dare!" Emma grabbed his arm. "I want at least one more go!" Avery grimaced but sat still while Emma probed his mental defenses once more. She battered at them and frowned. "I know I can do this," she muttered, kicking her heel back. She sucked in a sharp breath and held her breath while she struggled.

"Um...Gabriel..." Avery said a few moments later. Emma was turning faintly blue, her face screwed up in concentration.

Gabriel watched her intently. "She's trying to replicate what allowed her to succeed with Aoife. Give her a few more seconds."

Avery shrugged to hide his worry and stared at Emma. He twitched as he felt her presence brush his mind. He hadn't felt anything remotely like that for years, and a smile plucked at his mouth. "Well done!" he

198

exclaimed and grabbed her into a hug.

"Hang on," Emma breathed, putting a hand on his chest. With their minds open to each other this way, she could clearly sense Avery's feelings. An answering joy blossomed in her, so deep that she couldn't have formed words to express it even if she'd tried. She shared it with him through their new connection.

Avery went very still and listened. His freckles stood out starkly as his face turned pink, and a huge grin spread over his face. "I see. Thank you for sharing that." He leaned forward and shyly brushed her lips with his. When he looked up, he caught sight of Gabriel crossing the floor toward the tunnel. He chuckled. "Guess that's the end of the lesson. Want to go do something fun before rehearsal?"

"Sure." Emma stood up and stretched her arms over her head. She was aware of Avery watching her, so she stretched just a bit longer. "Davet is running around," she commented, hearing the young unicorn's thoughts flickering on the edges of her awareness. "Let's go play with him. He's always fun."

Emma sent out a call to Davet that she wanted to play, and he headed in their direction. They met in a tunnel a few minutes later. His eyes flicked to Emma and Avery's clasped hands, and he tossed his head. *Don't be like the pixies,* he thought scornfully.

Emma blinked. *Do the pixies hold hands a lot?* A few pixies clung to his mane, watching her and Avery with bright eyes. Davet usually had at least one or two with him. They thought him amusing.

Too often! Davet exclaimed and stamped his hoof against the stone.

"What are you two talking about?" Avery asked with a slight smile. Due to his connection with Emma's mind, he knew she and Davet were speaking but couldn't hear their thoughts. Emma frowned, wondering if she could manage to create a three-way mental conversation. Like a conference call.

Pay attention to me! Davet demanded, sensing Emma's focus had wavered off him. *We should go play outside! Mama said that I could if I have someone with me!*

Alright. Emma tried to remember where they were just then. Somewhere in Washington. Gabriel told her they were moving down the west coast for a few weeks. "Let's go look for newts and salamanders," she said out loud for Avery's benefit. "I've never seen one."

Davet's interest was caught, and he bombarded her with questions about what these were. She showed him an image of one, and he leaped. *Looks like a baby wingless dragon! I want one!*

We're not going to keep any! Emma thought sternly in reply, but Davet dashed ahead of them without acknowledging her reprimand. Emma shook her head, reflecting on how similar baby unicorns and human children could be.

She glanced at Avery. He watched her with a smile that made her feel like she walked on air. Now that Davet wasn't watching, she took his hand again. "Is this okay? I guess it's not that much fun for you."

"Nah, it sounds like great fun," he said cheerfully. "I love exploring forests. And it'll be even better to do it with you."

Emma looked away, feeling her face heating up. Avery bumped his shoulder into hers and squeezed her hand as they came out into the sunshine.

Davet continued to frisk ahead of them, and a cool, damp breeze blew between the trees they strolled through.

"We're near Seattle, aren't we?" Emma asked, shuffling some damp leaves under her boot.

Avery nodded, peering up at the trees with a wistful expression. "It's so cloudy and cool," he said and turned his face into the mist. "It reminds me of home."

Emma frowned, remembering Avery's story about their kidnapping. She looked up at the trees as well. "Would you like to fly?"

Avery's expression brightened. "You want to?" he asked eagerly and put an arm around her waist. "I would love to!"

"Hang on." Emma stepped out of his hold, chuckling. "Davet!" The unicorn skidded around a tree and cantered up to them, throwing his head and snorting in equine excitement.

I haven't found any wingless dragons yet. I'll keep looking!

Emma smiled and rubbed Davet's mane fondly. "You'll find some. Avery and I are going to fly up to the trees and look for the sky. You never know, some of the salamanders may have grown wing—"

Avery clapped a hand over her mouth. Emma stiffened in alarm, but when she twisted around to look at him, his eyes glittered with excitement. "I have a better idea," he said and put an arm around her waist. "Davet, want to play? I'll give you to the count of ten, and then we're going to fly after you."

Davet's eyes went wide. He spun on his back hooves and sped away, silent on the forest mulch.

Avery counted aloud. At eight, he glanced over at her. "Good to go?"

"Yeah," Emma said tremulously, remembering their last flight. "Just don't go too fast."

"Deal," Avery said with a playful grin. "But it'll be hard to catch Davet that way." He drove his wings down. The force of it lifted them off the ground, and they sped through the forest after the unicorn.

Rather than look at the ground falling away from her, Emma closed her eyes and turned her face into the mist to enjoy the feeling of weightlessness and Avery's steady arms supporting her. She let out a whoop as he flew them higher and saw Davet a good way ahead, his dark fur dappled with the sunlight as he sped onward.

They never did catch him, but his delight flowed through their mental link.

When they came to a meadow, Avery set her down. Davet frisked through the grass and cantered up to them. "Your turn," Avery said and held his arms open. Davet approached him tentatively. He carefully picked the unicorn up and took off, flying them high. Emma craned her neck back to watch and grinned at the joy she felt: both Davet's and her own.

"The pancakes are burning," Timaeus snarled. Nemo started and hastily took the pan off the fire. Smoke curled up from the blackened pancake. He made a face and scraped it into the trash before pouring more batter into the pan.

"What's on your mind, boy? You've been distant for a week now." Timaeus peered at him.

"Lian has gone into his room in her human form each morning this week," Donovan said from where he leaned casually against the wall on the far side of the kitchen. He kept well out of Timaeus's way, but he often hung around in the kitchen to make sure nothing caught fire. There was no fire alarm in this kitchen.

Nemo reddened while Timaeus chuckled. "Oh, so that's it. Decided on a mate, boy? Good. You're of age."

"Not like that," Nemo mumbled and bent over the pan, not wanting to look at either of the other men.

"Yes, it is," Donovan said blithely. "Or it will be, if Lian has any say about it. She has a voice attraction, and you're the best singer she's ever met. It comes from the amount of time she's spent as a bat. Even in her human form now, she can hear better than a normal human."

Nemo shook his head and didn't reply. He wasn't comfortable having this conversation. He could sense Timaeus and Donovan's knowing looks, and he stared resolutely at the growing pile of pancakes.

Lian's presence when he woke up each morning was causing feelings to stir in Nemo, but he didn't know her any better than before. She still barely talked to him.

As soon as the batter was gone, he fled from the kitchen with a plate of food. Lucien looked up at him as he went to sit down. Their eyes met, and the elf smirked. Lucien's hearing allowed him to overhear any conversation in the kitchen. Nemo fled the dining room altogether and was very close to his room before he thought better of it.

Lian would still be in there asleep. He swallowed and turned to go back to the dining room. Avery and Emma were walking the other way, carrying plates of food and holding hands.

Emma's face lit up when she spotted Nemo. "Hey, little brother!" she called and hugged him. "I haven't seen you in days, not since you've started your secret rehearsal. Let's have breakfast together!"

"Okay," Nemo agreed and took a resolute step in the direction he faced. "Can we eat in your room? I don't want to eat in my cave."

"Why not?" Emma asked. "The food will be cold before we get to my room. Your cave is right here." She strolled forward before he could protest and opened his door. Her eyebrows flew up, and the expression that came over her face made Nemo's heart sink. "Well, well. I see you've gotten *really* close to the acrobats."

Lian lay stretched out on his bed, sleeping peacefully. Nemo bit his tongue and shook his head. "Not like that," he muttered, wondering how many times he had said that now.

"Right," Emma said quietly and went into the room. A table and chairs appeared in a cluster at one end of the cave, as often happened when someone went to eat in their room. Emma pulled one chair out and sat down.

Avery grinned at Nemo as they followed Emma over. "I don't want to hear it. You two have been walking around all dewy-eyed for days now."

"I haven't fallen asleep on Avery's bed," Emma retorted lightly. Lian stirred, and Emma lowered her voice. "I'm not saying anything against it. I'm just surprised."

"It's really not like that!" Nemo hissed and plopped down across from her. "She's an insomniac, and my singing helps her sleep."

Emma chuckled, and Nemo flushed. "Anyways," he said, eager to change the subject. "The acrobats and I are premiering the new act soon. Will you help me bleach my hair again, Em?"

"Sure, sure," Emma agreed. "Although, you really should let your hair go natural. It looks much better that way."

Nemo touched his hair. "Maybe sometime soon. I want to have white hair for the premiere. It looks good against the dark clothing I'll be wearing for it. After that, I'll let my roots grow out."

"What color is your hair naturally?" The soft voice made Nemo jump. Lian blinked at them sleepily, holding Nemo's blanket just under her chin while she yawned. She sat up and rubbed her eyes.

"Sorry. We didn't mean to wake you," Nemo said, shooting Emma a look that dared her to say anything. She settled back in her chair, her face smug.

Lian rose lithely from the bed, glided over, and squinted at the top of Nemo's head. "I see what you mean. You would need to wear more colorful clothing with hair that color. White hair looks nice against the black."

A fourth chair materialized and Lian sank down into it. She put her head on his shoulder and poked at the plate of food that appeared on the table. Nemo's gaze remained on his plate the remainder of the meal. He couldn't help the happiness he felt over this position, but he didn't want to see the smug look he figured Emma must be wearing. She and Avery excused themselves only a few minutes later.

Lian only ate a little bit before she yawned and went back to Nemo's bed. "Sing for me again," she said insistently. "I want to sleep a little more before rehearsal." Nemo wouldn't look at her, but he obliged, singing as well as he could with his raw throat.

Tip and Neil sat in the empty sitting room, watching a fire flickering in the hearth. Neil shook his head, pressed his hand to the wall, and closed his eyes. His face scrunched up in concentration.

He sighed and dropped his hand. "Seth's lessons are hard. Even walking through the walls, I can't find a path to the center of the house without running into *someone* and being seen."

"Maybe if you tried in the early morning, when everyone is still sleepy?" Tip suggested.

Neil shook his head. "Seth said I have to be able to find a path from the very center of the house without being seen once. He's going to test me in a week."

Tip fidgeted with Balthasar's cell phone while Neil picked up a book. "What room is the center of the house?" Tip asked. "The library?"

Neil glanced at the grandfather clock that ticked audibly from by the door. "Not sure. I haven't gone to the library much," he admitted and flipped through the pages of the book. "The books in there are really dry. Rebecca said she would bring me some novels in a few days." He looked again at the clock.

"You that nervous about the test?" Tip asked teasingly and gave him a pointed look. Neil was acting way too nervous. "Next week is still a way off. You'll have time to figure it out."

Neil visibly relaxed and gave Tip a sheepish look. "No, it's just weird to be using my ability as much as I have been. I used it some when I was little but..." His voice dropped to a whisper. "It scared my parents really badly. Often when I was a baby, they wouldn't be able to find me, and they'd turn the house inside out before they found me behind a closed door. One night, I went into the neighbor's house to play with my friend. They thought I had been kidnapped. The police were involved. Nobody could explain how I'd gotten out of our house or into the neighbors' house. I can't remember how it was resolved exactly, but at least nobody was arrested. It scared me, though. I stopped using my Blessing much after that." He wiped his eyes.

Tip closed his eyes, took a deep breath, and exhaled a spell. His hearing sharpened. Irene and Gracia would be going into the Keeper's room with Rebecca right about now. He could hear their voices, soft as whispers through the walls. He glanced at the clock, turned the phone on and touched the screen a few times. The clock struck five. One stroke. The voices he could hear grew louder in apparent alarm. Two. Neil and Tip stood up casually. Three. A boom made Tip flinch and his ears ring. Four. Neil set his face and put one hand on the wall and grabbed Tip's hand with the other. Five. They strolled effortlessly through that wall and several more, navigating through the house. Then they were out in the open.

"You pass your test," Tip said breathlessly and began typing furiously. He raced down the porch stairs and looked back at the house to get the address, his thumb flying over the touch screen.

He got halfway through the message before, out of the corner of his eye, he saw Neil gesture frantically at him and melt back through the door. Horrified, Tip whirled around right before Balthasar knocked him to the ground. The phone flew out of his hand. He cursed and scrambled up to grab at it.

Before he could reach it, Balthasar grabbed his shirt and dragged him back up. The telepath, Virgil, was just running into the yard. He spotted the phone and dove for it.

Tip didn't have time to craft a careful hex. He shouted the first spell that came to mind, and the phone caught fire just as the telepath grabbed it. Virgil cursed and dropped it, then stomped on it to put it out before the grass caught fire. He succeeded in extinguishing the fire, but the phone was battered to pieces in the process.

Tip breathed a sigh of relief. They wouldn't get anything from that. His relief was short lived when he saw the shocked looks Balthasar and Virgil were giving him. The magic in the air was palpable. Virgil whistled, and Tip's heart sank. This would be a major setback. Then the grizzled old man grinned, and Tip blinked.

"Well, we have more on our hands than we bargained for with you," Virgil said. "Take him inside, Balthasar. This will take some thought."

19

The night of Nemo's premiere blew in with a rainstorm. Gabriel gave Emma a new job of surveying the thoughts of the audience and posting some of the accolades she heard on the show's website. To that end, wearing a new outfit Aoife had made for her the night before, she went out by the bonfire and joined the crowd. The fire burned brightly, hissing and sparkling blue and purple when the raindrops hit it. She walked through the tunnel into the amphitheater, scanning the spectators' thoughts while they went. It reminded her of the wonder she'd felt when she walked through this tunnel for the first time.

Two minds stood out to her, familiar as well-known voices in the crowd. Emma frowned and focused on those minds even closer. Why would there be anyone she knew here?

She realized what she was hearing and stopped dead. The person behind her bumped her, and muttering rose as the flow of people streamed around her. Once everyone walked past her and the voices were receding, Emma took a deep breath and straightened as she walked into the cavern. The stands were already filling up. She listened again and knew they hadn't noticed her. She couldn't ignore them though. Why would Gabriel do something like this?

Emma could think of a few reasons and each sent a thrill of nerves through her. She swallowed against her rising nerves and approached the couple. Whatever Gabriel's intentions, she would not be a coward.

"Mom! Dad! I didn't know you would be here! You didn't say anything the last time we talked!"

Elizabeth beamed. "Mr. Hightower invited us to the show as a surprise for Nemo's eighteenth birthday." They stood up and embraced her. Emma looked up into her father's face in surprise. His features were more lined than she remembered, his hair more frosted with gray.

"Nemo will be thrilled. He's been working really hard on a new performance." They made room for her on the bench in between them, and Emma sat. It had only been a few weeks since she had talked to them, but it felt so weird to see them again. They seemed out of place here, reminding her of the mundane right after the circus's magic entranced her anew.

"How have you two been?" she asked, struggling to match up the incongruous parts of this situation.

"Oh, you know," Elizabeth said airily, waving her hand. "Just day-to-day life. Working. Your father goes fishing almost every weekend now, and I've taken up painting again. It's been really quiet."

Since you left. The words hung unspoken in the air. Emma rubbed her arm and looked down into the arena. The performers were standing silhouetted, as they usually did before a show. More people were filing in, and their excited thoughts distracted her.

"What about you?" Richard asked and put a hand on Emma's shoulder. Her mind had wandered, and the sudden contact startled her. Her father raised an eyebrow. "Learning what you wanted to?"

"I am!" Emma said with a grin. "I've learned a lot. Gabriel is...well, he tries his best to teach me how to run a show. He's never taught anyone the skills he has before, so we've been learning from each other. I've made lots of friends, too. The people here are really interesting."

Her father nodded, his expression satisfied.

"Friends, eh?" Elizabeth asked with a suggestive grin. "Do tell. I want to hear more about this Avery fellow you keep mentioning!"

Emma turned pink and stood up hastily. "I have to go!" she said in a rush, and they stared at her. "I mean...I'll catch up with you after the show. I have to work." She spun around and fled along the benches to the far side of the stands. She could hear their thoughts following her, and she felt like a coward, but she needed to get away from that line of questioning.

She settled onto a seat near the back and scribbled down the audience's thoughts as she heard them, her eyes closed so she could listen better. It was a challenge to discern individual thoughts in the cacophony after the lengthy period of silence since the previous show.

Celeste's act started, and the amount of wonder that rippled through the audience made Emma peek. Davet gamboled around the arena, having a grand time. She had missed Gabriel's introduction, so she wasn't sure what the act was supposed to be, and Davet didn't know either. The joy he radiated was infectious, though, and entranced the audience. Celeste stood in the center of the arena, majestic and regal, her head held high and her horn glinting in the golden light. Emma could sense she was a little disgruntled to not be the center of attention, but she accepted it, and when Davet ran up to her side, she lowered her head and nuzzled him.

The light faded out, and they vanished into the gloom. Emma squeezed her eyes closed and scribbled down a handful of thoughts she quickly caught. Gabriel would notice if she didn't write any thoughts about Davet.

Watching the show through the minds and thoughts of those in the audience allowed Emma to see it anew, and she enjoyed it as the acts proceeded.

After Aoife's performance, the colored lights abruptly went out, leaving the cavern in darkness for several breathless moments.

A flicker of light attracted attention upward. A shower of sparks rained down out of the darkness, sputtering out after only a few moments but in that time glittering off the crystals on the acrobats' costumes.

Their laughter mixed with a merry flute tune as they sprang from one trapeze to another, much as they had in the first show Emma had seen. The theater lightened enough just to illuminate them, and she realized Timaeus was among them.

He leapt from one trapeze and caught Arielle's hand, her Blessing making him weightless so that she could easily support his bulk. The crowd inhaled in wonder as he swung around under her, flipping and twisting. The girl only grinned and hefted him up higher. Then she released him, and he flipped over to a trapeze swinging by.

Nemo appeared on a suspended platform, dressed in a tunic so deep blue that it was nearly black, contrasting sharply with his white hair and tan leather leggings. He sang as the light flared around him. Emma tried to catch the words, but they flitted just out of reach, beautiful but incomprehensible. He leapt from one swinging rope to another, often twisting and flipping in midair, displaying an agility and grace that made Emma grin.

His song continued in staccato bursts as he moved. The youngest acrobat, Adele, used her Blessing to flicker in and out of sight like a firefly, occasionally causing others to disappear as well, all in time with Nemo's song. Emma watched with fresh eyes through the minds of the spectators, sensing their breathless amazement, and remembered the magic of the show.

A drum pounded once. Timaeus's fingers skimmed the trapeze bar before it swung away, and he plummeted.

A red spotlight illuminated Martin standing on a platform high above, beating on the drum. His black feathers gleamed with a bloody tint enhanced by the crimson spirals painted on his arms, shoulders, and bare chest.

Smoke flickering with colored lights coiled around Timaeus as he fell; it expanded when he transformed.

The great black dragon uttered a thunderous roar and fanned his wings open just enough to land. Even so, a gust of wind struck the stands, and the audience cowered under Timaeus's glare. The drumming increased in tempo, and sparks dripped off the dragon's jaw as he let out a throbbing snarl. The terror that Emma could hear increased, and even she gripped the edge of the stone bench.

The high warbling of the flute returned, and a pale blue light showed Nemo standing on another platform on the opposite side of the theater, the trio of acrobats clustered around him.

He glared across at Martin. The drumming and the fluting picked up tempo. Below, Timaeus had his long neck craned upward, his head weaving like a snake while he watched them. Nemo pointed, and the three young women lunged forward, grabbing ropes and swinging toward Martin.

The music cut off, and Timaeus's head lurched down. Nemo grabbed a rope as well and slid down to the ground where he faced the dragon and boldly resumed the flute playing.

Timaeus glowered down at him and let loose a torrent of black tinged flame. The fire parted harmlessly and swirled around Nemo, who continued to play, unfazed.

A trill in the music caused Timaeus to twitch. Another, and he twisted his head in toward his chest. With each high note on the flute, Timaeus shrunk in on himself.

Meanwhile, the acrobats struggled with Martin high above. They shoved him off his pedestal, and then he flew in circles, still drumming, while they swung on ropes after him. Finally, Lian succeeded in grabbing the drum from him and tossed it down. It smashed with a clatter.

Smoke writhed around Timaeus once more, and when it cleared, he stood before the audience in his human form. He grinned toothily at Nemo, and they clasped one another's forearms.

The acrobats whooped and cheered and slid down to the ground, embracing Nemo and Timaeus and chattering like birds. Nemo put an arm around Lian and kissed her right before the lights went out.

Cheering and applause erupted, many spectators leaping to their feet and peering into the darkness for any sign of the performers.

Timaeus, Nemo, and the acrobats linked hands and bowed in unison. The other performers appeared around them, and all of them bowed once more before darkness fell. The applause thundered for several minutes.

Emma remained in her seat, grinning. After that kiss, their mother wouldn't be interrogating her alone. She listened for her parents' thoughts and heard their amazement over Nemo's act.

Emma waited until most of the audience filed ponderously out and then hurried down to Gabriel with her notebook. He accepted it and quickly skimmed the pages. "Very good," he praised and looked up just as her parents approached.

Emma's face grew hot. Her father's thoughts broadcasted his dislike of Gabriel. Not many of the spectators remained, so his resentment was particularly loud in the near-silence.

"Nemo is in his room, celebrating with the acrobats," Gabriel said calmly as if he couldn't hear her father's grumbling thoughts. "We'll go over your work tomorrow. Take the evening off to spend with your family. I'll tell Donovan they may stay for a few hours." He bowed gracefully to her parents. As he straightened, his eyes drifted over Emma's shoulder. A spark of amusement lit his face before he walked away.

Emma looked around and saw Avery approaching. *Oh no.* With her parents watching, she resisted the urge to make a warning face at Avery and instead forced herself to smile.

"What an amazing show!" Elizabeth gushed. "And those effects! The unicorns were one thing, although I am mighty curious how horses could be trained so well. But that dragon was something else!"

"I know," Emma said, a smile plucking at her lips. "Tim is great at that."

Her parents noticed Avery. Emma took a deep breath. "Mom. Dad. This is Avery. A friend of mine." She stressed the word friend slightly. "Avery, these are my parents."

They regarded Avery curiously, and he smiled shyly. "Nice to meet you."

"So, this is Avery. Are your wings real? They look like that man's from the show," Elizabeth reached out as if to touch his wing and then hesitated. "May I?"

"They're real. Martin is my brother." Avery extended one wing so

212

that it met her hand. His feathers ruffled up slightly, betraying his nervousness more than his expression did.

Richard stepped forward and offered a hand. "It's good to meet you as well, Avery. I see what my daughter meant about the interesting people here."

Avery grinned. "She's quite interesting herself, sir," he said and shot Emma a mischievous look that didn't escape her parents.

"Oh?" Elizabeth asked, with a playful look of her own. "Tell me more about how you find my daughter interesting. I'd love to hear your opinion of her."

"Mom!" Emma gasped. Avery opened his mouth, and Emma prodded him in the chest. "Not another word, you," she growled.

Her parents chuckled but fell into a hushed silence when Avery caught Emma up in a tight, squeezing hug. "You're so cute, Emma," he whispered to her. "Have a fun evening." He released her and grinned at her parents. "Again, I'm so glad to meet you. I hope to see you again soon." He bowed elegantly and marched off, leaving them all staring after him.

"Well then," Elizabeth said to break the silence. "You weren't kidding about making friends. And here I thought I might have to work some magic on a man for you."

"Leave the girl alone, Elizabeth," her father said. Emma could see a tenseness to the set of his shoulders, but he seemed to be taking this in stride.

"Thanks, Dad," Emma said. Her mother snorted. "Want me to show you around?"

"I'd rather go see Nemo," her mother said.

"Okay." Emma led them out of the cavern. There was a seamless shift that she could barely feel, and when she turned a corner, they were in the corridor leading to Nemo's room. She knocked on his door. "Nemo, we have visitors."

Nemo opened the door, and his eyes widened. He gaped like a fish as their mother pushed past Emma to hug him. "Oh, my baby," she breathed and squeezed him. Their father came up beside Emma, and she quietly closed the door behind them.

"Oh my." Elizabeth released Nemo and looked around the room. "Your room *is* a cave. I thought you were kidding when you told me that on the phone." She fixed her son with a stern look. "And yet it's still cleaner than you kept your room at home."

Nemo snorted. "I cleaned it for company." He nodded to the acrobats as the three women got gracefully to their feet. He introduced two of them but then hesitated. "So, you saw the show, huh?" he asked self-consciously.

"Oh yeah!" Emma broke into the conversation. "Why did you keep that from me, Nemo? Last I heard it 'wasn't like that.'" She grinned as she quoted Nemo's often repeated line about himself and Lian.

"Didn't mean to." Nemo rubbed his neck. "It just sort of…happened. While I was working with them on the performance."

The eldest acrobat gave a tinkling laugh and took Nemo's hand. He beamed at her. "This is Lian," he said to their parents.

"It is a pleasure to meet you," Lian said in her soft, breathy voice. She smiled at them all and then focused on Elizabeth. "You're so lovely!" she exclaimed and ran a hand over her own shoulder-length black hair. "Could you teach me how to do my hair that way? I keep mine short just because it's easier. I'd love to grow it out!"

Elizabeth stared at her in surprise. "She's adorable," she said and looked at Nemo. "If you don't keep her, I'm going to adopt her." She flashed a grin at Lian. "I would be delighted to teach you, dear."

Nemo turned cherry red up to his bleached hairline and covered his face with one hand, muttering under his breath.

Richard noticed the card game spread out on the floor and looked it over. "Poker, huh?" he asked Nemo.

"What? Oh. Yeah." Nemo looked down at the cards, obviously glad for the distraction. "The girls were teaching me how to play." He glanced at their blank expressions. "They're amazing at it. I can't keep my face straight enough."

"I could help you learn," Richard commented. "If you want."

Nemo stared at him, and their gazes locked. Richard looked away first.

"I would like that," Nemo said. He got the deck and dealt Richard

214

in before settling on the floor next to him. The acrobats sat down across from them. Lian stayed standing by Elizabeth, and after a moment Arielle folded Lian's cards back into the deck.

Elizabeth turned to Emma. "What about your room? Is it a cave as well?"

"It's not," Emma said with a grin. "I'll show you, if you want." That would give Nemo some time alone with their dad.

Elizabeth nodded and followed Emma out, Lian staying close to her side. The little acrobat waved to Nemo before the door closed and then skipped to catch up. Elizabeth chuckled and put an arm around the girl's shoulders. "Oh, I like you. Welcome to the family, Lian."

Lian beamed.

When they entered Emma's cabin-style room, Elizabeth gasped. "But this is lovely! How—" she glanced at Emma. "Trade secret, right?" Emma nodded. "You're so closed-lipped about all this stuff!" her mother protested. She went over to the mirror and beckoned Lian over. "Here, I'll fix your hair."

"So how is everything going at home?" Emma asked, sitting down on her bed. "I mean for real. Dad looks so tired."

"He's just gotten very stressed at work," Elizabeth reassured her. "He's fine. We're taking a long vacation soon."

"That's good," Emma said. "What about Gracia and Irene? How are they doing? I felt bad leaving them like that. I hope their mom found them a babysitter that didn't cost too much."

Her mother gave her a blank look. "Who?" she asked, her fingers deftly braiding Lian's hair.

"Gracia and Irene?" Emma didn't see any recognition in her mother's face and pressed on. "The little girls that lived next door? Their mother was single and worked multiple jobs, so I watched them in the afternoon after school?"

Elizabeth's face remained puzzled. "There are no children next door. There was a single woman. Her husband left...oh, three or four years ago now. She worked a few jobs trying to keep the house, but a few months ago she decided to live within her means and moved."

Emma stared at her in rising fear.

The acrobats wandered away after a few hands of poker, but Nemo and his father continued to play. Richard did his best to tutor Nemo on the finer points of the game. Nemo grew increasingly frustrated, and his attempts at a poker face failed miserably.

Richard dealt them new hands. Nemo huffed and threw his cards down. "I give up!" he said and fell back onto the floor. "I can't seem to get the cards I need!"

"And you never will if you quit." Richard set his own cards down and looked around the cave. "This is certainly not what I expected to see."

Nemo crossed his arms and glowered, irritated by the criticism. "What did you expect to see? It's not like you've gone to any show of mine since I was little."

Richard sighed and rubbed his face. "I know, I know. But I…we went to that show you were in. At the school. Even though you left, we still went. Your teacher told us you are a better actor than the kid who ended up with the part. I thought you'd be acting here. The show was quite impressive, don't get me wrong. Just not what I was expecting."

Nemo leaned forward on his knees. "I have been acting a tiny bit," he said. "This show doesn't really lend itself to it. Gabriel, the ringmaster, does most of the talking. We don't have the sound equipment that would allow much dialogue to be heard throughout the cavern. Gabriel can project his voice really well."

"I see," Richard said and fidgeted, rubbing his hands together. "So, you're still interested in acting? Maybe, when you're done learning what you can here, you can still move on."

Throughout the game, Richard had shot puzzled, hesitant sideways glances at Nemo. Now he seemed to reach a decision and stood up to dig through Elizabeth's purse. He pulled a worn paperback out and turned it over in his hands. "I have a gift for you. I wanted to…Well." He swallowed and tried again. "I've been doing a lot of thinking since you left. I know I wasn't there for you enough and I…I wanted to tell you why I named you Nemo."

Skepticism twisted Nemo's expression. "You picked my name?"

"I did." Richard stared fixedly down at the book. "Elizabeth named Emma after a character from her favorite book. She told me that I could name you after someone I admired." He smiled thinly. "I'm not much of a reader, but in school I read this book that I really loved. My favorite character in it was Captain Nemo. He was brave and clever. Like you've grown up to be."

Taking a deep breath, Richard wrenched his eyes up to look at his son. "I've never been able to relate to you, Nemo. When you chose to rehearse for a play instead of practice a sport, or didn't want to go out fishing, I didn't understand... But that's okay. I realize now we don't need to have those things in common. I'm still proud of you."

Richard took a card out of his back pocket, slipped it into the book, and handed the paperback to Nemo. "This is my copy of that book from school. I want you to have it now."

Nemo reached out and took it. Then he stepped closer and wrapped an arm around his father's shoulders. Richard stiffened and then relaxed and hugged Nemo back.

When the door burst open, Richard stepped back quickly, but Nemo didn't begrudge him that. *One step at a time.*

Emma rushed into the room. "Dad!" She darted up to him as Elizabeth and Lian came in, both looking perplexed. "Do you remember the little girls next door? Gracia and Irene?"

"Who?" Richard asked, mystified. He looked at his wife for help, but she only shrugged.

The stricken look that crossed Emma's face made Nemo worry. "G-Gracia and...Irene. How can...you not..." she trailed off, looking between their parents. Elizabeth looked concerned.

"What's wrong?" Richard asked and cast another look at his wife. She shrugged again and shook her head.

Emma bit her lip. "Nothing," she said and seemed to be struggling to find words, a crease between her eyes. "I was just...confused by something. You know." They didn't look reassured, so she smiled. "Forget about it. I don't want to worry you." Her parents again exchanged looks. "Really! It's not a big deal!"

"Okay," their mother said hesitantly. "If you say so. I'll let you know if I hear anything about those girls. Maybe you were thinking of some girls that live a few doors down." She didn't sound like she believed her own words. "So! Nemo. Tell us more about your life here!"

Lian melted away a short while later, but their parents stayed for another few hours.

Elizabeth prodded them for details about the show and the performers. She grinned when Emma told her about Davet's antics.

While Emma spoke, Nemo opened the book and looked at the card. It was thick, black card paper, with two gold towers topped with angels and gold lettering. *"Ark Light Company, CEO Dante Hightower"*. An address was listed underneath this heading. Coldness flooded into Nemo's chest, and he snapped the book closed before anyone else saw it.

"He seems like a lot of fun," Elizabeth said before she covered a wide yawn. "Oh my, I'm quite tired," she said in surprise. "I'm sure you must be as well after that show. I see Lian has disappeared." She climbed to her feet. "We'll take our leave." She hugged both her children and then put a hand on Richard's arm. "Have a good night, you two. Stay in touch."

Emma started to get up, intending to show them out, but her mother shook her head. "Oh. Don't worry about us. We'll find our own way out. We have a keen sense of direction." She waved, and they went out. Emma let them go, confident Donovan would handle getting them out.

The moment the door closed, Emma rounded on Nemo. "Neither of them remembered Gracia or Irene. From what mom said, I don't think Gracia and Irene's mom remembers them either. They must've been taken by the Company, Nemo! They must be Blessed!"

"We...don't know that," Nemo muttered. Emma gave him a sharp look, and he sighed. "It was months ago, Emma. Even if you're right...what can we do? Their mother has moved on and...we can't do anything about it."

Emma covered her face and groaned. "Their mother was so dedicated to supporting them and keeping them together as a family," she whispered. "To think she's out there and doesn't even remember them now. This is awful, Nemo."

"Yeah." Nemo crossed his arms. The business card screamed at him from within the book. He would do anything to throw it away and forget he ever saw that address. There was no way he was ever going to tell Emma he knew where Gracia and Irene might be. Gabriel was right, and he didn't want her to run off on a rescue mission and get herself captured by these people.

Emma couldn't sleep that night. She wandered the tunnels long after everyone went to bed. She knew the routes well now, having built a mental map of the caves over the last several months.

Guilt over leaving home ate at her. She'd abandoned those girls. Images of their smiling faces appeared in her mind no matter how hard she tried to banish them.

She barely knew she was heading toward Gabriel's room before she found herself outside his door. What was she going to do? She couldn't force him to tell her anything. Unless…she could break through his mental barriers and find the information herself.

The idea left her breathless. What other way was there, though? She couldn't just let this go.

Donovan and Lian materialized in front of the door before she could open it. "Gabriel isn't here," Donovan said. "He's still in his office, making plans for where the Circus should go next."

"How can he ignore this?" Emma croaked, her voice hoarse. She realized with a jolt that tears were running down her face. She looked away and rubbed her face. Donovan solemnly handed her a handkerchief. She buried her face in it.

"Avery is right," Lian said. "We can't take on the world. Gabriel is just trying to keep what he has."

"He's a coward," Emma muttered, but she didn't move to go toward his office. Neither of the mages corrected her.

"The elves will handle things," Donovan assured her. "Please just go get some rest. You'll feel better in the morning."

Emma shook her head and wiped her eyes again. "I don't

understand how all of you can just ignore this."

Lian stepped forward and put an arm around Emma. "I'll take you back to your room," she said and nodded to Donovan. "Let's be as sisters," she said. Her accent sounded stronger than when she spoke to Emma's mother before. "I will brush your hair and sing to you until you sleep. Things will seem better in the morning. You mustn't risk yourself, Emma. You're important to too many people here. We all need you. And if you are captured by the Company, they will use your Blessing to cause much harm. Please, just let things play out as they will for now."

Emma sighed and gave herself up to Lian's attention. They were in her room sooner than she expected, though she didn't notice Donovan providing a shift for them. She allowed Lian to help her out of the tight lacings of her outfit then fell into bed.

The mage sat down next to her and stroked her hair, crooning a lullaby. Emma couldn't identify the language Lian sang in, but her voice was lovely.

Emma's guilt and worry washed away. A sneaking suspicion that Lian was putting a spell on her stole over Emma along with the peaceful sleepiness. She didn't resist it though. Thoughts of the girls became distant, and her last lucid thought before she slipped into slumber was that Lian and Nemo should sing together some day. *They make a cute couple.*

Avery paused outside Gabriel's office and peered in. He frowned when he saw both Donovan and Timaeus. Had Timaeus ever come into Gabriel's office before? The dragon's presence certainly added formality to the situation, which he hadn't expected. His feathers fluffed up a bit as he stepped into the room. "Gabriel? Tristan said you wanted to talk to me?"

All three of them turned as one to look at him as one. The force of their gazes made Avery want to shrink back out the door. He wished Martin had come with him, but his brother had been too intent on his music and refused to leave the cavern they shared.

"Lian put a spell on Emma last night," Gabriel said. "To calm her down." He shot a dark look at Donovan. "We're trying to figure out what to do about Julia. In the meantime, we need someone to keep Emma's mind on other things. The sanctity of the mind and emotions is important. I regret breaking that rule with Nemo. I knew it would come back to bite me, and it did. I won't condone anyone tampering with Emma's feelings."

"Then make sure she doesn't run off," Timaeus growled. "She can endanger herself if she wants, but Nemo would go along to protect her. I will not allow the boy's safety to be jeopardized."

Gabriel glared at the dragon-man for the barest instant and then swiftly refocused on Avery. "Can you do it?"

Avery blinked, trying to catch up with the conversation. "Keep Emma distracted so she doesn't think about Tip, right?"

"Or the Company," Gabriel amended. "She got some news last night that they've taken a couple girls she babysat before she joined the Circus."

Avery flinched and rubbed the back of his neck. "Ouch. Well, I can certainly try. Maybe if I..."

He caught sight of Nemo standing in the doorway and trailed off. The teen's face was unreadable. There was no telling what he'd heard.

Nemo glanced around at the gathering. "Good morning. I thought Avery might want to know what day it is."

Emma stopped dead when she saw Julia waiting outside her bedroom. Her fingers tightened on the doorframe, and she fought the urge to close it in the woman's face rather than tell her Gabriel's decision.

"Good morning," she greeted. "Did you need something? Or are you lost? We can go to breakfast together. I slept in, but I'm sure there's still some food available."

Julia glared at her, and Emma hunched her shoulders. "Have you found out anything new about the Company?" Julia demanded. "I know you wanted to talk to Gabriel after what you heard from Aoife."

"Gabriel said no." Emma bit her lip and looked away. The words tasted sour in her mouth. It made her sound like she'd asked a parent something and been refused. She thought again of the two little girls and struggled to swallow past the lump in her throat. "Everyone is going to be fine," she said, trying to reassure herself as much as Julia. "The elves—"

"Donovan told me all about that," Julia cut in. "But why do we have to sit back and wait for them? We're a group of super people or whatever it is you want to call it! Let's do something, for Pete's sake!"

"They are Blessed too," Emma retorted, leaning back against the door. "Don't you remember what it was like for you that night? I saw it all in your head. They messed with your mind so much that you were barely sane when you got here. There's no reason to risk ourselves. It's not what Tip would want you to do."

Julia stared at her, her dark eyes narrowing and her hands balling into fists. "You're just as defeatist as that weakling Gabriel."

Emma took a step back in shock, but anger flared bright at the accusation. She glared right back.

"Forget it. I'll find my own way." The shorter woman whirled and stomped away before Emma could clear her mind enough to say anything.

Donovan appeared behind Julia, silent as a cat, and placed a hand on the young woman's shoulder. Julia yelped in surprise and tried to jerk away, but her knees gave out, and she slumped, unconscious, into Donovan's arms. He glanced up at Emma and nodded, his expression even more serious than usual. "I am not going to alter her memory. Gabriel's right. Some sedation spells will be enough to keep her calm until the elves get everything figured out."

Before Emma could ask what Gabriel was right about, Donovan vanished, taking Julia with him. Emma heaved a sigh, wanting to hide in her room and go back to sleep. Her appetite had dried up, but she trailed to the dining room anyway.

Donovan sat at one of the long tables, nursing a cup of tea. Now that Emma got a better look at him, she could see his eyes were more blood-shot than usual, the circles under them darker. Lucien approached and placed a steaming mug in front of him, snatching away the old one.

Emma dropped across from them and eyed Donovan. "Long night? You sure responded to Julia quickly. You seemed rather hands off with her before now."

"I didn't want to invade her space, and I knew it would garner Amadis's ire." Donovan rubbed his eyes. "It's been a long few days, keeping an eye on her in particular. Timaeus gave the order to keep her from reacting anymore." He took a long drink from his mug and made a face. "I need some coffee instead of this flavored water. Being Timaeus's Keeper has been more way more interesting than I expected. I came here to get away from people, darn it. I'm sick of all the drama."

Lucien tilted his head, something like sympathy in his eyes. "The Circus is a lot to keep track of."

Emma remembered the moment she had experienced what Donovan went through all the time and grimaced. "I bet."

Avery came up behind her and put a hand on her shoulder. She smiled tentatively up at him. "Want to go into town?" he asked her. He glanced at Lucien. "Timaeus asked me to go buy him some new books. He said you traded some of his gold for human cash while you were out and to get it from you."

Emma brightened. "I'd love to go book shopping!" It had been a while since she'd left the caves to explore one of the towns they passed through. She leapt to her feet and shot Donovan a grin. "I'll give you a few less people to keep track of, if you'll oblige us with a spell."

"Thank you," Donovan said dryly and flicked his hand at Avery. As the avian snatched up the wallet Lucien had placed on the table, his wings faded out of sight and his crest of feathers smoothed down into light brown hair. Emma reached over curiously and touched his head. His feathers shifted under her fingers. Invisible, not transformed. Avery grinned and grabbed Emma's hand, swinging it between them as they left the caverns.

Mist blew into Emma's face, damp and refreshing after the dry, stuffy air of the caves. Emma took deep breaths of it and brushed her foot against the thick greenery on the side of the road. Her tennis shoe came out dark with moisture.

"This place is beautiful." The fresh air cleared away the anger and confusion. Rays of sunshine blazed out from behind the clouds, and she stared at the dazzle reflected in the water droplets gleaming like diamonds.

"This is one of my favorite areas in this country," Avery told her, moving aside for a passing car.

"Does it remind you of home?" The sound of greater traffic roared through the trees, showing the direction to the main thoroughfare. Donovan usually told them if they needed to take a car or if the town was walking distance. Emma preferred walking when they could.

Avery didn't answer immediately, watching a pair of hummingbirds chase each other around a tree so large it made the birds look like gnats. They came to a fork and turned to walk downhill toward the town in the valley below.

"A little," he finally said, his eyes staying on the thickets of berries and vines. "Martin and I moved around a lot, so we never had much of a home. We'd only settled down for a few months, but that was enough for a group of Rangers to sniff us out." His lips turned down into a scowl that looked odd on his face. "There are limited places where people like me can live nowadays. We considered seeking out the elves, but Martin didn't want to. We thought we'd be safe in the wilderness, but magic seekers like the Company's Rangers often comb those areas for any hint of the old magic. They'll bleed the world dry, grasping at the little that remains at the edges of human society. The elves' cities are becoming the last bastions that can offer sanctuary."

"Lucien said the elves are considering removing the Blessing spell," Emma commented, her voice hushed. She squeezed Avery's hand, wishing she could do something for the pain in his eyes.

Avery nodded. "Technology has evened the playing field. Magic or a Blessing often pales in comparison to a gun, not to mention a bomb or a tank. A few mages, like Donovan, have trained to combat some modern weaponry, but most mages studying nowadays don't bother learning any combat magic. Instead, they experiment with magically augmenting mundane weaponry."

Emma shuddered at the thought. "That's awful. Do we really need more powerful weapons? I can't imagine what a combination like that could do."

"It can hold off people like the Company's Rangers," Avery retorted, grim pleasure creeping into his voice. "The people who still rely solely on a Blessing to hurt others." He squeezed her hand. "Enough of this! We're out here to have some fun!"

The discussion had distracted Emma from the approaching town, and she took a deep breath as the mental noise from the town washed over her. "Not as loud as my home town," she mused. "This must be a small town."

"As long as they have a bookshop and a burger place."

"Burgers?" Emma stared at Avery. "Why?"

A grin spread over Avery's face. "I like to spend Timaeus's money on fast food. It really burns him when I tell him I don't want the dinner he cooked."

Emma burst out laughing. "Be careful with that, or you'll be the one getting burned."

Avery shrugged. "A plate of hot, salty fries and a chocolate milkshake are worth risking a few first-degree burns." He paused. "Is there any fast food you miss? I'll let you choose."

"Oh man." Emma rubbed the back of her neck. "Can we find a Chinese express? That would be amazing!"

Avery pulled out a phone from his pocket, tapped something in, and stared at it for a minute. "There's a mall near the closest bookstore. Let's see what's available at the food court. I'm sure we can both find something. We can get as much as we want, and then I'll see what's left for Timaeus's books."

Emma grimaced. "You're really trying to push him, aren't you? I can buy my own lunch. Gabriel gave me my monthly allowance a few days ago."

"No way." Avery's face set stubbornly. "Not on—" he cut off and blinked before hastening to add, "I mean, we have more than enough for lunch and a pile of books. Don't worry about it."

"Okay." Emma gave him a puzzled look. Avery wouldn't meet her eye and launched into a list of possible books to get Timaeus. Emma shrugged and accepted the change of topic.

Gabriel twisted the brim of his hat in his hands and scowled, pushing up from the cavern wall. "Aren't Avery and Emma back yet? We're cutting this timing close."

The acrobats huddled nearby, speaking softly. Lian looked up and tilted her head. "You did ask Avery to keep Emma out and distracted."

"Not going to ask how you know that," Gabriel grumbled. His eyes roved to the other two girls beside Lian and then over to Tristan sitting by Celeste and Davet. "Your new act with Nemo was fantastic," he added, trying to distract himself. "Davet's debut caused some rave reviews, too."

Tristan stiffened. "I don't think we should subject Davet to the crowds very often."

Davet tossed his head and pushed against his mother's side. "Perhaps every other show," she told Gabriel and nuzzled her colt. "Davet's eager, but Tristan is right."

As the unicorn turned her head to regard Tristan, the electric lights winked against her horn, dazzling Gabriel.

He blinked and looked at himself, the out-of-body experience disturbing him for a moment before he settled into the vision.

Gabriel knelt in front of Timaeus, the mountainous dragon glaring down at him with smoke roiling from his nostrils.

Tristan stood on one side with Celeste, looking concerned. Donovan and Lucien stood on the other side.

The acrobats, Aoife, Martin and Avery, and the other Blessed who had left the Company with him stood in a cluster behind him, half in shadow.

"Please let us stay here," Gabriel whispered, his voice cracking with exhaustion. "If you'll even shelter us for a few weeks, I'll find another sanctuary."

A dark puff of smoke rose from the dragon's snout, and he drew his head back as Celeste paced forward, Tristan keeping to her side. "I will vouch for these Blessed," she declared. "They were employed by a wicked man, but they are fleeing him now, together with some of the other victims that were torn from their homes." She nodded to Aoife and the two avians. "If you allow them to stay, I will remain as well. I will give my word that they will not cause you undue trouble."

The dragon's eyes glared down at the unicorn. Tristan moved in front of her as if he could shield her.

Timaeus huffed out a laugh. "Very well. For a time. I challenge you, Gabriel Hightower, to come up with a proper cover for your people in that time. Be creative. If you manage to catch my interest, I might allow you to remain for longer."

The vision released Gabriel. He breathed a sigh of relief, feeling the tension from that long-ago day unclench inside him. This seemed far less stressful, in comparison to that memory.

Donovan appeared in the doorway. "They're coming. Timaeus instructed me to bring everyone to the dining room."

"How nice of you to tell us instead of just popping us over there," Gabriel growled, his mood still soured by the vision. Why did he only have visions of the past now? Was it the same for Michael?

Donovan tilted his head. He waved his hand and the room around them blurred. Gabriel's stomach flipped over at the transition. "Magic," he cursed and collapsed at the nearest table.

The lights dimmed. Gabriel felt a hand slide into his and squeeze his fingers. He put an arm around Aoife and drew her close, breathing in her salt water scent. It calmed his nerves.

The door creaked open. A rustle of feathers marked Avery's entrance. He passed into the darkness, and Emma stood silhouetted against the light of the passage.

"Avery?" she called, and a nervous chuckle escaped her. "Why are the lights off?"

"HAPPY BIRTHDAY!" The dragon's roar shook the caverns around them but didn't dissuade Aoife and Lian from dashing forward and throwing their arms around Emma. Davet trotted forward, just a few moments from the humans.

Emma laughed and returned their hugs and stroked the unicorn's mane as the lights came back on. Grinning, she looked around at everyone. "How did you know?" Her eyes landed on Nemo. He nodded. "Ah. I see." She glanced over at Avery, his wings fully visible now that they were back in the safety of the caverns. "Is that what today was about?"

Avery shrugged. "Nemo told us. It seemed right we should do something for it."

"May you have many more birthdays with us," Aoife said, kissing

Emma's cheek. "I made you a new dress for the occasion." She grasped both of Emma's hands and tugged her away from Avery. "And Timaeus has prepared a feast!"

"Easy there, Aoife," Gabriel said, approaching them. Aoife continued to bounce on the balls of her feet but took a step back. Gabriel beamed at Emma. She looked more than weary. He could hear the sadness that yet fluttered at the edges of her thoughts. "Happy birthday, Emma. I'm happy to celebrate it with you."

Emma paused, staring at him almost in shock before happiness blossomed over her features. Gabriel felt a tightness in his chest and glanced away, a slight smile plucking at his mouth.

"Thank you," she whispered.

Gabriel squeezed her shoulder and gestured to the table. "I'm sure you're hungry after a hike long enough for the feast to be ready. Let's eat."

Donovan continued to move them down the western coast into warmer climates. One afternoon, after rehearsal, Lian and Davet cornered Emma after a lesson. Davet darted forward and rammed Emma's legs, making her stumble and almost fall. She caught herself against the wall and rubbed Davet's head. "Hello to you, too," she said and smiled at Lian. There were dark smudges under the acrobat's eyes from lack of sleep.

Lian frowned in concern. "You are well?" she asked and peered into Emma's face. "Perhaps I should tell Nemo to come sing for you."

Emma chuckled. "No, I'm fine. Nemo's singing doesn't relax me that well." Lian's frown became puzzled, and Emma laughed again.

Let's go outside! Davet thought and sidled excitedly to the side. *Donovan said there are rabbits outside. I want to see one.* He tossed his head, nearly dislodging the trio of pixies that were clinging to his mane: two with sky blue wings, and one with bright red wings.

"Oh yeah, it's spring, isn't it?" Emma mused. "Yes, let's go outside. That sounds like it will do us all some good." As soon as she said this, she felt the shift that put them right by an exit. Davet dashed outside, calling to Emma to hurry. She glanced back and saw Lian hovering by the wall several feet back. "Are you coming?"

Lian hesitated and looked down. "I do not go out often," she muttered. "The sunlight hurts my eyes."

Emma studied Lian's pasty white complexion. "Hey, Donovan?" she asked into the air. "Do you have any sunglasses handy?" A pair of sky-blue sunglasses appeared, and Emma caught them before they clattered to the floor. "Thank you." She flashed Lian a tentative smile. "Really. I don't know where Donovan materializes stuff from." She held the sunglasses out. "Just try it. You can come back if you want."

"He is a powerful mage," Lian said, eyeing the sunglasses. "I'm still a beginner compared to him." She took the sunglasses from Emma and put them on as they stepped out of the cave.

It was one of the beautiful, sunny days California was noted for. Homesickness struck Emma, and she sighed quietly, trying to keep Lian from noticing.

They walked out into a picturesque meadow with tall grasses and flowers. The buzzing of bees and other insects was a low, persistent hum in the air. Davet ran through the grass, his joy palpable in Emma's mind, brightening her mood. He abruptly came to a skidding halt and lowered his head to nose a rabbit that hadn't even bothered to look up as he approached. It blinked at him and then raised its head to press its nose against the unicorn's. At the same moment, the pixie with scarlet wings tumbled down off Davet's mane and landed spread-eagled against the rabbit's back. She turned her head and rubbed her cheek against the velveteen fur, a huge grin visible on her miniscule face.

Emma snapped a picture on her phone and shook her head. "I feel like I just stepped into a fairytale."

Lian laughed, a melodic bell-like peal. "We have always lived in a fairytale. This is just a better setting for it than a cave." She picked some purple and blue flowers and motioned Emma over to the shifting shade under a tall oak tree. "Sit. I will braid your hair with these flowers."

Emma obeyed. She was just happy to be out in the sunshine and warmth. The caves could be oppressive and smothering if she stayed in them too long. She had been avoiding Julia, since she couldn't stand the fact that they were doing nothing about the Company, but in such enclosed spaces, complete avoidance proved to be an impossibility.

Judging by the bemused, dazed look Julia wore all the time now, Emma wasn't the only one who was being enchanted by either Donovan or Lian. Or perhaps Gabriel had blocked some of Julia's memories.

Emma sighed and put her chin on her palm, gazing out over the meadow.

"Do not sigh," Lian said. "This is a happy day."

"Okay," Emma said and smiled as Davet trotted over. The pixies were all gone from his mane now. Emma could see them hovering around the flowers along with the bees.

Davet sniffed the flowers in Emma's hair and watched as Lian put another in. *Ask her to do that with my mane!* He thought at Emma. *I'll have the pixies bring flowers for it.*

Emma relayed Davet's request, and Lian's face lit up. "I would be happy to, Davet!"

She dashed away into the grass to gather more flowers, disturbing both pixies and bees. A contentment washed over Emma, despite her worries. She lay back against the tall grass and closed her eyes, happy to relax in the sunlight for a little while. Tired as she was, she wasn't aware of dozing off.

A drifting cloud cut the sunlight sometime later. The day was immediately darkened and the wind, cool and pleasant before, now carried a chill suggestive of the late winter. Emma stirred and blinked up at the rustling foliage above her. A beetle was crossing her shirt, and she flicked it off before sitting up and rubbing her arms. Raised, unfamiliar voices drew her attention. She jumped up and circled around behind a tree before looking into the meadow. The scene that greeted her made her arms break out into goosebumps even faster.

Davet lay on his side on the ground, his legs tied. He gazed up at a trio of young men with wide eyes. Emma could sense his shock that anyone would do such a thing to him. It was unbelievably wrong to see the unicorn in such a state. His tumultuous feelings reached through their bond, making Emma's chest ache so much it was hard to breathe.

She forced her eyes away from the unicorn and looked instead at the young men who surrounded Lian. "Where is the mother?" one roared at the slight young woman, looming over her. Lian closed her eyes and resolutely shook her head. The man grabbed her and shook her in frustration. Lian's expression didn't change.

"Enough!" another man snapped with authority. "We'll just bring her back with us. Someone else can deal with getting some answers from her. We need to get this unicorn back to the Company before it tries to magic itself away."

Company. Emma's fear settled into a hard anger. She was not going to let these men take Davet away. She stepped out from behind the tree and ran at them. She tackled one to the ground before they could react and battered at his mental defenses, slamming into his mind.

His shocked thoughts tumbled around in her head, making her go rigid. The sensation was too familiar to share with a stranger.

"Get off!" he barked, unaware of her presence in his mind, and shoved her off. She fell back, and the other two men grabbed her arms and heaved her up.

Emma could sense their Blessings in the strength they displayed, and despair washed over her. She wouldn't be able to resist them physically.

"You mustn't do this," she whispered, looking straight at the man. "Ben, let the baby unicorn go." She said it both physically and mentally, trying to force him to obey. The young man's eyes widened, and silence fell.

Lian took advantage of the distraction to take off through the field. She ran bent over so that as soon as she dove into the grass, she was out of sight. One of the men turned to go after her.

"Stop!" the one named Ben ordered. "We have a unicorn and a telepath. We're heading home.

THE
BLESSED
ACT THREE

Nemo was setting tables in preparation for dinner when Donovan, looking panicked, burst into the dining room. Lian, red-faced and panting, was only a moment behind him. Nemo stared at them. Nobody crashed through doors like that here, least of all Donovan, who could will himself anywhere he wished to be.

"Lian, what's wrong?" Nemo asked, approaching the two mages. Lian blanched when she spotted Celeste and stepped behind Donovan.

"Davet and Emma have been taken by Company agents," Donovan barked at Celeste. Nemo stared at Donovan blankly, his mind trying to make sense of those words and failing.

A high-pitched keening escaped Celeste as she whirled and careened toward the door. Tristan somehow kept pace with her and stayed at her side. They both vanished mid-step, shifted out by Donovan. Lucien sprinted out from the kitchen and was likewise shifted out.

"Send me out!" Nemo insisted.

"No," Timaeus growled behind him, filling the kitchen doorway. "You're too slow. If those three can't catch up with them, they're lost."

Lost? Nemo sucked in a sharp breath. "Donovan," he said pleadingly, turning back to the man.

Donovan shook his head. "I agree with my lord," he said, not meeting Nemo's eye. "You'd just slow them down. Your Blessing would be useful, but your physical capabilities are lacking. You're human."

Nemo snarled and grabbed at Donovan's shirt. "You son of a—"

"Control yourself!" Timaeus barked, and Nemo stopped, his clenched hand still raised, just inches from Donovan's face. He let out an explosive breath and drooped. "I understand your feelings," Timaeus added in a more sympathetic tone. "But do not take it out on him. There will be a time and a place."

The dragon-man turned on his heel and marched into the kitchen. "Come with me, boy. There are preparations to be made."

"Preparations, my lord?" Donovan said, an uneasy note in his voice.

"I will not ignore this. That little one was under my protection, as is the Circus and its members. The Ark Light Company has crossed the line."

Nemo shoved his anger and impatience down into a grim resolve and followed Timaeus through the kitchen and into his library. He didn't see the stricken look Lian cast at his back, or the worried glances she and Donovan shared.

Celeste was inconsolable when she and Tristan returned to the caves several hours later. She collapsed onto her side and laid her head on the dusty floor of the amphitheater. Her eyes were dull, and she stared listlessly into the air. Tristan sat down, leaning against the wall of the stands, and put his head in his hands. Lucien did not return.

Nemo locked himself in his room. He sat at his desk with no lights on, his laptop playing music he wasn't hearing. When Donovan abruptly appeared in the cave, he looked up hopefully, but Donovan simply shook his head. Nemo rubbed his face and looked down at the business card that was sitting on the keyboard.

"Timaeus has not left these caves in…a very long time," Donovan said tentatively, knowing of the plans they'd made. "Be careful. Timaeus is not a subtle creature, and if he's found out it would have catastrophic results."

Nemo only nodded, wanting nothing more than to be left alone.

Soon Donovan's presence faded out of the room without a sound. Nemo had long since gotten used to Donovan's magic, but this time it seemed a little eerie. No wonder Emma gave Donovan such a tough time about it.

Tristan and Avery stood outside Nemo's cave when he walked out a little while later. Avery's face was drawn, his shoulders hunched and tense. He tugged on the feathers brushing his shoulder, staring at Nemo. "Tristan said you're driving to San Francisco with him. I want to go, too."

"No," Nemo said instantly.

Avery's eyes flashed, and his head jerked back as if he had been struck. Before he could speak, Nemo held a hand up. "Go talk to Timaeus. He wants you here with him. Martin, too, if he's willing to help."

"He is," Avery said. His wings drooped. He pulled one feather out, dropped it, and continued to tug at his plumage. "I want to go with you. I can't leave Emma to the Company."

"We're not," Nemo said decisively and walked past them. "Come on, Tristan." He felt a twinge over leaving Avery in the dark, but Timaeus would fill him in. Time was of the essence for him.

Tristan followed silently until he realized where they were headed. "I'm not going with you to speak to Gabriel," he said and stopped.

Nemo hesitated. "I could use your help. You know him best."

Tristan shook his head. "You might be right about that. I know he won't want to go or for us to go. If it was anyone but Davet or Celeste, I would obey him. If I go with you, I'll just feel guilty that I can't respect his wishes."

Nemo grimaced. "Okay. Make sure everyone is ready then. I'll meet you by the cars in a little while."

237

"Good luck." Tristan turned on his heel and marched off into the darkness.

Nemo watched him go and sighed. He would need the luck. He would have to have this conversation without using his Blessing, and he'd rarely been able to convince anyone to do anything without it.

Nemo knocked once on the door of Gabriel's office before going in. Gabriel sat on the floor surrounded by piles of books and stacks of papers.

"Have you ever considered getting a desk?" he asked, picking his way carefully over the piles and crouching down a few feet away from him.

"No," Gabriel said absently. "Desks and suits are too restricting." It sounded like something he had said many times before. He picked up a stack of papers and dropped it on top of another. "Donovan is preparing to shift us. What do you think of making a schedule of locations for our website? It could be broad. Maybe just the states we'll be in and add the cities in as we want."

"Donovan is shifting us close to San Francisco. We're going after Davet and Emma," Nemo said. Gabriel didn't look up from the papers. "Julia will probably go too, to get Tip. You must've known this was going to happen, Gabriel."

Gabriel only shifted his papers around.

Nemo slapped his hands down on the books in front of him. "You don't have anything to say? She's your student! Don't you care about this at all?"

"Of course I care!" Gabriel shouted and violently threw the papers away. "Oh God…" he pressed his palms to his eyes, his teeth gritted. "The Company finally got their hands on a telepath. Do you have any idea how hard it was to get away from them, with another telepath messing with my head all the time? I did all I could to keep Emma away from them, and now all I get is 'do you care?' Damn it, Nemo! I care so much it hurts!"

"Then help us," Nemo retorted. "We can get Emma away from

them. We don't have to just accept this!"

"I won't go back to San Francisco! I won't be subject to the Company and forced to constantly hear all the filth that spews from that city's thoughts! Never again!" Gabriel's voice rose higher with something like hysteria. He shook his head and got to his feet.

Nemo watched him march across the room, heedlessly knocking over piles of papers and books. He frowned and rubbed his shoulder. Where was the confident ringmaster they'd lived with all these months?

"You're no leader. Who would have to be taken before you would do something? Avery and Martin? Tristan and Celeste? Aoife? Would any of us be worth rescuing? Emma said you didn't want to risk your friends or your home. Well, your friends have been taken. If this continues, you'll have a home all to yourself. But you won't be in San Francisco. Congratulations."

Gabriel continued staring down at his hands.

Nemo shook his head and left him alone.

"Balthasar bagged us an untrained mage by accident." Tip's head cleared in time to catch those words. He blinked and looked around. He was in a large office with a desk on one side, a table with four chairs in the center, and a couch, television, and kitchenette on the far side. His eye flicked from the double doors to the large window overlooking the city. He didn't know what was on the other side of those doors, and judging from the view, the room was very high up. Neither seemed a good option for escape, so he focused on the conversation droning on between Virgil and Michael.

"The spells he cast were clumsy, and I thoroughly searched his memories. There's no hint of him having been taught by anyone," Virgil was saying.

"The worst part is the loss of the phone. If we don't know who he was trying to contact..." Michael looked in Tip's direction and saw he was awake. "Ah. He's with us again." Virgil looked darkly at Tip. "You may go, Virgil," Michael ordered. "I'll speak with him alone."

Tip's eyes met Michael's as the door closed behind the older man, and again Tip was struck by the power behind Michael's dual-colored gaze. Despite that, he felt no fear. There was no malice in the man's look.

"You've presented us with quite the conundrum," Michael commented, shuffling some papers around on his desk. "You're not a Blessed, so you don't really qualify to be here. We can't spare a mage to teach you...and we can't exactly just send you back to your home." He rubbed his face and grimaced. "So, the question is: what to do with you."

"I don't understand," Tip said, and Michael gave him a questioning look. "How does someone like you run a company like this? Do you really feel justified in taking these people from their homes and twisting their minds?"

Michael smiled crookedly. "Are you going to lecture me about morality while I decide your fate? The Blessed are better off here than other places. That is a fact. I don't need to justify myself."

Tip shook his head. "You think having money and power gives you the right to decide something like that for anyone? If that was true, why is it necessary to kidnap and block their memories? You justified yourself long ago, and it is a terrible thing you're doing. Yet you don't seem like a terrible person, Michael. You can—"

The door opened, and a middle-aged man advanced into the room. He wore a steel-gray suit with black shoes flashing underneath. His face and the curl of his graying hair closely resembled Michael, leaving Tip with no uncertainties about who the man was. His powerful presence, even greater than Michael's, brought both young men to their feet. Adah drifted in the man's wake.

"Father. I thought you were in a meeting until this evening," Michael said.

Dante Hightower nodded to his son. "I was. I excused myself when Virgil reported what happened." He turned his gaze to Tip, and Tip took a step back. The man's gray eyes were as cold and calculating as a snake's. "You are the mage?"

"Yes, sir," Tip whispered, his mouth drying with mounting fear. His instincts screamed at him to get away. Sweat beaded up on his brow, and he took another step back, clearing his throat.

"Father, please don't," Michael said and came out from behind his desk. Adah darted behind him, her face pale and her eyes frightened. "I can handle this."

Dante turned his gaze away, and Tip took a deep breath. "You are correct that he isn't Blessed," Dante said, as if Michael had not spoken. "However, he could not have accomplished what he has without training of some kind. Virgil is incorrect in that assessment, no matter what he was able to find in the boy's mind." He regarded Tip once more. "Who sent you?"

"Nobody," Tip croaked, his eyes darting around. Michael looked at his father in alarm. Adah cringed and covered her ears.

Dante put a hand under Tip's chin and forced him to meet his eyes. The instant their gazes locked, pain lanced through Tip's torso. He cried out, and his knees buckled. He fell sideways onto the carpet and clutched at his chest.

Somewhere above him, Adah sobbed.

The pain let up, and Tip went limp, panting hard.

"Who sent you?" Dante repeated in a bored drawl.

Tip sucked in a sharp breath and closed his eyes. The man was Blessed. He was Blessed, and he had twisted his ability for a purpose it was never meant for. *Is this really what has become of the elves' great gift to humanity? This man should be a Healer, with a Blessing that can physically influence others this powerfully.*

Tears leaked from Tip's eyes, more from sorrow than the pain.

"Answer me!" Dante snarled, and the pain resumed.

Tip locked his teeth and curled up. It lasted longer this time, and when it stopped, he groaned in agony. His arm stung from striking a chair when he fell. He cradled it against his chest and curled tighter.

"Who sent you?" the softly spoken words came from directly over Tip. Dante tapped Tip's back with his shoe and then placed his foot on Tip's shoulder. Tip shook his head, and the shoe pushed down harder.

"Father, stop it!" Michael protested. A ringing filled Tip's ears, and the voice sounded distant. His stomach churned, and he concentrated on preventing himself from vomiting.

241

He only caught snippets of the argument that followed. "There's no proof!" Michael said loudly at one point.

"Naïve boy," Dante snarled sometime later. Or maybe right after. Tip couldn't be sure.

Gentle, trembling fingers swept his hair back from his sweaty forehead. He inched toward that comforting gesture, vaguely remembering his mother comforting him after a rigorous day of training with his father. Pain abruptly shot through him again, and the hand yanked away.

"Don't leave," he begged. His heart fluttered in his chest and everything went dark.

Sounds of torment, both physical and mental, rammed through Emma's head. She jerked out of the hold of the man gripping her arm. He must have been equally shocked, or she wouldn't have managed it. Knowing it would be pointless to run, she stared uneasily at the heavy double doors.

The young man straightened, took a deep breath, and raised his hand to knock. Before he did, the door swung open and a middle-aged man stormed out. Her captors took several steps back and bowed their heads respectfully.

"I will send some men for him," the man said shortly over his shoulder. "Do not touch him. This isn't over." The man turned, saw the group, scowled, and stomped down the hall to the elevator.

Emma swallowed as she was tugged into the office. A man lay curled up on the floor, unconscious and breathing heavily. Emma recognized Tip from Julia's memories, and a gasp escaped her. A girl knelt next to him, wiping her eyes.

"Adah," Emma said with even more surprise.

The girl looked up, and her mouth dropped open. "Oh, you're..." she frowned and wiped her palm over her eyes once more before getting to her feet.

"Michael," said the man holding Emma's arm. Emma tore her eyes from Tip and Adah and followed the man's gaze.

A man in a suit stood with his back to them, looking out over the city, his hands clasped so tightly behind his back that his knuckles were stark white. He turned slowly.

Emma's mouth dropped open, and she took a step back. Gabriel's face, faintly puzzled, looked at her.

"Yes?" the man asked with Gabriel's voice. He frowned. "Aren't you Rangers? Why are you bringing me a Blessed?"

Emma's captor shifted and looked around. "We've guarded our minds. Like you've told us to do so that Virgil can't hear our thoughts." He bobbed his head. "We found her with a unicorn. She's a telepath."

The man in the suit stiffened. "I see. Thank you for bringing her to me, then. You may go." He frowned down at Tip. "Take that man out with you. Take him to my house and send a message to Caleb and Balthasar to bring their team to my house to guard him until I can come later."

Emma clenched her fists but didn't argue as they picked Tip up and went out. It didn't sound as if he'd be in any immediate danger. Besides, she was in no position to help him right now.

Adah tugged at the man's sleeve. "Michael," she breathed. "She was in that town when we heard about...you know."

Michael regarded her with Gabriel's eyes and walked over to her. *Not Gabriel,* Emma told herself. His hair was cut shorter and styled differently.

Gabriel wouldn't be caught dead wearing a suit, Emma thought, and despite the situation, a smile plucked at her mouth. Then she remembered Davet and her mirth died. "Where was the baby unicorn taken?"

"Baby?" Michael echoed, mystified. "That's not good." He rubbed his neck and grimaced. Adah stepped toward him, and he waved her away. "I'm sorry about that. I'll do what I can to help."

244

Emma blinked, caught off guard by his words.

"First, I need to ask if you know Gabriel Hightower? Judging by your expression when you saw me..."

Emma looked away and pressed her lips together.

"Answer enough," Michael commented. "Gabriel wouldn't have left another telepath to Virgil's tender mercy." The man clenched his fists and looked away.

Emma glared at him. She wanted to ask about Tip, but since she knew he was a half-elf agent, she decided to leave that alone. She didn't want to give him away.

Michael strolled back over to the window. "How is Gabriel?"

Emma remained silent. He didn't press her anymore but stared out the window thoughtfully. Her anger dwindled unexpectedly. She looked at Adah and realized what was happening. "Don't do that!"

Adah blinked, and the peaceful feeling faded.

"Adah, get my father's secretary on the phone," Michael said. He turned around with a resolute expression. "Tell him the Rangers brought in a telepath. That should distract him and Virgil from thinking about Tip for a few days, at least."

Adah hurried over to the phone on the desk, keeping her eyes down and not looking at Emma.

Fear made Emma's throat tight. "Your father. The man who was torturing Tip when we came in? I heard him screaming."

Michael walked across the room and put his hands on her shoulders. "You're Gabriel's student, right? Shield your mind. Virgil will try to get into it. Don't let him. Resist for just a few days, and I'll figure something out."

"Who are you? Why should I trust you?" She took a step back and knocked his hands away. "Those men tied Davet up! He's terrified right now! Take me to him!"

Michael's face went blank. "I am Michael Hightower. Remember to guard your mind. If Virgil gets into it, they'll find out about Gabriel and the Blessed that follow him. Collectors will be sent after them."

Emma's fury and anguish surged at this casually issued threat. Her hand shot out to slap him. The man caught Emma's arm and spun her around as the door opened.

"Take the girl to my father's office," Michael called. "Virgil is waiting for her."

Boiling in anger and helplessness, Emma was once more pulled away by force, but she kept her back rigid and didn't let Michael Hightower see her terror.

Tip swam into consciousness slowly. He ached terribly all over and didn't particularly want to be awake.

He could hear voices some distance removed from his location. He cracked an eye open to look around an unfamiliar room. The voices came from beyond a closed door.

Not wanting to alert them, Tip clenched his teeth to keep a groan from escaping and closed his eyes tightly. He gathered what strength he could muster and breathed a spell. It took several tries before the magic flowed.

"Are you sure?" Balthasar was saying when the spell allowed him to hear. "The Boss won't be happy about this. If he turns his anger on us for doing as you say…"

"We have no proof," Michael said stiffly. "I won't have him torturing the man on no grounds other than suspicion. He's been getting more and more paranoid ever since Gabriel left, but this is going too far."

"I don't think Gabriel would send a spy," Rebecca said. "It seemed like Tip was trying to send the address to someone. Gabriel certainly doesn't need that information. Come to think of it, I doubt Tip could've told him anything Gabriel doesn't know."

"I think you're overestimating Gabriel's intelligence," Caleb grumbled. There was a smacking sound, and Caleb yelped. "I don't take it back, Rebecca! Gabriel is a traitor!"

"Enough," Michael said coldly. His voice sounded so much like Dante's that a shiver went down Tip's spine. "I won't have you talking about my brother that way, Caleb. You have your instructions. I must go now. I'll be back later."

A door creaked open and slammed close, and Caleb sighed heavily. Tip released his hold on the magic, and exhaustion gripped him. It would seem he was safe for the time being. He couldn't make any sense of it other than that.

A rustling sound drew his attention. He opened his eyes and watched as Seth walked through the closed door, leading Adah and Gail. Seth paused when he saw Tip watching, leaving Gail half stuck in the wood.

"Seth!" she yelped. He hastily pulled her the rest of the way through. Tip managed a chuckle, but the sound was a rusty croak and turned into a painful cough that shook him.

Adah grimaced. "Crap, this feels terrible," she muttered. "Can't believe the boss did that. He really has gotten worse."

She came up beside the bed and dipped a cloth in some water on the bedside table. She placed it on Tip's forehead. It was an odd, old-fashioned gesture, but Tip couldn't deny it felt nice.

Gail and Seth exchanged looks behind Adah's back. It seemed they didn't find Dante's actions surprising.

"Sheltered much?" Seth muttered. "Guess cozying up to Michael has its—"

"Are you hungry?" Adah asked loudly, drowning out Seth's grumbles behind her.

"No," Tip rasped and coughed again.

Adah got a cup of water and offered Tip some medicine. "This will help with the pain and getting to sleep."

Tip nodded his thanks and gratefully swallowed the medicine. When she started to take away the water, he gestured, and she held the cup for him to drink the rest. His eyes drifted closed. The medicine, and his own weariness, dulled his awareness and senses for several hours after that. He knew the teenagers remained in the room with him, talking softly. There was music at one point, which made Tip dream he was in a video game as a non-player character, watching others moving around him while he stayed in place, unable to escape his programmed immobility.

Raised voices reached him, interrupting his dream. He jolted awake, and a trembling hand smoothed over his hair comfortingly.

"It'll be okay," Adah whispered, her voice shaking as much as her hand. The voices got louder and more abrasive, but Tip drifted off to sleep again, too weary and achy to deal with whatever was happening beyond the bedroom.

When he came to again, his mind was clearer, and he was able to focus on the voices. The door was open now, and the group were all together in the next room, talking quietly. Tip could hear them just fine without a spell this time. A small mercy.

"The boss is going to be so mad," Seth fretted.

"We just did what Michael told us to," Rebecca replied defiantly. "Nothing else matters."

Caleb made a disgusted noise. "Since when did we all become Michael's stooges?" he grumbled. "You just watch. Michael and the boss will kiss and make-up soon. And then we'll all be thrown to the wolves."

"Michael wouldn't do that to us!" Adah shrieked, and Caleb yelped.

It seems like someone is always hitting Caleb, Tip thought with a faint smile.

Tip's mind wandered. He was considering his predicament when a headache spiked. Something very powerful suddenly appeared at the edge of his awareness, like a great black thunderhead. Cold dread filled him as he sensed the power this creature emanated.

What is going on? Why would such a creature suddenly come so close to a city? Many possibilities filled his weary mind, each more fantastic and worrisome than the last.

He forced himself to sit up. The bed creaked, and silence fell. Adah flitted into the room, Rebecca, Gail, and Caleb following reluctantly, filling the room and making Tip realize how small it was. Seth stayed in the doorway, peering in.

"This is all very cute," he croaked and winced as his throat burned. "But I have a few pieces of essential information Michael will find very interesting. Is there a way for me to speak to him immediately?"

Thoughts pounded at Emma from beyond the walls of the office she sat in. Hundreds, thousands, whispering or shouting. The city was loud and terrible after the months of peaceful silence she had enjoyed in the Circus. What she could distinguish out of the roar made her stomach churn.

No wonder Gabriel refused to come back here.

The man sitting across from her, who had introduced himself as Virgil the evening before, rammed once more at her mental defenses. Emma gripped the arms of the chair until her knuckles stood out white. She stared fixedly at the glass of orange juice on the table in front of her, filling her thoughts with it and using it to repel the bombardment.

He blew out a frustrated breath. Leaning back in the leather armchair, he let up on the mental attack. "You have very good defenses."

Emma shifted, the various physical discomforts from being in this room all night clamoring for attention.

Her fidget didn't go unnoticed. Virgil put his hands on his knees and leaned forward. "This can all end right now. Let me see your memories, and you may eat..." he gestured to the plate of food between them. "And use our facilities."

"I know several Blessed. I'm not going to sell them out to you just so that I can use the bathroom."

"Why do you think it would be a betrayal?" Virgil asked, sounding genuinely curious. "The Blessed are brought here for their own good." He rubbed his bristly chin. "More than that, how do you know so much about the Company? Did you find out from the unicorn you were with?"

Emma flinched at being reminded of Davet. His misery and images of a a frigid, damp room leaked through their connection. Her throat felt tight, and she repressed tears.

Virgil scrutinized her face, a smile pulling at his scruffy beard.

"Let the unicorn go," she croaked. "He's just a baby."

He drummed his fingers on his knee. "It *is* sad for him to be separated from his mother, but we can't just let him go. What would he do alone, even if he was in a forest? If you would just tell me..."

Emma closed her eyes and repelled his next mental probe. She could sense his frustration as he pulled back. That gave her a small amount of satisfaction.

"He'll be sold soon enough," Virgil said. "We don't bring unicorns in very often. And an adorable baby, no less. He'll be auctioned off at quite a sum."

Emma's hands clenched into fists. She didn't open her eyes or let her emotions weaken her mind. As much as she hated Michael for putting her here, he was right. She couldn't let Virgil see her memories. She couldn't let him find out about Gabriel and the others. Images rolled through her mind: Avery and Martin on an auction block, followed by Aoife and Celeste in cages. Virgil breaking into Nemo's mind the same way he was trying to get into hers...No. Her resolve hardened.

"Enough." Virgil got to his feet, grabbed the plate, jerked a window open, and scraped the food onto the ledge. Pigeons descended as he slammed the window. Emma's stomach gurgled, but she kept her gaze on her hands, rubbing the grass stained knees of her jeans.

Virgil walked back toward her but lurched to a halt. His gaze went distant, and he tilted his head as if listening. Emma glanced up at him and listened as well. The thoughts were overwhelming, but she sensed several familiar minds nearby. She fought to keep her face calm.

"Looks like we'll have to continue this later," Virgil said, rubbing his hands together as he went to the door and opened it. He paused a moment and then clicked off the lights with light switches outside the door. Emma's fear spiked, and he nodded to her before stepping out.

She lurched up and ran after him. The door clicked closed before she got anywhere near it. She pounded once on the solid wooden barrier and then sank down onto the carpet.

"What do I do?" she muttered, rubbing her aching eyes. The dark walls pressed in around her, and she hugged her knees, repressing a whimper as her mind went blank with fear. She took a deep breath, and to keep from panicking, she concentrated on the minds moving somewhere several floors below.

Exhausted, she began drifting off despite her fears when a tapping drew her attention to the window. The pancakes had already been devoured, but a few pigeons still stood on the ledge. One of them, a black and white streaked bird, pecked the window, looking at Emma intently. There was something familiar it.

In a daze, Emma crossed the room and opened the window. The bird flew in, and she was enveloped in the cloud of magic the bird carried on its clapping wings. Her mind was laid bare, and she felt a fleeting gladness that Virgil wasn't in the room before her vision went blank.

Nemo had never seen San Francisco before, but the only impressions he got of it was the traffic and the difficulty finding a parking spot. After Tristan parked, Nemo circled the block twice before he found one. Between the stop lights and even more traffic, the endeavor took well over twenty minutes. Nemo's hands squeezed the steering wheel until his knuckles stood out starkly. Lian reached over and patted his arm a moment before they pulled up to the curb.

Frigid wind lashed at Nemo, Julia, and Lian as they walked to where Tristan and the acrobats waited. Nemo hunched into his sweatshirt and kept his eyes averted from the ragged people they passed.

Tristan nodded to the tall office building across from them. *"Ark Light Company"* read the big sign on the side of the building. "That's it."

Nemo studied the building. It looked so ordinary he found it hard to believe it dealt with magical creatures and Blessed humans.

Tristan tossed the keys to one of the acrobats. "You stay by the car. Have it running and ready to go. It's going to be hard enough getting a unicorn out without being seen."

She nodded and walked away.

Tristan focused on the youngest of their group. "Adelle, you stay with Nemo and make both of you invisible. Julia, you stay close to me. We'll probably have to use our strength Blessings to get Davet out of his cage. Lian—"

Lian's head tilted while Tristan spoke. Now she shook her head. "I'm going to search."

Before any of them could ask what she meant, she transformed into a pigeon and took off with a clapping of wings.

Julia watched Lian until she joined a flock of other pigeons. "Okay," she said, as if that happened every day. "And after we get Davet, we'll go to this House you talked about and get Tip."

It wasn't a question. Nemo shot her a smile, and they walked into the lion's den with the plain corporate sign over the door.

It was hard to be invisible in the press and flow of people in the building. Nemo clutched Adelle's slight hand, dodged as many people as he could, and hoped anyone he bumped would assume someone else in the press did it. Nobody looked up or said anything, so that seemed to be okay.

Tristan slipped out of the crowd and walked toward an elevator half-hidden by a tall potted plant in the small waiting area. He paused and looked idly up at the television while Nemo and Adelle joined him. Nemo touched his shoulder to signal they were there.

Tristan glanced casually at the receptionist desk to check that they were all busy with other people. He slipped a battered plastic badge out of his pocket and flashed it across the scanner next to the elevator. The light turned green and the doors opened. They all slipped quickly in, and Tristan breathed a sigh of relief when the doors closed behind them.

Nemo watched as the flashing numbers above the door told of their descent. They passed at least five floors, and Nemo couldn't believe there were that many beneath the building.

"What are all these floors?" he demanded.

"Extra housing for Blessed workers," Tristan muttered, his lips barely moving. "The House is reserved for the original group that was brought in years ago and newcomers. A lot of Blessed pass through the city while working for the Company, and they need to stay somewhere. This is cheaper and safer than putting them in hotels. There are also two floors used only for the creatures that are brought in."

Nemo tried to picture what that might look like, but then the doors opened with another cheerful ding, revealing a scene far grimmer than Nemo had imagined.

"Lian?" Emma said as her vision cleared.

She blinked and looked around. She was alone, her phone lit up in her hand. Emma frowned at it, seeing Adah's number.

That's right. Adah gave me her number that day at the college. What just happened, though?

Emma glanced around, disoriented and sure Lian had come in just moments before. As her confusion faded, her fear rose once more.

Emma, please talk to me, a voice whimpered in her head, distracting her.

Emma closed her eyes and plopped down before Davet drew her into his mind. He was lying on cold concrete. She could hear the rhythmic dripping of water nearby. A deep chill permeated through him, making him shiver.

Oh, Davet, she thought sadly and wished she could comfort him. She took a deep breath and shoved her fears away. At the very least, she could offer him calmness.

Davet opened his eyes and looked around. The room was like a parking garage but filled with lines of cages. Further away, she could see large tanks. Water seeped from these tanks, making the room damp.

A woman with long green hair and a dark-green tinge to her skin was in the cage next to Davet. She knelt, clutching the bars and crooning a lullaby. Her thoughts were so sorrowful and her song so sad tears stung Emma's eyes and rolled down her face. Davet leaned against the iron, trying to get closer to the woman.

It's okay, he thought to the dryad. *My companion will get us out. She is with me.*

Davet... Emma thought with some reproach. She couldn't bring herself to tell him that his confidence in her was unfounded. There was no way out for her either.

Echoing voices drew Davet's attention to a group walking through the line of tanks. The dryad leapt up and pressed herself back against the other side of her cage. Davet watched curiously.

"What use do they have for so many merfolk?" a woman asked.

Julia, Emma told Davet, recognizing the voice with a leap of joy.

"There are quite a few uses," Tristan said grimly. "Gabriel could tell you more. I was just a grunt worker when we were here."

They came into view. Julia and Tristan walked side by side. Nemo and the youngest acrobat trailed behind them. The girl clung to Nemo's hand and looked around so fearfully that he put an arm around her.

"Did the mermaid at the bar I worked at come from here?" Julia asked, peering at the empty cages.

"Most likely. I think the Company has a processing center on the east coast too, but a lot of merfolk are caught along the west coast," Tristan said absently. He spotted Davet and ran up to the cage. "Davet! Hang on, little one! We're going to get you out of here! Julia, come help me." They went up to the lock and gripped the panel it was on.

"One, two, three." Tristan gritted his teeth as they both pulled. Emma watched in amazement through Davet's eyes. She had never seen Tristan or Julia use their full strength. The panel bent forward with a screech of rending metal. Davet staggered to his feet and lunged out of the cage, scraping his shoulder on the gate.

Emma felt the pain, but the unicorn colt didn't notice, pressing his head against Tristan's chest. His thoughts babbled incoherently. Emma was pushed out of his mind in the confusion. The last thing she saw and heard was Tristan stroking the baby unicorn's mane and saying, "You're going to be okay now, Davet."

Back in her own body, Emma breathed a sigh of relief and stretched her stiff legs out under her. Then she heard another group of thoughts quickly approaching Davet.

Davet, tell them someone is coming! She shouted at him. His mind was still jumbled though, and she doubted he heard her. He did sense Tristan's unease when a ding sounded on the other side of the room and the elevator doors slid open.

Gabriel sat on a stone with his feet in Aoife's pool. She sat beside him, holding him tightly.

"I don't know what to do. We can't allow the Company to get another telepath. But it's madness to confront them…"

Aoife stroked his curls. "A choice has to be made. You can't keep walking this tightrope, or it'll unravel around you."

"I don't want to lose them. Why did they insist on putting themselves in danger? The elves would've handled everything. Although I suppose Emma wouldn't forgive me…"

Aoife slipped into the water and leaned against Gabriel's knees, her tail creating ripples in the pool. "The change wasn't coming fast enough. I can understand that." She cupped his face in her hand. He leaned into the touch. "Oh, my gentle angel, I know your pain. However, if you don't want to lose them, then it is time. You must confront Dante and the Ark angel."

Despair darkened Gabriel's face. "I haven't had many visions for a while. Michael was the one who saw visions regularly. Do you really think it's time?"

"Come what may, you must now jump into the fray. Protect what you cherish, just as you did when you left the Company."

Gabriel nodded slowly. "You're right. I must speak with Timaeus."

Michael's polished shoes clacked against the concrete floor. He frowned darkly and stepped over a puddle, glancing distastefully around at the leaking tanks. The atmosphere in this room was so miserably oppressive. He'd always hated coming in here.

He looked at Adah, needing to focus on a more pleasant sight. "How many intruders did Emma tell you there were?"

"She just said a group," Adah said, putting her hand in her pocket and gripping her phone.

"Alright." Michael nodded to Caleb and the others with him. "Spread out. Find them."

As they fanned out, Michael continued through the rows, followed by Adah and Tip. He spotted the mangled cage and frowned. "They took the baby unicorn," he called. "Be careful, everyone." He turned to Tip. "Tell me again what you sensed. Is that connected to this group?"

"I don't know," Tip muttered. "I just know there's a dragon somewhere nearby. Finish whatever you need to do here quickly so that we can figure that out. It should take priority." He wrapped his arms tightly over his chest and didn't look up from the floor. He could feel the dryad staring at him, and he resisted the urge to start screaming spells to free all these creatures. "What a horrid place."

"I agree," Michael said grimly. "But to stay on topic... Why would a dragon come to San Francisco? That doesn't make any sense."

"Can't say," Tip said and shrugged. "Dragons are a force unto themselves. There's no regulating a creature that powerful, and there's too few of them for much self-regulation as a species."

Michael felt someone brush his mind. His frown deepened, and he strengthened his barriers. Virgil wouldn't dare try to get into Michael's mind in normal circumstances, but things were far from normal.

A shout from the elevator made him whirl and start back that way. Balthasar, wearing a grim expression, dragged Tristan away from the elevator doors. The baby unicorn cowered inside the elevator. A white-haired boy came around the tanks and sprinted for the elevator, but Caleb barreled forward and grabbed him before he could reach it.

"Get Davet away!" Tristan bellowed. The doors closed. Seth dove through them and pressed the button to open them again.

Dropping Tristan to his knees under Caleb and Rebecca's guard, Balthasar went in and carried the baby unicorn back out. It trembled in his hold, but he kept his grip gentle and even stroked its mane, showing the tenderness that had allowed him to capture unicorns before.

"Is this everyone?" Michael asked Adah. Her gaze flicked to the elevator, but she nodded without meeting his eyes. "Okay," he said, deciding to let the deception slide. He offered Tristan a hand. "It's good to see you again, Tristan. I guess I shouldn't be surprised to find you involved with the baby unicorn."

Tristan glared at Michael and ignored his hand. "I shouldn't be surprised you're still going after unicorns," he snarled. "Didn't you learn anything? I thought Balthasar at least would've put a stop to—"

Caleb lunged forward and punched Tristan, who fell back, hitting his head against the concrete.

"Caleb!" Balthasar barked.

"He shouldn't dare say your name! After what he did to you!"

257

Caleb drew his leg back and kicked Tristan. "I refuse to stand here and talk to him like we're still friends! Do you have any idea the hell you put me and Balthasar through? I hope you get even a taste of what I did for trusting Gabriel!"

"Enough!" Michael snapped with such a commanding tone that Caleb froze. "We *are* still friends," he added in a quieter tone. "And nobody will be facing my father that way."

He took a deep breath and was about to continue when he felt someone pierce through his mental defenses. He went rigid and gritted his teeth, but then he realized it wasn't Virgil. He blinked, suspecting who it might be, and hesitantly lowered his hasty new defenses, giving up control for the first time in years.

Emma paced the office, frantically trying to do anything about the situation downstairs. The darkness pressed in on her once more, making her breath speed up. Michael was her best shot right now, and she threw all her mental energy into pushing at his mind, to no avail.

Closing her eyes did no good. Her fists were clenched so tightly her nails dug into her palms. That helped ground her. The fear receded, and she finally succeeded at breaking into Michael's mind. "Yes!"

Her desperate happiness faded instantaneously. Pained memories of him and Gabriel as children assailed her, giving her more information about them than she cared to know. She gritted her teeth and fought past them.

Gabriel hadn't taught her how to take control of someone's mind. He didn't even suggest such a thing was possible. But now Emma twisted and felt Michael's mind give in with little resistance. She could still hear him, but his thoughts were distant.

"Stop," she said through Michael's mouth, looking at Caleb through his eyes.

Caleb glowered. "I've had enough. I'm going to tell the boss everything." He turned on his heel and walked toward the elevator.

Emma followed him through Michael, but the words that came were Michael's own, making her realize he had allowed her to take charge of his mind. "If my father learns you kept this from him all this time, you'll all be punished. Gail, Seth, Adah, Rebecca. All of you. Do you want to go through that again, Caleb?"

Balthasar's head whipped around, and he grabbed Caleb. "You're not doing anything that will get Gail punished."

"We're going to let them all go," Emma said through Michael, reasserting her control. Michael huffed mentally. *That's not going to go over well.* She ignored him and cast a steely look around at everyone. Despite his disagreement, he spoke on his own after that. "I won't have Gabriel being forced into coming back. We're going to forget this happened."

"Unbelievable," Caleb said. "Even now, you're protecting Gabriel first! We wouldn't be in this mess if you had reported finding out about his dumb circus!"

Rebecca stepped close to Caleb, put an arm around him, and spoke softly to him. Caleb's face remained thunderous, but he took a step back.

"Fine, fine," he muttered to Rebecca and kissed her cheek. "Thank you." Rebecca smiled at him. He looked at Michael. "If I get a taste of the boss's Blessing for this, I will find a way to make you know what it feels like."

"I understand," Michael said solemnly and heaved Emma out of his mind. She gasped and blinked her own eyes. She could sense Michael in her mind and almost panicked, but his thoughts were gentle.

Gabriel's taught you a lot, but you still have a long way to go. I'm glad you made that effort, though. My telepathic abilities pale in comparison to my brother's, but when you linked our minds I could look through your memories. He seems quite happy. Thank you for allowing me to see that. Don't be afraid of the dark anymore. There's a light switch by the thermostat. I'll be up shortly.

Emma looked toward the door. Would anyone see the light? She couldn't risk that. She took a deep breath and settled herself to wait out the darkness. "I won't allow it to drown me," she said aloud and took courage from the words.

Tip crossed his arms, trying to puzzle out the man's odd behavior. Something didn't add up, but with the issue of the dragon, they needed to hurry out of here.

Michael rubbed his hands together and nodded to the man kneeling beside the unicorn. "Take the little one, Tristan. You always did have an affinity with unicorns."

Tristan glanced furtively at Balthasar and then pulled the baby unicorn close and they all followed Michael toward the elevators.

Tip couldn't bring himself to walk away from the dryad. "I'm sorry. I'll get you out very soon," he promised and turned to follow, but someone dodged around the cage and grabbed him. Tip sucked in a sharp breath and twisted in the human's grip. His hand went to her throat, but then he saw her face and went still. "Julia," he said, and joy lit his expression.

She stared at him in shock. He quickly let her go and stepped away, glancing over his shoulder. The others were almost out of sight among the tanks and hadn't noticed the brief struggle.

Tip's expression became distant. He couldn't help the happiness he'd already shown her, but he needed to do damage control now.

"You shouldn't be here," he said coldly. "Come along. You can still leave with the others. I don't know what's come over Michael, but you need to leave before the situation gets any worse."

Julia didn't move. Tip sighed in annoyance and tugged at her arm. She yanked free and glared at him. "What's wrong with you?"

"I am not the person you think you know," Tip said and grimaced. "The memories you have of me are the result of a spell, which I can undo now."

"I know." Those two words brought Tip up short. Julia gave him a small smile. "The spell has already been lifted. I just want to know why."

"We needed to investigate what was happening to the Blessed," Tip said mechanically, trying to digest this revelation. "So we found one that was likely to be targeted, and I was placed in a position close to her—

260

you." He shook himself and fell back on his training. "The investigation isn't over yet. You really must be on your way, human."

Julia recoiled, and Tip started to turn away, but she grabbed him again. "Wait! Let me think!" She held onto him and closed her eyes.

Tip could've pulled away, but he didn't. He glanced over his shoulder, wondering how long it would be before someone noticed he was gone. If the dragon was still on Michael's mind, which it should be, probably not that long.

"If that's true," she said, "then why did you help me get away? If it was just an investigation, it would've been easier for you to let me be captured."

"I don't know." Tip kept his gaze on the floor. "Now come on." He pulled out of her hold and then gripped her arm tightly and pulled her after the others. Half of the group had already gone up.

"Found another one. Let's hurry this up," he said to Michael.

Once in the elevator, Michael struggled to zero in on Emma's mind, wishing he knew more about his second Blessing. He eventually found her mind unguarded and resumed going through her memories. He paused over her recollections of Aoife, particularly the time when she found out that Gabriel and Aoife were in a relationship.

"Can you stop?" she snapped at him mentally and physically, even though she was still alone in the office. He chuckled, causing the others in the crowded elevator to stare at him.

Sorry. I've missed my brother a lot the last few years. He shared his thoughts about Gabriel's sudden disappearance. *As soon as I get things settled down here, I'll come up and help you,* Michael added, sensing her physical discomfort. *We still have a few hours.*

Before what? Emma asked.

The elevator dinged. Michael stepped out into a ring of waiting security guards, and the awareness of Emma watching through his eyes went to the back of his mind.

Dante stood at the head of the group, his arms crossed grimly.

Michael forced a wooden smile onto his face. "Father. I thought you were still at Mass," he said, keeping his voice and face calm despite his rioting thoughts.

"I skipped it today. Same as you, apparently," Dante replied, his eyes narrowing. "I didn't want to go while we were still at odds over the young mage. Virgil sensed the intruders and called me at home to tell me what was happening. It is a good thing I didn't go, I suppose."

A sharp prick of pain and another feather came to rest on top of the pile between Avery's feet. He scowled down at the feathers and then at the welling blood speckling his wing. His fingers brushed over his stained plumage, and then he forced his hand to drop onto his leg. His knee started bouncing.

"Are you unable to stay still?" Lucien asked from the driver's seat, his voice laced with curiosity. He waved his hand, and Avery's wings vanished. "Stop undoing the spell."

"I don't care about that," Avery snapped.

Martin reached over and squeezed his shoulder.

Avery huffed and leaned back to watch the road pass. His knee continued to bounce. "How did you learn to drive, anyway?"

"I've learned many things to better serve my lord dragon in the modern age," Lucien said with a hint of smugness. "When you have centuries…"

Avery's scowl deepened. "Jerk," he muttered and crossed his arms. Lucien chuckled and said no more as they came into San Francisco.

He parked in front of a tall, skinny house that looked like two towers squashed together. Identical houses pushed in on either side. "Why do humans choose to make things so similar? Like ducks in a row," Avery said, eyeing the light-blue house. "This is it?"

"Yeah." Lucien took a deep breath and got out of the car. "Follow the plan now." He nodded to Timaeus, who reclined in the passenger seat. "We'll be just a few moments, my lord dragon."

Timaeus nodded, examining his nails.

The two avians flanked Lucien as he marched up the porch steps to the door. Avery could sense the spells on the house, wrapping the owers like a thick net. The elf put a hand on the doorknob and light lared around his fingers.

A pigeon swooped down and collided with the elf's head, gripping his hair and leaning forward to peck at the door. Lucien cried out and grabbed at the bird. It pecked his fingers and squawked when he wrapped his hands around it.

"Not a word," Lucien snapped, seeing Martin's shoulders shaking with repressed laughter. He tucked the pigeon under his arm and turned once more to the door.

This time, when he put his hand on the doorknob, the light was dimmer although the brass under his fingers glowed with heat. The pigeon resumed pecking at the wood, its neck extended out to reach.

The spell broke with a hiss like escaping steam, and the door swung open. They filed inside, and Avery held his breath, goosebumps breaking out over his arms as they crossed into the House Keeper's domain.

A wild cry rent the breathless silence. A young woman charged into the entrance hall, a silvery substance flowing from her hand. It solidified into a dagger aimed for Lucien's heart.

He twisted out of the way and grasped the woman's arm, allowing her momentum to carry her past him. The pigeon, freed from Lucien's hold, disappeared toward the next story of the house with a wild clapping of wings.

"Filthy elf!" the woman shouted and tried to pull away. Lucien twisted her arm behind her back until she cried out and dropped the knife. It evaporated away into nothing before it hit the ground.

"Interesting." Lucien pressed a hand to the back of the woman's head, and she went limp. He lowered her to the floor and straightened. "Well, Keeper? Are you going to allow your charges to fight your battle? Come face me!"

Only silence greeted him. Lucien nodded to Martin and Avery, and they moved toward the stairs.

High-pitched singing floated down. Avery, in the lead now, stared at the two little girls standing at the landing. One sang in Spanish, the other looking on. After a moment, the second girl hesitantly added her

263

voice to the song. A faun appeared and galloped down the stairs toward them.

Lucien breathed a spell and made a throwing motion. A black orb left his hand, but it passed through the faun, which disappeared as abruptly as it had appeared.

"An illusion," Martin said grimly. "Must be one of their Blessings."

Avery's wings snapped open, and he flew toward the girls. Their singing broke off into startled squeals, but as he neared them, a spell slammed into him. He slumped down onto the stairs, his breath knocked out of him. The girls fled out of view as Martin rushed over and helped him to his feet.

A young man had appeared in the girls' places. "What do you want?" he demanded. He stood firmly but his voice wavered, and Avery could see fear in his eyes.

"We are here to undo the travesty you and your fellows are perpetrating on those who are Blessed."

"What?" the man blinked, and then his expression settled into a scowl. "You have some nerve to come barging in here and—"

The pigeon descended onto his head, beating him with its wings.

Lucien grinned. "He's an amateur," he told Avery. "No Keeper worth his salt would have failed to notice that."

The young Keeper stumbled and fell, the bird still gripping his head. Colorful lights flew from the bird's wings and wrapped around the man, leaving red marks on his arms and face. He toppled onto his side, flailing blindly with one hand and covering his eyes with the other as the spell streamers flicked over his face.

A crack rent the air and the walls rattled. The bird ceased its assault and flew toward the door. The Keeper drew himself up onto his hands, his face paling. "No."

Timaeus strolled in and ascended the stairs. The pigeon landed on his shoulder and turned its head to preen itself. The trio moved behind him as he regarded the prone human. "Well done, Lian. You provided the perfect distraction while I broke the Keeping spell on the house. Now what to do with the mage…"

The dragon-man's grin widened to show more teeth.

The door creaked open to admit two security guards. Emma charged at them. One of them caught her and almost lifted her off the floor. She struggled helplessly and kicked at him. He held her out further from himself, his face carefully neutral. A third man led her brother in.

"Nemo!" she exclaimed and pulled against the man's hold. He let her go, and she barreled into her brother.

He grunted but hugged her tightly. "Are you alright, Emma?" He looked her over as if searching for injuries.

"I'm..." she trailed off and looked longingly at the closed door.

One of the men cleared his throat. "Virgil instructed us to bring you some food and escort you down the hall for a few minutes." He nodded to Emma, and she could see the understanding in his face.

"Be right back," Emma said and hurried out, flanked by two of the men.

When she came back, two sandwiches, thickly wrapped with cellophane, sat on the table. Her stomach growled, and she hurried over as the men left the room, locking the door. Emma glanced at the barrier between them. She could sense their minds just on the far side. "They locked Davet up again," she said, feeling his renewed misery. "Where are the others? Why did they bring just you here?"

"I'm not sure. I think it's because that Michael guy told them I'm Gabriel's student."

"He did?" Emma frowned. *What is Michael playing at?* That question plagued her while they sat in the uncomfortable office chairs and watched the clock on the wall tick the time away. There was nothing they could comfortably say for fear they'd be overheard, so she was only distracted by wishing she could do something for Davet.

It was evening before the door opened again. The same three security guards entered. "The boss wants to see you." As before, Emma was ready. She stood up regally and sailed past the men. One of the young men quickly dodged around her so he could lead the way. His disgruntled air gave Emma quiet satisfaction.

They were shown into a spacious office where Dante sat at a desk by large windows with a magnificent view of the sun setting over the ocean. Emma's eyes were riveted on Dante, though. Virgil was in the corner, trying to probe her mind, and it was all she could do to ignore his loathsome presence.

Michael sat in the first of three chairs across from the desk, looking perfectly at ease. Dante gestured at the other two chairs. Emma shot Michael a glare and reluctantly sat down. Nemo sighed and followed her lead. They didn't have much choice.

"You two are Gabriel's students?" Dante asked, nodding to them.

"Yes," Emma said and silently told Nemo to agree. He nodded after a moment. She tried to scan Michael's mind but found it closed off even more securely than earlier to guard against Virgil, she guessed. She couldn't read anything in his face either. He stared straight ahead at the sunset, his expression blank.

"Really. That boy." Dante huffed. "If he wanted to instruct some Blessed, he could've just asked. Virgil doesn't get many students, but Gabriel could've helped teach some of our workers who are Blessed with mental abilities."

"Do you really think that's why Gabriel ran away?" Nemo asked incredulously. Emma shot him a warning look, but he ignored her. "It sounds like you're making a wild guess to me. You must've never connected with him very well. Some father." Nemo's voice was bitter, and Emma knew he wasn't talking just about Dante.

Dante's eyes narrowed dangerously, and Emma's unease grew. "I take it you're speaking from personal experience, boy," he said, catching the same thing Emma had. "Don't project your own petty experiences onto my son and me. Our relationship is different."

"So you say," Nemo sneered.

What are you doing! Emma thought at him urgently.

He continued to ignore her. "But he ran away just like I did. Doesn't sound all that different to me."

Silence fell like a stone. Dante glared at Nemo, and Emma felt a charge in the air, like gathering thunder. Nemo stiffened but glared right back at the man.

"Do you think you're special, boy?" Dante asked in a dangerously silken tone. "Is it because you were taught about your Blessing by my son's small group, instead of my company? Do you have any idea how many Blessed have been educated at my facility? You're nothing but a grunt, and you'll take your proper place soon enough."

"I get it." Nemo smirked. "You made your sons feel like they were no more important than all the other Blessed who work for you." Michael made a sound that might have been agreement. Dante shot him a scathing look.

Dante didn't say anything, though. He put a hand to his temple, a puzzled look on his face. Realization dawned slowly. He started to his feet and slammed his hands down on the desk. "How dare you use your ability on me! Who do you think you are!"

Nemo sucked in a sharp breath and gripped the edges of his chair as sweat beaded his forehead. Emma looked at him anxiously. "I am Nemo Reeve," he said, getting to his feet as well and balling his hands into fists. "I am Blessed, and I am a dragon's student. You will remember my name, and you will stop using your Blessing to hurt people!"

Power built up in Nemo's voice as he spoke until there was a jolt and something like a flash of light at the very end. Dante staggered and leaned heavily against his desk. Emma wiped her eyes and blinked to clear away the dazzle, confused as to what had just happened. "Was that magic, Nemo?" she asked. It seemed like a little more than just his Blessing. Nemo only shrugged.

"Sir!" Virgil ran around the desk. "Are you alright?"

Dante waved Virgil away, breathing heavily and running a hand through his hair until it stood in uneven clumps. He glared pointedly at Nemo, who stood tall and regarded him with distaste. Then Dante's eyes widened, and his face paled.

"Father?" Michael went around the desk as well and hovered.

"What have you done! What sorcery is this!" Dante howled, ignoring both his subordinate and his son.

"You will never use your Blessing to hurt people again," Nemo repeated, a note of exhaustion in his voice. Emma quickly put an arm around his shoulders to support him, and he leaned gratefully against her.

Dante straightened and regained his composure with effort. "We shall see. Virgil, take them away. Block their memories and put them with the others in the House."

Virgil started toward them, his face set in a dark frown. Emma and Nemo backed away, and she jabbed at Virgil's mind so hard he paused.

"That won't be happening," a voice said lightly. Everyone in the room stared as a small black mouse scampered up onto the desk, stood up on its hind legs, and looked around. Seeing that it was the center of attention, it preened and drew itself to its full height of three inches. Once its whiskers were perfectly arranged it regarded everyone with its shiny black eyes. "The House is under new management."

"Lian?" Nemo furrowed his brows in confusion.

In the same moment, Michael leaned forward. "What do you mean?" he asked in an alarmed voice.

"Just what I said," the mouse said. "I challenged the House's Keeper and subdued him. I have freed the residents of the house and enchanted them to come here."

Michael twitched back and stared at the mouse in horror. "The Keeper. Is he alive?"

"We killed no one."

"I've heard enough of this nonsense!" Dante snarled and swatted at the mouse.

There was a flash of light, and Lian crouched on the desk, smirking and gripping Dante's wrist. "Want to try that again, old man?" she breathed and raised a hand filled with golden fire. Dante cried out and jerked back. Virgil took a step between him and Lian.

"Don't!" Michael said and reached for her. She turned her gaze on him and angled her hand in his direction, her smile widening.

The doors sprang open, making them all jump. Emma would've sworn those doors were locked, and she watched in bemusement as a troop of elves strolled in.

This is getting extremely weird. Her exhausted mind couldn't keep up with the rapid succession of happenings.

Lucien and an elf whose face showed just the slightest signs of age led the elves. Tip and Gabriel followed closely behind. Michael's eyes

268

were riveted on his brother, and he didn't seem to notice anyone else.

"Dante Hightower," the older elf intoned.

Dante shrank away, and Virgil moved protectively in front of him.

"The Council of High Elves has charged you with abusing your power and abducting children bestowed with the Elves' Blessing. We are here to confiscate your Blessing."

"Too late," Nemo said, grinning despite himself.

The elf looked down his sharp nose at Nemo. "Excuse me?" The other elves fanned out around them, studying Nemo with interest and watching Dante warily.

"I've already taken him down a few pegs. Do you want to be next?" Nemo's voice crackled with power, and the elf took an involuntary step back.

"Who are you?" he demanded and cast his gaze around at the assembled group. It was clear he didn't want to look directly at Nemo.

The elevator dinged again, and Timaeus came in, followed by a few Company agents Emma recognized from the basement. "He is my student."

The elf looked at Timaeus incredulously. Timaeus grinned and shifted into his draconic form. This pushed everyone else to the edges of the room to make space. The floor creaked and Timaeus held himself very still and coiled, the air shimmering around his middle marking where he compacted himself to fit into this space. He huffed and snaked his head around, bringing his burning copper gaze on the quaking elf.

"Forgive me, my lord!" The elf dropped to his knees and bowed his head. Satisfied, Timaeus changed back before the floor gave out beneath them.

Emma dashed past them and went to Gabriel. "You came!" she said, grinning.

Gabriel looked pained, and she knew he must be getting a headache from the city noise, but he smiled crookedly at her. "When I heard that Lucien went to send word to the elves about the Company, I knew it was past time I acted. They were still waiting for word from Tiberius." He grimaced. "I'm sorry I let it get so bad."

"It's not your fault," Emma said and hugged him. Gabriel stiffened for a moment but then smiled slightly and put an arm around her.

"Gabriel," Dante interrupted and stumbled over. "Why?" he croaked. "How could you do this to me?"

Gabriel regarded his father impassively. "If you have to ask, you'll never understand." He looked like he would've said more, but Virgil launched a mental attack on both him and Emma. Gabriel went rigid, and his face reddened with rage. Virgil jabbed at his mental defenses. Emma clenched her fists and counterattacked with her Blessing, shattering Virgil's defenses a moment before Tip hit him with a spell. He collapsed to the floor, his eyes wide and furious.

"Well done," Gabriel said, surprise evident in his voice. "Adversity really does seem to be the best teacher on how to use a Blessing." He glanced down at Virgil and shook his head. "That isn't always true, though. The main thing your treatment taught me was how to defend myself. Did you really think you'd be able to break into my mind again?"

Virgil looked away, unable to speak with the spell on him.

An elf woman came to Gabriel's side. "We cannot allow your father to go unpunished after all that he has done."

"I know." Gabriel glanced at his father, who was staring down at Virgil, looking as equally stunned as his assistant. "Please allow me to see to it. Being retired forcefully from the Company and put under house arrest by some of the very people that once served him should be punishment enough. As for Virgil..." He glanced down at his former teacher and rubbed his face. "I'm not sure. But I'll figure something out. This is a human matter and should be judged by humans." The elf woman tilted her head but didn't argue. "I would appreciate your people's help with getting the Blessed back to their homes though. Most of them have been here too long, and we'll have to find them new situations, but there are some that can be sent home."

"Of course." She spun on her heel and began issuing orders which the elves hopped to obey. Even the pompous elf acquiesced to her authority.

"You'll never get away with this," Dante croaked. "The Blessed will fight. This is their sanctuary."

"And it still will be. I'm taking over." Michael advanced bravely past Timaeus up to Gabriel and Dante. Two of the elves flanked him, but he seemed at ease. Gabriel tensed as Michael approached but didn't move. Michael pulled him into a hug and pressed his forehead to Gabriel's. "I've missed you, brother," he said softly. Emma could hear them communicating silently. Feeling out of place, she wandered away.

Nemo stood with his arm around Lian while Timaeus glowered down at her. "Donovan told me he instructed you to bring everyone together," he growled. The Company agents backed away, and Dante shot the dragon-man a horrified look. "This could've been disastrous if the older Hightower boy wasn't amiable to our cause."

"I know," Lian admitted. "I took that chance. I'd heard Gabriel tell Aoife about Michael before, and I got the feeling things between them could be mended."

Emma was confused for a few moments, and then what she was hearing clicked into place, explaining the events of the morning. "You put a spell on me to call Adah!"

Lian glanced at her with a guilty expression. "Yeah. I was going to get you out, but then I saw you had the Company girl's phone number. I wasn't sure how to contact Michael to come to the building, and that was exactly what I needed. I wasn't expecting their father to come around, but it worked out."

Emma glared at Lian, too furious for words. Lian smiled sheepishly. "Sorry. It seemed like the best course."

"It all worked out," Timaeus interrupted and patted Lian on the shoulder. "You did well. You've earned a place for yourself, not simply as Donovan's student. You are welcome in my home."

Lian beamed, but Emma grumbled under her breath. She really didn't appreciate being used like that. The conversation moved on to Nemo's accomplishment against Dante.

Feeling put out and still out of place, Emma went out into the hallway and almost walked into Tip.

"Tiberius," she blurted, and he looked at her in surprise.

"Do I know you?" he asked, frowning in confusion. Like the other elves, he seemed aloof and distant; much different than the charming, friendly person Emma saw in Julia's memories.

"Well, no," Emma mumbled, rubbing her neck. "When Julia arrived at the Circus, she was sick. I used my Blessing to look into her memories to find out what had happened. So, I guess I feel like I know you."

"I see," Tip said absently. The elevator dinged behind them, and Julia emerged. Tip sprang forward and drew her into a hug. "Thank God you're safe," he breathed against her hair. "I was so worried when you were taken to the House."

Emma took a step back, wishing she could be somewhere else. Maybe she would go outside and get some fresh air. She was caught up suddenly from behind, and gasped. Feathers brushed her cheek, and she relaxed and grinned up at Avery. His expression was as relieved as Tip's.

"Are you okay?" he asked. "Timaeus told me to help get the House under control. He said he and Gabriel would take care of things here and you would be fine, but then I heard you were separated from everyone else and were alone with Dante Hightower—" his voice cracked, and his arms tightened around her.

"I'm fine, Avery." She returned his hug. "Everything's fine," she added, reassuring herself as much as him. A realization struck her, and she reached out mentally. *Davet! Are you okay?*

"It will be now," Avery said seriously. "Oh. I have a surprise for you." He stepped back and gestured at the still-open elevator. Two little girls peered out, keeping it from closing. Davet darted out from behind them and threw himself against Emma.

"Davet!" Emma dropped to her knees and wrapped her arms around his neck. The little unicorn pressed his nose against her chest. Emma looked up at the two girls, and her hand tightened around Davet's mane. "Gracia! Irene!"

The girls simply stared at her, no recognition in their faces.

"Their memories are blocked," Gabriel said behind her. She looked up and found him watching them grimly. "All the Blessed that were brought in had their memories blocked off. To keep them from trying to run away and go home."

"But there's a way to fix that." She didn't make it a question, scowling at him. "You wouldn't teach me before, when you blocked some of Nemo's memories. You will now."

Gabriel smiled, and his eyes narrowed with repressed laughter. "Oh, yes. It's time for that lesson. And we have a few hundred Blessed for you to practice on. Congratulations."

26

G olden sunlight poured in through the large window. Emma groaned and pulled the thick feather-down blanket up over her head. Giggling and high-pitched chatter reached her even through the fabric. She pulled it back down and gazed sleepily around the room.

The walls were a pale gold, echoing the sunshine. Gracia and Irene played with dolls on the floor a few feet away. After she'd fixed their memories, they asked to share a room with her, so Michael had given them this room in the Hightower mansion. Gabriel had looked askance at his brother but hadn't said anything.

It was a grand room, with a window that took up all of one wall and looked out onto the garden. The four-poster bed was even larger than the one in Emma's room in the caves, made of dark wood and carved with flowers. There were two smaller beds on the other side of the room, by the door.

Emma suspected this room had belonged to Gabriel's mother at some point.

Most of the Circus members had gone back to the caves to tell Donovan what had happened. Michael had put up the few who remained in this mansion. A week of unblocking memories had left Emma exhausted and with no time to even look around before now. Climbing out of the gigantic bed took some effort and her feet sank into the plush carpeting when she stepped down. She wiggled her toes, enjoying the feel of it.

"Good morning." She yawned and smiled at the girls. They echoed her and darted away to put the dolls on their rumpled beds.

Emma went over to the window and looked out. Celeste stood in the middle of the yard, her horn crossed with Davet's. He sidled away and then darted forward, jabbing his horn at her. She swung her head to catch his shorter horn once more on hers. When she tossed her head upward, much like she had done to disarm Tristan many times in the shows, Davet lost his balance and tumbled onto the grass.

Teaching him self-defense? Emma wondered. "Let's go have breakfast," she called to the girls. "Will you show me the way down to the garden?"

"Easy!" Irene piped. They each grabbed one of Emma's hands and showed her down a hallway, descended a grand staircase, and then went out through a glass door.

The garden was beautiful, with an open lawn bordered by roses against the wall of the house. A grove of fruit trees stretched to the fence, providing extra privacy.

Gabriel and Michael sat on the patio eating breakfast. "Want to join us?" Gabriel asked.

She nodded and sat down at the iron table. The girls ran out onto the lawn to play with Davet.

"I thought Celeste took Davet back to the caves," Emma commented. "I'm surprised she'd bring him back after what happened."

"I asked her to come along," Timaeus said and strolled onto the patio with Nemo and Lucien tailing him. "For the occasion."

"Occasion?" Emma asked. Gabriel made a face, but before anyone could answer, a group of men and women crossed the lawn, led by Aoife and an older man with an arm protectively around her shoulders.

They paused to watch Davet, and Aoife spoke softly to the man. He cast Michael and Gabriel wary looks every few seconds as if they might move while he was distracted.

Davet skittered away, and they continued along to the patio. Lucien bowed to the man leading the group. Timaeus nodded. Celeste surged up and came to the edge of the tiles, calling Davet to her side.

"We have come for negotiations," the man said to Michael in a heavily accented voice. Emma had never noticed Aoife's slight accent. Now she realized it was a milder version of this man's. "All of my people have been freed?"

"All of the ones we have here." Michael turned his mug in his hand. "My employees are looking through the records for the ones that were sold or taken elsewhere. It will take time to track them down and make deals with the companies we sold them to."

A young man that Emma had seen trapped in one of the tanks approached Michael. He looked very similar to Aoife and the older man, and Emma guessed he was a member of their family. "You will get it done," he said, his accented voice rasping harshly.

"I will," Michael said. "I promise. Now for the requirements for an alliance we discussed last night..."

Gabriel held up a hand and got to his feet, his chair scraping against the cement. "I don't want to discuss this over breakfast."

The older man gave him a dark look, but Aoife smiled and patted his shoulder, whispering something to him.

"Later then," he relented.

"I would like you to sample my cooking," Timaeus said with a toothy smile. "I am curious if it is to your people's taste."

"I would be honored to," the man said and led the group into the house. Lucien fell in step with his entourage. Aoife's gaze lingered on Gabriel, but he didn't look at her, so she went inside as well. Nemo waved to Emma and then slipped in after them.

"Gabriel," Michael said, giving his twin a reproachful stare.

Gabriel just shook his head. "I didn't come back so that you could run my life. I realize we need to make peace with the merfolk, but how medieval can they get with that demand? I don't want to discuss it right this moment, considering what else we have to deal with today." He stared down at his mug. "I don't appreciate being forced into this. It's not how I wanted to do it."

Emma looked questioningly at Michael, but he only shook his head, so she sighed and resigned herself to the silent meal that followed. At least the girls were having fun. Their laughter drifted to her over the lawn as they chased Davet through the fruit trees.

After they finished eating, Gabriel took a deep breath. "Please come with me," he said shortly to Emma and led the way into the house. Michael followed, his expression grim.

They stopped outside a door where Tip stood guard, and Gabriel faced Emma. "I have to ask a really big favor, Emma. It's been decided that Dante's punishment will be to have his memories of the Company blocked permanently. Will you do it, please? I will show you how."

Emma took a step back and shook her head before he finished speaking. "No."

The blocks that Virgil had placed on so many memories felt unnatural and disturbing. She had been physically sick after only undoing the first few. She didn't want to put such a thing in place herself.

"Please," Gabriel said again. "If you won't, then I'll have to."

"Isn't there another way? The elves or some other telepath? With all the Blessed working for the Company—"

"Telepathic abilities are one of the rarest Blessings," Michael cut in. "Virgil and Gabriel are the only ones that the Company found in the last fifty years. Your ability is a treasure, Emma. Though it must feel like a curse at times."

Emma swallowed and looked at Gabriel. He crossed his arms, his face closed off. She could only imagine what he must be feeling. "I told the elves we needed to handle the human matters. If we ask them to help here, they'll want to step into other areas as well. We either keep all the boundaries or we won't have any."

Wrapping her arms around herself, Emma looked down. Pain and uncertainty warred with the desire to not place the burden on Gabriel. She pictured having to do this to her father. That bolstered her resolve.

She would not make Gabriel do this.

"Show me what to do."

They practiced on Michael for a little while. Gabriel showed Emma how to block a portion of his memories, and then she unblocked them again. The portion got larger and larger, and each time, Michael's face got more strained. Emma saw memories of him and Gabriel as children, playing in that large garden. Michael gritted his teeth and clenched his hands into fists when she blocked those memories.

She saw their mother's uncertain, confused face as she was confronted with their unusual abilities and their almost constant silent communications. She saw the day their mother left, and their father shut himself away in his room. They stood outside and called uselessly to him. Emma felt tears start to her eyes, but she held them back and averted her eyes from the guarded door. It looked the same now as it had back then.

"Enough!" Michael exclaimed when they got to his memories of when Gabriel ran away. Sorrow etched deep lines into face. "I can't take this anymore. Isn't that enough practice?"

"It'll have to be," Gabriel said. He looked at Tip. "Will you cast a spell to reinforce her work? This will be her first time doing something of this magnitude. She'll need the help." Tip nodded and opened the door. "I'm sorry for leaving you alone," Gabriel said softly to Michael as Emma walked in ahead of them. "It was selfish of me."

"Things needed to be changed," Michael replied wearily. "I refused to acknowledge that, and it drove you away. I've done my best to make things better since then. I should've done more before you left." He clasped Gabriel's shoulder, and then they turned as one to survey their father.

Dante sat by the window with a book. Unhappiness lined his pale face. Still, he raised his head and regarded them proudly. "So nice to see you, Gabriel. Now that I have fallen from grace, you actually come to visit."

"You may have fallen from power, but you're far from falling from grace," Michael said. "I'll go with you to Mass tomorrow, father."

"Escorted by this demon-spawn elf?" Dante cast a loathing look at

Tip. "I'm ashamed of you, Michael. That you would make alliances with these creatures and then go to Mass is beyond disgusting."

"They are God's creatures too, father," Michael said. "But perhaps you're right. I think—" Gabriel elbowed Michael to silence him, apparently having seen something in his mind.

Dante's eyes popped wide.

"Stop provoking him," Gabriel snapped. "Don't make this harder than it has to be."

"I was being serious," Michael muttered, but Gabriel ignored him, and Dante didn't seem to hear him.

"Make what harder?" Dante said and got to his feet, clutching the book like a weapon. "I may have lost my Blessing, but I am not powerless."

Tip murmured a spell, and Dante sat down again with a thump. His face reddened with outrage and shame. "Will you not let me retain any dignity at all?"

"The elves will leave very soon, Father," Gabriel promised. "After we deal with this matter." He nodded to Emma.

Wanting to see no more of this, Emma closed her eyes and listened for Dante's mind. He possessed the strongest barriers she had yet encountered. This was a man that wanted his mind to himself.

"Don't do this!" she heard him protest when she picked at his defenses. "Tell her to stop!"

Nobody responded. Gabriel helped Emma get past the older man's defenses and then recoiled when they heard his dark, furious thoughts. They were like a poison, and Emma's stomach roiled. She regretted having such a large breakfast before starting.

Delving his memories, she learned all about the Company. The Blessed Scouts and Collectors that were sent out to locate and capture others. The fishing ships that netted and dragged merfolk from the ocean. The Rangers that were sent into forests to find other creatures, such as unicorns, satyrs, and nymphs. With each piece of information, Emma's pity for the man shrank.

That helped her when she began the task of blocking those memories. She saw a memory from years before of Balthasar in a bed with Gail crying over him, after he was blinded while unicorn hunting. She skipped from this memory to Dante's rage shortly after he learned Gabriel had slipped away, taking several Blessed with him. She swallowed and stopped paying too close attention to the memories she skimmed over. She would go mad if she took in any more information from this man.

The sun was sinking low and the shadows in the room were growing before Emma finally finished. She swayed, and Avery caught her. She hadn't heard him enter the room. Gabriel was just walking back in. Michael was nowhere to be seen. Dante's eyes were closed.

"Father?" Gabriel moved closer and touched the man's hand.

"I cast a sleep spell on him partway through," Tip said. "To make it easier on him. It was too cruel to have him awake through the process. He will be adjusted to the change when he wakes up."

"Thank you," Gabriel said gratefully. Tip nodded and left the room while Avery helped Emma over to the other armchair. "I owe you so much for this, Emma. I can't tell you how much I appreciate it."

Emma nodded, feeling too sick to speak. Avery crouched down beside her chair. "You did well." He clasped her hand and turned to Gabriel. "How did the arrangements with the merfolk go?"

"Well enough, I suppose," Gabriel sighed. "They have every right to be outraged. I'm surprised they didn't act out before this. Well, I suppose they did in small ways. But this is the first time they've organized. That means our timing was good. It would've been terrible for our sailors if things had continued the way they were."

"So, you're taking responsibility for it," Emma croaked. Her mouth was terribly dry. Gabriel raised an eyebrow. "You said 'our sailors.'"

"I pulled my fair share of merfolk up while I worked the ships as a teen," he replied. "I was there when Aoife was captured. I'm not proud of it, and I'm doing my best to help Michael make amends."

"You're going through with the arranged thing, then?" Avery asked. "Timaeus and I have a bet going on that."

Gabriel shot Avery a sour look.

"Going through with what?" Emma asked, feeling like she missed something. Gabriel made a face. "What is it?" she asked anxiously and sat up straight. Avery took her hand and ran his thumb over the back of it reassuringly.

Gabriel rubbed his face. "Preparations are being made for us to go back to the Circus. We should be able to leave in the next day or two. Several of the Company's Blessed have chosen to go with us. A few others will go with us to be taken home when we pass through their areas. Like Gracia and Irene. They asked to spend some time with you." Emma brightened. "There are a few more loose-ends to tie up here first, though."

Emma stared at him. After what they worked on that day, she couldn't imagine what else would have Gabriel acting so morose. "What are you dancing around? I don't have the energy left for guessing games."

"The merfolk asked for a few gestures of good faith to solidify an alliance. Michael can handle most of them, but there was one they demanded of me and Aoife." Gabriel crossed his arms and glowered at the fading light outside the window. "I have to get married."

The words didn't compute. Emma felt her brain short-circuiting. It was just too much to take in, mentally exhausted as she was.

Avery gave her a concerned look. *Emma? Are you okay?*

She didn't look at him. "I don't get it. What's the punchline?"

"I am going to get married," Gabriel repeated, slowly and clearly. Emma gaped at him, and Avery chuckled.

Gail looked out the window of her bedroom and drummed her fingers against the windowsill. Adah lounged on her bed. Seth sprawled on the floor, a game in his hands but his eyes staring up at the ceiling.

"Stay at the House and await orders," Michael had told them. Then he had gone off with Balthasar, Caleb, and Rebecca.

Gail hated waiting. Especially now, with the House so quiet. It had never been this quiet before. There was always someone in the living room watching TV or groups of children playing. Now everyone had disappeared, even the Keeper, and they hadn't been told what had happened after Dante had apprehended the intruders.

"How long do you think we're going to be kept in the dark?" Gail muttered. "Where the heck did everyone go?"

"Don't know," Adah mumbled, as unruffled as ever. "Michael will come back soon. He promised he'd keep us safe."

Seth huffed and rolled over onto his side. "Your faith in your boyfriend is disgusting."

"Your life would be a lot calmer if you had a little faith in him yourself," Adah retorted and threw a pillow at him.

Seth muttered something mostly indiscernible, but Gail caught what sounded like "hit you with meat." Adah ignored him.

The floorboards outside creaked, and Adah started up with a grin. "That must be Aoife, the new girl!" she squeaked.

"Who?" Gail asked blankly and watched as a young woman not much taller than her entered. The woman's black hair flowed around her, rippling with more than just her movement. The air rippled around her. Gail blinked, trying to clear her eyes.

Adah darted forward and hugged the stranger. "She's staying at the estate. I met her the other day when we got instructions, and she gave me some fashion tips."

Terror gripped Gail as she realized it was magic she was sensing. She started to her feet and cast her shadow around her and Seth.

Adah blinked, standing too close to the woman for the shadow to encompass her. "Gail?"

"Get away from her!" Gail shouted. "She's a mermaid!"

Seth cursed and leapt to his feet, looking around wildly for anything to use for defense.

"I know," Adah said, and Gail felt the other girl's Blessing trying to calm her. "But she's Michael's guest and my new friend. He told me to make her feel welcome if she came around."

"Traitors," Seth growled, and Adah flinched.

"No!" Adah protested. "Michael is the new boss. Dante is going senile."

"I'm getting married to Gabriel," the mermaid interrupted. Adah's jaw dropped, and she stared at the young woman. "I would like you and Gail to be my bridesmaids. Balthasar is among Gabriel's groomsmen,

283

and he's said you're a wonderful girl, Gail. He wants you to join us at the estate, so we can all figure this out together."

"Then why didn't he come?" Gail demanded, backing away. This had to be a trap. But Adah would never betray them. *You believed the same thing about Gabriel and Tristan,* the anxious part of her mind taunted. She squeezed her eyes shut, confused and wanting to drown out the voice of her anxiety and Adah both.

"I did." Gail's eyes flew open at the sound of her brother's voice.

Balthasar stepped around Aoife and advanced toward Gail's shadow, struggling to push against the darkness. "Adah's telling you the truth. Michael wants to make an alliance with the merfolk, so Gabriel has accepted an arranged marriage with this woman."

Gail allowed her shadow to dissipate and stared up at Balthasar, feeling her world tumbling down around her. "Things have been dealt with, and it's safe for you and Seth to come to the Estate now." He smiled. "We can get our memories back, Gail. We can find our home."

Gail shook her head. "This is my home," she whispered. Her shoulders slumped, and a few tears slipped down her dark skin. "But I'll go where you want us to be. Just please don't leave me again."

Balthasar wrapped Gail in a fierce hug and then looked up at Seth, hovering as if also wanting to reassure her. Her brother grinned and gathered Seth into the hug as well. "Come on. It's time we all found our true places without any restrictions on our minds."

Emma slipped the dark blue dress over her head and looked at herself in the mirror while Adah zipped the back up. Blue always complimented her fair complexion, and her light hair contrasted with the deep shade. She curled it up into a bun and pinned it in place.

Adah darted over to help Gail with her dress. "These dresses are so beautiful. I'm glad we were able to find bridesmaid dresses on such short notice."

"Money helps," Emma said dryly. Michael was paying for this affair.

Adah didn't seem to hear her. She tutted over Gail's hair and helped the younger girl to arrange it better.

"Money and style," Aoife commented, looking out the window at Gabriel standing on the lawn with the groomsmen. "The dresses are exactly what I wanted."

Emma still couldn't quite believe this was happening. She surveyed herself in the mirror while Gail and Adah chatted behind her. The dresses were indeed beautiful, made of dusky, twilight-blue satin. The bodices were studded with tiny crystals that glittered like stars. It suited the bride very well, short notice as it was.

They were doing their makeup when Seth strolled in through the closed door. Adah spotted him first. "Seth!" she shrieked and threw a hair brush at him. It bounced off his head, and he fell back through the door with a yelp.

A moment later, there was a tap on the door. "It's Seth," he said politely. "Are you decent, girls?"

"You know we are," Gail said, covering her smile. Adah sniffed and wouldn't look at Seth when he came in.

"Michael sent me to say everything's almost ready." He shifted his weight. "I brought our games from the house if you need a break from the party later, Gail."

Adah shot him a scathing look, and he fled back through the door.

"That's almost as bad as Donovan," Emma said in reply to Adah's mental fuming over the ways Seth used his Blessing. She finished her makeup and stepped away from the mirror so Gail could get closer and adjust her makeup with a tissue.

"Donovan?" Gail asked curiously.

Emma sat down stiffly on the edge of an armchair, feeling restricted by the tight dress, and told them about Donovan and the caves. They listened in wonder.

"That's amazing," Gail said. "I'm excited to see it."

"You're coming?" Emma said in surprise. "I didn't think Balthasar would want to." He had seemed so loyal to Michael that she had thought for sure he would stay with the Company, and Gail would stay where he was. She thought uneasily of the memories she saw in Dante's mind. "Is he going to be okay with Tristan? I mean…the accident that happened…"

Gail looked down and twisted the tissue tightly between her fingers. "I'm not sure. He's said before he didn't blame Tristan. The unicorn's magic made him do it."

Emma was silent. She knew that wasn't true. Tristan had acted to protect Celeste. Gail looked up and smiled thinly. "It's better this way. Tsar needs to make peace with Tristan. They were close friends before it happened. I think losing Tristan affected him more than the injury itself."

"Cheer up!" Adah commanded and swamped them with a burst of joyful energy. "We're going to a wedding! This isn't the type of thing to talk about before such a joyful occasion!"

"Okay, okay," Emma said. "Stop with the positive vibes, please."

Adah stuck her tongue out at Emma and finished her makeup. "Let's go! The bride is waiting for us!" She grabbed Gail and propelled her out the door.

Emma paused, watching them. How quickly things changed. Aoife and Adah had become fast friends while Emma dealt with the Blesseds' memories. It made Emma happy. She sensed that everyone, both from the Company and the Circus, was relieved. There had been multiple rifts between friends, not just the one between Gabriel and Michael, and they were slowly being repaired now.

Half an hour later, Emma took her place among the bridesmaids in the garden. Julia joined them a few minutes later, having gotten dressed separately. "How is Tip?" Emma whispered, her eyes roving over the people gathered.

Julia beamed. *We've come to an understanding,* she thought and showed Emma a few memories of what happened.

It was mostly Julia talking while Tip listened and nodded. A griffin hovered in the background, glaring daggers at Tip. Tip had smiled suddenly, dazzlingly, and began to speak…Julia cut the memory, embarrassed.

That's great! Emma thought. *I'm really happy for you two!*

The wedding party was certainly unique. Celeste walked daintily over and joined the bridesmaids. The groomsmen included Timaeus, Lucien, Avery, and Martin. Michael stood right beside Gabriel, holding the rings.

The music started up as Gracia, Irene, and Davet came down the aisle, sprinkling flowers. When they got to the altar and dumped their baskets, Davet put his head down and gingerly lipped up a few of the petals. Emma heard him clearly thinking how sweet they tasted, and she covered a smile.

Gabriel watched Aoife walk down the aisle between the Blessed humans of the Company and the Circus on one side and the merfolk on the other. Dante sat in the front row on the human side, leaning on a cane and looking quite serious but serene.

The man leading Aoife didn't look any more cheerful than when Gabriel had seen him at breakfast two days before, but his gaze softened when he looked at Aoife. They stopped at the altar.

Gabriel held a hand out to Aoife.

The man hesitated. "You take care of my daughter. Or we will reconsider taking vengeance on your ships."

"I promise," Gabriel replied, his voice thick with emotion. The man took Aoife's hand and placed it in Gabriel's hold and then took a position in front of the altar to perform the ceremony.

Gabriel responded promptly to each vow, but his mind wandered to the night before. This really hadn't been how he had intended it to go with him and Aoife.

Wanting to make amends for the rushed nature of the event, he had sought her out privately in the evening.

"Having cold feet?" Aoife had asked when he came into her room. She smiled when she said it, but he sensed the concern in her mind.

"Not at all," he had said softly. "I just wish it had gone differently. So, I got you something today."

"Oh?" Aoife turned away and rifled through the closet absently, her thoughts casual.

Gabriel got down on one knee and proffered a ring. Aoife whirled, her eyes widening. "Aoife, will you marry me? You've been at my side for years now, and I should've asked you long before now. I truly want to spend my life with you."

Aoife stared at him, her mouth gaping open, her eyes wide, and seemed speechless for once. She dropped to her knees and hugged him. "Of course, my angel," she whispered, pressing her face against his chest. "You didn't need to ask."

He took her hand and kissed it, slipping the ring onto her finger. "Too much has happened to both of us without our consent," he said, rubbing her back. "It's time we got to choose our fate."

"Do you take this woman to be your wife?" The question broke through his reverie, and for a moment Gabriel found himself speechless.

"I do," he whispered, and the rest of the words washed vaguely over him until Aoife leapt forward and kissed him to hoots and cheers.

A reception followed the ceremony, with a feast and dancing. The garden smelled of flowers, roast meat, and rich chocolate. Nemo sang for Gabriel and Aoife's dance, accompanied by Martin playing guitar. After the first dance, Gabriel sat with Dante, Aoife, the merfolk leader, and Michael, excitedly weaving dreams with Aoife, imagining the things they could do with the Circus now that they didn't have to keep themselves hidden from the Company.

Avery pulled Emma onto the dance floor, despite her reluctance. She was still suffering from the headache that started when she was brought into the city. She wanted nothing more than to retreat to her dark and, at least physically, silent bedroom, take some pain medication, and sleep. Gabriel had begged her to stay, and since he was suffering similarly, she agreed. Now, with Avery's arms around her, she was glad she had. Lian and Nemo circled past them. Emma frowned but decided not to let her displeasure with Lian ruin the evening.

When Aoife threw her bouquet, Julia caught it. She looked across the lawn at Tip and grinned wolfishly. Laughter ripped through the assembly. Tip fidgeted and rubbed the back of his neck.

Emma laughed with the rest. Julia had her work cut out with that.

Avery squeezed Emma's hand and led her away to a dark edge of the garden. "This garden is so huge," she commented as they sat down beneath an apple tree. "This whole place is absurdly huge." Avery was watching her intently and didn't reply.

She glanced at him and then away nervously, clutching a fold of her dress. "Stop staring."

The avian smiled, his face lighting up. He put an arm around her shoulders and hugged her close. "I'm just so happy you're okay," he said, pressing his lips to her hair. He put a finger under her chin to make her look at him and kissed her lightly.

Emma sucked in a sharp breath and then put her arms around him and relaxed into it.

A few minutes later, they returned to the reception hand in hand. Avery remained close to Emma the remainder of the party, and with each caress, light kiss, and grinning glance, made the horrible memories of the last few days recede further. There was a glow to the night. That and a supply of champagne that never seemed to dwindle combined to make her feel lighter and happier than she had since she had found Julia.

The next morning Emma's head pounded worse than ever, and she regretted indulging so much with the champagne. After a good portion of the morning had slipped by, Gracia and Irene jumped on her. She groaned and flailed at them. They dodged out of her reach and continued to bounce on her until she got up.

The Circus members were gathered in the foyer when Emma found them nearly an hour later. It had taken her that long to make herself even somewhat presentable after she'd given up on hiding the dark smudges under her eyes and how drawn she looked from the persistent headache.

A pile of luggage was next to the group, and Lucien spoke with an elf about a spell that would transport everything.

Gracia and Irene rushed off to play with Davet, and Emma watched them, smiling. "Their mother will be so happy to have them back," she commented to Nemo. He nodded, his expression distant. "What's up?" Emma asked. "Penny for your thoughts," she added with a smirk.

Nemo snorted. "I was just thinking about how much has changed," he said. "This is the longest we've been away from the caves since we joined Circus Phantasm. It feels like we're going home now."

"That's true," Emma mused. When she had fallen sick before, she had wanted to go home to their parents. That passed, though, and now she only felt a pull from the caves. She smiled and looked contentedly around at everyone that was gathered: the friends she had made at Circus Phantasm and the new members who were joining from the Company. Gracia and Irene stood by Davet and a few other children.

Emma laughed aloud as a thought struck her. "I'm getting my daycare after all." She reached over and fondly ruffled Nemo's hair. "Let's go home, little brother."

I owe so much to the creatives in the Realm Makers Consortium. The support I found among them was critical to finally finishing this story. I've learned so much about writing and self-publishing from them.

Savannah Jezowski, author and graphic designer, has been so patient with all my questions, and helped this story unfold from the rehearsal drafts.

Lauren Salisbury, author, has been wonderful enough to share her knowledge with me as she continues along the self-publishing path, just a few books ahead.

Arielle Bailey, editor, worked hard to make this show come off without a hitch. I'm still a little stunned how many misplaced commas she caught.

Many thanks to my handful of volunteer beta readers for catching plot holes in my story's weaving.

38691732R00182

Made in the USA
Lexington, KY
10 May 2019